CATHERINE'S CODE

CATHERINE'S CODE

West Avenue Books

Catherine's Code.

Printed in the United States. For information about subsidiary rights go to: rich@richardbognar.com

The characters and events in this book are fictional and any resemblance to actual persons or events is coincidental.

ISBN-978-0-9890962-3-2

Library of Congress Control Number: 2013935000

REMEMBRANCE

For Marilyn Graham, my mother. I still see you pulling the wagon down West Avenue, knocking on doors and asking neighbors if they could spare extra food. You then placed it on the porch of the family who was going through hard times. The neighbors called you the Queen of West Avenue, and you were, Mom.

ACKNOWLEDGMENT

My thanks go to Stephanie J. Beavers, my editor. Stephanie edited my first book, *The Event,* and she has performed just as brilliantly on *Catherine's Code.* My thanks also go to C. J. Barnard for designing another superb book cover for me.

DEDICATION

For
Cyndy

My Muse

CATHERINE'S CODE

Prologue

On December 16, 1999, three extraordinary events occurred that changed my life forever. The first took place while I was in the Brazilian Rainforest researching rare plants. Nothing I can recall has ever terrified me more than what occurred that afternoon. The second event—clearly the greatest tragedy to befall me—was the loss of my wife Catherine. As you will see, it began my search to find whoever was responsible for the death of this most extraordinary woman. The third and final event of that ominous day is one that will take a great deal more courage to put on paper. But I am compelled to tell you everything. My challenge will be to remember it all in the short time I have left. Let me begin.

Chapter One

It was six p.m. and, like clockwork, the jungle's darkness crept in, forcing daylight to retreat. I had surprised myself, going almost the entire afternoon without thinking of Catherine, and not once recalling the promise she'd broken or that she was still in New York, thousands of miles away. What was she doing at this moment? Did I invade her mind as she invaded mine? Has she forgiven me for being selfish and for leaving? I had walked away from Memorial. What had stopped her from doing the same?

One bite more of mango and those thoughts faded. I lifted myself off a tree root, one of many that snaked along the black earth of the Amazon basin, and walked to where it tapered toward the river to drink. My shadow was cast onto the calm, dark water. For a moment I considered camping there. The place was peaceful, but I felt compelled to wring out every moment of daylight.

"Let's move out!"

Three Kayapo Indians rose from the jungle floor. I gripped my machete and began to cut a trail through the thick, green vegetation. We had a system: each man in turn at the lead, chopping until exhausted, when another then took his place. For a long twenty minutes I wielded my machete with as much force as the natives.

One of the Indians that spoke English yelled out, "Jack has *Loagi*."

A faint smile crossed the faces of the other Indians. I knew about *Loagi*, the god who enters the body of worthy warriors and gives them the courage to bravely fight their enemies.

"No," another Indian yelled, "no *Loagi*, much *Menpati*." All three Kayapo laughed at the thought of me drinking their favorite intoxicant, perhaps dancing through the night until collapsing from exhaustion.

A quiet breeze stirred patches of green-white orchids, and I avoided cutting those in my path. These elegant flowers reminded me of Catherine—a face oval and classic, with two hazel-flecked eyes peeking out at me, and, like Catherine's, flawed only by a wisp of bangs that eternally found their eyes, and beneath them, an intelligent gaze.

I was living my dream, having traveled to the deep jungle in search of a single plant that would heal just one disease. Impractical, yes, and my chance of discovering even a second-rate plant was remote, but I was living the dream, every researcher's dream. I pulled my shirt up to wipe sweat from my brow and a hand pressed against my back. It was Raoni, one of the Kayapo.

"Enough, Jack. Enough!"

Raoni was right. I was exhausted and stepped aside. Raoni took the lead and got to work, cutting our path through the plants with his swift, compact swing. He was my chief guide and friend, and we had learned to communicate with few spoken words. None of this surprised me. Raoni was brilliant, especially where plants were concerned. He was not formally educated in botany, but he understood the intrinsic nature of plants better than most trained experts. The jungle was his home and, like his father and grandfather before him, he found pleasure in the sanctity of this garden.

"Quiet!" Raoni lowered his machete and stood alert.

I stepped up beside him and we listened to the sound in the distance. His reddish-brown five-foot stature contrasted in every way to my larger frame and lighter skin color.

Raoni motioned for the men to sit. Then, in his sweet, high voice he said, "Chainsaws."

"Loggers? Out here?" People come to harvest trees, in particular, the valuable mahogany. Rapid changes were taking place in this part of the world, with the population exploding and new roads crisscrossing into the heart of the rainforest. What concerned me most was the rapid extinction of many of the rainforest's precious, indigenous plants.

"Why doesn't someone stop this? They're killing this world. Killing it!"

Raoni and the men stared at me with fear in their eyes. I shook my head and collected myself to focus on the impending danger. Harvesting mahogany trees was illegal, and some loggers had been known to dispose of a witness or two in order to avoid jail time.

We soon heard the sound of machetes cutting through the undergrowth. Raoni whispered something and the Kayapo men scrambled into the thickets. I scrambled as well. "Are they coming toward us?"

Raoni nodded.

I was about to give the order to retreat when the machetes went silent. Raoni motioned that the loggers and their Indian guides knew we were in the bushes.

"How could they?" I whispered.

He rubbed his finger across his chest and then under his nose. Somehow, from a distance of fifty yards or so, the Indians had picked up our scent.

Raoni stood up and yelled out in his language. I caught a few words about "jungle people," as he told them not to be afraid.

A voice yelled back, too quickly for me to understand. Raoni motioned for me to stay put while he spoke with the loggers. I tried to stop him, but he disappeared into the jungle. Then, for the first time of this expedition, I removed a holster from my knapsack and buckled it on. It held a .38 Special. I ran after Raoni, but stopped when I saw him in a clearing some thirty yards ahead. "Get out of there!" My words were silenced by a gunshot and a piercing scream. Raoni clutched his stomach, spun around, and fell to the ground. Fear overwhelmed me. I knew that to run and aid him made me a target as well.

A man stepped from the thickets and approached Raoni. He was Indian and, by the looks of his clothing, from one of the local towns. As he moved in Raoni's direction, I saw him remove his knife from its sheath. I pulled my .38 from the holster and took aim, uncertain if I would be able to squeeze the trigger. A doctor was committed to saving lives, not ending them. "Stop! Just leave him alone and go!"

We locked eyes. He studied me briefly and without a second thought continued toward Raoni. There was an explosion and both our bodies jolted. The echo of the blast beat through the forest. At first, the Indian stood motionless; then a look of surprise crept across his face. He stumbled to one knee and fell to the ground a short distance from Raoni. I lowered my weapon. My body began to shake. *This can't be real! Things like this don't happen.* Just as quickly, I regained my senses. There were more loggers in the forest and this was not the time to panic. I squatted under a rubber tree with leaves wide enough to hide me. *Catherine, thank God you're not here. Thank God you stayed home!*

The forest had turned silent. Was it possible one gunshot had frightened the loggers away? Were they content with the bloodletting that had just taken place? One of theirs for one of mine? Instinct took hold. *Just run and save yourself.* I looked to where Raoni lay face down in the clearing; he might still be alive. Twilight had now fallen and was the cloak I needed to pull him out. But once again, my instinct screamed, *flee.* After all, Raoni was probably dead. *Why risk my life to prove it?*

I crawled under a Jacaranda tree and waited, shivering, as dusk settled in. If Raoni was still alive, each moment counted. Finally, an adrenaline surge pushed me into the clearing where I took hold of Raoni and lifted him onto my shoulder. From the corner of my eye I glimpsed a mane of red hair. The man who owned it stood calmly with both hands on his hips. Two more men stepped into the clearing and flanked him. Their eyes were more intense, like predators waiting to pounce. I turned and hurried from the clearing.

The forest was dark and my thrashing had drowned out all other sounds, including that of loggers who might be chasing me. Raoni had begun to weigh me down and my legs were giving out. I stopped and listened for sounds of men in pursuit. Nothing. Had they abandoned the chase?

I laid Raoni on the ground and placed my ear to his chest. A faint heartbeat. *Thank God!* I opened my knapsack and pulled out a small pouch that held a scalpel and a pair of tweezers. Perhaps not the best tools, but better than nothing for extracting a bullet.

My objective was to locate where the bullet had lodged itself and then remove it without Raoni bleeding to death. In a hospital I'd grab a liter bag of intravenous solution and pump it into his stomach, wait a minute, then suck it out. If the solution had filled with blood, I'd know the bleeding was life threatening. There was no bag of solution or pump in my knapsack, so I had to rely on my instinct and guess right.

My next concern was infection; I knew the chance for it flourished in this place even though, when a bullet is fired, the friction of traveling through air sterilizes it. I gripped a penlight in my teeth and, shining it into the medical bag, I found the Alchonone, a greenish gunk. The sticky disinfectant would keep bugs from crawling into the wound. At least, that was my hope. I slipped on latex gloves and removed the scalpel from its casing.

"Raoni, can you hear me?" There was no response. *Good.* I made a four-inch vertical incision down his stomach. To hold the intestine in place, I pushed two sponges into the incision. I shone the penlight into the opening and probed. The bleeding was severe, and the jarring of his body while on my shoulder had not helped matters. I followed the source of blood to a ruptured artery, clamped it, and then searched until the light reflected off a dull metal object lodged in his stomach lining. I grabbed the tweezers and delicately dislodged the bullet.

I bit down on the penlight once more and threaded the suture. Minutes later the ruptured artery was stitched, as was the tear in his stomach lining. Even with perfect surgery Raoni's chance of recovery was slim at best. If the blood loss didn't kill him, an infection could, only more slowly and cruelly.

As I started to suture the incision, everything went dark. The penlight had died. "Damn it!" My hands probed Raoni's stomach until I found the outline of the incision. Stitch by stitch I began to close him up. There was a moan. *"Please, don't wake up now."*

Raoni's breathing became rhythmic again. I sutured the final stitches, bandaged the wound, and stabbed him in the thigh with a syringe of antibiotics. There was nothing more to do. I pulled a shirt from my knapsack and covered the wound. I leaned against a Caoba tree, still afraid the loggers might stumble upon us or that Raoni would awaken in the darkness to discover his belly had been ripped open.

The pounding in my chest was relentless and I took deep breaths to calm myself. Then, I closed my eyes. Catherine appeared, and with her vision came a twinge of pain. Her broken promise to come with me played throughout the night, until sunlight trickled through the braided Acacias. When the sound of tree animals began to scream morning into existence, I knew sleep was no longer possible. I removed the shirt from Raoni's wound and checked the sutures—not perfect, but they would hold. I rose to my feet, gently lifted Raoni and laid him over my shoulder. The sun was due east. I followed it, knowing it would lead to the Kayapo village. Two hours later, Raoni lay in a hut with his family around him.

I returned to my bungalow where I found Brother Johanas from the mission waiting for me. He held a telegram in his outstretched hand.

"I took the liberty of reading it, Jack. Try to stay strong."

I looked at him, then grabbed the piece of paper. *Jack, sorry to tell you this by telegram. We failed to reach you by telephone at the mission. Return to New York immediately. There's been an accident. Catherine has been killed.*
Colter Malone

Chapter Two

"Jack!" Two large, flaccid arms engulfed me and a ruddy cheek pressed into my face. "It's so horrible. I can't believe Catherine's gone." Frances McQueen pulled back to look at me. "Sweet Jesus, how are you holding up, Jack?" She pulled me close again and wept.

It was midnight on a Tuesday night, and we were standing in the hallway on the fourth floor at Memorial Hospital. Nurses inside the station turned to look when they heard the sobbing. Frances had always been a woman of great emotional force; whether laughing or crying, tears always found their way down her cheeks. She was a large woman, and her two hundred pounds of girth pulsated against my body as she squeezed me and wept.

I pushed away. "How did it happen?"

She composed herself. "Crotalus durissus. They found it in Catherine's blood. The doctors don't know how it got there."

"Crotalus? How could it harm her? It's not poisonous." I had used Crotalus in the past and knew it well—venom milked from pit vipers. Once the toxins are removed, Crotalus is used as an agent to separate gene strips from a DNA strand.

"That's all the hospital would say, Jack. Talk to the doctors, maybe they'll—"

"Where's Catherine now?"

Frances was startled by the question. "You don't know?" She teared up again. "She was buried three days ago."

I went numb. "Catherine already buried? How could it be? Colter's telegram didn't mention she'd been buried, only that the services were tomorrow."

"Because you weren't here, her parents made the burial arrangements. Colter and Mitch arranged the memorial service and scheduled it for tomorrow, expecting you'd be back by then."

I sat down and cupped my face in my hands. I didn't know what I was feeling at that moment.

"I'm sorry you missed the funeral, Jack. Only the immediate family and close friends attended, but the ceremony was touching."

To hear Frances describe Catherine's funeral that way made me both angry and upset. When those feelings subsided, self-hate took over. I had failed on every count to provide as a good husband and protector.

Frances's hand came to rest on my shoulder. "You look exhausted, Jack. Why don't you go home and get some rest before the service in the morning."

"I can't go there."

"It's your home. Why not?"

I didn't answer her. To sleep in a room filled with Catherine was, well, and to touch even one item of hers would...

"If you can't go there, maybe get a room somewhere for the night."

* * *

I entered a spacious apartment on the forty-sixth floor of Olympic Towers, located in midtown Manhattan. Every hotel had been sold out for the upcoming millennium celebration, but a late cancellation had made this apartment available. At a thousand a night it was hardly a steal, but at this point the money was of little consequence.

The bellhop followed me into an apartment that consisted of a living room, bedroom, kitchen, and bath. As he was setting my duffel bag down, I walked into the bathroom and closed the door. I held the sink and dropped my head. I remained motionless for five minutes. Or was it thirty? I had the sensation that blood was coursing through my veins much too fast, as though I were on amphetamines or something. But how would I know? I'd never taken a stimulant or even a tranquilizer in my life. There was a rap on the door.

"Are you all right, sir?"

I looked into the mirror and two bloodshot eyes stared back at me. Catherine could have had any man she wanted, but she had chosen me.

Had she married anyone else, she might still be alive. There was another rap on the door.

"Sir, can I get you something? I'll be happy to run downstairs."

My face and scalp began to burn. I stuck my head under the water tap and kept it there until the cold began to numb me. After I dried myself off, I left the bathroom and rejoined the bellboy. "Sorry I kept you."

"It's no problem, sir. I hope you're feeling well."

I walked to the window and looked out over the city. Only a thin pane of glass separated me from the blistering cold and the streets below filled with holiday bustle. It was almost Christmas, the most joyous time of the year.

"I placed your bag near the sofa, sir."

It was rude of me to make the bellboy wait. I should have given him a tip and let him go. I reached into my pocket and pulled out a twenty.

"Thank you. That's very kind, Doctor Lewis. If you need anything, anything at all, sir, just call down and ask for Jimmy."

The door closed behind him as I remained at the window and looked out across the evening sky. A full moon had started its voyage from Brooklyn to Battery Park. Where was Orion's Belt? Not within sight. Not with the glare from so many city lights spoiling the view of the constellations.

I called Colter Malone and then Mitch Cochran. Neither picked up, so I left messages on their answering machines. Exhausted to the point of collapse, I walked into the bedroom where my head fell onto the first pillow it found. Gravity tugged gently at my body. Faint sounds from the street drifted up to the forty-sixth floor, and I listened to the clamor that had made its way into the room. Weight pulled my eyes closed and Catherine appeared. She began to walk toward me and I—

RINGGGG!

Opening my eyes, I tried to adjust to my unfamiliar surroundings.

RINGGGG!

I fumbled the phone to my ear. "Hello."

"Is this Jack Lewis?"

"Yes."

"My name's Vanessa Boulay, a friend of Mitch's. I work for him at Rosetta."

"You work for Mitch?" I said, waking up.

"Yes. I apologize for disturbing you at a time like this, but I got your number off Mitch's answering machine." There was a pause. "He said you'd call once you arrived."

The woman seemed nervous. I sat up on the bed. "Is anything wrong?"

"Well, Mitch was arrested and taken to the Sixth Precinct."

"Arrested?"

Another pause. "He's being questioned as a suspect in Catherine's murder."

I rose to my feet. Her words cleaved into my brain. "What? Catherine was murdered?"

"Oh, my God! You didn't know?"

Chapter Three

Catherine had been murdered and a stranger called to tell me. A close friend was a suspect, and I remembered the woman rattling on about Mitch being innocent and incapable of harming a fly, but it was too late. The buzzing in my head had drowned her out and the room began to spin. I slammed the phone down.

I arrived at the Sixth Precinct at three a.m.

The sergeant at the desk lowered his newspaper and gave me the once-over.

"I'm looking for information on the death of Catherine Lewis."

"You are?"

"Her husband."

"The detective assigned to the case?"

"No idea." He folded the newspaper neatly and set it down before swiveling his chair around and typing a few words into his computer. It took a while for the screen to populate.

"Detective Gravers is assigned." The sergeant looked at his watch. "It's pretty early, but take a seat and I'll find out if he's on duty."

I sat on a wooden bench and waited impatiently, maybe ten minutes or so, with no response from the sergeant. I returned to the desk. "Anything on Detective Gravers?"

The sergeant looked at me over the top of his newspaper. "I doubt he's around. But I did place the call, Mr. Lewis. Give it a few minutes."

With that, he lifted his newspaper in my face and continued where he left off. I was shocked at the treatment I was receiving. It angered me to be so casually dismissed. My wife had been murdered and for that reason alone I deserved better. The longer I stood at the desk, the more infuriated I became, so I walked to the pay telephone on the far wall. If Catherine's parents were staying in town for the memorial service, they might be at our condo. I dropped a quarter into the phone and began to dial.

"Mr. Lewis." The sergeant waved me back to the desk. "Detective Gravers won't be available until late morning."

I walked back over to where the sergeant was sitting. "Someone here must know something about what happened to my wife."

"I wish I could help, but Detective Gravers has the paperwork."

"My wife's dead and no one can tell me anything?"

The sergeant looked at me without saying a word.

"Is Mitch Cochran being held here?"

He typed Mitch's name into the computer. "He's no longer in custody."

"All right, then. Leave a message for Gravers. Tell him I'll be here at noon tomorrow. Would you tell him that?"

"I'll see he gets your message, Mr. Lewis."

I left the precinct and walked up Seventh Avenue. The lights from Times Square were blinding. A digital display hanging on a building read three degrees above zero. My limbs and fingers felt stiff, but I wasn't cold. It then occurred to me that my body was probably in shock. I wasn't even dressed for the cold although I had winter clothes at the condo. I flagged a taxi. "Hudson and Bank Street."

I slipped my key into the lock and heard the tumbler rotate. If Catherine's parents were here, they would hear me enter. The light from the street cascaded through the window and onto the hall closet where my overcoat should have been hanging. When I opened the closet door, however, I didn't see my coat. In fact, I didn't see anything of mine. Looking around the condo, there was little evidence that I had ever lived in this place.

There was no luggage or other sign that Catherine's parent were staying here, so I walked into the bedroom to check if my clothes were in the closet. I noticed the answering machine blinking and pressed the play button. The first message was from the dry cleaner's informing Catherine that they were unable to remove the stain from her skirt. The next was from the maintenance man saying that the water would be shut off on Saturday to correct a plumbing problem. The last message came from the dentist's office advising she had missed her appointment, and that she should call to reschedule.

I turned the machine off and continued to the closet. Catherine's dresses and suits hung there neatly, and on the floor shoeboxes were stacked three high and eight across. She loved buying shoes, but mostly they sat piled up in their boxes, rarely ever worn. An open jewelry box sat on her vanity and I picked up the diamond stud earrings I had bought her, held them in the palm of my hand for a moment and placed them back where I had found them. A cheap red plastic bracelet was tangled in her gold chains; the bracelet was a prize I had won for her at the San Gennaro street festival.

I sat down slowly on the corner of the bed. Thoughts of Catherine flooded my mind. Then, a sound in the hallway broke that train of thought and I looked up. "Catherine!" She stood in the doorway. When I had spoken her name, she walked across the room. Her hazel eyes smiled down at me, and she touched my cheek.

"You're cold, Jack. Did you forget your gloves again?"

"I came to get them, but they weren't—"

"Why did you go? I never thought you'd really do it."

"I told you time and again. Sixteen hours of research every day was too much. It caught up with me. It wore me down. You should've left Memorial when I did. The rainforest was your dream, too."

She lay down on the bed and I was drawn to her side. I ran my finger down the contour of her nose and when her lips puckered, I kissed them. I moved closer so her warm body pressed against me, and the cold melted away.

"Catherine, I..."

Her finger touched my lips. "Shhh. Not a word. I know." Her mouth curled to form a delectable smile and she tugged at me. "Love me, Jack."

Morning's first light woke me and I looked over at Catherine's side of the bed. The blanket was still tucked in as if no one had slept there. "Catherine?" I ran out to the living room and then to the bathroom. Apprehension hit me when I realized she was not here. I leaned against the wall feeling a sense of gloom build within me. How was it possible? I felt the touch of her hand on my face. The warmth of her body pressed against mine. And then there was the love more sumptuous than I deserved. It *did* happen, didn't it? I looked at my watch. "My God! Catherine's memorial service!"

Chapter Four

Frances McQueen stood on the rectory stairs in a half-opened pea coat with her white nurse's uniform showing beneath it. She hurried down the steps and threw her arms around me. "Did you get some sleep, Jack?" Her body shook, even more than at the hospital the night before. The rectory door swung open and Monsignor John Carradine made his way down the stairs. The elderly priest used the handrail to navigate around the icy spots. "My deepest sympathy, Jack," he said, taking hold of my hand.

"Thank you, Father." The monsignor had married us in this church three years earlier, and now he had to preside over Catherine's memorial service. Frances took my hand and we followed him into the rectory. I pulled her to the side. "Have you see Colter or Mitch? I need to talk—"

The monsignor stopped, turned, and looked me in the eye, which caused me to stop in mid-sentence. "The church is full, Jack. I'll start the mass in about ten minutes. After communion I'll say a final prayer and nod for you to come up and give the eulogy."

Catherine's eulogy had not occurred to me. I was not prepared to give it, or for that matter, to accept communion. I was no longer a practicing catholic. Even if I were, killing a man was a mortal sin that required more than a few *Hail Marys* to wash away.

"Are you all right?" the monsignor asked.

I deliberated on whether to tell the monsignor right then and there, but Frances was standing beside me. "Can I speak with you in private, Father?"

We walked into the next room and the monsignor looked at me expectantly. Just then I froze. It became abundantly clear that admitting to killing a man was much more difficult than I thought it possible.

The monsignor broke the ice. "I know how hard this is for you, Jack, being out of the country only to learn that Catherine's been taken from you."

"I can't take communion, Father. I, well, haven't been to confession and—"

16

"Ah, not to worry, Jack." A knowing smile came to his face as he led me into a smaller room at the back of the rectory. We sat down at a card table where only the dim light from the hallway bled into the room. In his most pious self, the monsignor whispered a few words in Latin. "Now, my son, confess your sins before God."

* * *

While sitting at the card table, I confessed only to taking the Lord's name in vain and to swearing on a regular basis. The monsignor sensed there was more going on inside me, that I was holding back, and he implored me to clear my conscience. "Confession is good for the soul," he said. That was when I stood up and walked out.

Frances and I watched as the priest made his way through the passageway that connected the rectory to the church. "We should go, too, Jack. He'll start the service as soon as he reaches the altar, whether we're there or not."

Frances had appointed herself to do the thinking, and I was comfortable with that arrangement. She took my hand and led me into the tunnel.

"There's lots of people in the church, Jack. Not just from Memorial, but half the research industry is here to pay their respects as well." She stopped to wipe a budding tear.

"You all right?" I was barely capable of caring for my own emotions, but I felt compelled to say something to her.

"I've run out of tissues," she said, rummaging through her purse. But it was too late; the dam had burst. I had run out of the condo and never thought to bring tissues. My mind was in no form to plan things out, let alone to remind me to stuff tissues in my pockets. "Just let it out, Frances."

"I'm sorry, Jack. I didn't want to make it harder on you, but it's so painful, and I miss Catherine so much." Her voice echoed in the tunnel. "She came to my rescue when I hadn't a friend in the world. You'd gone by then, but Catherine came and got me and the kids. Oh, *Jesus, Mary, and Joseph,* I was a mess, my face all puffed out like that, and not showing up for work for an entire week. I knew rumors were spreadin' that I was on a binge, but I'd kicked drinkin' long ago, and it wasn't fair that I got pink slipped by the hospital for not showing up. No one knew what was going on, how he hit me, hit the kids, and then he'd lay there in a drunken stupor stinkin' to high heaven on that couch in his underwear and empty bottles of whiskey on the floor. I didn't think we'd ever get away—but Catherine came looking for me. She knocked on the door and saw what I looked like and ... and she grabbed me and the kids and put us in the car and took off. Next day she told Memorial that if they fired me, she'd quit on the spot. And then she got me into that woman's program and, *sweet Jesus,* I wouldn't be here now, Jack. I just wouldn't be here if she'd never come looking for me. Now she's gone and there's this empty spot. I don't know what I'd have done without her, I just don't know. I..." She wiped her nose on her coat sleeve.

The monsignor had stopped at the far end of the passageway and was looking back at us. The light coming from the church silhouetted his body. A moment later the silhouette disappeared when the monsignor turned and walked into the church. Frances was still a wreck and I was unable to comfort her. I needed what little strength I had to get through the service. "Not sure I'll make it on my own, Frances. You may need to help me."

Her eyes lit up. She looked at me and took my hand. "You can count on me, Jack."

We entered the church and I sat in the front row next to Catherine's mother. Frances sat behind me in the second row. I embraced Mrs. Prescott and kissed her on the cheek, and then reached across her and shook Mr. Prescott's hand. Catherine's father was in his mid-seventies and her mother a couple of years younger. Both of them looked more wrinkled and gray than I had ever seen them, and it distressed me to see the pained look on their faces. My presence offered little solace since, to them, I was the person who had abandoned their daughter and gone off on some adventure.

Hundreds of people were in attendance. So many, the church doors had been kept open so those standing on the steps could hear the service. I looked about and saw neither Colter nor Mitch in the first couple of rows. But I was confident they were inside the church somewhere. The monsignor started the mass. He spoke lovingly of Catherine and how fortunate he had been to know her both as a child and as an adult. He spoke about how she had grown up in New York and touched so many people with her warmth, her kindness, her compassion, and how she possessed that wonderfully rare gift of brightening the lives of all who had come to know her. Heartfelt regrets were extended to Catherine's parents and to me for our tragic loss. "Catherine is in God's house now."

A procession of people filed past me to receive communion at the foot of the altar. After the monsignor had placed the host on the last person's tongue, he ended the mass with a final prayer and nodded for me to come up and give the eulogy.

I remained seated until Frances patted my shoulder, urging me on. I rose and faced the congregation, but the few words that floated in and out of my mind had not composed themselves into any speakable form. After a minute, I began to collect my thoughts. I wasn't sure what to say, but I was resolute about one thing. My feelings for Catherine would not be placed on public display. What I felt for her belonged to me, and only me. These guarded memories would resonate only within me. Still, I owed the congregation something, maybe a few words about Catherine's passion for science and medicine, or how she opposed an industry where multinationals wielded so much power over the development of new drugs. Instead, I inexplicably blurted out the sentiment that hung heaviest in my heart. "I left New York six months ago. That was a mistake, as I left Catherine alone and unprotected. I'll never forgive myself." After those three short sentences, I just stood there, looking at no one or nothing.

Frances began to cry again. Suddenly, I felt a hand come to rest on my shoulder. I turned to see Colter Malone, garbed in a royal blue sport coat, his hair wild and blonde as ever. He'd removed his sunglasses to look me over. Colter was handsome, what some might call Hollywood handsome.

"Have a seat, Jack," he said softly, slipping his sunglasses into his pocket. Colter turned to address the congregation. "I'm Colter Malone. Catherine was a colleague and dear friend, and, as many of you know, a remarkable person. A woman not only blessed with charm and intelligence, but one who cared deeply and who touched people in a special way. And, when it came to science, well, Catherine had *the* gift. Her knowledge and wisdom in and around the laboratory was uncanny.

"Many of us here today had reached out to Catherine at one time or another when a project had hit bottom and we'd exhausted every possible avenue to get it moving again. Yes, we turned to Catherine and, step by step, she would dissect the pieces of a project and reassemble them until it had been resurrected. And then, as all fine teachers do, she would walk us through the critical stage where we had miscalculated or overlooked something, and point out the necessary correction. Scientists were an important part of Catherine's family, and she loved nothing more than helping each and every one of us. Her loss has left a gaping hole in our community, a hole that will never be filled. We will never forget her. May Catherine rest in peace." Before walking away, Colter once again placed a hand on my shoulder. I could say nothing else. The monsignor thanked everyone for attending and, row by row, people began to file out of the church.

Frances walked around to the front row. "Are you all right?"

"I'll be fine."

She handed me a piece of paper. "I'm late for work, Jack, but call me if you need to talk to someone." She hugged me and walked away as Colter approached. We embraced. It was comforting to be in the company of a good friend. Colter was the first scientist I had hired for the LEC Enzyme project at Memorial. Three grueling years later the importance of this enzyme had finally received the credit it deserved. Colter was there the night I received the Einstein-Betchel Award and the check for $400K that went along with it.

After we sat down in the pew, I searched for the right words to ask. "How did she die?"

Colter was taken aback by my directness. "You don't know? No one's told you what happened?" His powder blue eyes examined me, as though he were afraid to speak words that might offend me or cause me more pain. "The hospital should've reached out to you."

"Crotalus was found. That's all I know."

"I heard she accidently injected herself."

"Catherine? Inject herself? She was too good to make that kind of mistake. Besides, the police are calling it murder."

"Murder? Are you serious?"

"A woman called last night and said Mitch was being questioned."

"Mitch? My God! I know he's a little wacky, but he'd never harm Catherine."

"Was it...did she...how long did it take?"

Colter lowered his eyes a moment, and then looked back up at me. "About four hours from what I've heard. After they found her on the lab floor in a coma, they took her to a room on the fourth floor. Little could be done at that point. I don't think she suffered, though, if that's what you're asking."

"You know for a fact that she didn't suffer?"

"Well, no, but she was in a coma, and the doctors couldn't bring her out of it. I got to the hospital as soon as I heard. With you out of the country, I wanted to be there for her. By that time, the poison had been in her body a while and her vital organs were shutting down. There was little anyone could do. Well, then Mitch showed up and all hell broke loose. He wouldn't accept the doctors' diagnosis. So, after they had left the room, Mitch took Catherine to the basement to have her contusion x-rayed."

"What?"

"I know. It's crazy. The doctors had already performed a blood test and confirmed that Crotalus was in her system and nothing could be done, so taking x-rays made little sense at that point. It's no real surprise that Mitch thought he knew more than the doctors."

It was not a surprise. Mitch thought he was right about most things, and once he got an idea in his head, little, if anything, could be done to dissuade him.

I badgered Colter with more questions: Who were these doctors? Was someone else in the laboratory with her? Who found her on the floor? Given the circumstances, he answered the questions with great deference to me. Finally, his weary expression told me he had had enough, and I was convinced that he had told me everything he knew about that morning. I sat back and looked across at him. His back was arched, waiting for my next barrage of questions, but instead, I changed the subject. "Are you still at Memorial?"

"Not for much longer, Jack. I'm leaving the city right after New Year's."

"Where to?"

"I've an offer from a research firm in Los Angeles. The lifestyle on the west coast has always intrigued me. Besides, Memorial just isn't the same."

"What do you mean?"

"It's been a steady exodus of the top scientists there. Simmons and Suzaki are gone, and they're only the tip of the iceberg. With the multinationals playing catch-up, most biotech scientists have their résumés out on the street. Suzuki received stock options that will make him a millionaire before he even shows up for work. I'm hoping to negotiate a similar package."

Half of my brain listened to Colter and the other half tried to make sense out of what he had conveyed about Catherine's death. I needed to question other people if I ever expected to understand what happened on the day she died.

The monsignor came over to where Colter and I were sitting. "Mr. and Mrs. Prescott are waiting for you at the door, Jack. And there's a woman asking for you."

I excused myself from Colter and headed for the front of the church. On the way, a woman wearing a black veil approached me.

"How are you, my darling?" I recognized Michelle's throaty French accent before she lifted her veil. We held each other and stood motionless without speaking a word. It would challenge me to define Michelle, as I cannot fit her into any one or two particular categories the way I do most people. I had known her long before Catherine had ever come into my life, and looking back, I cannot recall at what point I first flirted with her. All I remember was my subtle overture, and then her kind and gracious rebuff. Our relationship traveled down a different path from that point on. Over time a deep friendship blossomed, where Michelle, as my confidante and occasional sounding board, was the one person I could trust to share my deepest doubt or an aspiring thought or two. She was the one woman who, for reasons unspoken, gave freely of herself to me, and to this day she still does. As we held each other in the church it was no different on that day. Michelle took on the role of mother to me, and the strength I drew from her embrace was considerable. A moment later I stepped back and looked into her eyes. "Catherine's parents are leaving and I need to say goodbye to them. Can you wait for me?"

"No, darling, I must leave now. And besides, there are many people you need to speak with today. Come to the restaurant later. We'll spend time together there." Michelle Chavier was the proprietor of La Vie en Rose, the restaurant in SoHo where we had met many years ago.

She looked me up and down. "You're so thin. You need your strength, my dear. Come, and I'll cook for you." She kissed me on both cheeks, lowered her veil and left the church.

The Prescotts were surrounded by people when I finally reached them. Catherine's father saw me approach and reached into his coat pocket. "Here, take this, Jack. It's directions to Catherine's gravesite. Her headstone will be erected tomorrow so you needn't worry about that." Without another word he turned and rejoined his wife.

His comment and abrupt dismissal pierced me. If I had doubted for one moment his anger with me, it was now apparent that I would likely never be absolved of my sin against his daughter. Here I was, holding directions to my own wife's gravesite, and the manner in which Mr.

Prescott had slapped them into my hand was another indication that he intended to inflict pain. He had succeeded. The Prescotts were in pain as well, I reminded myself. They had entrusted their daughter to me, and how did I repay their trust? I had left Catherine and traveled to the Rainforest. It was hard to justify that to them, or even to myself. Not when you consider that the Prescotts were here the day Catherine and I got married. And on that day, I had promised to love, honor, and protect her until death do us—

"Jack!"

A short, stocky man with curly, dark hair approached me. It was Mitch Cochran.

He threw his arms around me. "I'm sorry, Jack, so very, very sorry."

I pushed him away. "Why did the police question you?"

My question had surprised and maybe even hurt Mitch. He looked around to see if people were watching us. "I'd rather not discuss that now, Jack. I—"

"Answer me. What did the police want with you?"

Mitch stepped closer and spoke softly. "All right, if you insist, here it is. The police are not convinced that Catherine's death was an accident. They interrogated me, and let me go."

"That's it? No more than that?"

"Let's not talk here, Jack. I was grilled enough at the police station. If you want more information, speak with Detective Gravers."

I looked at my watch. "Gravers!"

Chapter Five

It was 12:05 p.m. when I arrived at the Sixth Precinct for my meeting with Detective Gravers.

"He's not in the station right now."

"He was supposed to meet me at noon."

The officer looked at his watch. "Well, sir, he's only a few minutes late. Knowing him, he'll be here soon. Have a seat and I'll let you know when he arrives."

I walked over to the bench and sat down. The station was active with people coming and going, some handcuffed, and others talking loudly, letting their displeasure be known. Several minutes had passed and Gravers remained missing in action, so I walked back to the sergeant's desk.

"Look, is there anyone here who can help me?"

"You must be Jack Lewis."

I turned around and saw a nondescript man of medium build. He was wearing a dark suit.

"I'm Detective Gravers. Sorry to keep you waiting. Would you follow me?"

Gravers led me down a hallway lined with filing cabinets and into a small office.

"Have a seat, Doctor Lewis. Coffee?"

"No, thank you."

Gravers had been one rip away from opening a fresh packet of coffee, but he tossed it on the desk and sat down. "My condolences, Doctor Lewis. I know this hasn't been easy for you, losing your wife that way, and then having to come here twice to get information on the circumstances surrounding her death." He pulled his folder on Catherine from a tall stack and began looking through its contents as though he were piecing together a puzzle. "Your wife died after being injected with a venom by the name of Crotalus durissus. A puncture mark on her back led doctors to believe it was an accident, thinking she had somehow backed into the needle. The certificate lists your wife's death as an accident as well. But,"

Gravers paused, "we need to look at these findings more closely, as she also had a head injury and multiple bruises on her arms and back. May I ask you a couple of questions?"

"First, let me ask you about something that's been bothering me. Was Mitch Cochran brought in and questioned?"

"Yes, he was, but I'd like to go over the information we have on your wife's case first."

I nodded for him to proceed.

Gravers looked down at the folder. "Do you know anyone who disliked Catherine, or would want to harm her?"

"No one. I've never met anyone who disliked her. She was quite remarkable that way."

"Was Catherine a physically active woman?"

"I'm not sure what you mean."

"Did she play sports, study karate, or indulge in physical contact activities?"

"Catherine rarely exercised. Like most of us, she intended to, but never found the time."

"Was she seeing anyone while you were out of the country?"

I wasn't sure how to answer him. The question had crossed my mind on more than a few occasions, but I refused to believe that she would find comfort in another man's arms. "I don't believe so. Why do you ask?"

"I need to establish whether your wife had bruises on her body prior to the morning of her death. If so, she may have had an accident at home, or, well, she may have been in an abusive relationship."

Those words hurt. "Catherine would never allow anyone to abuse her."

"It's only speculation, and I had to ask it." Gravers looked at the folder again. "There was a break-in at Memorial that morning, and we're looking into any possible links to your wife's death. The hospital's been robbed twice in the last three months, and the morning of your wife's death two laboratories were ransacked and equipment stolen. Often the thieves are drug addicts who sell the equipment to buy their next fix."

Gravers paused. "Doctor Lewis, I'm going to assume your wife was not in an abusive relationship, and that she received those bruises at work. That leaves us with two scenarios. Scenario one: Catherine may have been working with Crotalus in her laboratory when burglars entered. Maybe she confronted them, or panicked, but a struggle took place where she was pushed or backed into the syringe sitting on her bench. She was knocked to the floor, or fell, accounting for the contusion on her head and bruises to her body. Then there's scenario two." Gravers stared over at me. "Someone intended to harm your wife and, after knocking her to the ground, they injected poison into her body."

Gravers picked up two sets of pictures that had been taken of Catherine. "I normally don't do this, but since you're a doctor, I have no issue letting you see these pictures before they're cleared for release. The first set was taken shortly after your wife was admitted into intensive care. The second set was taken after she had expired. I'll caution you that these pictures are not pleasant to look at, especially the second set, where your wife's body had bloated from the Crotalus. You may not recognize her."

He placed the pictures on the desk and I deliberated whether or not to pick them up. "I'll look at them another time. Do we have anything else to talk about?"

"Just one thing more. The official medical report states the cause of your wife's death as respiratory failure. Crotalus contains a lethal protein called alpha-neurotoxin that paralyzes the respiratory muscles. It was only a matter of time before her breathing was disrupted."

I struggled to push the image of Catherine fighting to breathe out of my head. I began to analyze the two scenarios Gravers had described. I did not accept the first scenario in which Catherine had been accidently stabbed with the syringe. You don't accidently empty the entire liquid content of a syringe into your body. It was more likely that someone had intentionally injected her. I couldn't stop the horrid vision I was having of Catherine on the floor struggling with her attacker. Did she yell for help? Did she call out my name? Did the killer place his dirty hand over her mouth?

"Doctor Lewis, are you all right?"

"Yeah, I'm fine." Gravers continued to describe more details surrounding Catherine's death, but I had reached my limit. My brain was incapable of storing any more information. Finally, he stopped talking. "You've convinced me."

"Convinced you of what?"

"That Catherine was murdered. My question to you is, how do you plan to catch her killer?"

Gravers closed Catherine's file. "Officially, I can't say to you that she was murdered, but I'm going to approach the investigation that way. First, we'll question everyone who came into contact with your wife that day, to uncover a motive. Anyone suspicious will be questioned in greater detail. The goal is to link them with the break-in at your wife's laboratory; and if we can do that, there's a good chance we'll squeeze a confession out of them. Short of that, we'll continue to compile as much information as possible, and with a little luck, at some point we'll piece together what really happened that morning."

"And if you fail to piece things together?"

"I won't kid you. If we complete our investigation without any evidence of foul play, then your wife's case will remain unsolved. That doesn't mean we won't reopen it if new evidence comes to light."

"How long will it take to investigate?"

"It's hard to tell, but I'd say about two weeks. Most of the facts should be collected by then."

"That's it? Two weeks is all murder cases get these days?"

Gravers glared at me for my condescending tone. "I can sit here and tell you that a crack team of detectives will work around the clock and won't stop until your wife's killer is found, Doctor Lewis. But I'm not going to do that because I've been down that road. If I work twenty-four hours a day for the next year, it's still not enough time to handle the case load sitting on my desk."

He stood up and ripped open the packet of coffee he had tossed aside earlier. He poured it into the machine. "You seem like a man with some means, Doctor Lewis. Do yourself a favor. Hire a private investigator. It'll save you the grief of calling me every day and asking questions I can't answer. I get too many of those calls now."

I had seen a hundred movies where a cop says, *my hands are tied, there's nothing I can do.* I just never thought I'd be the one to have them said to me. I got up and walked to the door with the feeling that this might be a story with a bad ending. I turned and looked at him. "You never answered my question about Mitch Cochran. Why was he questioned?"

Gravers poured water into the coffee machine. "He was a close friend of your wife's and took it upon himself to remove her from intensive care to be x-rayed. He's not a doctor, and that's an unusual thing for someone to do. Then, after that, he was found in your wife's laboratory where, admittedly, he was removing confidential files that belonged to the hospital. I'd say those are two good reasons to question him."

"Was he charged with anything?"

"No charges were filed against him. Cochran told us that when he took your wife for x-rays, he was trying to save her life. Since nothing he did at that point further harmed her, we had no grounds to book him. And, since he returned the hospital files, Memorial agreed not to press charges. Cochran got off scot-free, except for a restraining order. He's not allowed within five hundred yards of the hospital. We found nothing else to charge him with in the six hours he was here."

"You questioned him for six hours?"

Gravers turned and faced me. It was the first time he showed any emotion. "During the questioning, one of our detectives accused him of putting those bruises on your wife's body. Cochran lost it and had to be restrained. We cooled him off in the tank for a couple hours."

Chapter Six

A biting wind stung when I left the precinct and stepped onto the street. I was torn between going back to the condo or to Olympic Towers. I flagged a taxi.

"Olympic Towers."

I collapsed on the sofa when I arrived, trying to make sense of it all. The advice Gravers had given me to hire a private detective played over and over in my mind. Not only did this advice make good sense, it resonated with me. I knew I'd have to hire the best detective possible. One with honed skills and a track record for solving murder cases.

A knock on the door startled me. No one knew I was staying here except for Frances. When I opened it, Mitch Cochran was standing in the hallway.

"I thought you'd be at the condo," he said, allowing himself in and looking the place over. "What are you doing here?" He walked to the window and looked down at the bustling street below. "Monsignor's worried about you, Jack. He doesn't think it's good for you to be alone right now. He asked that I keep an eye on you, maybe convince you to see a doctor."

"Why would I need a doctor?"

"I don't know. He said, and I agree, you're under a lot of stress, and maybe you blame yourself for Catherine's death. It must've been some conversation you two had. And you refused communion, too, he said."

"The church must've changed since I've been away. Used to be priests weren't allowed to discuss your private business with people. Maybe the monsignor needs a refresher course."

Mitch smiled. "Maybe a refresher course wouldn't hurt him, you're right. But maybe older people don't deal with pressure too well, either, especially when they care about someone. Don't worry; the monsignor didn't give away any secrets. Although, now that I think about it, maybe one did slip out."

"What one was that?"

"I don't recall his exact words, but the gist was that you're dealing with multiple sins. He didn't say much more, but it was enough to concern me. Maybe if you're not feeling right, a therapist isn't a bad idea."

"I don't need a therapist. I need answers." Gravers may have grilled Mitch at the station, but I had my own questions for him. "Why did you remove Catherine from intensive care?"

"She had bruises on her body and a contusion on her head, and those three geniuses that call themselves doctors hadn't x-rayed her. What if she had survived the Crotalus poisoning only to have a fractured skull kill her? The doctors should've covered all their bases. Catherine deserved every chance, and that's what I gave her."

"Three doctors said Catherine wouldn't survive the day, and you thought they were wrong and you were right?" My blood began to boil and I wanted to throw Mitch out, but instead I turned away. After a minute, I turned to face him again. "All right, you did what you thought was right. Your actions were bizarre and unorthodox, to say the least, and I have to believe you tried to help her, so let's just leave it there."

"Okay. Now that that's over, can we talk about you? What in heaven's name are you doing in this place, Jack? And are you going to stay mad at me, or can we talk like we're actually friends? Why are you here? You should be with people who care about you. You can't go through this alone."

"I'm hiring a private investigator."

Mitch raised an eyebrow and looked at me as though I had a screw loose. "Investigator?"

"Gravers gave me the idea. I want a P.I. and I want the best money can buy."

"Where's this coming from, Jack? Let the police handle it. You need to work on recovering from the most horrific event of your life. Don't pile more stress on yourself." He paused, but continued to search my face. "Unless there's something you're not telling me? Is there?"

Mitch walked closer and we stood nose to nose. Well, not exactly. My nose was six inches higher than his, but his was larger. His eyes searched mine to see if he could discover something, anything. Mitch was a master at getting people to open up, and at that moment I felt vulnerable.

I mentioned at the beginning of this story that three extraordinary events had occurred on December 16th. Two of them I've already mentioned: killing a man in the Rainforest and finding out that Catherine had been taken from me. The third event had occurred earlier that same day when I met with my oncologist in Manaus. The news I received was not good.

The more Mitch spoke, the more the pressure inside me mounted. I had been given some heavy baggage to carry, and I needed to unload some of that pressure, which meant confiding in someone. It meant trusting Mitch to keep my secret no matter what. There were only three people in this world that I trusted. Mitch was one of them. And so, just like that, I blurted it out. "There's something I haven't told you. I have a brain tumor. It's inoperable. I've got two, maybe three weeks. That's it."

Chapter Seven

Rutger Dobler hurried down the hallway to his forty-sixth floor corner office at Nine West 57th Street. He opened an envelope stamped 'Personal and Confidential' and read the bad news: Europe's losses were greater than expected, and might reach $100 million. He walked to his desk and pressed the intercom. "Get Daniel."

Daniel Von Hoff, Rutger's Chief Financial Officer, entered the office minutes later. "Welcome back, Rutger. I didn't expect you back from vacation for another week."

"I hadn't planned to cut it short, but this company has urgent business issues that need serious attention. The bleeding has to stop." Rutger walked over and held out the telegram for Von Hoff, who was short and portly in stature next to him. With his sleek blonde hair, chiseled features, and perfectly tailored blue suit, Rutger displayed an amount of elegance most other men wished they possessed.

"Whew! Europe's down $80 million for the quarter, and getting worse. That's more than I expected." Von Hoff sat down on the leather sofa and poured himself a glass of water from the pitcher on the table in front of him.

Rutger sat on the corner of his desk. "What can we expect stateside?"

"I won't have those figures for another two days."

"Ballpark it."

Von Hoff set the glass down on the table. "I'm not sure I can. This company hasn't seen a losing quarter in twenty-five years. I'd be guessing."

Rutger gazed coolly at him. "Then guess."

"Since you're holding my feet to the fire, I'd say we'll lose another $50 million in the U.S., give or take $10 million."

Rutger didn't flinch. "What's done is done. But we need to protect this company from these kinds of losses ever happening again. I've outlined a strategy that requires approval from the others."

"You mean the multinationals?"

"Yes, but Grandfather doesn't think they'll go along with us."

The intercom buzzed. Rutgers leaned over his desk to answer it. "What is it?"

"There's a Robert Farrington in the lobby to see you, sir."

"Tell Farrington that I'm in meetings all day, and inform him to *never* show up at this company again without an appointment." Rutger turned back to Von Hoff. "Now, I want you to work with my father to develop a reduction plan for the European workforce. Try not to touch our plants in Germany or the Netherlands. We're in the middle of some rather delicate negotiations there."

"What about Brazil? We're losing our shirts there."

"I'll need to think about Brazil. There are a few diplomatic feathers we can't afford to ruffle. For now, stick to Europe, and if we —"

There was a knock at the door. Rutger's secretary poked her head into the office. "I'm sorry, Mr. Dobler, but Mr. Farrington will not leave. He's demanding to see you. He's yelled at the receptionist and she's afraid he'll get violent. Should I call security?"

Rutger looked at Von Hoff. "Get started, Daniel. I'll meet with you later. I'll expect to see a draft of your plan by the end of the day." He turned to his secretary. "Show Farrington into my office."

Rutger stepped into the hallway to meet Robert Farrington. His tattered suit and frail appearance were visible even at the other end of the corridor. His appearance was wraithlike—cheeks gaunt and ashen, and his wan body was markedly undernourished. To pass Farrington on the street you would be hard pressed to believe he was an accomplished scientist who had developed an important drug. As Farrington entered the office, Rutger saw his bloodshot eyes, and flashed a smile to ease the moment.

"Robert, good to see you again. It's been too long."

Farrington walked past Rutger and stood stiffly in the middle of the room.

"Have a seat, Robert. Can I pour you a drink?"

"That's not why I'm here."

Rutger walked to the refrigerator and filled two glasses with ice. He dropped a lime wedge and poured Pellegrino into each, then set one of the glasses down in front of Farrington.

"You look upset, Robert, so why not put everything on the table, so to speak." Rutger sat down on the sofa and sipped his drink.

"You *know* why I'm here, so don't act like you don't."

"Please, Robert, let's not quibble. What's on your mind?"

"It's been two years since I sold you the rights to Procelium, and still it hasn't reached the market. I doubt it ever will. All I get from your people is the runaround, and I get the same from you."

"We are working diligently to get FDA approval, Robert, but it hasn't been easy. They keep asking for more data to support our claim that Procelium actually reduces brain swelling in encephalitic patients, and that the drug will not induce toxic side effects. We lose another three months each time information has to be sent to them. You know how cautious the FDA can be in these matters."

"Procelium passed every toxic side-effect test long before I sold it to you. All you had to do was pay the FDA approval cost to get it to market. Procelium hasn't advanced one iota under your control, and it sure as hell isn't going to reach the market with your family controlling it."

"You seem to forget, Robert, that you lacked the funds to complete the research. That's why we agreed to assist in getting Procelium approved and to market."

"What you mean to say is that's when you stole my drug to keep it off the market!"

The telephone rang and Rutger lifted the handset. "Yes, send it through." Rutger kept his eyes on Farrington while he waited for the call to come through. "Darling, how are you? ... No, not at all. Tell me what you have in mind.... Sounds wonderful. I'll see you at eight, then.... Love you, too." Rutger placed the telephone down and turned back to Farrington. "Let's stop this nonsense, Robert. You did agree to the terms and conditions of our contract, didn't you?"

"You and your grandfather were very clever. You knew I was desperate to see Procelium succeed. You took advantage of me!"

"We do not take advantage of desperate and, may I add, exhausting people, Robert. We—"

"You lied. You promised to get FDA approval within six months. That never happened. You said I'd receive royalty checks. That never happened. And now you want me to believe it's not your fault that Procelium hasn't reached the market. I was a fool to trust you—" Farrington paused. "I want Procelium back. I've worked too hard and sacrificed too many years to be cheated by you."

"We have not broken any terms in our agreement, Robert, and repurchasing Procelium is out of the question. We've invested far too much—millions—in its development. We believe that, in time, once we weave through this FDA mess, Procelium will be highly successful." Rutger took a sip of water and set the glass down on the table. "Now, think, Robert. You really don't want to pursue a hostile relationship, do you? Besides, it's perfectly clear in our agreement that we have total say as to how Procelium is developed."

Farrington's lips tightened. "You love saying that, don't you?"

"Accept the fact, Robert. You don't own Procelium any longer. You receive only royalties from this drug, and that's not counting the $25,000 given to you by Grandfather and me. The money we so generously—"

"Procelium would have been approved by now if I still owned it, and—"

"You were flat broke when we met you," Rutger said. "You hadn't even pocket change. We put food on your table and a roof over your head. You should be grateful."

"I know what you're doing. You're trying to distract me again, but it won't work this time. You think I don't know what's going on? That Procelium competes with your own drug? A drug with eight years of patent protection still left on it? That's the reason Procelium hasn't reached the market. You're protecting the profits on that garbage drug you sell!"

"You had better watch—"

"I want Procelium back, or I'm going to the Attorney General. I'll tell her what you're doing, and a lot more, too. I'm not the only one you've cheated. I know others —they'll back me up."

"Are you threatening me, Robert?"

"People are dying because Procelium hasn't reached the market, and for what? So you can make millions off your own worthless drug. Is money all you care about?"

Rutger lifted his eyebrow. "I think this meeting is over, Robert. You're getting that desperate look, and I don't want to be accused of taking advantage of you again."

"You're going to be sorry that—"

"Good day, Robert. I'm already late for my next appointment." Rutger walked to the door, opened it, and waited.

"You'll hear from me, you and your grandfather both. I'll see you in front of a senate sub-committee. Just you wait!" Farrington stormed out.

Rutger picked up the telephone and dialed his grandfather's number. "Farrington just paid me another visit. He made his usual threats, but this time he said he's going to the Attorney General."

"We need to keep an eye on him."

"I agree, Grandfather. There goes my intercom. I need to run." Rutger hung up and took the call from his receptionist. "It's Mr. Tsai on line four. He says it's important that he speak with you."

"Tell him I can't be disturbed right now. I'll speak with him tomorrow, or at the convention." Rutger sat behind his computer and began to add the final touches to the presentation he'd written the night before. Farrington's visit had inspired him to add another strategic point to the presentation that he would be giving to the other multinationals. Point Five: *The FDA drug approval process can be used as a tool to slow the rapid growth of biotechs.* He deleted the title "The Four-Point Plan," and renamed it "The Five-Point Plan."

Rutger picked up the phone and called Daniel Von Hoff. "Daniel, have you finished the cut-back plan for Europe yet?"

Chapter Eight

I told Mitch my story from the beginning. It had started with vision problems while in the Rainforest, and was followed by two hallucinatory episodes. I traveled to Manaus and had a physical examination, which led to a brain scan, and then an MRI and emission tomography test. My doctor had consulted with two other doctors before sharing the diagnosis with me. In the end, they all agreed that I have a glioblastoma multiforme grade-IV incurable astrocytomas. In short, an incurable, malignant tumor, and, as happens with this type of tumor, I have three options for handling it. Palliative: receive medical care in a hospital to comfort me until I expire. Operate: I might live longer, but my mental and physical abilities would be significantly impaired. Do nothing: which is what I chose. In other words, to live each day the best I could for as long as I lasted.

Mitch was silent. The news depressed him, but only briefly. Ever the optimist, Mitch believed no mountain was too high to climb and no illness too severe to remain uncured. "You're back in New York, Jack, with the best doctors in the world."

Once more I explained to him that no one had ever survived a malignant astrocytomas tumor, and there was no sense looking for a doctor to cure me. Finally, it sank in with Mitch and he slowly accepted the truth of my fate.

* * *

Later that day Mitch called me. His voice was subdued, and he told me he had planned to wait a couple of weeks before sharing some news with me. He wanted to wait until I was back on my feet, he said, when I had recovered enough to handle what he had to tell me. But learning of my grave condition had changed everything. He said it was imperative that we meet at Rosetta first thing in the morning.

"Why?"

"Just come in the morning. Actually, there's two things we need to discuss, but one of them I'll need to show you."

"Don't say that and then not tell me. You need to show me what?"

After a long silence, Mitch spoke. "If Catherine was murdered, I might know the reason why.

* * *

Outside the Towers the doorman ushered me into a waiting limousine. Before driving down Fifth Avenue, the limo driver introduced himself as Eddie. I got the impression that the doorman had guided me to this particular limo and I suspected the driver and he were working a small-time hustle. As a rule, it annoyed me whenever someone tried to pull the wool over my eyes, but this morning I let it pass. I was obsessed with getting to Rosetta to hear Mitch's reason why Catherine might have been killed. I leaned back and closed my eyes. Last night had been difficult. Catherine's death had hit me especially hard once I was alone. I was up and down most of the night. Easily, it was the worst night of my life. Pain in my head had ebbed and flowed most of the night, and just when I started to drift off to sleep, it blasted me yet again.

"We're here, Doctor Lewis." The car came to a halt in front of Rosetta Laboratories on Waverly Street in the Village. Eddie turned around and asked. "Should I wait?"

It was the first time I saw Eddie's face. He was young, twentyish, and Italian-looking, with dark, curly hair, and straight, white teeth. He spoke with a distinct Brooklyn accent.

"No, that won't be necessary. I'll be a while. How much?"

"Twenty bucks. Should I pick you up later?"

"I'm not sure when I'll be leaving."

"Here, take my card, Doc. Call me when you're close to leaving. If the number's busy, call Jimmy back at the hotel. He knows how to reach me real fast."

Eddie jumped out and came around to open my door. The din from the city rushed into my head. It allowed me to appreciate the quietness I had found inside Eddie's car. As he closed the door behind me I turned back and looked the limousine up and down. It was a chariot from the seventies—a vintage Cadillac in perfect condition.

Back inside the limo, Eddie rolled down the side window and yelled out, "Tap your knuckle against the fender, Doctor Lewis."

I did, and heard a heavy thud. "Pretty thick metal."

"*Very* thick metal, Doctor Lewis. This limo has quite a story. Remind me to tell you some time." Eddie rolled up his window and said something else, but I couldn't hear him through the glass. Slowly, the limousine slipped away from the curb and rolled down the street.

I walked up the brownstone steps that led into the Rosetta Laboratories. Once inside, I found myself staring at an empty reception desk in the foyer. I waited there for a minute, but no one came out to greet me. It was unlike Mitch to allow such easy access into his building, especially as it was located across the street from Washington Square Park, renowned for its drug dealers and transients.

"Hello? Anyone here?" When no one answered, I walked past the reception area, down a narrow hallway and then down the stairs to the laboratory. It had been renovated since the last time I was here. It may seem odd, but I viewed research equipment as friends who labored alongside me to uncover hidden secrets buried deep within the fold of a molecule.

There was an ultracentrifuge analyzer against the wall, and I failed to recall the last time my hands had touched one. Petri dishes lined benches and a stack of culture flasks sat beside a small vortex mixer. A shelf full of reagents colorfully decorated another wall while an incubator sat quietly in the corner, most likely growing freshly spliced bacteria cultures.

The inside of the refrigerator bloomed with the biology of enzymes, gene snippets and human cells. Beyond that stood dozens of file cabinets filled with folders, each crammed with research reports. There was some scribbling on a lone chalkboard. I knew that scribbling was no less important to the scientist who had rendered it than were brush strokes to an artist's unfinished canvas.

"May I help you?" A voice broke the silence. A matronly woman stood in the doorway to the laboratory.

"I'm here to see Mitch Cochran."

"Who shall I say is calling?"

"Jack Lewis."

"Oh, Doctor Lewis," she said, allowing her shoulders to relax. "You gave me a start. Mitch said to expect you. We were broken into the other night and I'm still a bit shaky. If you'll follow me, I'll take you up to Mitch's office."

As we passed through the vestibule I heard the voices of two men who were on their way down the stairs. There was no mistaking the high-pitched trill in Mitch's voice, a foible of his that occurred when he became emotional. He and the other man had stopped halfway down the staircase. The other man sounded upset about something.

"I'm telling you, Mitch, I'll quit before I work with him again. I mean it."

"Now, Isaac, be patient. Franz can't help it. He's a perfectionist."

"Tell him I need that model today. And if you don't, I'll—"

"Now don't say anything you'll regret, Isaac. I'll speak to Franz, I promise. Go back to work and let me handle it from here."

The man hesitated for a moment, then turned and walked back up the stairs. I stood at the bottom of the staircase in plain view of Mitch.

"Jack!" He ran down to greet me. "Welcome to the new and improved Rosetta Laboratories." Mitch was proud of the renovations and began to point them out.

"I've already seen the new laboratory downstairs."

"You have? Let me take you back down there and show you what you missed."

I was about to remind Mitch that I was here about Catherine and how she might have been killed, not to discuss his renovation, but I held off when he asked me to follow him upstairs. As it turned out, that was only so he could introduce me to one of his prize scientists.

"Jack, meet Franz Weber, our most senior scientist and crystallographer."

From six feet away he appeared cherubic. I forced a smile, stepped closer, and shook hands with him. I felt his fleshy, damp palm and the pointy, fat fingers that shook my hand back. Standing much closer to him now, it became clear there was nothing cherubic about this man at all. In fact, I was struck by the painfully serious look on his face. Weber looked about fifty, and his short, round body contrasted with, what seemed to me, a rather large, square head.

"It's a pleasure to meet you, Doctor Lewis. I am familiar with your work on the LEC Enzyme."

Weber was German but spoke English quite well, and was formal in both manner and dress. Under his white lab coat he wore a black suit and tie, suggestive of how scientists had dressed forty years earlier. I was flattered that Weber knew my name and had knowledge of my research, but there was something queer about him that made me uneasy in his presence. It was nothing I could pinpoint exactly, but he seemed off-kilter in some odd way.

"Now, if you would excuse me," Weber said, "I have a pressing schedule today." He bowed his head slightly and disappeared down the hallway.

"Unusual man," I said, with the hope that Weber's was the last introduction I would have to suffer through this morning.

"Yes, a bit. But we're fortunate to have Franz at Rosetta. He's from Heidelberg, where he was a Professor of Genetic Engineering at the University there."

"Really? What brought him to New York?" I was immediately sorry I'd asked, as I really had no interest at all in how Weber had found his way from Heidelberg to New York.

"I'm not really sure. He has no family here, but apparently he's always wanted to live in New York. Actually, I had no openings for a geneticist when he showed up six months ago and applied for a position. But I was in desperate need of a crystallographer. I just happened to mention that opening to Franz, and he said, fine, he'd take it. As you might guess, I was skeptical of course, knowing the training of a genetic engineer is worlds apart from that of a crystallographer. But Franz assured me that I wouldn't be disappointed. I agreed to hire him on a thirty-day trial, and, well, he's still here."

"That's quite a story. It's rare that a scientist walks in off the street to fill a position like that. You'd be hard-pressed to find a top crystallographer even if you had advertised for one." Before Mitch could utter another word, I took him by the arm. I had reached my limit with the small talk. "We need to get down to business. I—"

"You don't need to say another word. Follow me."

Mitch handed me a file when we reached his office. I could tell from the handwriting on it that it had belonged to Catherine. "Someone broke into Rosetta last week and tried to steal this file. Did you know that Catherine was working on a cure for the common cold?"

"The common cold? You're kidding."

"That file contains most of her research. It's impressive work."

I skimmed through four or five pages and saw that Catherine had been experimenting with a way to protect blood cells from becoming infected by the cold virus. "What's this? She named her drug Cold?"

Mitch laughed. "It's a reasonably good name."

I dropped the file on his desk. "You're saying someone broke into Memorial and killed Catherine for this file?"

"I can't say that for sure, but yes, that's what I think. And when they didn't find it there, they came here to look for it. But that's only half the story. Come with me."

I followed Mitch to the downstairs laboratory and, once inside, he pulled down the sliding door he'd installed as extra security. He locked it. He inserted a key into a metal box on the wall and a panel slid open to reveal a small room.

"Pet project of mine during the renovation. I've always wanted a secret room."

I walked into a mini-laboratory. It had a workbench, refrigerator, file cabinet, sink, and a scanning-electron microscope.

"Nobody knows about this room. Well, my assistant Vanessa knows, and now you."

Mitch walked to the refrigerator and took out two petri dishes. He set them on the workbench. "Before I show you this little miracle, I want you to know that, after you left for South America, Catherine and I began to speak on a regular basis. She told me about her project, and that it was nearly perfected. The day she died, Colter and I bumped into each other at Memorial. We shared our disbelief in hearing about Catherine's death and even found solace in each other's company. Colter had no knowledge of Catherine's project, and after we finished talking, I walked down to Catherine's laboratory for the purpose of locating her Cold file. I found it, along with a flask of the Cold serum from her refrigerator. I have no idea how Memorial found out that I'd removed these two items from Catherine's laboratory. Maybe the security camera caught me carrying it out of her office, or Colter might have seen me enter Catherine's laboratory and then leave with the folder and serum. I wouldn't put it past him to report me to the hospital."

The familiar high-pitched trill resonated once again in Mitch's voice. Just the mention of Colter's name was enough to trigger it. For reasons I never understood, Mitch and Colter failed to get along. And those occasions when they did confront one another, Mitch usually ended up on the short end.

"Well, enough about him. Are you ready to see a miracle?"

Chapter Nine

Mitch possessed the skills of an on-stage actor. A gift he used well. His charm had enticed investors to not only bankroll Rosetta, but also to recruit the finest biotech minds from the top schools.

"All right, let me show you. This first petri dish contains healthy human cells which have been contaminated with a common cold virus. The second dish contains the same healthy cells and cold virus, but Catherine's serum has been added."

Mitch placed the first dish under the microscope and invited me to observe it. I saw the virus attack the human cells for the sole purpose of commandeering their DNA. It produced young viruses that multiplied and spread until the host immune system sent an army of antibodies to wipe them out. I nodded to Mitch that I had witnessed the cold virus contaminate the cells. He then placed the second dish with Catherine's serum under the microscope. When I observed it, I saw something quite different taking place. The virus was clearly unable to commandeer the human cells. "The cells remained untouched."

"That's right, Jack. Now, here's what's truly remarkable." He walked to the refrigerator and removed a third petri dish. "This dish contains four different strains of cold virus, thousands of healthy human cells, and Catherine's serum." He placed it under the microscope and I saw that, inexplicably, the serum had restricted activity in all four virus strains from attacking the human cells. This was unfathomable to me, since there are close to a hundred known rhinoviruses, each with its own destructive personality. What I saw in the petri dish looked like the demise of one of mankind's greatest natural enemies. I stepped away from the microscope. Mitch had made his point—Catherine's drug was extraordinary and the commercial value was greater than I could even begin to imagine. Great enough for someone to steal this drug, or even kill for it.

I opened Catherine's file and checked her entry dates. She had begun her research in December 1998, a full year ago, and six months before I had left for Brazil. That explained why she had remained in New York: Catherine had chosen her research over me. Mitch picked up the petri dishes and returned them to the refrigerator.

"Why hasn't Memorial placed more security around this drug?"

Mitch walked back with a smile on his face. "You just asked the billion dollar question. And the answer is: because Memorial doesn't know Cold exists."

"Impossible. They have to know. The research took place right under their nose."

Mitch rubbed his hands together. "Catherine never discussed her research with Memorial. She received no funding from them. But then, nor did she seek approval to use their facility for her project."

"But you returned the Cold file to Memorial, right? Once they read the contents they'll claim ownership."

"Well, let's say that I returned *a* file to Memorial. Need I say more?"

Mitch listed a litany of possibilities pertaining Catherine's drug. He went on and on, and the more he talked, the more excited he became.

"Where's this leading to, Mitch? I get the feeling there's another reason you asked me here."

Mitch looked me straight in the eye. "If I didn't feel as though we were brothers, I wouldn't even broach this subject with you. Still, it's a delicate matter to discuss."

"What's spinning around in your head?"

"All right, here goes. Rosetta is doing okay. We have contracts with a couple of pharmaceuticals to do their grunt work. That's what pays the bills around here, but if we landed something really big, it would put us on the map. The way I see it, you have legal rights to Catherine's drug and, whether you want it or not, you're responsible for its future, its survival. I don't have to tell you that a drug like this doesn't come around that often."

"Now I get the picture. You want to make sure you get a piece of this drug before I kick off."

"Don't talk like that, Jack. You're not looking at this the right way. This drug is Catherine's legacy. She gave everything she had to develop it. All I want is for—"

"You're missing one thing, Mitch. Memorial will claim rights to this drug at some point, and I'm sure patents have been filed by now."

"None have been filed. Catherine was gathering the patent material and expected to file for it in the next thirty days. I had that conversation with her two weeks ago."

"I see." Mitch took a deep breath and allowed the conversation to rest for a moment. I got the feeling there was more in store for me, but I wasn't sure what to expect.

"Don't you see? The wheels have been put in motion, Jack, and this drug needs to be developed. Here's my proposal. I arrange for the patent, in your name, of course, and I'll also provide all the resources for the trial testing. When the drug's ready, I'll file for FDA approval. But, before I start anything, we need an agreement."

Mitch had planned things perfectly. It took a lot of balls to stand across from me and say what he had just said. Catherine was barely gone and he was already on to the next thing. Anger boiled up inside me over his crassness and lousy timing. Mitch must have sensed my anger because he said nothing. After a minute I cooled down and tried to look at it from Mitch's point of view. First of all, he could have taken the drug for himself and I would never have known it. Second, because of my failing condition, he didn't have the luxury of waiting two weeks before putting his proposition on the table. Third, and most importantly, this was Catherine's drug and clearly he, and I, wanted it to succeed. Her legacy was all she had left now. "Tell me your proposal again?"

"I'll raise the capital to pay for the research, the testing, and to cover the cost for FDA approval. Raising money is never a walk in the park, but this drug changes the rules of the game." He paced the narrow width of the room. I could almost see the wheels turning in his head. "What we need is an *angel*. A large multinational with deep pockets that's willing to commit $50 million without batting an eye."

"That's a pretty big number. It'll make a lot of people blink."

"Not if this deal is set up right. I'll arrange for a press conference. *The Wall Street Journal, The New York Times, The Science Review,* everyone. We'll make a big splash. I can't wait to see their reaction when they hear about a drug that can conquer the common cold. The media is going to love this story! And, with a little luck, we'll have our share of multinationals eating out of our hands."

"Slow down, slow down. This drug hasn't even been tested on mice yet, has it? It might be years before it reaches humans."

"Trust me, Jack. Once a major drug company gets behind us, it'll happen a lot sooner."

Mitch was on a roll and his ideas kept flowing. My mind drifted off topic as Mitch droned on. I wondered how to go about hiring a private investigator. Only when Mitch ran out of breath and stopped talking did my focus return to him.

"So what do you think about those ideas?"

"Sounds good, Mitch. I have a few ground rules to add. I want to be kept in the loop as long as possible, and all major decisions need my approval. The Catherine Prescott Lewis Foundation will be launched and all rights to this drug will be controlled by the foundation."

"What about Rosetta? I want a crystal clear agreement before I assign any resources."

The next hour was spent negotiating a deal where Mitch agreed to assume responsibility for raising the capital and managing the day-to-day project requirements. In return he would receive fifteen percent of my share. We left the downstairs laboratory and headed back to his office.

"On the phone you mentioned two things we needed to discuss. What was the other?"

"Well, it's a delicate subject, and we've never discussed your thoughts on this kind of matter before. But I've attended a couple of cryonics conventions over the last year or so. The field of cryonics is growing in popularity, mostly because technology is advancing rapidly and it's projected that in thirty or forty years cancer and Alzheimer's will be a thing of the past. Many scientists believe we're closing in on immortality. Who wants to miss out on that? Cryonics is an interim step that many people are now considering. If I were diagnosed with an incurable disease, I wouldn't hesitate a minute to make arrangements for my body to be frozen. What could I possibly lose by waiting thirty or forty years for a cure that might give me immortality?"

I stopped and stared at Mitch. "You're not going off the deep end, are you? I just placed Catherine's drug in your hands and now you're scaring me."

Before Mitch could respond, we heard footsteps in the hallway. Mitch looked out to see who it was. "Hold that thought, Jack. This looks like trouble." It was the man who had complained to Mitch earlier on the staircase. "What is it, Isaac?"

"Franz Weber still hasn't delivered my model. I have a deadline to meet!"

Mitch placed his hand on Isaac's shoulder. "It's my fault, Isaac. I've been tied up this morning and haven't spoken to Franz yet. I'll talk to him right now."

Isaac was clearly upset. "Do it as quickly as possible. Please." He stormed off down the hallway.

As we walked back to Mitch's office, my mind went back to Weber, the man with impeccable credentials. I wondered why he had given up a professorship at the University in Heidelberg to work for a small biotech in Greenwich Village. It was a step backwards to say the least, especially at Weber's age where a job at Rosetta did not offer the security that a fully tenured professorship might. Why uproot at his age and move to New York? "Your prize scientist creates quite a stir around here, doesn't he?"

"Weber's done that from the beginning. As I'm sure you've figured out, Isaac doesn't like him much." Mitch lowered his voice to a whisper. "In fact, most of the team doesn't like him."

"What's his problem?"

"He's a perfectionist. Franz won't release a single analysis until he's absolutely certain it's correct. Not a bad quality for a scientist, but sometimes he drags things out for weeks at a time. It drives people mad. And, he's so quiet and deliberate, like a surgeon, it unnerves everyone. Isaac thinks he'll show up with a shotgun one day and finish us all off."

"Are you serious?"

A wry smile came to Mitch's face. "Hey, I live in the Village. If they think Franz is strange, they should meet my neighbors. They'll find out what—"

"I've been looking for you, Mitch." A tall, attractive woman entered Mitch's office. She had sleek, black, shoulder-length hair and wore a black skirt cinched at the waist. Her white silk blouse was buttoned to the neck, and a long gold chain hung deep between her breasts.

"Jack, say hello to Vanessa Boulay. She's my right-hand woman around here."

"So very good to meet you, Jack."

Vanessa moved across the room and offered her hand. There was a refined quality about her that was instantly apparent. "I apologize for my call to you the other night. I upset you, and that was the last thing I wanted to do. Please accept my regrets. Catherine was a remarkable woman."

"Thank you. There's no need to apologize. Mitch was in trouble and you were just helping him out. I would have done the same under those circumstances."

Vanessa turned to Mitch. "There's a Julia Marshant waiting downstairs."

"Good. Show her to the conference room. Jack and I will join her there in a couple of minutes." Mitch waited for Vanessa to leave the room. "I arranged this meeting for us, and I know you'll be very interested, but before we go to the conference room, promise me that you're open to having a discussion on cryonics. You need to keep your options open, Jack. There's a lot more to cryonics than meets the eye."

"Who's Julia Marshant, and why are we meeting with her?"

"First promise me that we can have another cryonics discussion."

"All right, I'll discuss it with you again. Now, who's this woman?"

"Julia Marshant. She's a private investigator. One of the best, I've been told. She's going to help you find Catherine's killer."

Chapter Ten

With sirens blaring, four police motorcycles, two in front and two at the rear, guided a limousine swiftly through the midtown traffic. Vehicles on Eleventh Avenue pulled to the side as the sirens approached. The procession came to a halt in front of the Jacob K. Javits Convention Center. A hand inside the limousine waved to the motorcycle cops. They signaled back and then, as a unit, sped off down the avenue.

All doors to the limousine opened and two large men stepped out. Bystanders gathered in front of the exhibition center to see who might emerge. Two men dressed in black suits moved briskly from another car that had arrived moments earlier, while the limousine driver hurried to the trunk and lifted out a wheelchair, placing it curbside. Rutger Dobler was the first to step out of the limousine. He waited until the wheelchair was secured, then reached inside and assisted his grandfather, Heinrich Dobler, out of the vehicle and onto his feet.

The crowd watched a frail, elderly man with silver-gray hair balance himself on the curb's edge. He scanned the crowd before turning and lowering himself into the wheelchair. His team of men moved him swiftly into the building and away from the spectators.

"Are you comfortable, Grandfather?" Rutger asked, leading the way into a specially prepared room with a large glass window that overlooked the convention floor. There were a table and four chairs in the middle of the room. A certificate of recognition hung on the wall, thanking Dobler Pharmaceutical for sponsoring this annual convention.

"This will do," Heinrich said, in a pronounced German accent. He wheeled himself to the window and looked down onto a convention floor that bustled with people. There were scientists, genetic engineers, representatives from large pharmaceutical companies, doctors, Wall Street investors, reporters, government officials, and every kind of drug industry entrepreneur imaginable. Heinrich could see lines of people at the main entrance, standing at registration booths waiting to pick up their badges. One end of the floor was lined with conference rooms and at the other end speakers stood on raised platforms giving lectures and demonstrations as proof their company had made an invaluable breakthrough or developed an unheralded new treatment. Investors flocked around the most passionate and convincing speakers, those claiming their company had discovered one of nature's most guarded secrets.

Heinrich watched with interest as one conference room filled with people. Next he observed two apparent FDA officials in the middle of the floor sharing a bag of popcorn and strolling aimlessly. Directly below his window, Heinrich saw a salesman darting from booth to booth, perhaps looking to find the latest Fountain of Youth drug or cure that he could profitably peddle. Two distinguished-looking gentlemen in blue suits, Wall Street types, stood at a biotech booth and looked intrigued as the scientist in the booth, appearing somewhat animated, explained the potential of his new drug. The men listened intently to each word the scientist spoke, most likely to determine whether the drug could garner enough interest for a public offering.

Heinrich remained at the window and watched them all. Everyone on the floor was there to make a deal. Of course deals were not restricted to only the convention floor; they were also made in hallways, behind closed doors, and even in the men's room.

The Dobler Convention was an event that most small biotech companies could ill-afford to miss, that is, if showcasing their under-financed drug was important to them. Biotechs were here to raise money, and in some cases, new funding was necessary to keep the doors of their small laboratories open for another twelve months. Like polished apples, scientists glimmered inside their booths, waiting for that special investor, an "angel," a multinational, or whoever was interested in taking a not-too-deep bite out of them. Heinrich watched them all from his lofty perch, just as he had done for the past five years.

"Grandfather, the reports have arrived."

Heinrich wheeled himself away from the window as a group of employees filed into the room. Five men and one woman, all young and well dressed, took turns piling information on the small table in the center of the room.

"Good morning," Heinrich said to them, his eyes fixed firmly on the literature, "Is this all of it?"

"Yes, sir. It's data from every company on the floor," one of the men said.

Heinrich looked at the sizable stack of information. "Thank you for your diligence," he said, and then dismissed them peremptorily with a subtle hand gesture. Only Rutger remained in the room with his grandfather. Heinrich placed his hand on the mountain of information, patted it twice, and then wheeled around to face his grandson. "This should keep us busy for the next couple of weeks." He glanced over to make sure the door was closed. "I have some items we need to speak about, Son. How is your 'Five Point Plan' coming along?"

"It's completed. All we need now is to arrange a meeting with the other multinationals and present it. Once they ratify it, we'll have the clout we need."

"You're wasting your time trying to unite those greedy bastards, but I won't stand in your way. You need to learn for yourself."

"Things are moving, Grandfather. And, so you're not surprised, I've asked Randall Whitestone to join us this morning."

"Whitestone? Here?"

"I know you have your differences, but Randall's the right person to deliver our message to the others. He has influence over them, and—"

"He'll rake you over the coals, Son. Couldn't you have chosen someone else?"

The door to their room opened. "Excuse me, Mr. Dobler. There's a Mr. Whitestone to see you."

"Please show him in," Rutger said. He smiled at his grandfather and walked to the door to greet Whitestone. "Thank you for coming, Randall."

"I can't stay long," Whitestone said. Then, with noticeable hesitance, he walked over and shook Heinrich's hand. Neither man exchanged words.

Heinrich looked up and was quick to notice that Randall had aged considerably. He remembered Randall as taller and with thick, dark hair; the man before him was hunched and had thinning white hair. It occurred to Heinrich that the swiftness of the years had taken its toll on them both. It seemed only yesterday that they were eager young men, always challenging each other and perhaps driving each other to achieve. In those days, Whitestone Pharmaceutical had been the powerhouse company. Heinrich remembered the day he had wrestled the number one spot away from Randall, and it brought a smile to his face.

"Now, what's all this about?" Whitestone said gruffly, turning his back on Heinrich to address Rutger.

Rutger needed to show deference to this man and to deliver his ideas with caution. He knew Randall Whitestone made quick decisions, so he chose his words carefully. "Take a look down there." Rutger pointed to the convention floor.

"What am I supposed to be looking at?"

"The world is changing, Randall, And if we're not careful, we'll be left behind."

"If you're referring to this biotech thing, I wouldn't be too concerned about it."

"And why is that?" Heinrich said, wheeling himself around while still maintaining distance between Whitestone and himself.

"Genetic research isn't going to affect people like us in the long run. Financial clout, market share, and distribution channels control the drug industry, not a bunch of undercapitalized start-ups."

Rutger glanced at his grandfather. Their eyes met only briefly, but in that moment he knew they were both thinking the same thing: if Whitestone was underestimating the emergence of these biotechs, then other multinationals were most likely doing the same.

"I disagree with you, Randall," Rutger said.

"Oh, you do?" Whitestone said, with a touch of annoyance in his voice.

Rutger needed to be careful here. He was talking to a man who had built a dynasty out of a dream, while Rutger would one day be handed his empire. Whitestone was more than twice his age and known for walking out of meetings for the slightest reason. "Yes, I disagree with you," Rutger said. "Many of these small companies are developing superior drugs. To ignore them is to put ourselves at risk."

"Then we'll *buy* them up," Whitestone said, his voice booming off the walls. "We'll just *buy* them up."

Rutger knew that Whitestone, his grandfather, and others had held control over the drug industry by acquiring those companies that posed a threat. But the world was changing, and the men in those booths on the convention floor were not only biotech scientists, but astute businessmen with MBA degrees. They understood the value of their drugs and were less likely to fall prey to the powerful money people. "It's too late to buy up a thousand biotechs, Randall. We need a different strategy, or face—"

"I think you're reading too much into this," Whitestone said.

"Maybe," Rutger responded. "But, and excuse my directness here, you may not be reading enough into the war being waged against us." Rutger paused, sensing that Whitestone was willing to hear him out. "I'll confess something to you. In the last ten years, Grandfather and I have stopped a good share of biotech drugs from reaching the marketplace, mostly by buying them up. In time, some of those drugs will reach the marketplace, but others, well, you know what I'm getting at here. Every multinational has done the same. It's a practice we never discuss, but it's one that benefits us all. My Five Point Plan is a structured approach to slowing down the biotechs."

Whitestone squinted at Rutger. His glance moved to Heinrich and once more down to the convention floor. He then searched Rutger's face. His tone became somber. "You're an intelligent young man, and I know you didn't drag me down here to talk nonsense. What do you expect me to do?"

Rutger smiled. "Get the other multinationals to meet with us."

"That's impossible. You know how they feel about you ... well, about your grandfather. And I can't recall when the top seven CEOs have ever agreed to meet. Everyone's too busy. With all the lawsuits flying back and forth, most of them can't stand being in the same room together."

"It's in their best interest to meet with us," Rutger said.

"If I'm not convinced these biotechs are a threat, why would the others think they are?"

Heinrich lunged his wheelchair closer. "He's talking about a problem that could ruin us all!" he yelled.

"And why would you care what happens to me or the others?" Whitestone yelled back.

"Because," Rutger said, calmly stepping between them. "The in-fighting has to stop. We need a strategy that everyone can agree to follow."

Whitestone looked confounded. "And I'm supposed to get them to this meeting?"

"They're smart men, Randall. The balance of power is changing. Once we show them how the biotechs can be controlled, they'll embrace it. No one wants to relinquish the power they have over this industry."

Whitestone searched Rutger's eyes again. "You're asking a lot of me."

"Trust us, Randall. Be assured that everyone's best interest has been accounted for. And be sure to tell the other CEOs that my grandfather has personally requested their attendance."

"Hmm." Whitestone looked down on the convention floor once more. "I'll see what I can do, but I won't promise anything."

"They'll listen to you, Randall. You're held in high esteem." Rutger played his trump card—Randall's ego.

"I'll call them. But you'd better know what you're doing. That's all I'll say." He looked at his watch. "I'm late." He shook Rutger's hand, and left without saying a word to Heinrich.

Rutger sat at the table next to his grandfather. "What do you think?"

"He knows it's important. He's smart enough to know that much, but enough about Whitestone." Heinrich took a breath and then looked over at Rutger. In an even tone he said, "Tell me about that business in the hospital. What happened to that woman?"

"I don't know. I was told someone was killed and that it happened the day the Sumataika had broken into the hospital."

Heinrich hit his fist on the table. He yelled, "Cut our ties with Tsai and those people. They're savages! Just end it, you hear? We manage our affairs just fine without them."

"I'll see to it, Grandfather."

"Now, about that cold drug. Is it the real thing?"

"It has enormous potential. In time, it may become a big competitor. But maybe we should pass on pursuing it, Grandfather. The accident is a bad omen."

"You said it hasn't been patented yet, so at this point it's anyone's drug. We can't just walk away from it. But, I do understand your point, Son. Find out from Tsai if those savages had any involvement with the death of that woman. And, either way, let's pursue the drug, even if we buy it outright. We don't need another cold drug on the market."

A well-dressed middle-aged man appeared in the doorway. "Hope I'm not disturbing you." William Dobler was tall and slender, with grayish-brown hair worn longer than most of the others on the executive team at Dobler Pharmaceutical.

"Of course not, Father. Grandfather and I were discussing the convention," Rutger said.

"Could I have a word with you, Son, alone?"

Rutger turned to Heinrich. "I'll only be a moment." He walked into the hallway.

William reached over and closed the door. "Your mother and I haven't seen you in weeks. Why haven't you called?"

"Sorry, Father. Between vacation, the downsizing in Europe, and the convention, I've had little time for much else. Tell Mother I'll visit soon."

"She's having a little get-together this Sunday. You know she'd be thrilled if you could make it. Maybe you could surprise her."

"Sunday isn't possible. Grandfather and I are working through the weekend."

"I see."

Rutger glanced at his watch. "I need to finish up with Grandfather right now. How about we meet for coffee in the morning? We can talk then."

"That's fine. I have to leave now, anyway. Speak to your grandfather and see if you can change your plans for the weekend." William placed his hand on Rutger's shoulder for a brief moment and then walked away. Rutger rejoined his grandfather at the table.

"What was that all about?"

"Mother's having a small party this weekend, and father invited me to—"

"From the look on his face, I thought something was wrong in operations."

"Everything's fine. Things could be better if you two would speak to each other once in a while."

"Not that again. Your father has had every opportunity to take the reins of this company. Don't think I didn't try. What father wouldn't want his son to step into his shoes?"

Rutger's cell phone rang. "Hello. Okay, I'll meet you there in forty-five minutes. He stood up. "I'm meeting with Tsai."

"Don't forget. I want it ended with Tsai and those animals!"

Chapter Eleven

It was no surprise that Mitch had friends at the FBI; he had friends everywhere. He had taken it upon himself to call John Tuttles, the Investigative Director at the Bureau, and to explain the circumstances of Catherine's death. Tuttles had Mitch contact a former FBI agent with good credentials.

Julia Marshant was waiting in the conference room when Mitch and I entered. When she turned and looked at us, her generous smile and large green eyes made a good first impression. She was tall and blonde and wore a loose-fitting business suit that did little to hide her toned body. After the introductions, Mitch prepared to leave the room, but I insisted that he stay. I knew very little about what makes a good investigator and neither did Mitch, but I valued his opinion.

We sat across the table from Julia, who sat erect with her hands folded in her lap. "Tuttles explained everything to you about Catherine?"

"Yes, and please accept my deepest sympathy for your loss."

"Thank you." I stood up, walked around to her side, and leaned against the table. "Catherine's death is being called an accident. But after meeting with the detective assigned to her case, I'm convinced she was murdered. I've nothing against the police, but this detective can't handle the workload already sitting on his desk. And when we spoke about finding her killer, I didn't detect a great deal of optimism on his part. That's why you're here. I need an experienced investigator, someone willing to dedicate themself to finding Catherine's killer. Does this sound like something you can handle?"

"First, you have a right to demand the best investigation possible from the NYPD. I'm sorry you don't think you're getting it. But to answer your question, yes, I'm qualified to handle your case. I'll start by contacting the police and requesting a copy of their investigative report. I'll retrace their footsteps to uncover anything they may have overlooked. Then I'll question everyone who came into contact with Catherine that day, and compile a list of your wife's friends and acquaintances, both at Memorial and outside the hospital. I believe it makes sense to perform background checks on everyone. Anyone with a checkered past will get more of my attention. The phone company will supply Catherine's home and work telephone records, and I'll go over that list with a fine-tooth comb. I'll ask Memorial for a list of any disgruntled employees. If there are any, I'll question them. All local gangs, known criminals, and dope dealers that operate in the vicinity will be identified and investigated. Collecting solid and relevant information is what we want to achieve during the first phase of the investigation, and once I complete it, we'll know much more than we do now."

Julia's approach was detailed and more scrupulous than what Gravers had presented to me. It was what I had expected to hear from a private investigator. "Mind if I asked a few questions?"

"Not at all."

"How old are you?"

"Thirty-two."

"How long were you with the FBI?"

"Seven years."

"Why did you leave?"

"Do you want the long or short version?"

"Whatever you feel comfortable with."

"I accidently killed someone."

"Okay, how about the long version?"

Julia placed her hands on the table and briefly rolled her eyes to the ceiling. "I was assigned to a team that had to stake out the house of a suspected abductor and killer. I'll spare you the details of what this man did to his victims. I was posted at the rear of the house while two agents entered through the front door. A few minutes later a man who fit the killer's description ran out the back door. I drew my weapon and yelled for him to stop. When he kept coming, I fired a shot and hit him in the chest. Ten seconds later, I heard a barrage of gunfire inside the house. An agent ran out and told me the killer was dead. The young man I shot was a victim that had managed to escape. I had only a split second to make a decision. I made the wrong one. The next couple of months were difficult. They told me it would go away in time, but it never did. I resigned from the Bureau three months later."

"I'm sorry you had to live through that experience, but help me understand something. I mean, you quit the FBI because you killed someone. Now you're back in the same business."

"As an investigator. I collect and analyze information. I don't apprehend criminals. The police perform that after the criminal is identified."

"How many cases have you handled since leaving the Bureau?"

"This will be my first."

"Your first?" I looked at Mitch. "Did Tuttles mention that to you?"

"No, he didn't. I would have remembered that."

I turned back to Julia. "Do you have the experience to handle this case?"

"Yes. Seven years at the Bureau is experience enough."

"You're on your own now. The Bureau isn't around to back you up, and you quit because the pressure got—"

Julia raised her hand and stopped me. "First of all, until you know what it's like to point a gun at a human being and pull the trigger, you really shouldn't pass judgment on someone who's done it." My mind raced back to the jungle—my finger also pulled the trigger and took a life. To say so to Julia would be inappropriate, but I knew what she felt like inside. "I merely—"

"Second, I know how to investigate a crime. I can do that as well, if not better, than most."

Julia was quick to stand up for herself, and I respected that quality. But I had trepidations about her ability to perform under pressure. The bigger concern boiled down to my limited time of two, maybe three weeks, and if this woman had the skill to find Catherine's killer in that timeframe. I was not certain of her ability, but the thought occurred to me that I could take an active role in the investigation. That way, if Julia performed poorly, or fell down on the job in any way or shape, I could dismiss her and keep the investigation going. "I'd like to hire you to conduct the first phase you just mentioned. I'll evaluate your progress once the first phase is completed and decide whether or not we'll continue together. Also, I'll need the phase one information completed within the next four days. Can you do that?"

A look of concern crossed Julia's face.

Mitch stood up. "Jack, can I speak with you?" We walked into the hallway. "Aren't you being a little heavy handed? I'm no authority on investigating, but that sounds like a lot to ask someone to complete in four days. She knows how long it'll take. She's a professional. Treat her like one."

"You don't get it yet, do you?"

"What?"

"I won't be around much longer. I need this done quickly. I'm dealing with a finite timeline. Can I make it any clearer?"

Mitch opened his mouth as if to say something, but caught himself. "Okay, I'm sorry. But if she doesn't accept your terms, you're back to square one with no investigator. Tuttles swears by her. He said she's one of the best he's seen in twenty years at the Bureau."

"All right. You've made your point. Let's go back inside." I sat back down across the table from Julia. "Sorry if I come across a bit strong, but I've got a lot of pressure on me. Let me re-phrase what I said a minute ago. How long will it take to complete the first phase of the investigation?"

"Well, if I can contact everyone, possibly a week. But two weeks would be better."

"Here's what I want to do. Hire you for a week and see how the investigation goes. We'll decide at that time whether things are moving in the right direction. Also, I'm willing to help with the grunt work, if you need that kind of help."

"I'm sorry, Jack, but I'll be more productive working alone. And completing phase one in a week, well, you do realize you're asking for an enormous amount of work to be completed in a very short period of time, don't you? And after the information is collected, it will need to be analyzed."

"Do you accept my offer?"

Julia thought it over. "I'll accept on the condition that you give me a free hand and remain out of the investigation until the first phase is completed."

I was not thrilled with her conditions, but time was ticking away and I wanted the investigation to begin. "All right, I'll stay out of the way."

Julia stood up and gathered her briefcase. She started for the door.

"Julia," Mitch asked, "one last question. From the limited amount of information you have on this case, is there anything you can tell us now?"

Julia looked at me and then back to Mitch. "Ask me that question when phase one is completed." She turned and walked out of the room.

Chapter Twelve

Heinrich wheeled himself to the window and watched the biotech representatives hustling around the convention floor. In the distance he saw Rutger. It pleased him to watch admirers surround his grandson, and the grace that Rutger exhibited in their presence. The years of training had paid off splendidly.

Heinrich spotted William standing on the convention floor by himself. How was it possible for someone to have so little in common with his own son? William had been a difficult child, even when his mother was alive. If not for Rutger as their go-between, Heinrich's brittle relationship with his son would be non-existent.

Heinrich thought back to when William had married Elizabeth and soon after bore Rutger. William knew how much his father had wanted a grandson, but cruelly he kept Rutger from him. When the couple had trouble raising the boy, having to discipline him on a daily basis, they had reached their wits end. Afraid they might stigmatize their son by bringing in a therapist, William finally permitted the six-year-old to meet his grandfather, a strict disciplinarian. Elizabeth had taken Rutger to Bashakill herself, since William had sworn years earlier to never set foot upon that piece of earth again.

It was a wonderful first meeting. The boy had taken an immediate liking to the resort, and he was at ease when his mother left him alone with his grandfather. Heinrich and Rutger walked the hillside together and spent hours in the orchard. Under an apple tree they became steeped in conversation. Elizabeth watched from the pool, keeping her distance and allowing them to explore each other. Heinrich found the boy not stubborn at all. Rutger asked intelligent and thoughtful questions.

That evening, when Elizabeth told Rutger it was time to leave for home, he told her he wanted to stay with his grandfather. Elizabeth promised they would visit again, but Rutger ran off and hid in one of the large rooms. His grandfather found him in the rear of his bedroom closet while Elizabeth was searching the other rooms.

"Come out here, boy," Heinrich said.

Rutger crawled out from under the coats and over Heinrich's shoes. He stood up and walked over to his grandfather, who was sitting on the edge of the bed. His young eyes cast on the floor.

"We had fun today, didn't we?"

"Yes."

"But you must go home with your mother now."

"I want to stay here."

"Your father wants to see you at your house."

"You can be my father."

Heinrich laughed. "But that would make your father very sad."

Rutger was still looking at the floor.

"Do you know how to play make-believe?"

"Yes."

"Okay, then. I will pretend to be your father, and you can be my son."

Rutger looked at him. "Okay."

"But you must go home with your mother now. And when you come back next time, I will call you *Son*."

"And I can call you *Father*."

"No. Always call me grandfather, that way nobody will ever know our secret."

"So, there you are," Elizabeth said, walking into the room. "What are you two talking about?"

"Oh, nothing," Heinrich said. "I think he's ready to go home now."

Heinrich led Elizabeth and the boy to the waiting car. "I'm glad you two got along so well. William will be pleased to hear it."

"Yes, well, you'd better be on your way. It's a long drive home."

"You're right. Thank you for letting me bring Rutger to visit," she said as she stepped into the car.

"Bring him back again." Heinrich leaned over and looked into the back seat where Rutger sat close to his mother. "So long, Son."

Rutger looked up and smiled. "Good-bye, Grandfather."

That was twenty-five years ago, Heinrich thought. On the convention floor below, he saw William quicken his pace toward the exit. Rutger pulled himself away from an attractive young woman, probably a reporter, and left through another door. Heinrich wheeled himself back to the table piled with biotech information. He began the process that he went through each year: find drugs that show promise, as well as those that pose a threat. With those thoughts, his heartbeat quickened.

* * *

Rutger entered the Plaza Hotel and took the elevator to the fourth floor. At the end of the hallway, he knocked on a door and entered the room. Once inside, he sat down on the chair that Kajara Tsai had pulled up to the table for him.

"Thanks for coming, Rutger," Tsai said in perfect English, a fine accomplishment for a man born in China and raised in Japan. Tsai was

65

diminutive with straight black hair, and weighed no more than one hundred thirty-five pounds. His double-breasted suit hung long on his torso and gave him the appearance of being even smaller than his five-foot-four stature. He was the President of Nasashi Drugs, a small, relatively unknown company. Tsai had been fortunate to meet Rutger, who took him under his wing and helped Nasashi develop a presence in the States. The generic painkiller manufactured by Nasashi was nothing special, but it had gained a decent market share in the States with Rutger's assistance.

"Can I get you something to drink?"

"No. Tell me what happened at the hospital."

"Well, the Sumataika gained access to the laboratory, but they could not locate the file."

"I want to know about the woman."

"I heard there was an accident that morning, but the Sumataika had left the hospital by then."

"Are you sure about that? They had no involvement?"

"God, no. That would be a horrible thing to have happen." Tsai glanced down at his watch.

"Are you in a hurry?"

"I'm catching a flight to Tokyo this afternoon. It's my tenth wedding anniversary. I'll be back in five days."

"Congratulations to you both, but I don't understand how you botched this up. You're the one who sold me on the Sumataika. Asking them to grab a couple of folders isn't so difficult, is it?"

Tsai cleared his throat. "No, it shouldn't have been difficult."

"I heard about another break-in the next night. This one took place at Rosetta Laboratories. Was that the Sumataika?"

"Yes. We found out that a Mitch Cochran had removed the file from the hospital and taken them to Rosetta."

"And?"

"The Sumataika were unable to find the file there, either."

"So, you broke into another laboratory after that woman was killed?" Rutger stood up. "Did it ever occur to you that breaking into a second laboratory might raise a few eyebrows? Did you stop to think of the danger this witless act might expose me to?"

"I understand," Tsai said, "but the Sumataika know what they're doing. They took every precaution."

Rutger glared. "I don't believe this! You assured me these people were professionals. Now you're telling me they broke into two places and still failed to get a simple file."

"There were no witnesses and none of this links back to you. The Sumataika are—"

"On the contrary," Rutger said, pointing his finger in Tsai's face. "You may have drawn *considerable* attention to us. Even if the Sumataika had no involvement with what happened to that woman, the police will go over every detail with a fine-tooth comb. Even one strand of hair can come back to haunt us. If, or should I say when, the cops piece together that two laboratories were broken into to get that file, they'll intensify their investigation."

Tsai looked up at him, but had no response.

"Contain the damage. Find out how much the police know and what type of investigation is planned."

Tsai looked at his watch again.

"Oh, regarding your flight. Well, it's not a good time to leave New York."

"But, my wife, I promised to be home for our anniversary."

"You promised me, too. Don't go anywhere until this mess is cleared up. And, starting today your Asian friends are out of my business. I want nothing to do with them. I'm holding you personally responsible for keeping my family's name out of this mess."

Tsai dropped his head for a moment and then looked up at Rutger once more. "This is not going to please you, but the Sumataika contacted me this morning. They have requested a meeting with you."

"What? How do they even know of me? My family's name was never to be mentioned."

"It never was. They had to have learned it another way."

"I have no desire to meet with some mobster. What is it they want, blackmail money? I will not be intimidated."

"Wait, Rutger, please. The Sumataika don't want to blackmail you, I'm sure of that. Meetings have been arranged here with other companies, and they want to include you."

Rutger turned. "What are they doing, opening a Manhattan office?"

Tsai's expression never changed. "That's exactly what they're doing, and the meeting with you is to avoid any conflict of interest."

"Conflict of interest? What the hell does that mean?"

"They want to solidify existing relationships. No different than what a law firm does before taking on a new client."

"That's ridiculous."

"Stealing information is a trillion-dollar business, and New York is home to many powerful companies."

Rutger studied Tsai for a moment. "Tell me more about these people."

"The Sumataika are not limited to corporate espionage. They've been known to perform some vile acts as well. You know, Rutger, your grandfather has his share of enemies, and it wouldn't be pleasant if one of them employed the Sumataika."

Rutger glared back. "How dare you threaten me!"

"I mean no disrespect. But, the fact is, a relationship exists between you and the Sumataika. It's in your best interest to have a cordial meeting with Jito Sumataika. He heads the family."

Rutger wondered what would happen if he refused to meet with this man. He concluded most likely nothing. On the other hand, would he ever forgive himself if one of his grandfather's enemies struck a deal with this Sumataika?

"I want to know everything about them."

"*Sumataika* means 'warrior god.' For almost a century they've derived income from gambling, prostitution, and extortion. They're very powerful with over ten thousand members, and no one in his right mind would go up against them. Every so often a politician decides to make a name for himself and tries to go after them. The Sumataika retaliate by kidnapping someone from a prominent family or burning down a building. With that kind of message sent, the politician usually backs down. This gang has had a symbiotic relationship with Japan, much like a parasite that sucks nourishment from its host, but never enough to kill it. The gang's stranglehold over Japan has waned somewhat in recent years, and that's why Jito Sumataika has created new business opportunities for the family. He plans to export his services to Europe and the United States. The U.S. is their prime target, and once they establish themselves here, it will bring a whole new meaning to the term 'organized crime.' One more thing: Dobler Pharmaceutical is their first U.S. client, so it places you in a position of importance to them."

Rutger was sickened by Tsai and the Sumataika. How risky could it really be to actually meet with them? He negotiated global drug deals with brilliant businessmen every day, so meeting with a gang leader shouldn't be that difficult. "Call me tomorrow and I'll tell you where Jito Sumataika can meet me." Rutger left without saying another word. Outside the Plaza, he stopped to light a cigarette, and made the conscious decision that any meeting he would have with the Sumataika would not be divulged to his grandfather, who was up in age and under too much stress right now. He stepped into his limousine and took a deep drag off his cigarette. This would be a first—to hide the truth from his grandfather.

Chapter Thirteen

I was alone in a large garden. A faint breeze stirred patches of green-white orchids, and I was careful not to step on those in my path. They were elegant flowers with hazel-flecked eyes that peeked out at me, some with the shape of Catherine's face, oval and classic, and flawed only by the wisp of bangs that found her eyes. Beneath all that was her intelligent gaze. Then, before my eyes an orchid transformed itself into a cylinder of swirling light, and the light took the form of an exquisite figure. Catherine. *Our night was magic, Jack. Always remember.*

I awoke to the sound of a loud knock. The second knock brought me to my feet with Catherine still resonating within me. On the third knock, I realized someone was pounding on the door, and it forced my dream to float away.

Colter Malone was leaning against the archway, his arms crossed. He looked like a Brando character out of the Wild Bunch, with wild hair, dark sunglasses, and a black leather jacket. He walked in, dropped his jacket on the floor and then flopped onto the sofa. "You have coffee or do you order up?"

I walked to the kitchen and poured water into the coffee machine. "What's the occasion? You're not an early riser."

"When you don't return my calls, it forces me to leave the warmth of my bed to track you down in person."

"Yeah, well, sorry. I've been tied up at Mitch's."

"You know Memorial's banned him from the hospital after the caper he pulled there?"

"I heard." Colter made small talk as I watched the coffee brew. When the small pot was full, I poured two cups and carried them into the living room.

Colter sipped from his cup. "Not Starbuck's, but I won't complain." He placed the cup down. "How are you holding up?"

"What do you think?"

"Sorry, that didn't come out right. Someday I'll learn to keep my mouth shut. I want you to know I'm here for you, that's all."

Colter was not one to volunteer his shoulder to cry on. His tendency was to escape the presence of people in pain. In uncharacteristic fashion he had rescued me during Catherine's eulogy, and now this morning he tracked me down. It was the kind of support that does not go unnoticed, and it spoke volumes to me. "Thanks for checking in on me."

"I changed my flight plans and don't fly to L.A. until after the New Year. And, if you're not back on your feet by then, I'll change them again."

"Don't stay on my account. You're starting a new job. It's a big transition. Besides, New Year's is ten days away, and everything should fall into place by then."

Colter lifted one eyebrow. "Why are you being so standoff-ish? Can't you just say thank you, and accept my measly help? You're going through hell right now." He picked up his coffee and sipped it. "I've never had a brother, but you're the closest thing to it. I'd like to think you feel the same way."

I was grateful for his sentiment. I debated telling him about my condition, but having told one person was enough. That alone relieved the pressure from me. Besides, it was painful having to tell someone I was going to die soon. I did not want to relive that experience.

"You know, since coming to New York, I've spent more time with you than with anyone," Colter said. "*Whew.* The hours we spent on the LEC Enzyme boggles my mind. And then the evenings with the gang at *La Vie en Rose.* Catherine was as exhausted as we were, but just one drink and she'd be turning a serious matter from her day into a hilarious story. And then laugh out loud. It was contagious. Once she got on a roll, we were mesmerized, waiting for her next story. If someone showed up late, all they had to do was follow the laughter to find us. Those were the days. We were young and vibrant—all of us—trying to make our mark in the world." Colter hit himself in the head. "Sorry, Jack. I shouldn't have brought that up."

"No. It's okay. Those were incredible times. We were inseparable, especially Catherine and I. I don't remember when it changed or how we lost it."

"Hold on. You never lost anything. Couples go through ups and downs. Catherine loved you. Don't ever forget it." Neither of us said anything for a long time after his remark. Finally, Colter looked at his watch. "Oh, man, I have to go. I don't want to, but I have a meeting in twenty minutes. Promise to stay in touch, okay?"

"I will." Colter stuck his fist out and we pounded knuckles. He scooped up his jacket and was out the door.

I didn't move from that spot. I was trying to remember when things had changed between Catherine and me. How do you go from being in love, knowing your wife's every thought and action, to a place where she's become a complete stranger? Her smile never changed whenever she looked at me. Her kiss never lost its passion. At night, we lay in each other's arms before falling asleep. And once we pulled apart, she often reached for me during the night, touching me to be sure I was still beside her. Even during a dream she often took hold of my arm, as if to pull me into her special world, so I, too, could explore what she saw there. Then, in one brief moment I was dealt a painful blow, and came to realize she'd been working behind my back the whole time to develop some new drug. She had concealed it from me for more than six months, and never once did she slip up and mention it. That was not the Catherine I knew. The woman I knew shared every moment of her day with me each evening over dinner. How was it possible for her to sit across the table from me night after night and keep such a secret? I would give anything to know the answer to that question.

On the street corner I tried to flag a taxi, but snow had been falling hard for days and there were none in sight. A horn blared behind me. When I turned around, I saw a black limousine pulling up to the curb. Eddie smiled at me through the windshield. Before I could take another step, he had jumped out of the limo and was holding the rear door open for me.

"Where ya going, Doctor Lewis?"

I slid into the back seat. "Same place as before, Eddie."

He took off down the street. "You wanna hear about her now, Doctor Lewis?"

I had no idea what Eddie was talking about. "About who?"

"Not who. *What.* You know, the limo. You're sitting in a very famous spot. I betcha didn't know that." He smiled at me in the rearview mirror. "Here, let me show ya." He pulled something out of the glove compartment and handed it to me through the sliding glass panel. It was a photograph. "That's Fidel Castro. He used to ride in this limo—can you believe it?"

The photo was of a fully bearded Castro sitting in the limo. The photo was so clear I could see the smoke suspended mid-air from his trademark cigar. "That's him all right." I handed the picture back to Eddie.

"There's more, Doc. This limo used to belong to the Cuban Embassy. It's got steel plates in the doors. Even the windows are bullet-proof."

"Are you sure that's enough protection in New York?"

"Ha, I'll have to remember that one, Doc. You really don't have to worry, though, not in this limo, it's made for protection. I could take you through Bed-Stuy in the Iron Lung, and you'd be safe as a baby."

"The *Iron Lung.* Is that what you call her?" I rapped my knuckle against the window, but it didn't sound much different than a regular car window.

"Jimmy named her the Iron Lung and I guess it stuck."

"Jimmy?"

"You know, the bellboy at the Towers, the guy who steered you to me in the first place. He's my cousin."

"Now I get it. You two work this Iron Lung gig together, right?"

"One hand washes the other, Doc. Besides, you're getting the safest ride in town. This baby's sealed airtight. No one's gonna break into her, that's for sure. That's one reason I bought her—that, and she's also a good conversation piece."

I leaned back and closed my eyes, hoping for a few moments of peace. We were on Fifth Avenue in mid-town New York, where cars, cabs, and buses fought for every inch of street. I had to admit one thing: it was quiet inside the Iron Lung, and it helped me to relax. Colter came to mind. It touched me that he'd changed his flight plans to stay in New York. He had worked diligently on the LEC Enzyme project for over two years, and I felt ashamed for never acknowledging his contribution. I had walked away with the award, the money, all the credit, and he received nothing but a pat on the back. I should have, after all that, made some gesture of recognition. At that moment I decided to make a list of the things I needed to complete before it was too late. Acknowledging Colter was at the top of my list.

"We're here, Doctor Lewis."

My eyes opened to the sight of graffiti sprayed on the archway leading into Washington Square Park. I paid Eddie and told him not to bother getting out to open the door for me. I stepped from the limo into the cold morning wind. Eddie rolled down his window and yelled out, "What time should I pick you up?"

"It'll be another long day, Eddie. Can't say when I'm leaving. I have your number."

"Okay, Doc. Call me if you get stuck. They're calling for more snow, so it might be tough getting a taxi tonight, too." Eddie flashed a smile and rolled the window back up. The muffler rattled as the Iron Lung pulled away. The sound reverberated off the brownstones that lined the street, its thrumming soaked up and softened by the falling snow. The faint staccato beat held me there until the limo turned off the block.

I ran up the stoop and pulled out the key Mitch had given me. When I unlocked the door and entered the foyer, I noticed a light reflecting down the staircase. It was not quite seven a.m. and I knew the staff didn't arrive for another hour and a half. I heard a door close on the second floor, and as eager as I was to look at Catherine's drug in the downstairs laboratory, the noise caught my attention.

I climbed to the top of the landing and looked down the hallway, but no one was there. You could hear a pin drop, and now the thought of an intruder made my heart race. With more reluctance than I care to admit, I began my search by looking in each of the rooms. They were all dark, and my nerves started to get the better of me. I wasted little time flicking on the light as I swung each door open. Mitch's office was locked when I tried the doorknob. I continued down the hallway. When I reached the last office on the floor, I noticed the door was ajar. I pushed it open and looked inside.

There was a faint, unfamiliar odor, and the radio played classical music. I stepped inside the room and walked over to the desk. I picked up an open folder that was lying on top of the desk and saw that it contained the results of a drug called Glaxomin, a drug I'd never heard of. The odor grew more pungent, filling the room. I sensed someone watching me. When I turned around, I saw a short, stocky man staring at me.

"May I help you, Doctor Lewis?"

Chapter Fourteen

I caught my breath after being startled by the sudden appearance of this man. "Doctor Weber. Good morning. I heard a noise up here, so I came to look." Weber's eyes lowered to the folder I was holding. Knowing full well I'd been caught off guard, I said, "Looks interesting," and placed the folder back on his desk. Then, trying to keep the conversation light, "What time do you usually arrive?" I asked.

"Six a.m." Weber said.

I forced a smile. "That's early. I doubt we'll bump into each other at that hour."

"I wouldn't imagine I'd see anyone here at that time. I am here until six p.m. as well. You might say I work half a day." I believe Weber had taken a stab at humor, but it didn't work. He stood there a moment longer and when I failed to keep our conversation going, he turned and left the room. If anything, it was his office and I should have been the one to leave.

Clearly, the man made me uncomfortable. I now understood why the scientists at Rosetta felt the way they did about him. He lacked the simplest of social graces, and without them in New York, things can get lonely quickly. It still baffled me why he had come to the city in the first place—why leave the security of a teaching position at the University of Heidelberg? Certainly, not for the glamour of working for Mitch, or the meager salary Mitch must be paying him. No, not reason enough, I was sure of that, but my thoughts drifted away from Weber as I left his office and headed toward the downstairs lab. After all, I had come to take a closer look at Catherine's incredible drug.

Inside Mitch's hidden laboratory I removed Cold from the refrigerator. After placing a small amount of the serum into a petri dish, I set it underneath the scanning electron microscope. I adjusted the lens to one ten-thousandth of an inch and took a look at the mosaic that made up Catherine's drug.

Speak to me, Catherine. Show me what you've done here, and why you never told me. I did not expect to understand it all in one day. After all, it had taken Catherine a year to create her drug. But I did want to understand the drug's basic architecture. This was Catherine's creation, and in many respects I understood her thinking process. I was optimistic this morning, too, because my mind was clearer than it had been at any point since returning to New York.

* * *

Nine hours later my breakthrough came: Cold conquers viruses because it binds to a hydrophobic pocket in VP1 and stabilizes the protein capsid to such an extent that the virus cannot release its RNA genome into the target cell. I was now certain Cold detected the virus as it entered the body, possibly three to five days sooner than a person's antibodies could react to the invader. Cold destroyed the virus's appetite to attack human cells, and in short, rendered the virus powerless to reproduce.

At the core of the drug was an elegant molecule that had been masterfully assembled to "gut" the harmful nature out of the virus shortly after it entered the blood system. Remarkably, this molecule had been taught to seek out and destroy the virus's reproductive machinery. It was an amazing creation. As I read through the final pages of Catherine's research document, however, I saw references made to improving the drug by coating the surface of human cells with a substance that would make them slippery and thus impossible for a virus to cling to and penetrate. Those notes scribbled in the margin were not in Catherine's handwriting. Apparently Catherine had collaborated with another scientist. I stepped back from the bench, exhausted. Looking out through the barred window, I saw that evening had arrived. I was grateful to Mitch for allowing me free access to his laboratory, and I had accomplished enough work for one day. I went back upstairs to Mitch's office, where he was in a meeting.

"Jack, don't leave. Come in and meet David Goldfarb, Science Editor for *The New York Times.*"

A heavyset man with a scant patch of hair on the top of his head turned to greet me. "It's a pleasure, Doctor Lewis. I covered your discovery of the LEC Enzyme a few years back. I'm delighted to hear you're heading up the Cold project for Rosetta."

Surprised by his statement, I glanced over at Mitch as Goldfarb continued.

"If Mitch sends me the information within the next two hours, we can get your Cold article in Tuesday's *Times.*" Goldfarb put on his coat and wrapped a scarf around his neck. "It was a pleasure, Doctor Lewis, and congratulations on getting the FDA to consider preferential treatment for your drug. That is a rarity."

I kept my cool until Goldfarb was gone. "Since when am I heading up the Cold project? And what's this crap about preferential treatment from the FDA?"

"Relax. I'm just painting a picture for the press. If you don't give them a bit of dazzle, they won't print your story. Your history with the LEC Enzyme project doesn't hurt either. Investors always look for that type of stuff."

Vanessa entered the room. "Sorry to disturb you." She handed Mitch some papers and looked over at me. "How are you, Jack?"

"Fine. Thanks." Actually, I was not fine, and I suspected Vanessa knew that. "I have a question for you."

Vanessa nodded. "The last time we spoke, you said that Catherine was a remarkable woman. You knew her?"

"Why, yes, of course. Mitch introduced us when she first came to Rosetta. We had lunch on a few occasions and became friendly. The more I got to know her, the more remarkable she became. Extraordinary is a better way to describe her." At that moment Vanessa became self-conscious and stopped speaking about Catherine as though they were truly old friends. "Well, I've got to get back to my desk. Mitch, don't forget to sign those papers before you leave tonight. It was good to see you, Jack."

Mitch followed Vanessa with his eyes as she left the room. It was clear there was an attraction there. I knew Mitch well enough to know he was smitten with her. I dropped Catherine's file on the desk to catch his attention. "I found some scribbling on the last pages of Catherine's research folder. Did you ever notice it?"

"No. Scribbling?"

"Did Catherine ever mention she had a collaborator?"

"No. Why? Do you think she did?"

"The scribbling outlines an alternative design for the drug outside of what Catherine had created. I believe another scientist is involved."

"Scribbling in her folder doesn't prove that. Maybe she had a consultant look the project over."

"What, to suggest coating the exterior of human cells so the virus slides off? It's an odd suggestion, don't you think? A consultant would evaluate Catherine's design, not suggest an alternative one. Besides, the drug is exquisite on its own. Why would anyone suggest changing it?"

"I don't know, but let's say you're right about a collaborator. Why haven't they come forward to—"

"Ah, you may have hit on something, Mitch. If we find Catherine's collaborator, maybe we find much more. Maybe even her killer. How difficult can it be to track this person down? Whoever it is, they have to be a scientist and have spent time with Catherine. They probably even visited her laboratory on a regular basis."

"You make it sound easy."

"I'm just thinking out loud."

"Can we talk about this later? If I don't send Goldfarb the information he's requested, our article won't make the paper."

"About that, Mitch. Why go out of your way to mislead the press? I'm not heading a team to develop this drug. They'll find out sooner or later, so why start out on the wrong foot?"

"You'll need to trust my judgment when it comes to marketing, Jack. Meanwhile, I have a request of you. What are you doing tomorrow?" He slapped an airline ticket in my hand. "The FDA expects us first thing in the morning. We're on the early bird."

I looked at the ticket to Washington. "A seven a.m. flight?"

"It's the only way to make our nine-thirty meeting. You'll go, right?"

"Let's get one thing straight. I'll go, but I don't want to. I need you to understand one thing: this will be the first and last time I'm involved with this project. Are we clear?"

"We're clear. But now, I have something to say to you. Don't drag me into your investigation. My nerves are already shot from the break-in, and

I'm not sleeping well. Something tells me things are going to get worse before they get better."

"Okay, then. You keep me out of the research, and I'll keep you out of the investigation. Deal?"

"Deal. And now that that's settled, let me get Goldfarb his information and then I want to finish my spiel on cryonics."

"Not again, Mitch. I know where you're going, and I appreciate it, but save your breath. I don't buy into the cryonics hype."

"Forget about cryonics for the moment, and let me paint a bigger picture for you." Mitch walked to the bookcase, pulled down an eight-inch-thick folder, and set it on his desk. "Do you ever get the feeling everything in life is speeding up? That we're forced to do more things in less time?"

"At times."

"Well, they *are* speeding up, and here's why. Technology is evolving at an astounding rate. A multitude of medical discoveries occur each and every day. While it's virtually impossible to be kept abreast of them all, we still feel their impact. And the impact produces change in our daily lives and more information for us to absorb. As we compress larger quantities of new information into our brain it creates the sensation that things are moving faster. So what does all this mean? The rate of discoveries we make will continue to increase exponentially, and people who are alive on this planet in, say, thirty years, may never have to die."

"Mitch! I'm not understanding anything you just said. You sound like the leader of some cult!"

"Let me finish, Jack. Biotechnology, nanotechnology, and artificial intelligence are evolving at a ridiculous rate. At some point, they're all going to blend into one, single technology. And when they do, the result will be the eradication of most major diseases."

"That may happen, but people will still eventually die of old age."

"Not thirty years from now. Open your eyes and look at what's happening. The human genome is on the brink of being deciphered, and the experts are convinced our genes can be re-instructed to not shut our bodies down. Death is *only* a disease. Nature has programmed human beings so the older of our species die off at one point. This allows the younger of the species to have enough food to survive. In the not too distant future, man will replace nature's role and take control of our own evolution. We will then re-program our body so the old no longer need to die off. Whether you believe it or not, every bit of research that takes place on this planet is driven by our subconscious for the single purpose of finding a cure for death. I believe that to be the truth."

"You lost me somewhere along the way. But, mostly, I'm stunned. When did you start thinking this way? You were the good Catholic, even an altar boy, and believed in life after death. What changed you?

"Nothing has changed me. I'm still Catholic, but maybe God intends for us to conquer this universe, and maybe another part of His plan is for mankind to discover immortality. It makes sense that He would empower us to evolve to that level. Otherwise, why would he have created disease and death, and this barren universe, if not for us to overcome it? There's a passage in the Bible that really caught my attention and touched me. I need to go back and find it. It's where God said, "Heaven is on earth." I think He said that for a reason. He's laid it all out for us, Jack."

"Okay, I get the big picture, and can understand why you're pushing cryonics. I just don't buy into it. Cryonics sounds good on paper, but it's a last-ditch hope for people who can't accept death, and none of those frozen cadavers will ever be revived." I looked at my watch. "I'm late for a meeting! I listened to your cryonics spiel, so let's never discuss it again."

Chapter Fifteen

I stepped into the entryway of what was once Catherine's favorite restaurant. A server walked past carrying a tray laden with plates. I breathed in the bouquet of these freshly cooked meals and was reminded that my taste buds had never been disappointment in this bistro. In fact, Michelle's culinary creations were capable of intoxicating just about everyone who dined here. It was comforting to know that at least one thing in New York had not changed.

"Jack!"

I opened my arms and let Michelle wrap herself around me. Her head came to rest on my chest. No words were needed between us. We both understood: Catherine was gone and the world would no longer be the same. Michelle was family, or as close to family as I had, and to hold her brought me to the brink of tears. Michelle pulled away and looked at me. For a woman in her fifties, she was stunning. With flowing red hair, high cheekbones, and flawless skin, she was as attractive now as when I'd first met her twelve years ago.

"Your friend is waiting at a table in the back. She's been here quite a while and appears to be getting impatient," Michelle said, to alert me. She curled her fingers into mine and led me to the table.

Julia was seated with a half-empty wineglass in front of her. I glanced at my watch and realized I had arrived an hour past our appointment time. Petrie, Michelle's longtime waiter, saw me from the other side of the room and made his way over to greet me.

I turned my attention to Julia. She was wearing a simple black dress and a string of pearls. It worked well with her blonde hair and green eyes in the semi-dark room. "I apologize for being so late."

Her nostrils flared. "You know, Jack, your schedule may take some getting used to."

Petrie arrived and placed his hand on my arm. "My deepest regrets, Monsieur Jack. *La Vie en Rose* will never be the same without Catherine."

"Thank you, Petrie."

"Your usual, Monsieur?"

The doctors had instructed me to avoid alcohol, but said nothing about the pleasure of ordering it or the enjoyment of watching Petrie fill my glass. "Yes, and bring a new glass for the lady." When Petrie left, I once again turned my attention back to Julia. "Thank you for waiting."

Julia began to sort through her papers without answering me. Years of experience had taught me that a good bottle of wine can smooth over most anything. Petrie returned with a bottle of Châteauneuf du Pape, and as he was about to pour, I gestured toward Julia's glass. "Please, allow the lady to taste it."

Skillfully, Petrie poured a splash of wine into the bottom of Julia's glass. She swirled the wine in the glass, lifted it to her nose to smell its bouquet, and slowly tasted the wine when her lips touched the glass. "It's very good, thank you." Petri filled both glasses halfway, set the bottle down on the table, and walked away.

I held up my glass, "To punctuality." My attempt at levity had fallen on deaf ears.

Julia placed a folder filled with papers in the middle of the table, still refusing to make eye contact. "I've been placed in a position where I need to work very hard to meet your deadlines, and I've practically killed myself to collect this much information." Julia stopped, inhaled deeply, and looked me straight in the eye. "If I tell you that I'll be somewhere at seven o'clock, you can expect to see me there ten minutes early. What I expect from you is that you show up on time."

I nodded. "It won't happen again."

Julia stared at me while she composed herself. She also wanted to make sure I explicitly understood her point. After a moment more of silence, she added, "If I were the police, you'd be my prime suspect."

"What? How can you say that?"

"Catherine was poisoned by Crotalus durissus, which is pit viper venom indigenous to the Rainforest in South America. Coincidentally, that's where you've spent the last six months. And, Catherine had a life insurance policy worth a million dollars with you as the sole beneficiary."

I was infuriated. I had hired her to help me track down Catherine's killer, and all she could come up with were motives as to why I might have killed my own wife. "Yes, Catherine and I did take out life insurance policies. So do millions of married couples. That doesn't make me a suspect. As for Crotalus, I'm not aware it exists solely in South America. Last I heard, pit vipers live on most continents, including the U.S."

Julia looked at her notes. "Let's move on. Crotalus should not have killed Catherine because the toxins are removed before it's shipped to the hospital. But, the fact of the matter is, it *did* kill her. I contacted Memorial and asked for an explanation as to why toxins were found in the Crotalus, but I haven't heard back from them. We may not hear back at all, as they may sense a lawsuit, something no hospital wants."

"Lawsuit?"

"Yes. They may be negligent on a number of counts: Crotalus filled with toxins, no antivenin in the hospital, their security system failed to protect Catherine when someone broke into her lab... You don't have to be a lawyer to see that Memorial is running pretty scared about now."

"I have no intention of suing anyone. Aren't we getting off track?"

"Let's continue then. When I visited Memorial, I noticed a camera that watches the back door to the laboratory. I requested a copy of the video taken on the morning of Catherine's death, but they haven't produced it yet. I imagine they want their attorneys to look it over first. Whoever broke into Catherine's laboratory had to go through that back door. The only other way to reach her laboratory is from the elevator, where a security guard is stationed. According to the guard, he didn't see or hear anything that morning. Anyway, I let the hospital's attorney know that if we're denied access to that video, we'll file a court order against the hospital. I don't think they want that kind of negative press. Any questions on that?"

"No. It looks like you covered it well. I'd certainly like to see that video too."

"I've also interviewed most of the people that had contact with Catherine the morning of her death, but I've been unable to reach

Frances McQueen. I've left four messages for her and she hasn't responded back yet. I'd say she's ducking me."

"That doesn't sound like Frances. I wonder why she'd do that. She was one of Catherine's closest friends. She wants this case solved as badly as I do."

"She's gone out of her way to avoid me, so my report on her is incomplete. There's one event in particular I want to ask her about. On the day of Catherine's death, a young woman on the intensive care floor where Catherine was taken. She also died. That woman's body disappeared."

"What do you mean it disappeared?"

"It just vanished. She was a Jane Doe, a prostitute and drug user. After she died, her body was being transported to the morgue in the basement, but never made it there. Frances had floor duty that day and had ordered the woman's body moved to the morgue. This probably has nothing to do with Catherine, but it's unusual because this Jane Doe died around the same time as Catherine. I want to hear what Frances has to say about it. Any questions?"

"No. Except I don't see the connection between this Jane Doe and Catherine."

"And there may be none, but we need to check it out. Now, as you may have guessed, the background searches have not been completed, and it might take another week to get them all. But, I've completed the searches on Mitch Cochran, Colter Malone, Vanessa Boulay, and a report on Franz Weber."

"Well, Mitch and Colter are the least of my concern. Since I've known them for years, there's little new you can tell me about either of them."

A devilish smile crossed Julia's lips. "Tell me about Mitch."

"Okay. He grew up in Hell's Kitchen. He attended Saint Agnes High School, and from what he told me today, he's still a good Catholic. He studied pre-med at the University of Buffalo, and received his Ph.D. in Microbiology at Minnesota. School was never Mitch's strength, and to his credit, he worked harder than most in his class. And now he owns his own company and appears to have a promising future. Mitch is well liked by most, and I doubt he's ever had a run-in with the law. Oh, there was a family tragedy that affects him to this day. When Mitch was ten years old, his older brother was shot and killed. Because of that, he abhors all forms of violence, and that includes weapons. He can be a bit high strung at times and prone to anxiety attacks. Business pressure doesn't bother him as much, but if he senses danger, he's been known to collapse like a house of cards. And, although Mitch has gone out of his way to help me find you, my investigator, he has asked me to keep him as far away from the investigation as possible. How close is that to your report?"

"Not bad. There's much more in his report, but nothing in Mitch's background concerns me at this time. Care to share your insights on Colter?"

"Sure. He was raised in Chicago by free-thinking parents. They gave him freedoms most young people rarely see, like at age fourteen traveling alone to visit museums in Washington D.C. At fifteen he had a Europass and was riding trains across Europe. His parents considered him advanced and took pride in his maturity. It was no surprise that he got a full scholarship to Loyola at the age of seventeen. He earned a degree in chemistry, and then a fellowship to the University of Chicago, where he earned his Ph.D. in microbiology. He also picked up a Ph.D. in chemistry. Needless to say, the man's brilliant. He's also a free spirit and, to be blunt, a ladies man. He doesn't act, look, or dress like a scientist, but he's capable of practically anything he puts his mind to. I would venture to say Colter's never crossed paths with the law either."

"I guess you don't know him too well. He was arrested twice for assault and battery, and a female was on the receiving end both times. He avoided prosecution because he was under age at the time."

"Colter once said he got into trouble a couple of times as a teenager, but he never elaborated."

"Well, he draws a red flag because of his history of battering women. Needless to say, Catherine had bruises on her body, and Colter's laboratory was next to hers, which gave him easy access. Let's just leave it there for now. Any questions?"

"Actually, I'm surprised. And quite frankly, I don't know how to deal with what you've just said."

"Don't over-think anything at this point, Jack." Julia reached into her briefcase and pulled out another file. "Vanessa Boulay was hired by Mitch five months ago, while you were in South America. Frankly, she's a person of interest as well. Outside of Mitch, she's the only person with complete access to Rosetta's books. She knew Mitch was at the Sixth Precinct the night Rosetta was broken into. She was friendly with Catherine and admittedly had regular contact with her. None of this incriminates her, but she's managed to place herself in the middle of a lot of things." Julia turned the page. "Here's a little more about her. Vanessa was born in Nice, France, in 1967. Her mother died giving birth, and her father, Doctor Vincent Boulay, raised her alone. The two moved to New York when she was seven years old, and she attended Saint Ann's, a private school in Manhattan. Doctor Boulay practiced internal medicine at New York University Hospital. Vanessa graduated from MIT with a Ph.D. in microbiology. She then went back to school, and got her M.B.A. in finance from NYU. Her father died in 1992, just before she received her final degree. She has no known relatives in the United States. She's never been married, has no children, and no criminal record."

"I was impressed with her when we met. She comes across as having a good heart. But I'm even more impressed with your ability to gather as much information on her as you did in such a short timeframe, given the fact she was born in France."

"Having friends in the right places makes an investigator's job much easier."

"Have these same friends gathered any intelligence from Germany?"

"You're asking about Franz Weber?"

"That's right."

"Well, I'm afraid you're going to be disappointed. All I know about Weber is what you told me, which is that Rosetta Laboratories hired him six months ago. My people checked every university in Heidelberg and found that Weber never taught at any of them. In fact, they couldn't find anyone from Heidelberg that fits Weber's description."

"What? They must've overlooked something. Mitch told me himself that Weber had been a professor at a university there."

"Not according to my report. Just so you know, my people in Europe are the best."

"Hmm. I knew it! There was something about Weber that didn't ring true with me. Nobody with his credentials just walks into a biotech off the street to ask for a job. He must've lied to Mitch. Wait until he finds out his star scientist is a fraud."

"Be careful, Jack. We need to confine this information to Catherine's investigation."

It took a moment for her words to sink in. "I get it. Keep my nose out of Mitch's business. That might be hard to do, since Mitch is my friend. For now I'll keep quiet. But this means we also need to collect more information on Weber. Now that I think about it, your report on him is timely. Today I discovered that Catherine must have relied upon a confidant when developing her drug. She visited Rosetta on occasion, and Weber probably befriended her. I don't think it's too far-fetched to believe he's involved. He might even be trying to peddle her serum. We need to look into this more deeply. See where he goes, who he meets. Maybe he'll slip up."

Julia slid the papers into her briefcase and snapped the lid closed. "Our arrangement was for me to collect information on Catherine's case, not to go on a wild goose chase that will only lengthen the investigation. Weber's not a prime suspect. In fact, no one is right now. Let's stick to completing the first phase of the investigation as agreed. Then, if you choose for me to remain on the case, we'll review the findings and decide the next steps to take."

"I know, but Weber—"

"Jack, I understand how you feel, but maybe Weber isn't from Germany, and that's why he didn't show up on our radar screen. And even if he is from Germany, there could be a hundred reasons why he didn't tell Mitch his real name. That doesn't mean he was involved with Catherine's death. I could make the case to incriminate Mitch from the information I've collected. But running an investigation means you gather the facts first, evaluate them, and then take the appropriate next step."

"Incriminate Mitch? How?"

"Well, he has no alibi. All we really know is that he showed up at Memorial an hour after Catherine was taken to a private room. He then had her wheeled to the basement to be x-rayed. But, technically, he had time to commit the crime earlier that morning and return home."

"Wasn't he at Rosetta that morning?"

"No. He didn't go to Rosetta that day. He said he was home alone all morning. But, understand my point. Just because Mitch hasn't got an alibi doesn't mean I'm going to shift the focus of the investigation to him."

"Mitch always goes to Rosetta first thing in the morning. It's not like him to stay home."

"Let's not dwell on it right now, all right?"

"You're right. I'm sorry. Let's get the facts first. I'll reach out to Frances for you, too."

"No, I don't want you interfering. We agreed that you will stay out of the investigation until I've completed the first phase. I expect you to honor that agreement."

"All right, I'll stay out of your way, but tell me one thing. Do you really believe I could have had anything to do with Catherine's death?"

"I ran a search with the airlines and know exactly when you left and when you re-entered the country."

"So you know that. Why did you accuse me then?"

Julia ran her finger around the rim of her wine glass, and then looked across at me. "You made me wait an hour, Jack."

Petrie approached the table. "Mademoiselle, Monsieur, would you follow me, please?"

Julia looked startled. "Where to?"

"Please, Mademoiselle, just follow me."

Chapter Sixteen

Michelle's face brightened into a welcoming smile when she saw Julia and me enter the kitchen. She wiped her hands on her apron. The half dozen chefs working alongside Michelle also greeted us with smiles. To our left, a small table had been set with all the accoutrements needed for a fine meal. The centerpiece was a beautiful flower arrangement.

"Bonsoir, Mademoiselle," Michelle said, motioning Julia to the table.

"Good evening. Your kitchen smells wonderful."

"It should," Petrie said, pulling out Julia's chair. He bent over and whispered into her ear a few words akin to a trade secret. "Michelle is an artist, and you are about to taste her *sampler extraordinaire*. It's served only in the kitchen, and only to a select few." Petrie then grabbed his tray, loaded it with plates of food, and left for the dining room. Michelle placed four crystal wine goblets on our table. She then returned to the pan-seared steak she'd been overseeing at the stove.

"I'm a bit curious—why are we eating in the kitchen?"

"At Michelle's invitation. We've been friends for years. The kitchen is the only place we can visit when the restaurant's busy. You're not vegetarian, are you?

Julia laughed. "Hardly."

Michelle appeared at the table with a bottle of Pinot Noir. She splashed a little into her glass and tasted it. "Excellent." She filled the other three goblets. "Petrie," she called, handing him a goblet as he re-entered the kitchen. "To friendship," she said. We all toasted.

Petrie set his goblet down and again vanished through the double doors with another tray full of dinners. One of the chefs served us *beggar's purse*, an appetizer comprised of crème fraîche and beluga caviar piled atop a thin, elegant crepe. When wrapped up and tied with a green scallion, it took the shape of a small money bag. I popped the bite-size 'purse' into my mouth, bit into it, and enjoyed the medley of flavors that exploded from within. Michelle gave us time to savor our appetizer before dishing us each a serving of pepper-seared venison steak from a copper pan. She topped the steaks with sun-dried cherry sauce just as one of her chefs arrived to serve us butternut squash *timbals*.

"Bon appétit," she said, and returned to her stove. The samplers were small portions intended to tantalize your taste buds without filling you up. Fifteen minutes later Michelle served us grilled *poussins* with a warm vegetable salad and tomato-herb vinaigrette. "Eat while it's hot," she said. We consumed that dish with delight. Michelle's next surprise was a small portion of *salmon roulade* with gazpacho sauce.

I looked across at Julia. "I hope you're enjoying this."

Julia stopped chewing for a moment, "Epicurean." She devoured the last morsel on her plate.

Michelle watched over us from the stove and smiled as we cleared our palettes with a second goblet of Pinot. Another twenty minutes had passed before she carried over the ultimate experience of the evening. "This is *soufflé Michelle*." The rich, vanilla soufflé was topped with *Grand Marnier* sauce, whipped cream, and a light sprinkling of powdered sugar and shaved chocolate. Petrie appeared with freshly brewed coffee. By then I had reached my limit on food and drink, but I tasted the soufflé and sipped my coffee before pushing away from the table. Michelle walked up behind me and placed her hands on my shoulders. She whispered, "We need to speak soon." Something on the stove began to sizzle and she returned to oversee it. Julia observed the affection Michelle had shown me. Curiosity got the best of her.

"How long have you two been friends?"

"Twelve years. I stumbled upon this restaurant by accident one day and discovered that the chef was a culinary genius. I've been hooked ever since. Once, many years ago, I was laid up for days with the flu. There was a knock on my door and I dragged myself out of bed to answer it. Michelle was standing there with a huge pot of soup. She rushed past me and placed it on the table. 'Eat it all, my darling, and by tomorrow you'll be better.'"

"Did you eat it?"

"Every spoonful."

"And...?"

"The next morning the flu was gone. My lungs were clear and my body felt strong. So, when I say she's a genius, you're hearing it first-hand from someone who knows her."

Julia's eyes opened wide as she looked over at Michelle. "I love magical stories."

There was more to the story that I had not shared, as our history together had taken more than one turn. One afternoon twelve years ago, while walking down West Broadway, I collided with a woman wearing coveralls and a dust mask over her face. Out of breath, she pointed to a large object that needed to be dragged from the restaurant. Minutes later, I found myself hauling an old stove to the curb. Later that week I was recruited again, this time to move a sink and a rusty old refrigerator. With most of her face covered with the dust mask, it was only the charm from her eyes that compelled me to help her. A week later, I received an invitation to the Grand Opening of the restaurant. When I entered, a beautiful redhead walked over and planted a kiss on my cheek. I looked into her eyes and knew it was Michelle. You see, she was a new chef with limited funds, and was forced to renovate the restaurant herself, with only the help of a few friends. The kiss was in appreciation for my helping her out. After the restaurant closed that night I stayed and piled chairs onto tables, and even mopped the floor. Once we left the restaurant and she locked the doors, we stood outside under a full moon and looked into each other's eyes. My heart was racing, but it broke moments later when Michelle said it had been a long day for her. That night, we went our separate ways. The next morning I awoke to being totally in love. A couple of days later I visited the restaurant only to be devastated. She broke it to me delicately. She explained that she was much older than I. That she had experienced just one deep love in her life, and he had been taken from her. I was a young man starting out, she said, and her ingredients mixed with mine rarely worked in the long run. I lived under her spell for almost a week, until one morning I awoke to find her spell had released me. I realized she was right. From that point on, I became a regular customer and our friendship grew in ways I had never thought possible. In time, I forgot about falling in love with her. Then, when Catherine came into my life, it was crucial that these two important women become friends.

I looked at my watch and then across the table at Julia. She looked as tired as I felt. "It's late and I have an early flight. Mitch and I are meeting with the FDA in Washington tomorrow morning."

She hesitated for a moment and then spoke. "Can I ask a question, Jack? If I'm stepping over the line, just tell me to mind my own business."

"Ask away."

"Have you been to the cemetery yet?"

The question caught me off guard. Visiting the cemetery should have been the first thing on my mind, but it had never occurred to me. "Not yet. I plan to go soon. With the investigation and everything, I..."

"No need to explain. But it's important to heal, Jack. An investigation like this puts pressure on a person." Julia paused. "Let me take you to the cemetery tomorrow. I'll drop you and wait near the gate, if you like. What time do you return from Washington?"

I removed the airline ticket from my pocket. "We land at two o'clock, but this might not be a good idea. You'd have to come from the city to pick me up, and traffic that time of day—"

"I'll be there at two o'clock," Julia said in a way that made it final.

Michelle approached as we got up to leave the restaurant. She asked when we could meet to spend more time together. I promised to call her the next day. Moments later I was outside putting Julia in a taxi.

"Thanks for my first kitchen extravaganza, Jack. It was wonderful."

"Get home safely. I'll see you tomorrow." I closed the cab door and tapped the roof.

As the driver pulled away, Julia rolled down the window and stuck her head out. "Get some rest, Jack. See you tomorrow."

After the taxi drove off, I fell into a state of depression. I had been in New York for five days without once thinking to visit Catherine's grave. If I was blind enough to block out something that important, what else was I not seeing?

I walked up West Broadway toward Houston Street. The frigid air felt good on my face, and I once again debated whether to return to the condo or go back to the Towers. I continued to walk and think as the snow crunched almost musically under my feet. My eyes teared, perhaps from the biting wind whistling by or maybe because I was feeling sorry for myself. I tried to think good thoughts. One: I was still alive. Two: I was not confined to a hospital bed with an intravenous needle stuck into me. Three: There were no doctors around to poke, probe, or play twenty questions about how I felt. Four: I was not waiting to be rolled into an operating room and turned into a turnip. Five: There were no young interns standing next to my bed writing down every small change that occurred while my body succumbed. And finally: I was not choking and near death within earshot of a nurse who had no real desire to revive me.

I told myself to knock it off. Those thoughts were morbid. I turned my attention back to Julia, our evening together, and what she had revealed in the course of her investigation. A story was unfolding that involved Mitch, Colter, Vanessa, Frances, and Franz Weber. Not one of them was squeaky clean: Mitch had no alibi; Colter had a history of battering women; Vanessa had planted herself in the middle of everything; Frances was avoiding Julia; and Franz Weber, well, he was just a small, fat mystery to me. Did one of them kill Catherine? Or was it a random burglar who happened to break into her laboratory? Will Julia be able to push this investigation to completion in two short weeks?

Even in my exhaustion from the day's events and the cold of the night air, it occurred to me that not Julia, not any person, had the ability to investigate every aspect of this case in two weeks. I needed to accelerate the investigation, and that meant scrutinizing the day-to-day operation. I planned by starting with one thing that really gnawed at me. Why was Frances McQueen ducking Julia? Frances needed to be questioned, and if Julia was unable to get answers from her, then I would.

Chapter Seventeen

Rutger stepped from his town car and fought a punishing wind on the East River tarmac. The steel-blue backdrop of the Manhattan skyline was at his back. When he turned to face it, all he saw was the harsh morning sun reflecting off a wall of skyscrapers. He gripped his collar and stepped inside the waiting helicopter which the wind rocked with force from side to side.

The pilot yelled, "Fasten your seat belt," and Rutger braced himself as the blades propelled the vehicle off the ground. Earlier that morning, the pilot had called Rutger to suggest they delay the trip due to the poor weather. Since Rutger had agreed to meet with Jito Sumataika and Kajara Tsai regardless of the brewing storm, the appointment stood.

Rutger removed the science section from *The New York Times* as wind bounced the helicopter around. He cringed when he read the lead article. "Damn it!" The article was not long, but it was there for the entire world to read. *Rosetta Laboratories Announces Drug that May Cure Common Cold*. He read on. *Owner of Rosetta Laboratories Mitch Cochran invites industry leaders to attend a demonstration of the new Cold drug early next week*. Rutger decided then and there to attend. After all, he had promised the drug to his grandfather. It was clear Cochran was looking for investors. Who better than Dobler Pharmaceutical, the market leader in cold remedy drugs, and whose premier service was to also help small companies launch their new drugs?

The helicopter set down on the snowy-white surface in Bashakill, New York. Given the remoteness of his grandfather's summer resort, Rutger knew it would be the perfect place to meet with Jito Sumataika. Heinrich kept the hotel's penthouse for the family's personal use year round.

Rutger recalled the holidays he had taken at this resort with his mother. He spent mornings in the company of his grandfather, who told him story after story about his drug industry dynasty. In the afternoons, while his grandfather worked, Rutger raced his bike through the massive hallways of the hotel, which to him were wider than a football field.

Bashakill had been a remarkable place to spend his summer vacations. The swimming pool was filled with noisy children, and the adults became just as noisy after having a drink or two around the pool.

In the winter, though, Bashakill was a paradise lost. The empty corridors of the hotel were eerie in their silence. Rutger remembered sensing a low, hollow murmur as he walked past the locked doors, always expecting one to creak open. The hotel's massive kitchen had lost its aromatic luster, its rows of stainless steel cold and still in their emptiness. When a draft of cold air swept through the kitchen, the tympanic kettles swung on their ceiling hooks, at times brushing up against each other and giving off a hollow, desolate sound.

Rutger felt the solitude of the hotel most as he passed through the elegant dining room with its sea of unoccupied tables and chairs. As summer and sunlight nurtured the spirit of life at Bashakill, winter with its dreary emptiness reduced this majestic structure into a dark, lonely, cavernous dungeon.

"May I take your bag, Mr. Dobler?" Tony said, as Rutger entered the lobby.

"Thank you, Tony." A skeleton crew worked the hotel during the winter months. Rutger pulled Tony aside and out of earshot of the others. "Any problems with the catering instructions?"

"None at all. Everything is prepared." Tony was a local who had been working at the hotel since high school. He was reliable.

Tony accompanied Rutger to the penthouse. When they stepped off the elevator, Tony opened the door and placed Rutger's briefcase on the table. He tossed a few more pieces of wood into the fireplace, which he had kept going since early morning.

"I'm expecting two guests. Show them to the penthouse when they arrive."

"I'll take care of it, Mr. Dobler."

"Thank you, Tony." He removed a fifty from his billfold and held it out.

"Thank you, Mr. Dobler. That's very kind."

"Wait for my guests at the front door and be sure to send them up on the private elevator. And, Tony, call me before you send them up."

"I will, Mr. Dobler." Tony hurried out the door.

Rutger walked to the fireplace to warm his hands. Part of him wanted to call his grandfather and tell him about the meeting, but he thought better about creating unnecessary stress for him. The time would soon come when his grandfather would no longer be part of it all, and that, indeed, would be a sad day for Rutger.

The sliding glass door beckoned and Rutger looked out past the terrace to the rolling hills. A barren, white landscape surrounded Bashakill. The apple orchard on the hillside was dried and withered, its parched, brown branches cracked and lifeless. On the terrace, the wind tugged at a green and white striped awning that the staff had neglected to take down at season's end. Several small icicles snapped off the bottom edge of the awning and crashed against the glass door. The telephone rang. "Yes?"

"Your guests are on their way up, Mr. Dobler."

"Thank you, Tony." Rutger walked to the video monitor to view Kajara Tsai and Jito Sumataika as they entered the elevator. Grandfather always told him, "Watch the actions of a person's face and body for ten seconds. It will tell you everything you need to know." Rutger watched Tsai cordially step aside to allow the slightly taller Jito to enter the elevator. A well-dressed, distinguished-looking man in his mid-forties appeared in the monitor. Jito's black hair and mustache were flecked with gray, and his demeanor showed that, while he was serious, he was perfectly at ease with himself. Rutger turned the monitor off and moved to the elevator. When it opened, Jito Sumataika took one step out and stopped. Rutger approached with a smile, but the solemn expression on Jito's face remained steadfast.

Tsai squeezed past Jito and positioned himself between the two men. "Jito Sumataika of Sumataika Family, please meet Rutger Dobler of Dobler Family."

Rutger and Jito held each other's stare without blinking. After Tsai's introduction, Jito placed his hands together and bowed. His head and upper torso bent below his waist, and he held that position for a prolonged time. Gracefully, he stood back up. Rutger understood Japanese culture and knew that the deeper one bows, the greater the respect he has bestowed upon the recipient. Jito's bow was deep. Rutger placed his hands together and bowed in similar fashion to Jito. Tsai then bowed to both men, being careful not to bow as deeply as Jito, so as to not deprive him of the high honor he had shown to Rutger.

"Please, join me," Rutger said, escorting the men to a small table set up with a bottle of hot sake and three porcelain cups. Rutger poured the sake and lifted his cup in Jito's honor. "Welcome to America." It amused him to watch Jito portray himself as someone who was raised in a heritage of refinement. He was, after all, nothing more than an extortionist, and most likely a cold-blooded murderer. Rutger flashed a convivial smile and sipped his sake.

"You honor me by accepting me in your home," Jito said. "I bring you the gratitude of my father, who honors you."

"Thank you. Please convey my regards to your father." Rutger poured more sake and waited for the business discussion to begin. Japanese business etiquette called for a waiting period before mentioning business matters. Jito finally opened the conversation.

"Has Sumataika pleased Dobler Family?"

Rutger smiled, but he was hardly pleased. The Sumataika had botched a simple burglary and deprived him of gaining important industry information. To express his dissatisfaction, however, would be rude. "Your family has provided only one service for us to date."

"The Sumataika very pleased in friendship with Dobler Family. Thousands of patents lose protection soon, many belong to Dobler Family. Competition great from biotechs. No good for your business."

"Yes. You are quite right, Jito. Many biotech companies will challenge us with new drugs."

"I take time to know American business, Rutger Dobler. Much can be done to help you."

Jito became more aggressive in his tone and asserted himself. Rutger would not allow that to occur, and the battle to control the meeting had begun. "Jito, let me ask you a question. Are you content with our arrangement?"

"The Sumataika Family very pleased."

"Well, forgive me, but, are you looking for more out of our relationship?"

"The Sumataika and Dobler families share much in common. We, too, must survive. We, too, compete for new markets. America is future opportunity."

Jito's words sent a chill through Rutger, and it confirmed the Sumataika did, in fact, plan to invade America. "I'm still a bit confused. What are you expecting from our relationship?"

"Your friendship very important. We want to keep business with you. We always protect you. We must also increase cost to one hundred thousand."

Ah, finally, there it was. "From twenty-five thousand?" Rutger knew Jito was an extortionist, so why should Jito's attitude toward him be any different? Rutger looked over at Tsai, the one who had delivered this animal to his doorstep. Perhaps Tsai was part of the extortion plan that would allow the Doblers to be their next sacrificial lamb.

Rutger filled their cups once again. "I need to ask you something, Jito. Your men broke into the hospital last week and a woman was killed there that same morning. Did your men have anything to do with it?"

"Yes, woman killed. Very sorry. Sumataika not responsible."

"You're quite sure about that?"

Jito looked up at him. "I would not lie to you."

Rutger studied Jito's face. He looked at Tsai. But nothing on either man's face led Rutger to believe he was being lied to. "I will take you at your word, Jito. I'm relieved that you were not involved in this woman's death. It allows us to go forward, but under three conditions. First, you did not get the file that was promised me, and I will not pay for something I did not receive. Second, I'll pay the higher fee for future work, but there will be no further increase in your fees. Third, your services are never to be offered to another pharmaceutical company. Now, if you accept those terms, we can continue our relationship."

"Hai."

"Can I trust the Sumataika to do what we ask?"

"Hai."

"How do I know you will keep your word?"

Without the slightest change of inflection in his voice, Jito said, "I sooner cut wife and children's throats than dishonor you."

Those were the coldest words Rutger had ever heard spoken. That Jito had spoken those words without hesitation was even more chilling, and it forced Rutger to keep his emotions in check. "You will have the opportunity to prove yourself, Jito. Stay in New York for a couple of days. I have a few things that need to be done."

"One moment, Rutger Dobler." Jito pulled out his cellular telephone, dialed a number, and gave an order to the person on the other end. He slipped the telephone back into his pocket and waited. A minute later the elevator door opened and a man stepped out. It was hard for Rutger, or, for that matter, anyone, to not notice the large size of the man who just entered the room.

Jito motioned the man closer. While the man crossed the floor with a certain grace, there was no complementing charm to be found in his face or any other part of him. His eyes were small, dark, and cold, and his air sent a clear message that he was dangerous. Rutger calculated him to be well over six feet tall and weighing in excess of three hundred pounds— not the average Japanese.

"I cannot stay in America," Jito said, "but I leave Juntaro Yashida. I speak through his actions. He will do all you ask, Rutger Dobler."

Rutger considered the possibility of Jito having outsmarted him. One of his men had entered Rutger's world, but there was no graceful way to refuse his offer.

"Well, then," Rutger said with a smile. "Please join me in the dining room." He escorted the men to a table that held a large assortment of sushi and sashimi. Juntaro Yashida waited at the elevator. Once Jito and Tsai were seated, Rutger went out and guided the giant back to the dining table.

Twenty pounds of raw fish was beautifully arranged on three large platters. Jito served himself first, followed by Tsai, and then Yashida. Rutger placed a few pieces on his plate. He was struck by the loud eating sounds around the table. Most of it came from Yashida, who devoured large slabs of sashimi, akin to a shark disposing of a seal. He was a veritable eating machine, snapping up and swallowing everything within reach. Through it all, Yashida's eyes remained cold and lifeless, and he neither looked at nor spoke to anyone during the entire meal.

Before leaving, Jito handed Rutger a telephone number to link him with Yashida. The entourage then descended in the elevator. Rutger watched from the penthouse window as their town car departed through the outer gate. Today, a line had been crossed. There was no turning back.

Chapter Eighteen

The coffee shop across from Memorial was busy when I slid into the booth. I looked up as Frances brushed snow off her blue pea coat and then took a seat across from me.

"Thanks for meeting me so early, Frances. I'm catching a plane this morning and wanted to speak to you first." The waitress slapped down two cups and filled them with coffee. "Julia said she left four messages for you. Any reason you haven't returned her calls?"

Frances cradled her cup in both hands. "She's that investigator you hired, right? I think I saw a message or two, but the hospital's been shorthanded and I've been doubling up."

Her answer surprised me. Working two shifts was a poor excuse for someone like Frances.

"Besides, a detective came around last week and I told him everything I knew."

"Mind telling me what happened that day?"

Frances put her cup down. "I don't mind at all, Jack. It's just that I know how painful it is for you to hear about that day, and I get emotional even thinking about it. But here's what I know. Catherine was found unconscious in her laboratory and taken to intensive care on the fourth floor. When I got there three doctors were trying to figure out why she was in a coma. They ran an EISA test and that's when they found Crotalus in her blood. Memorial's supposed to have antivenin, but there was none where it was supposed to be. Then, one of the doctors said not to bother looking for it, because she was too far gone. He didn't even give her another hour. I called Mitch to tell him what the doctor had said, and he was at the hospital in ten minutes. The doctors weren't allowing anyone in Catherine's room, but he barged in anyway. They asked him to leave and he refused. The door was ajar and I pushed it open a crack more to look inside. Mitch was sitting on the bed. I saw him push Catherine's hair off her face. He took her hand and began to talk to her, saying that he was there now, and she shouldn't be afraid. Then he leaned over and kissed her on the forehead and said he wouldn't leave her no matter what. Sweet Jesus and Mary."

Frances's lips began to quiver. She picked up her coffee cup, but rather than take a sip, she set the cup back down. "Mitch asked the doctors some questions, but they were irritated and didn't answer him. One of them told Mitch that because he wasn't a doctor or family and had no right to ask any questions. On their way out of the room, I heard one doctor tell Mitch that if he was still there when they returned, he'd have security escort him out.

"After they left, I went into the room. Mitch was reading through Catherine's chart. He almost lost it when he saw no x-rays had been taken for the contusion on her head. He told me to have an orderly bring a gurney and take her to the x-ray room in the basement. I never questioned what Mitch asked of me, mostly because I wasn't thinking straight. I even went to the nurse's station and got him a temporary badge so he'd have authorization to get down to the basement and past the morgue. I went down with Mitch and the orderly, but didn't stay long because I was still on duty. By the time I got back upstairs, the doctors were outside Catherine's room and they were furious. They wanted to know what happened to her, and I told them she was being x-rayed. They had me send another orderly down to bring her back up. After the orderly returned Catherine to her room, he found me at the nurse's station and said she was gone—she had died. It must've happened on the way back to her room, maybe even in the elevator, because when I spoke to the technician later, he said she was alive when they x-rayed her."

"Where was Mitch?"

"I don't know what happened to him. But a little while later when I looked for him, I found him in Catherine's laboratory. Colter was there too, and they were going through Catherine's stuff. I didn't stay long because the police were waiting for me on the fourth floor. Someone else had died that morning and her body had just disappeared. I had to answer a lot of questions that day."

"Julia said a woman died on Catherine's floor, a Jane Doe, and her body just vanished. Who was she? Did they ever find her?"

"No, we never did. She was unconscious when they brought her in, and she had no identification. Only needle marks on her arms and legs, so we knew she was a drug user. After the doctor examined her, he said she had been a prostitute, too. The only thing in her possession was a worn out picture of little boy, maybe four years old. I was in the room when we took her clothes off. I was the one who went through her pockets and found the picture. I still have it." Frances opened her purse and pulled out the photo.

"You can hardly recognize his face, but even this crumpled up photo can't hide his beautiful, translucent blue eyes."

I took the picture from her, looked at it briefly, and handed it back to her.

"I'm going to hand it over to social services to see if they can identify the boy. Maybe he's in foster care, and with luck they can track the family down.

"Did someone take the Jane Doe from her room?"

"No. After she died, I had the orderly take her down to the morgue. When he got to the basement, he parked the gurney in the hallway and went to the men's room. He said he was only gone a couple of minutes, but when he came out, she was gone. Security searched the entire hospital, but they never found her."

"That's very strange that her body could just disappear like that."

"I don't know why someone would take a corpse." Frances finally took a sip of her coffee, set the cup down, and put her coat on. "I've got to get to work."

"Do you know if Catherine was seeing anyone while I was gone?"

Frances's eyes widened. "How could you ask that?"

"Was she, Frances?"

"Dating? Catherine? Is that what you're asking?"

"Well, yes. Was she seeing anyone?"

"Catherine would never! Besides, there weren't enough hours in the day with all her research."

"What about Mitch or Colter? Did she see them?"

"Why are you asking these questions? Don't torture yourself like this. It does no good now." Her face turned flush red. "Look here, Jack. Catherine's gone. Now let her be. I won't have a conversation like this!" She buttoned her coat and stormed out.

* * *

The shuttle to Washington landed on schedule. Our meeting with the FDA took place with little fanfare and, as expected, no favors were granted. Mitch's attempt to accelerate the approval process for Cold had fallen on deaf ears. In fact, one mid-level manager scolded Mitch for trying to strong-arm them into giving special treatment to a drug that hadn't even gone through trial testing. *"Federal laws must be obeyed. The Agency will not cut its process short for any drug!"* At that point I wanted to pull Mitch aside and tell him to back off, but the throbbing in my head had reduced me to a mere spectator for most of the meeting. We were promptly escorted out of the building. Thankfully, by the time we boarded the plane back to New York the pain within me had subsided.

"What a waste of time. I'm sorry I dragged you down here," Mitch said.

"What did you expect? The drug's not close to being ready. I'm surprised they didn't throw us out sooner."

"They could've at least shown a little excitement over the drug. Is that too much to ask?"

"Mitch, the meeting's over. Forget it." We sat in silence for a minute. Then, "Mitch, I have a few more questions for you about the day Catherine died."

"What do you want to know?"

"You gave me the impression that you had taken Catherine's file right after she died. Frances told me you took it later that morning."

Mitch looked at me for a moment. I could tell my question had confused him. "You think I intentionally misled you? About what? I told you what happened. I took the file later that morning."

"I'm having a hard time putting the timelines together."

"Why don't I tell you what happened from the beginning. This way you'll hear the whole story again, and once and for all."

"That would help me a great deal."

"Frances called and said they'd found Catherine. She said she was in a coma and that they had taken her to intensive care. I got to the hospital as fast as I could. I didn't know what room Catherine was in, but I walked into the room I thought was hers just as a nurse was pulling a sheet over a woman's head. I pretty much lost it because the woman looked like Catherine. The nurse calmed me down and said she was a Jane Doe and that Catherine was in the next room. There were three doctors attending to her when I went into the room. They were young interns and it concerned me. I asked a couple of questions, and they suggested that I leave. Well, I wasn't going to do that. No way a couple of junior doctors were going to throw me out, and they knew it. After mulling around for a while, the way interns do, they finally left the room.

"Catherine had a contusion on her head, so I grabbed her chart and saw they hadn't taken any x-rays. I told Frances to call the x-ray department and let them know we were going to be taking Catherine down. While waiting for the x-rays to be taken, I received a call from the office that Isaac and Franz were at each other's throats. In short, all hell had broken loose. The x-ray tech told me it would be about twenty minutes before they'd be able to get to Catherine, so I ran back to Rosetta to put out that fire. I wasn't gone long, but it was long enough. By the time I'd returned, Catherine had been taken back to her room. I went to the nurse's station for an update and they told me it was too late. She had died.

"I must've gone into shock at that point because the next thing I knew was I was roaming around the parking lot. I really don't know how much time had passed before I went back into the hospital, but when I did, I went to Catherine's laboratory. Colter was already there, and then Frances showed up and told me security was looking for me. On that note, Colter bolted. He wasn't sticking around to help me, that's for sure. But it actually worked out for the best, because it allowed me to find Catherine's Cold folder and serum, which, as you already know, I took to Rosetta."

"What about the Jane Doe in the room next to Catherine's?"

"Yeah, I heard about her, too. She disappeared on the way down to the morgue."

"Frances said she died around the same time as Catherine." At that, Mitch didn't say anything, so I tried to connect the dots myself. I finally reconciled that the two deaths occurring at the same time was a coincidence. Yet, I couldn't let it go completely. More importantly, Mitch's account of what happened that morning was the same as Frances's. Between getting up early to meet with Frances, then the flight to Washington, and now the flight back to New York, it had exhausted me and I must have dozed off. The next thing I knew, Mitch was shaking my arm.

"What?"

"You fell asleep and we've got another thirty minutes before the plane lands. It'll give us time to finish our cryonics discussion."

"We discussed it yesterday and I asked you not to bring it up again. Remember?"

"Yeah, but I don't think you really understood it."

"Let me make it clear then. Cryonics is not for me. It doesn't work. You can't freeze a person and expect them to come back to life. It's never happened, and in my opinion, it never will."

"It hasn't, because science hasn't evolved to that point yet. But it's going to happen much sooner than you think."

"Doesn't it strike you as strange to place a body in a steel vat and have it float around for fifty or a hundred years? Or, you can select option B, where they decapitate you and place your head in a vat to bob around with dozens of other heads. You know what this reminds me of? The movie *Poltergeist*. Remember that scene when JoBeth Williams falls into the unfinished swimming pool in her backyard and all the skeletons start attacking her? Remember how creepy that was? Well cryonics is even creepier. And if you can't see it, I don't know what else to say."

Chapter Nineteen

The sky radiated blue against an orange sun that traveled low in the west. It was bitter cold when we reached the cemetery. The rear wheels of Julia's Chevy spun when we hit an icy patch of unplowed road. I reached into my coat pocket and took out the map Catherine's father had given me. "Pull over. This looks like it here." I opened the door to get out.

"Wait. Take these with you." She reached into the back seat and handed me a bouquet of red roses. "I figured you'd want to place some flowers at her grave but wouldn't have time to pick any up."

It had never occurred to me to bring flowers. "Thank you." With the roses in hand I left the car and looked at the field before me. Every headstone was blanketed with snow. I spotted a small knoll in the distance that looked like the landmark circled on the map of where Catherine's grave rested. I trudged toward it, dusting off pieces of granite along the way in search of her name. The snow was deep and I had come unprepared. My shoes were soaked within minutes and my pants were drenched to the calf. I started to feel a prickly numb sensation in my toes. Wiping snow from headstones without gloves was numbing my hands, too.

I soon realized I had misread the map. Catherine's headstone was not in this section of the cemetery at all. I turned and plowed in a different direction until I came across a fresh set of footprints. I followed them over a small knoll into another section of the cemetery. In the distance, the man who had made those footprints was planting a bouquet of white roses in the snow. He then stood motionless in front of the headstone. I walked in his direction, passing dozens of headstones with icy petal tips pointing out though the virgin snow. The man crossed himself and walked off in the opposite direction. I continued toward the place where he had been standing. I looked down at the neatly planted white roses and then raised my eyes to the engraved headstone. It read: Catherine Prescott Lewis.

I stood frozen at the sight of my wife's name etched into the stone. Catherine lay in the ground beneath my feet, and the carved letters that spelled her name held me in a trance. I bent down and picked up the card that had been left with the white roses. *Rest in Peace Lovely Child*. There was no name on the card. I turned to locate the man descending the other side of the knoll. "Hey! Hold up a moment!"

I ran to the top of another knoll and saw the man get into his car. "Hello!" I waved my arms but the man was facing the other direction and did not see me. When I heard his car engine start my heart sank, as my chance to speak to him was lost. From the top of the knoll I took in the lay of the land. The road was circular, and if I headed straight for the gate I might reach him before he left the cemetery. I took off running across the graveyard. The snow was deep and it was like running in knee-high water, but I needed to reach the gate before he did. It was my right to know who had placed flowers on my wife's grave.

Only one more knoll to climb over and I would reach the gate. I saw the car was nearing the gate as well. I flailed my arms to get his attention, but in my pursuit, I failed to pay attention to the steepness of the knoll. I barreled down the icy slope and was now on a collision course with the car. The man slammed on his brakes as I slid onto the road just as his car approached. I ended up on the other side of the road with my legs stuck in a snow bank. After I pulled myself out and got back on my feet, an older man with a frightened look on his face rolled down the car window. "Are you all right?"

"I'm fine. Sorry I startled you." I brushed the snow off. "I saw you place flowers on Catherine's grave. Have we ever met?"

"No. You don't know me. I just deliver flowers here. Our truck is on the blink, so I used my own car today."

"I see. I noticed no one signed the card that came with the flowers. Can you tell me who sent them?"

"Are you related?"

"Catherine was my wife."

"Oh. I'm very sorry. She was so young."

Overhead a murder of crows flew by. Their racket was loud and piercing. I waited until they were gone. "Can you tell me who sent the flowers?"

"I wouldn't know that. You'd need to speak to Carl. He could tell you."

"Carl?"

"That's right. He owns the flower shop." He held out a business card and I walked over and took it. I looked at the card and thanked the elderly man. He nodded and rolled up his window, but then immediately rolled it down again. "I can tell you this much. It's the second time I've brought white roses out to her. People don't send 'em much this time of the year."

I followed my footprints back to Catherine's grave. Along the way I picked up the roses that I had dropped while racing across the cemetery. I placed them in the snow next to the white roses, all the time aware of the fact that under my feet was the casket that held Catherine. I waited for my emotions to overtake me, but her life force was strong inside me. She just couldn't be dead.

I caught myself. It was insane to think that way. I had attended her memorial service. There was a headstone with her name carved into it. The pain in my head returned. It was brought upon by thinking irrational thoughts, and I was powerless to stop the throbbing. Not long ago my brain had been the source of my strength. Now I no longer trusted it. I dropped to my knees in the snow. Still, the tears did not come.

I looked up and saw Julia crossing the field toward me. When she reached the gravesite she laid her hand on my shoulder. She knelt on the snow beside me. When my body began to tremble she took my hand in hers. Daylight was melting away and my very sanity was now in question. I had visited Catherine's grave on a day when the crows screamed across the darkening blue sky. The evening air had settled on the fields of snow around me and a light wind tugged at the roses, taunting their red and white petals to break free and tumble along the hardened crust. Kneeling in silence our warm breath struck the cold air at her gravesite that sat between two icy knolls. I looked back up at the headstone. *"Catherine!"*

Chapter Twenty

"Thought this show was supposed to start at one o'clock," a reporter said to his colleague. Dozens of other reporters were also waiting in Rosetta's downstairs laboratory.

"Who knows," another reporter said. "Maybe Cochran found a bug in his cold serum." A few within earshot of the reporter chuckled at his comment.

Mitch knew a large group had assembled in the laboratory as he waited at the top of the staircase. One hand rested on the railing and the other held a flask containing a bit of the Cold serum. This afternoon he would prove to the world that Cold was the real thing. If he expected investors to pour millions into the drug, his performance today would have to be extraordinary.

"Mitch? I thought you'd be downstairs by now," Vanessa said.

"I'm just heading down."

"Are you all right? You look a little piqued."

"I have to admit, I'm a little nervous. I thought Jack would be here to help out with the presentation, or at least to offer some moral support."

"Where is he?"

"He had a doctor's appointment and then he was meeting with Colter about something."

Vanessa placed her hand on Mitch's arm. "I know how important today is for you. Frankly, I'm a little surprised Jack isn't here to support you. After all, this is Catherine's drug."

"Well, he hasn't been feeling well. I'm glad he's seeing a doctor. I'm not sure why he's meeting with Colter, but it's none of my business."

"He's very lucky to have you."

Mitch looked at Vanessa. "I'll take all the compliments I can get. Walk down with me?"

Vanessa took his arm. "I'd love to."

The excitement mounted in Mitch as he descended the staircase with Vanessa. He was certain he had a winning combination if he could both capture her heart and develop Cold successfully. Mitch knew that retaining even a small piece of this drug would make him a wealthy man. The discovery of Cold rivaled that of penicillin, and would certainly lead to recognition from the global science community.

Mitch entered the first-floor laboratory and walked to the front of the room. He looked out over the crowd of reporters, businessmen, critics, and potential investors. "Let me begin by thanking you for attending today. You are about to witness an extraordinary breakthrough in science. As you can see, microscopes have been positioned around the room for you to observe how Cold disarms a virus before it can infect a human cell. For those less technically inclined, we've stationed staff members at each microscope to explain the significance of what you are viewing. Enjoy this day because you are about to witness history in the making."

Scientists and reporters lined up to look into the microscopes. Resounding "ooohs" and "aaahs" filled the room. The Wall Street investors and other non-scientist types needed help to understand the significance of what lined the bottom of the petri dish. Mitch's confidence grew as distinguished scientists agreed that Cold just might be the next important drug. All the while, Vanessa remained at his side. He leaned over to her. "How do you think it's going?"

She placed her lips close to his ear. "You just hit a home run. The fun part will be watching the sharks rip each other apart for a piece of Cold."

"I can't wait for that. Too bad Jack isn't here to see it."

Mitch opened the floor for questions. For the next twenty minutes he and his staff fielded dozens of them. Then, a senior analyst from Smith Barney stepped forward and asked a simple and direct question.

"Is Cold ready for the market? Too many biotechs have failed us with supposed wonder drugs, and the stockholder is left holding the bag."

Silence fell over the room. Mitch's staff looked to him for the answer. Mitch had two answers. One, the truth, that Cold had never seen the light of day outside of a petri dish and would require years of trial testing before

FDA approval was given. That answer might chase a potential investor or two out the door. Mitch decided to give them the second answer. "We are very close to bringing Cold to market," he said in a cool, composed manner.

Colter and I walked into the back of the room just as Mitch spoke those words.

"Did Mitch just say the drug's ready for market?" Colter said. "I thought you told me it was years away."

"I must be mistaken, then. Mitch wouldn't *dare* mislead the press or the investment community." Colter smiled, having enjoyed the sarcasm directed at Mitch. I walked out of the room and kept a cool head.

Keeping a cool head was the advice given to me earlier that morning by Doctor Frankfort, a psychiatrist from Sloan-Kettering who specialized in brain tumors like mine. I wanted to understand more about my hallucinations and what medications were available. Since Doctor Frankfort was considered an expert with treating grade IV astrocytomas, I sought his opinion. He said I had a sixty percent chance to live a full year if I elected to have an operation. The bad news was that there was no guarantee on my mental or physical state after the operation. With that, I told him surgery was not an option for me. After that, Doctor Frankfort asked detailed questions about my hallucinations. I told him about Catherine visiting me at the condo, and how I didn't believe she was buried in the cemetery. That maybe she was even alive.

Catherine showing up at the condo, the doctor said, was a hallucination. For me to not believe Catherine was buried in her grave was a delusion. He further explained that hallucinations are seeing things that don't actually exist. Delusions are different, and in my case rather unique. Because the cancer was located in the right hemisphere of my brain, it forced the left hemisphere to overwork. The language structure in the left hemisphere created a story that could not be edited or corrected by the right side of my brain, which is what occurs in a healthy brain. My view of reality was distorted. Maybe not every thought or event, but some events that seemed real to me were actually a delusion.

I accepted morphine for my pain, but refused medication to reduce the number of hallucinations and delusions. I knew I would suffer more events, but it was better than walking around in a stupor all day. The doctor noted my decision and advised me to keep my hallucinations to myself. It would be less frightening for others that way. He left me with a final warning. Avoid stress at all cost. It weakens the immune system and accelerates the growth of the cancer.

Colter joined me in the hallway. "I have to hand it to Mitch. They're eating right out of his hand. I just hope he's not turning this into a circus act."

I was less concerned with Mitch at that moment, and more about laying my cards on the table with Colter. That was why I had asked him to meet me. I proceeded to tell him about the background check Julia had run on him. He was surprised that I had chosen this particular time and place to bring it up. Even more surprising to him was how Julia had gained access into his juvenile records, which he knew had been sealed by the court. He had received extensive counseling as a teenager, he said, and has never struck a woman since.

"How much contact did you have with Catherine over the last six months?"

"We bumped into each other from time to time," he said. "That was the extent of it."

I had caught Colter off guard and embarrassed him. His eyes welled up and he expressed how deeply he cared for Catherine. I remained silent, but his words rang true with me. It was now time for me to come clean with Colter.

"I need to tell you something." I paused a moment and thought how odd it was to use terminating language about myself. "I've been diagnosed with glioblastoma multiforme. It's malignant. Mitch already knows, and now you know, too."

Colter's expression changed from one of embarrassment to one of utter helplessness. It was clear he wanted to help me, but he knew he couldn't. He embraced me. "I knew something else was going on with you, but I never would've guessed this. It means a lot that you're confiding in me. What are the doctors doing for you? How many have you spoken to? There's doctors, and then there's doctors. I want to help you get through this."

Just then, Mitch walked into the hallway with Vanessa. "Did you catch the reaction?"

"Great job, Mitch," Colter said. Then in typical Colter fashion, he flashed a smile at Vanessa. "Hi. Colter Malone."

"Vanessa Boulay," she offered her hand.

I turned to Mitch. "Still telling investors that Cold's ready for market?"

"The people in that room only care about one thing: if Cold is real or not. That's all they'll remember in the morning."

"And not that you misled them?"

"Excuse me," Vanessa said. "Mitch has taken on an enormous burden here, one he's lifted off your shoulders, Jack. He knows what he's doing. I don't think it's fair to criticize him, especially in front of others."

Mitch's receptionist approached. "There's a Rutger Dobler in the lobby to see you, Mitch."

Chapter Twenty-one

Rutger's arrival gave Colter the excuse he needed to bow out of the contentious bantering in the hallway and to leave Rosetta. Vanessa bowed out as well and returned to her office. Mitch and I went to his office and

Rutger Dobler appeared in the doorway a moment later. He had a commanding presence.

"I hope I'm not interrupting."

"Not at all. I'm Mitch Cochran and this is Jack Lewis."

Rutger shook Mitch's hand and turned to me. "Doctor Lewis, please accept my deepest sympathy for your loss."

"You're very kind."

"And please forgive me for dropping in unannounced. I was unable to attend your presentation earlier, but fortunately, I was able to get away from my office before the entire day got away from me."

"I'm afraid the demonstration is being dismantled. But if you—"

"I wouldn't ask you to go to any trouble, Mr. Cochran."

"Please. Call me Mitch."

"Well, Mitch, I'm sure your demonstration was quite successful, and I would like to discuss this new drug of yours. I have another matter to discuss as well. Let me get right to the point. If this drug is anything close to what *The Times* has claimed it to be, my family is interested in purchasing it. As you know, Dobler is the largest manufacturer of cold remedy products in the world, and we have the largest global distribution channel. Billions of people will be able to benefit from this drug. Of course, strategic marketing is required so that people are made aware of its value."

"I was just explaining that very thing to Jack. How marketing a product correctly will attract interest," Mitch said smugly, looking over at me.

"It's refreshing to know that you understand the challenge," Rutger said. "Many smaller companies—and, please, don't take this the wrong way—fail to grasp the complexity of marketing a drug that's destined for worldwide consumption."

"It still needs significant testing. And the public has the right to know it'll take time, maybe even years to complete," I said, looking back at Mitch. "And, of course, there's the FDA hurdle."

"Well, you're the experts in genetic engineering," Rutger said. "Our value is to provide the financing of the drug's development and then support getting FDA approval. For example, if this drug is developed, in say, six to nine months, we can arrange for FDA approval within the calendar year, or possibly sooner."

Mitch's eyes opened. "Is that possible?"

Rutger smiled. "It's possible with the full weight of Dobler Pharmaceutical behind you."

"In fairness," I said, "we've only begun to look for a partner. The decision will take a while. But please—"

"Quite understandable," Rutger said. "You are businessmen. You must consider your drug's worth, and feel you're exacting a fair price for it."

"We don't want to rush into anything," I said. "Was there something else you wanted to discuss?"

"Yes. It's my grandfather's eightieth birthday this weekend, and we're having what you might call a 'gala event' at his estate. Many of our colleagues from the industry will be in attendance, many people you may know, and I want to personally extend and invitation to you both to join us. I would consider it an honor if you accepted my invitation. It's short notice, I know, but getting to know each other on a social level is much more enjoyable than meeting in some drab board room. One thing's guaranteed: You'll have a marvelous time."

"We appreciate the invitation. Give us a day or so to get back to you with an answer, if you don't mind."

"Of course." A wide smile flashed across Rutger's face. He added, "Look, if your intention is to sell this drug outright or to enter into a partnership, we don't plan to be outbid by another company. If you're considering a deal with Wall Street, well, remember that their loyalty is always to their stockholders. They care most about profits, not medical research. And if the drug fails to develop according to their plan, expect to be put on the hot seat. Few understand what it takes to create a drug. It is an art form that needs to be sketched and perfected before being placed on a canvas, because there are always setbacks. Dobler is prepared to spend whatever it takes to make this drug work, and we're also committed to making it a household name. That's not just a promise—it's a guarantee from my grandfather and from me."

I looked at Mitch and he was smiling from ear to ear.

"Well, I must leave. I'm pleased we had this time to speak, even if it was brief. I'll have the invitations delivered tomorrow, and we'll look forward to seeing you both on Saturday." Rutger slipped on a pair of black leather gloves and bowed gracefully. "A pleasant evening, gentlemen." He was down the stairs and out the door as quickly as he had arrived.

"Quite an impressive man," Mitch said.

"We finally agree on something."

Chapter Twenty-two

Rutger's chauffeur dropped him at the Pierre Hotel, where he owned an apartment on the sixth floor. He poured himself a Scotch before calling his grandfather.

"I'll be staying in the city tonight."

"Very well, then. I'll have dinner brought up to my room. How did it go?"

"Better than expected. I invited them to your birthday party."

"Splendid. Did you share our interest in buying the drug?"

"Yes. If I had stuck a contract under Cochran's nose, he would have signed it right then and there. Lewis was more distant, probably still in mourning. He'll come around. Our timing is perfect."

"Well done. I'll see you in the morning, Son."

"Good night, Grandfather." Rutger placed the telephone down and before he had a chance to take a sip of Scotch, the lobby rang him up.

"Ms. Shelby to see you, sir."

"Bring her up."

A burgundy-suited doorman escorted the young woman to Rutger's door.

"Hello, Susan." She was a reporter for *Science Today Magazine,* and had approached Rutger for an interview while on the convention floor at Javits. He'd flirted with her, and she flirted right back—the attraction was instant. When she spoke, Susan evoked an innocent, mid-western charm, and it didn't hurt that she was slender and attractive.

"Drink?"

"White wine," Susan said, with a touch of nervousness in her voice. She stood in the middle of the room, her hands clasped together. "Actually, I've surprised myself by coming up here. When I first entered the lobby, I immediately walked back out."

Rutger carried two drinks across the room and handed one to her. He leaned over and kissed her lips. "But, you came up after all, didn't you?"

Susan looked into his eyes. "Yes, I did."

She had taken only one sip of her wine when Rutger removed the drink from her hand and set it on a table. He led her into the bedroom. Susan did not object. He sat her on the edge of the bed in front of him and observed her. Her hands were tightly intertwined, her eyes as wide and bright as a doe's in headlights. At the same time, she was accepting of whatever might happen. Rutger relished the tension and anticipation he saw building within her. He waited patiently without speaking a word. Only when her carotid arteries began to pulse did he address her.

"Take off your clothes," he said softly. "Your blouse first."

Susan glanced up at Rutger, then unbuttoned her blouse and took it off. Next, she wiggled out of her skirt, and was on the bed in front of Rutger in just panties and bra. Rutger pulled her bra straps down to her waist and slipped off her panties. He removed his shirt and slipped out of his trousers and briefs before pushing her back so she lay flat on the bed. She sought eye contact with him but Rutger did not reciprocate. She simply closed her eyes and surrendered. His full weight came to rest upon her. A minute or two later he moaned. Within seconds the telephone rang.

"Hello? Yes, darling ... No, I haven't forgotten this evening. I'll be on time ... Me too." Rutger placed the telephone back on the receiver.

Susan pushed Rutger off and jumped off the bed. She picked up her clothes and ran into the bathroom. Moments later, fully dressed and trembling, she reappeared in the bedroom doorway. "You bastard!" She turned and ran out of the apartment.

Chapter Twenty-three

Maple trees lined the road that led to Heinrich Dobler's estate. Eddie drove the Iron Lung up to the twelve-foot-high entrance gate and waited. A security guard approached. "Your name, sir?"

"Jack Lewis and guests," Eddie replied.

The guard looked at all six passengers and checked the number against the guest list. He walked back to his post, mumbled something into an intercom, and then opened the gate.

"Stay on the main road to the mansion," the guard said, as he gave the Iron Lung the once over. Eddie shifted the car into gear and entered the property.

Eddie smiled. He'd spent hours shining the Iron Lung up after being hired to chauffeur the trip to Connecticut. He could not wait to mingle with the other drivers, to watch them bang on the Lungs' fenders and tap her bullet-proof windows. But the *pièce de résistance* would be telling the drivers how he had outbid a room full of people at the Cuban Embassy to win her.

Mitch leaned forward to get everyone's attention. "Listen. One of my scientists said he might have stumbled on the gene that causes male pattern baldness. Think about it, add one gene back into the DNA mix and, presto, you just put a thousand hair clubs out of business." Mitch broke into laughter, as did Vanessa, Julia, Colter, and his date, Margo. As for me, I didn't find the story particularly funny. Mitch was in a good mood because Vanessa had agreed to attend the party with him. Julia, on the other hand, had refused to attend at first; she was upset with me for going behind her back and questioning Frances. It came down to last minute heroics by Mitch to convince her to come. As for me, there was nothing about attending Heinrich's birthday party that thrilled me, but Mitch had played the guilt card—the future of Cold was at stake, and my attendance mattered greatly.

"Listen, Jack, I've been thinking."

"You like to live dangerously, don't you?" I said.

"Seriously. If the Doblers give us any sign they want to bankroll Cold or buy it outright, I say we make that deal. Something good is going to happen tonight. I can feel it."

Rutger had sent six invitations for the birthday party, so I invited Colter and his date to join us. Mitch wasn't thrilled at having to spend the entire evening with Colter, but Mitch was Mitch, and most things eventually rolled off his back. Meanwhile, Julia deflected each attempt I made to engage her in conversation.

As we wound around the estate road, tall cypress trees blocked our view from just about every angle. We finally reached the top of a small hill that gave us our first look at the property. The mansion lay on a long stretch of land adjacent to the Long Island Sound. There were no other structures in sight. Exterior lights illuminated the reddish-brown fortress walls and cornering towers. Flags of green, yellow, and crimson waved proudly over Heinrich Dobler's palatial mansion, bestowing upon it a sense of preeminence. From the hill, it appeared as though Camelot had been dismantled stone by stone and rebuilt into the Connecticut countryside.

Eddie brought the Iron Lung to a halt in front of the main entrance, where men fully clad in Renaissance garb waited to assist us. Julia stepped out first. She wore a black silk, off-the-shoulder evening gown with a plunging back, and long black gloves. A strand of Austrian crystals looped around her neck and cascaded down her back. It was hard to tell what was holding the gown in place. It seemed to defy gravity.

Vanessa emerged next, wearing a strapless, ruby-red velvet gown with a full skirt. The sash that tied at the back of her waist was a crisscross of beads that draped to the ground. A diamond necklace with a single teardrop ruby adorned her neck; it was complemented by a ruby and diamond bracelet and matching earrings.

Mitch and I wore off-the-rack black tuxedos with black bow ties. Colter sported a black Armani tuxedo with a gold and sapphire vest and matching tie. Margo, who had been blessed with a flawless figure, wore a sleek silver sheath gown that left little to the imagination. On the drive, Colter had whispered to me the details of how he and Margo had met the night before at one of his Upper East Side haunts.

We entered the mansion through an enormous oak door where four large men in dark suits gave us the once-over. Once inside the ballroom, we encountered at least four hundred people dressed to the nines. A twelve-piece orchestra played a Benny Goodman tune while couples jitterbugged on a large oval dance floor. On the left side of the ballroom, a pair of ten-foot-high, white French doors opened to a magnificent terrace that overlooked the sound. To the right, a rose-covered trellis scaled up to a second-floor balcony.

"There are a total of forty rooms here," Rutger said, appearing unexpectedly. He looked dashing in his ivory tuxedo jacket, black slacks, and classic bow tie. When I introduced Julia, he lifted her hand to his lips and bowed. He extended the same courtesy to Vanessa and Margo.

"Thank you all for coming. This is an extraordinary night for my family, and Grandfather has insisted on meeting you all." Rutger offered his arm to Vanessa and led us across the room.

"I am so very pleased you came tonight," Heinrich said from his wheelchair, dressed in a black tuxedo. He looked at the women and smiled. "Thank you, ladies. You add immense joy to an old man's birthday bash."

A line had formed behind us as other arriving guests awaited their turn to be greeted by Heinrich. Rutger, in his role as the perfect host, escorted us to our table. "Michael, take very special care of my friends," he said to the waiter. "Bring them whatever they desire, starting with a bottle of our best champagne."

"Yes, Mr. Dobler."

"I must get back to my post," Rutger said. "Enjoy yourselves, and I'll join you the first chance I get." He left as the champagne cork popped and the waiter filled our crystal flutes.

Margo looked in the direction of the dance floor and smiled at Colter.

"Excuse us," Colter winked for all to see. "Margo is in the mood." On the dance floor he spun her with precision, and I was immediately reminded of him once telling me that he was an excellent dancer.

"To beautiful women," Mitch said, lifting his glass. Julia and Vanessa looked at each other and smiled. "What do you think of Rutger?"

"Very charming," Vanessa said.

"It's nice to meet a man with manners," Julia added.

I suspected that Julia's comment was intended for my benefit. But then, since we'd barely had a chance to speak at all, I may have been reading too much into what was probably just a casual comment. Julia sat on the edge of her chair and watched the people on the dance floor. I caught her glance only once in my direction, but I knew what she was thinking. The furthest thought from my mind was the dance floor, but if twirling Julia would help mend the bad karma, then dancing it would be.

I walked around the table and held out my hand. Julia took it and rose from her chair. I led her to the dance floor as the orchestra began to play a waltz. I slid my right hand around her waist and she placed her left hand on my shoulder. We cupped our other hands together and began to move around the floor. Compared to Colter, I'm certain I appeared to be plodding around the dance floor in a circle, but I was content to stay in the slow lane. Julia still refused to make eye contact, even when we had relaxed a bit and our bodies moved a smidge closer. I was surprised at how light I felt on my feet, but knew it was not the effect of the champagne, as

I had not even had a sip. Whatever it was, however, it must have rubbed off, as Julia finally looked me in the eyes. She even smiled, which prompted me to admire how radiant she looked, now that she had engaged me. When the waltz ended, I escorted her back to our table. The others had all disappeared. As we were alone, I thought it a good time to clear the air. "Care to see the view from the terrace?"

Julia nodded and we walked through the French doors. She placed her elbows on the marble railing and looked up at the gibbous moon that hung over the sound. "Gorgeous," she said, "how the moonlight glimmers on the water. It's so poetic."

"All of a sudden you don't sound like a private investigator."

"Why do you say that?"

"The way you express yourself."

"There's no rule that private investigators can't be poets. We're no different from other people. Or, do you think we are?"

"No, of course not, and I didn't mean to insinuate otherwise."

Julia turned and faced me. "We need to talk business for a moment. I was going to break the news to you on the drive up but thought it better to wait until we were alone. Phase one of the investigation is complete, and that completes our agreement. I've accepted another assignment and leave tomorrow for Chicago."

Chapter Twenty-four

Some words stun; others devastate. "Are you serious? What about the investigation?"

"I wasn't sure where we stood or if you wanted me to stay."

"I see. I do one dumb thing and you're out."

"No, and you're not being fair. You placed me in a tough position. You demanded I get information in record time, but never once did you speak to me about staying on. When this new assignment was presented, I had to either accept it on the spot or turn it down. I accepted."

At that moment I could hardly believe what I was hearing. I hoped Julia would reconsider, but the expression on her face told me it was not going to be the case.

"I have a lot to do before I leave, and the sooner we can wrap things up the better it will be for both of us. Can we schedule a time?"

She was already gone. I could hear it in her voice and see it in her eyes. I had no one to blame but myself. "Sure, let's wrap up loose ends."

"How about meeting for breakfast in the morning?"

"In the morning, then."

Vanessa hurried out onto the terrace where Julia and I were standing. She looked concerned. "Jack!"

"What's wrong?"

"I think Mitch has had too much champagne. He's in the men's room. Would you mind checking on him?"

Vanessa waited for a response. I looked at Julia and knew that our conversation had ended. "Yes, I'll see how he's doing."

"Thank you," Vanessa said. "I'll be at the table." She walked back through the French doors and into the ballroom.

"Did you notice her necklace?" Julia said.

"Yeah, it's very pretty."

"Pretty expensive, you mean. Those are real diamonds, and the ruby hanging around her neck is at least four carats."

"Well, frankly, I've seen a lot of pretty necklaces hanging around necks tonight. Yours is very pretty, too."

Julia gave me an odd look and grabbed her necklace. "There's a difference between Austrian crystals and diamonds. Vanessa's wearing the real thing, and I can only imagine what they're worth."

"Well, maybe we can talk about it over a drink some time. Right now I've got to check on Mitch. You coming inside?"

"No, you go ahead. I want to stay here and look at the sound a while longer."

Mitch was leaning against the wall when I opened the door to the men's room.

"You all right?"

"I don't know. I'm a little dizzy."

"How much did you drink?"

"That's the funny thing. I didn't drink much at all."

"I haven't drunk anything. Maybe you're coming down with something."

"Maybe. Or maybe Colter dropped something in my drink."

"Come on, Mitch. You know he wouldn't do that."

"I know. But he acts so cool. Did you see him on the dance floor with his hands all over what's her name? Talk about God's gift to women."

"You really are jealous of him, aren't you?" Mitch was reluctant to answer me. A look of annoyance crossed his face. "You know, Colter has nothing on you. Vanessa's not exactly chopped chicken liver. Why do you find it necessary to compare yourself to him?"

"I don't!" Mitch pushed himself away from the wall, but he was unsteady and I had to take his arm.

"You'd better sit down." I led him to a sofa. "Can I get you something?"

"No, I'll be fine. Go back and have some fun."

"Sure, Mitch, I'm having a ball tonight."

"I'm sorry. This is the second time I've dragged you someplace you didn't want to be."

I pulled a small plastic bottle out of my pocket, opened it, and took out a pill. I opened my mouth and placed the pill under my tongue.

"You okay?"

"Nothing a little morphine won't remedy. Doctor Frankfort gave me this free sample bottle. I'll have to buy my own from now on." I winced and waited. "Whew. Feels better already. This might not be the best time to be bringing this up, but the doc gave me a new prognosis."

"What did he say?"

"Expect headaches, lots of them. My memory will start going, and I'll probably get grouchier. Oh, I almost forgot: blindness, too. I'll know the end is approaching when my sight goes."

My latest news had a sobering effect on, Mitch. "I'm an idiot. Look at me. I walk around pretending nothing's wrong with you. And all the time you're... I don't know why I act this way. I'm sorry."

"Hey, you're doing fine. There's no recipe on how to act when someone gets sick. Just don't start feeling sorry for me. That'll piss me off. And for Pete's sake, don't mention my condition to anyone. You haven't, have you?"

"No. I haven't, and I won't. I promise."

"Good. All right, then. I'm going back in there to have a ball. You coming?"

"Not just yet. Give me a few minutes. I'll be out soon."

"Okay. You have ten minutes, or I'm coming back to get you."

"Do me a favor when you get back to the table. Ask Vanessa to dance. She's been waiting for me to take her out on the dance floor, but I'm not sure I can now."

"I'll ask her." I turned to leave.

"And Jack..."

"Now what?"

"Make sure Colter doesn't dance with her."

"I'm out of here."

Julia was alone at the table when I returned. "Where's Vanessa?"

She pointed to the dance floor. "Rutger was too irresistible."

I sat down and watched them dance. There was a difference in Vanessa as Rutger propelled her across the floor. He was a splendid dancer, and Vanessa was radiant in his arms. Her eyes came alive every time he flashed his smile at her. They were quite good together, almost as though they had danced in each other's arms before. Even when Rutger escorted her back to the table, I noticed how at ease they were in each other's company.

"Thank you," Rutger said, holding Vanessa's hand until she was seated. Then he looked over at me. "I understand Mitch is a bit under the weather."

"He'll be all right."

"I'm glad to hear that." Rutger looked at Julia and Vanessa. "If you ladies don't mind, I'd like to steal Jack for a couple of minutes."

"Only if you bring him back soon," Julia said. "We're running low on escorts."

"I won't keep him too long. I promise," Rutger said. I stood and followed him out of the ballroom. As we headed toward the study, one of the stewards approached.

"Excuse me, sir. Sorry to disturb you. We'll need to bring up more champagne."

"Of course," Rutger said. "Would you like to wait in the study, Jack, or join me in the dungeon?"

"Dungeon? I'm not sure I've ever seen one. Do you mind?"

"Just as I thought, a true adventurer at heart. I'll bet we had the same childhood heroes." Rutger led the way down a wooden staircase and along a corridor of inlaid cobblestone. There were six rooms on either side of the corridor. Each had a Moorish-style door with black metal strips studded across it, and above the strip a port window. I craned my neck to look through the windows, but most of the rooms were empty. When we reached the wine cellar, Rutger pulled out his master key and unlocked the door. The steward walked inside while we waited in the corridor.

"You don't allow the stewards down here alone?"

"You may not have noticed, but the lower level of this mansion was constructed with oak. One-hundred-year-old oak, to be exact, and it's very dry and dangerous. We caught an employee smoking down here last month and had to dismiss him. They know the rules, but even good employees can be careless. Next month all this oak will be ripped out and replaced with a fire-retardant material. I'll sleep much better once it's completed."

"Excuse me, sir," the steward called out, "we're out of the *Taittinger*. Shall I bring up something else?"

"I'll just be a moment," Rutger said, and joined the steward.

Left alone, I walked farther down the corridor, peering through the portholes of each door I passed. At the end of the corridor I came upon a large door that was different from the others; it had no porthole. I tried to open it, but it was locked. Just then, Rutger came out of the wine cellar. He saw me at the end of the corridor and gave me a curious look. I walked back and rejoined him.

"This is quite fascinating," I said as we headed upstairs.

"Yes. If you can believe it, I find it exciting as well. As a child, I used to play in many of those rooms."

"I don't mean to be nosy, but what's in the room at the far end of the dungeon, the one without a porthole?"

Rutger chuckled. "Sorry to disappoint you, Jack. I have no insane half-brother shackled to the wall there, and it's not a diabolical laboratory where I experiment on virgin maidens, although that last thought does have some appeal. I'm afraid the most exciting thing we do in that room is store old furniture."

I followed Rutger into the study. It was impressive—a man's room with fine, leather chairs, a large fireplace, a billiard table, and wall-to-wall bookshelves that scaled the height of the twelve-foot ceiling. It was the perfect place to escape the mass of people milling about in the ballroom.

"Make yourself comfortable," Rutger said as he reached into a humidor to select a cigar. He struck a match on the fireplace and lit it, then took a long puff and exhaled the smoke upward. "Care for one, Jack? I have them flown in from Havana."

"Sure. Why not?" I was in a room filled with leather and oak, and a cigar seemed natural at that moment. Rutger lit my cigar. I pressed back into one of the leather chairs and plopped one foot on the ottoman. In the background I heard the faint sound of the orchestra, but the thick walls filtered out most the ballroom chatter. Rutger poured cognac into two snifters and handed me one.

"You strike me as a man who knows how to enjoy life, Jack." Rutger walked back and stood near the fireplace. "Too many people miss what little joy life has to offer them."

"And how do you rate yourself?"

"The same as you, Jack. Live every breath to its fullest. We are put here to live by both our intellect and our instinct, a kind of controlled recklessness, if you will. Whether you realize it or not, that's why you've been successful. You taught the world the importance of the LEC Enzyme, and that put Memorial on the map. And then you moved on to new adventures."

"I don't view it quite that way."

"Of course. You wouldn't. Men like you never do. You went to the Rainforest, something most men lack the spine to do. I suspect many of your colleagues hate you for the life you live."

"I don't know about that. I do have regrets."

"Maybe, but you have courage. Most men wake up to find the best part of life has passed them by." Rutger sipped his cognac. "You're a free spirit, Jack. Now you're back with a revolutionary drug in your grasp. In the end, there's little regret for any man who has the ability to stay on top. But I'm rambling. It's a Dobler trait. And it's my way of getting to know you better, especially if we're going to conduct business together, which is why I asked you to join me in the study."

"Then you need to speak with Mitch."

"You're not involved in the decision making?"

"Ultimately, yes. But Mitch is the business mind and runs the show."

"Well, since Mitch is under the weather, I'll cut to the chase. We believe you have an important drug, and we're prepared to offer you $250 million for it."

Chapter Twenty-five

No one said a word. They were startled after hearing the news. Finally, Colter picked up his champagne glass and made a toast. Mitch downed his sparkling water and signaled the waiter for another.

Rutger came over to the table. "Grandfather has requested that we get together after the party. Hopefully, no one has early morning plans?"

I looked around the table and no one objected. "We'd be delighted."

The orchestra conductor tapped on the microphone to get everyone's attention. Rutger excused himself.

"Ladies and gentlemen, please welcome our guest of honor, Heinrich Dobler."

The lights dimmed and loud applause erupted as Rutger wheeled his grandfather to the center of the room. Heinrich smiled and waved as the lights went out and a multi-layered birthday cake was rolled into the room. The orchestra played "Happy Birthday" and everyone sang along. William and Elizabeth joined Heinrich and helped him to blow out candles. One candle remained lit.

"Let Grandfather blow out the last one," Rutger said, as he wheeled him closer to the cake. "Make a wish, Grandfather."

Heinrich took a breath and blew. The room went completely dark. In that split second of blackness, a gunshot rang out. The lights came back on and a single scream filled the ballroom. Heinrich was slouched in his wheelchair. Blood soaked his tuxedo shirt. The screaming intensified as guests clutched one another and ran from the ballroom. I started to cross the dance floor to attend to Heinrich, but it occurred to me that the shooter might not be done. Mitch and Vanessa ran onto the open floor, and I yelled. "Get down! It's dangerous in the clearing!" They looked confused and returned to the table.

Rutger stepped in front of his grandfather and glared into the crowd. "I need a doctor!" Three security guards entered the room with weapons drawn. This prompted us all to sit down. The guards moved from table to table, and within minutes they had secured the ballroom while a doctor who had been sitting close to Heinrich attended to him.

"We need to lay him down," I heard the doctor say. With that, Rutger lifted his grandfather out of the wheelchair and carried him from the room. William and Elizabeth followed, with a bodyguard close behind them. Elizabeth was hysterical and William tried to calm her.

I was frisked by a security guard when I left the ballroom. I walked down the hallway to where Rutger was standing with his mother outside the study. I stayed a respectable distance away and watched him place his hands on his mother's shoulders and encourage her to gain control of herself. "Mother, we need to be strong now."

Elizabeth wiped her tears. "I will, Son. I will." She turned and walked into the study.

I approached Rutger. "Is there anything I can do?"

"I don't think so, Jack. The doctor said it's a shoulder wound. It could have been much worse. He's dressing it now, but thanks for offering." Rutger looked into the crowd that gathered in the hallway. "A monster is in our midst," he said. He opened the door to the study and returned to his grandfather's side.

I caught a glimpse of Heinrich as he lay on the couch. His skin was drained of color, but he appeared conscious and alert. Elizabeth had regained her composure and was placing a pillow under Heinrich's head when the door closed. I rejoined the others.

The mood was somber on our trip back to the city. Even Mitch had little to say.

Chapter Twenty-six

Eddie had dropped everyone off before driving me to the Towers. The ordeal had been exhausting, sapping me of strength. As I pushed through the revolving doors I noticed a man in a dark overcoat and brown fedora standing just inside the hotel. Our eyes made brief contact and he looked away. He followed me to the elevator, stepping inside behind me. I pressed the button for the forty-sixth floor. The man neither selected a floor nor asked me to push a button for him. It was reasonable to think his room was on the same floor as mine, but my senses were heightened after the shooting this evening. In this frame of mind, I would not rule anything out.

The man was short and slight of build. He was standing perfectly still. His coat was fully buttoned and both hands were in his coat pockets. When the elevator doors opened, I stepped out and walked down the hallway. He exited the elevator behind me. I turned right at the first corridor, and he did as well. The hallway was quiet except for the scraping of his feet on the carpet. As I neared my door, I pulled out the room key and picked up the pace. I hurried to unlock the door and step inside. As I was about to enter, the man spoke.

"Excuse me, Doctor Lewis. May I have a word with you?"

A pang of fear riveted my body and I fought to conceal it. "Have you been following me?"

"My name is Peter Bastianich. Forgive me if I alarmed you."

His accent sounded Slavic. "What do you want?"

"May I come in and speak with you?"

"What do you want, Basterich?"

"That's Bas-ti-a-nich. Could I have just a moment, Doctor Lewis?"

"What is this about? Who are you?"

"I waited for you outside the hotel most of the evening. Allow me a moment, please."

His eyes expressed urgency. He sounded educated and looked harmless. I stepped inside and looked back at him. "I'm sorry, it's late." I began to close the door.

"It concerns Catherine."

I opened the door a crack. "What did you say?"

Bastianich did not answer right away. He just looked at me. "It is important, Doctor Lewis."

I stood looking at him for another moment. "You have five minutes."

I motioned for the man to move his arms away from his body. I had never frisked a person before, but I wasted little time patting him down. I even checked the lining of his hat and the elastic stitching of his socks, but discovered no concealed weapons. I placed a chair in the middle of the room and motioned for him to sit there while I sat a distance away on the sofa. Bastianich looked to be in his forties. He now appeared shorter than when I first saw him. Probably five-foot five at most, and no more than a hundred and thirty pounds. His black hair had receded, and his suit pants had not been recently creased. He sat on display in the middle of the room and appeared perfectly at ease with himself.

"Let me formally introduce myself," he said in a pleasant voice. "I am Doctor Peter Bastianich. I was a doctor in the Czech Republic, but here I work as a chemist for a small biotech company in White Plains. I attended your wife's memorial service. Please accept my deepest sympathy for your loss."

"Thank you. Now what is it you want?"

Bastianich nodded. "Yes, of course. Crimes against humanity are being committed, Doctor Lewis, and I am one of many scientists making a stand against it."

"Can you be more specific?"

"We want to expose pharmaceutical companies that are buying up new drugs and keeping them off the market. Many are important drugs that have been developed by the biotechs, and they're simply not reaching the sick."

I was now concerned that I'd allowed a crackpot into my apartment. "That's quite a claim. Most drug manufacturers will walk through fire to get their drugs in the marketplace."

"That's true for ninety-eight percent of drugs. But two percent never reach the market. And these are the ones that make a difference."

"I've never heard of anyone keeping a drug off the market."

"When they pose a threat to a multinational, they disappear. Patent protection allows these companies to earn hundreds of millions off their own drugs. The last thing they want to see is a more effective drug, at least not until they get the full economic life out of their existing drug, even if it's a poor drug. It's a cold-hearted business, Doctor Lewis."

"What does this have to do with Catherine?"

"Your wife is not the first scientist to have created an important drug and pay the consequences. Her drug is troublesome for many multinationals. It's alarming to think that a person can be harmed for their brilliance, but it has happened. Over the last year, I've compiled a list of valuable drugs acquired by multinationals. Very few of them have reached the marketplace. These drugs can save lives, but they've vanished."

"Have you any proof?"

"Not on me. I would have to be insane to carry information like that around. But I can produce the list, which brings me to why I'm here tonight. Our goal is to draw attention to these crimes, but the drug cartel is powerful, with lawyers that can squash us. We're small men, Doctor Lewis, and not trained to fight them. We don't know if our arguments will hold up in a court of law. Maybe they will listen to you."

"Why would they listen to me? You have information. Take it to the Attorney General. Besides, I'm the wrong person to fight your battle."

"Why is that, Doctor?"

"I don't have enough time, and that's all I can say about it."

Bastianich pointed to his parched lips. "May I trouble you for a glass of water?"

I got him a glass of water. He drank it down and placed the glass on the floor.

"Doctor Lewis, these are not white-collar crimes like insider trading. In those cases a judge fines the guilty party or sends them to jail. There are no laws pertaining to the medical industry that punish a company for keeping a drug off the market, even if that drug could save millions of lives. When madmen like Hitler and Stalin killed millions of innocent people we called it genocide! But there is no legislation that *requires* multinationals to deliver new drugs to the marketplace once they're developed. Ask yourself a question, Doctor Lewis. Where are all the new drugs? With all our technology, there should be thousands of new drugs flooding the marketplace. Where are they all? It's not difficult to slow down a drug's development if a multinational decides to do so. We simply cannot allow this practice to continue. They have to pay for what they've done."

I watched him flinch, as if he were in pain "Are you all right, Doctor Bastianich?"

He whispered something under his breath and looked up at me. "Your two-year-old daughter suffers from encephalitis and you stand helplessly by her bed. After weeks of agony, the terrible morning arrives and she dies in your arms. I am a doctor, and I could not save her. Then I meet a man named Robert Farrington, a scientist who tells me he had developed a new drug for encephalitis, a drug that may have saved my little girl. Hard times had forced him to sell his drug to a multinational. They promised him everything, but the drug never reached the market. That multinational already had a drug for encephalitis, an inferior one, but it generates hundreds of millions of dollars for them. My daughter took their drug and now she's..."

Bastianich's eyes glazed over as he removed his wallet and handed me a picture. A beautiful young girl with pigtails was sitting on a woman's lap. "My daughter Tanya," he said. "She died one year ago this month, and I break down each time I remember what Farrington told me."

"Is this your wife in the picture?"

"Yes. Raija. She still wakes in the night and whimpers under her breath, 'Tanya, my Tanya.' I try to calm her, but there's nothing I can do for her pain." Bastianich removed a handkerchief and wiped his eyes. "We must stop these animals, Doctor Lewis. I am a doctor! I know better. You, too, took an oath."

Bastianich lifted himself from the chair and stood in the middle of the floor. "Where have things gone wrong, Doctor Lewis? Has the world become so monstrous that we fail to see the pain of our fellow man?" His eyes glazed over again. "I swear by Apollo, the physician, by Asklepios, Hygieia, and Panakeia, and I take to witness all the gods, all the goddesses, to keep according to my ability and my judgment the following oath:

"To consider dear to me as my parents, him who taught me this art; to live in common with him and if necessary to share my goods with him; to look upon his children as my own brothers, to teach them this art if they so desire without fee or written promise; to impart on my sons and the sons of the master who taught me and the disciples who have enrolled themselves and have agreed to the rules of the profession, but to these alone, the precepts and the instruction. I will prescribe regimen for the good of my patients according to my ability and my judgment and never do harm to anyone. To please no one will I prescribe a deadly drug, nor give advice which may cause death. Nor will I give a woman a pessary to procure abortion. But I will preserve the purity of my life and my art. I will not cut for stone, even for patients in whom the disease is manifest; I will leave this operation to be performed by practitioners (specialists in this art). In every house where I come I will enter only for the good of my patients. Keeping myself far from all intentional ill-doing and all seduction, and especially from the pleasure of love with women or men be they free or slaves. All that may come to my knowledge in the exercise of my profession or outside my profession or in daily commerce with men, which ought not to be spread aboard, I will keep secret and will never reveal. If I keep this oath faithfully, may I enjoy my life and practice my art, respected by all men and in all times; but if I swerve from it or violate it, may the reverse be my lot."

Bastianich finished reciting the Hippocratic Oath, and put his hat and coat on. He turned to me. "One multinational in particular has purchased many of these drugs. If we ever get our hands on their records, we could bring them down." He walked to the door. "I must go now. Raija worries when I stay out late. We shall meet again, Doctor. I know this now." He closed the door quietly behind him.

Chapter Twenty-seven

Out of breath, I chased a man who had mumbled Catherine's name in the subway station. I yelled for him to stop, but he did not heed my warning. He only turned and smiled at me. A sinister look filled his eyes as he ran from Grand Central Station.

"Stop! Who are you? Why are you speaking Catherine's name?" The man looked familiar to me. But he wore a trench coat with the collar up, and the brim on his hat was turned down, his face hidden in the hollow. I ran fast, to where the sound of wind cut into my ears, but the man pulled away, only to make a mistake—he turned into an alley and I had him trapped. His posture reeked of guilt as he scurried like a rat, darting from one corner of the alley to the other. Then, he stopped dancing and lifted the brim of his hat.

I recognized his face, but from where? He had a red mane, and he placed both hands on his hips, as a confident smile spread across his face. Then, a faint breeze stirred the air. Patches of green-white orchids sprouted in the alley, and I avoided those in my path. These were elegant flowers that had hazel-flecked eyes that peeked out at me. Some with the shape of Catherine's face, oval and classic, and flawed only by the wisp of bangs that eternally found her eyes, and beneath all that, her intelligent gaze.

Catherine rose out of the orchids and blocked my path. She walked toward the man, speaking to him, but her words were soft and low, and I could not hear her. He pulled out a gun and his smile twisted into a crooked grin. "Catherine! Be careful! Please, don't shoot her!"

"Why not? You left her all alone, didn't you? You never watched over her." He pointed his gun at her, and I was helpless to stop him. His laughter bounced off the brick canyon walls.

Catherine turned and gazed at me. "He can't hurt me, Jack, and I won't allow him to hurt you. Leave now. You don't belong here."

Ringgg! Ringgg!

I sat up and clutched my chest.

Ringgg! Ringgg!

Maybe the morphine from the night before was too strong a dose. My body was paying the price. I glanced over at the clock—six forty-five a.m. I had instructed the front desk to wake me at seven fifteen. Why the hell can't they get it right? "Hello?"

"You up, Jack?"

"I am now."

"Are you coming to Rosetta today?"

"I don't know. I'm not feeling that great."

"I want to talk about last night. And there's something else we need to speak about."

I asked Mitch to tell me over the telephone, but he refused, saying we needed to speak in person. "You okay? You sound a little funny."

"Well, last night made me put things into perspective."

"Okay, then. I'll try to stop by later." Mitch hung up. I pulled myself out of bed and jumped into the shower. If I made it to Rosetta at all today, it would be my third appointment. The first was breakfast with Julia, to collect the case documents before she left on her new assignment. After that I was off to Sloan-Kettering for my appointment with Doctor Frankfort.

When I left the Towers, Eddie was waiting there for me. He had become my full-time driver, which meant I no longer had to stand on the street corner to flag a taxi. It reassured me to know the Iron Lung was at my disposal the weaker my body grew. "Prince Street. I need to get there quickly."

Eddie cranked up the Lung. "Don't worry, Doc. I'll getcha there real soon."

At eight a.m. sharp the Lung eased to a halt in front of Gannon's Restaurant.

"I ate here once," Eddie said. "Terrific breakfast—the only ham and eggs joint I know where you need a reservation."

"Don't go anywhere. I won't be long." I walked into Gannon's and slid into the booth across from Julia. She looked at her watch and smiled. "I'm impressed. Right on time."

I was unable to manage a smile. I wasn't exactly overjoyed at this moment.

"The cheddar omelet and decaf coffee," Julia said to the waitress.

"And you, sir?"

"Just coffee." She filled our cups and left.

"You look tired, Jack. Are you all right?"

"I'm fine. What do you say we get this over with."

Julia pulled out a thick file and slid it to my side of the table. "It's the complete report. Interviews from doctors, lab technicians, nurses, orderlies, you name it."

I flipped through several pages in the folder. "Will I understand this or do I need to hire an interpreter?"

"It's pretty straightforward." Julia reached over the table and grabbed my hand before I turned another page. "There's two sets of pictures in there. The first set was taken right after they moved Catherine into intensive care. The second set is, well, after she had died. Her body had swelled up considerably. I didn't want you to just stumble across those pictures without knowing what to expect."

I didn't look at the pictures when Gravers gave me the chance, and I wasn't going to look at them now. I went straight to the reports. "What's this about Crotalus?"

"That's our first topic of discussion. Memorial produced receipts to show that Catherine had purchased Crotalus in its lethal form and had been purifying it herself. There had been a shortage of Crotalus at Memorial, and her team needed it to complete their projects. That explains how the venom got into the hospital in its raw form, but obviously, not how it found its way into Catherine's bloodstream. Proof that Catherine purchased it takes Memorial off the hook. Any other questions?

"Not really. I'll read the report in more detail later."

"All right, then. Let's move to the Jane Doe mystery. The hospital never found her body. But I've thought about this long and hard, and in my opinion, there's no correlation between the disappearance of this woman's body and Catherine's case."

"I think you're right. What's next?"

"Memorial's attorney called me back about the security camera pointed at the back door. On the morning of Catherine's death, the video captured three masked men entering and leaving through that door. It shows two of the men hauling hospital equipment away when they left, and the third man pulled off his mask before leaving the hospital. The camera got a good shot of him. He's Asian."

"Asian? What do you make of that?"

"It's hard to say if they were thieves, drug addicts, or professionals concealing their real intent, which may have been to steal Catherine's files. The police received a copy of the video and it's being looked at by their mug-shot people. The video is also going to air on the local TV stations. Maybe someone will recognize that character. "

"Good. I'll contact Gravers to see if his team has identified him or if any viewers have called in."

Julia closed the file and nothing was said for the next minute. I think she felt awkward about the way things had turned out. I know I did.

"If you like, Jack, I'll run a background check on the Doblers for you. It's not part of Catherine's case, but since you plan to enter into business with them, it may be useful to know more about them."

"I would like a report. Thanks."

"I'll have to mail it to you, since I'll be out of town." Julia paused for a moment. "Also, you should know, I'll be back in New York in four days or so, as soon as I'm done in Chicago. I haven't committed to any other case yet, so if you're interested in rehiring me, I'll be available at that time."

Her words surprised me. "You mean that?"

Julia smiled. "Yes, I do. But there's still one small matter to settle." She pulled out an envelope and slid it across the table.

I opened it and saw the bill for her services. "Whew! That's some price tag."

"I have people to pay, and they don't come cheap."

I pulled out my checkbook. "Who should I make this out to?"

"Julia Marshant."

"Julia Marshant, in the amount of thirty-two thousand, five hundred dollars." I signed the check and slid it across the table. "I hope you're buying breakfast."

"I insist on it. You also need to sign this contingency waiver." She stuffed the check into her briefcase and placed the waiver on the table.

"What is this?"

"It authorizes me to act on your behalf while I'm gone. It's not likely I'll need to, but if something comes up and I can't reach you, it gives me permission to perform as I see fit. You should read it over."

"I don't need to read it," I said, and signed it.

Julia put the letter in her briefcase and snapped it shut. "I hate to leave so abruptly, but packing is my Achilles' heel."

"What about your breakfast?"

She stood up, put on her coat, and then wrote a telephone number on her business card. "Here, take this. If anything happens and you need me, leave a message at this number. I check it on a regular basis."

I took the card and looked up at her. "You know, we got off to rocky start, and I blame myself for that. I could've handled it better. We could've gotten to know each other better. "

Julia smiled. "I think we've gotten to know each other pretty well. A few questions more doesn't really matter."

I stood up to say goodbye to her.

Julia looked over my shoulder and into the street. "Well, I'd better go. I have a lot to do. Be careful while I'm gone. Don't run into any burning buildings. Not unless you check with me first."

"I'll try to remember that."

She turned and walked out. A minute later she was on the curb hailing a taxi. I ran outside and grabbed her arm, startling her for a moment. I led her over to the Iron Lung. "Take her where she needs to go, Eddie. Catch up with me at Rosetta." I closed the car door and Eddie pulled away. Julia turned and looked back at me. A faint smile crossed her face and then she was gone.

Chapter Twenty-eight

I was barely on time for my appointment with Doctor Frankfort at Sloan-Kettering. When I arrived, he gave me a physical, asked me how I felt, wrote a new prescription for me, and then asked that I tell him a story about Catherine and me. I did not understand what he was getting at, but one vignette came to mind: the time Catherine and I escaped to Woodstock.

We jumped into the car that weekend and made the two-hour drive from Manhattan. Catherine loved the area, and she oozed joy as we strolled around the town and through what seemed like dozens of art shops. She talked me into taking an impromptu art class. It was not how I had expected to spend the afternoon, especially since there was not one artistic bone in my body. I thought the same was true for Catherine, but she painted the most beautiful portrait of a young boy's face. At the time,

I thought the portrait was her subconscious speaking, and the child was the image of the son we would have one day. The instructor asked where she had studied, and Catherine told him she only dabbled. For me, another facet of her tapestry had come to light. I had grown to accept the fact that nothing about Catherine should ever surprise me.

When I finished the story, Doctor Frankfort made some notes. I wanted to ask him why he insisted on knowing about Catherine, but his telephone rang and he motioned that I could leave. On my way out his secretary handed me a card for my next appointment with him.

I hailed a taxi outside the hospital. As we sped down First Avenue, I flipped through the file Julia had given me at breakfast. It included a copy of the file Mitch had taken from Catherine's laboratory. I noticed some code scribbled on the file jacket. It contained only eight letters, and was nothing a detective or investigator would question. *My God!*

A couple of years back, Catherine had become obsessed with a new concept called *Computer DNA* that used the human body as a computer. It was all the rage and was being called the next generation of microprocessors. Our body contains millions of natural supercomputers that have the ability to store billions of times more data than any man-made computer. Catherine could not get enough of this stuff, and some nights I'd have to drag her away from her computer and back into bed. In no time at all she had created her own program and begun to store messages inside the DNA of human cells. Playfully, she challenged me to find them. Sometimes I could, but only with great difficulty. It now occurred to me: Did Catherine leave a message for me inside Cold's DNA?

Mitch was in a meeting when I arrived at Rosetta, so I went into the conference room to wait for him. I considered going to the downstairs laboratory to look for a possible message in Cold, but it was an arduous task that required both strength and endurance, two qualities I no longer possessed. Mitch had plenty of researchers on staff, and maybe he would assign one for me. I paced the floor, impatiently waiting for Mitch to finish his meeting.

I walked to the window that overlooked Washington Square Park and gazed down at the huge snow drifts. Even with snow piled to the knee, people still congregated in the park. I slipped my hand into my pants pocket and pulled out a business card I had forgotten was there. It was the card the flower delivery man had given me at the cemetery. I picked up the telephone and called the number on the card. "Carl, please."

"This is Carl."

"My name's Jack Lewis. I'm Catherine Lewis' husband. Your driver delivered white roses to my wife's grave at Rose Mount last week, and I noticed the card that came with the roses was not signed. Can you tell me who sent the roses?"

"Are you the man my driver almost ran down?"

"Well, yes, I'm afraid so. I slipped on the ice as I was running down the hill trying to catch him. Can you tell me who sent the flowers?"

"I'm afraid I can't, Mr. Lewis. I don't have the person's name."

"How could you not have their name?"

"All I can tell you is that I received an envelope. It contained a hundred dollar bill and a note saying: *White roses for Catherine Lewis at Rose Mount Cemetery.*

"Was there a return address on the envelope?"

"There was a stamp, but no return address."

"What about the postmark? Did you see that?"

"Yes, I did look at the postmark, Mr. Lewis."

"Where was it sent from?"

There was a pause before Carl spoke. "Mr. Lewis, I don't know why someone would buy flowers in this manner, and it's really none of my business; I'm just a florist. But I think whoever sent them doesn't want their name known. I think we should respect that. Someone's gone to great lengths to remain anonymous, someone who apparently has great admiration for your wife's memory."

I tried to think of something to say, some way to convince Carl to tell me the postmark, but I realized that no matter what I said, Carl was not going to give me any information. "If you change your mind and decide to tell me, I can be reached at Rosetta Labs in Manhattan. Thank you for delivering flowers to Catherine's grave in the snow." I hung up and sat down with little hope that I would ever hear back from Carl. A moment later the phone rang.

"There's a call for you, Mr. Lewis," the receptionist said.

"Send it through.... Hello."

"I apologize for calling you at Rosetta, Dr Lewis. I tried your hotel, but you were already gone."

"Who is this?"

"Peter Bastianich."

"How did you find me here?"

"I've seen the *Times* article about Rosetta and the Cold drug, and that you're heading up the project."

"There's an article in the *Times* that actually said that?"

"Something like that, yes. But I want to follow up on what we discussed."

"You were going to provide some evidence—"

"Please, Doctor, not over the telephone."

"Should we meet in person? How about coming to Rosetta?"

"Yes, I can do that. I'll be there in thirty minutes or so."

Bastianich hung up and I walked down to Mitch's office.

"Sorry, Jack. It's been a hectic day. Have a seat." Mitch closed the door. "I didn't sleep well last night. I was back and forth between pacing the floor and looking out the window I can't tell you how many times. I can't believe Heinrich was shot, and we were seated only tables away. I'm still rattled. It got me thinking and..." Mitch ran his fingers through his hair. "Look, I need to come clean on something—"

"What happened last night is traumatic for everyone, I can see you're upset and I don't mean to cut you off, but I've a favor to ask." Mitch would talk for another hour about last night's incident if I allowed him, but my sense of urgency needed to prevail at that moment. "Do you remember Catherine's obsession with that computer DNA stuff? Where she wrote her own language?" I saw a sense of relief come over Mitch, as if he had dodged a bullet. It was an uncharacteristic expression for a man who usually dominated the first and last words in most conversations.

"I can see you're pent up and haven't listened to a word I've said." Mitch looked down at the papers on his desk for a moment and then up at me. "Yes, I believe you're referring to the language that Catherine wrote to store messages inside the DNA of cells."

"Exactly. Now, I doubt this has anything to do with Catherine's case, but I'm wondering if she wrote a message for me inside Cold."

"Are you planning to look? You want laboratory space?"

"I'm not sure about my endurance for something like this. Would you be able to assign a researcher?"

"You're kidding, right? To look through a hundred thousand genes? They'd have to work around the clock to even begin to make a dent in it. Besides, I just can't pull someone off a project. Wait a minute, Weber might be available."

"No, I don't want him near Catherine's work."

"Wow. I didn't expect that response from you. Did you have a run-in with him or something?"

"No. I'd rather not go into it. Can I bring someone in from the outside?"

"I don't know, Jack. It's a liability to give outsiders access to what we're working on."

"What about Colter? You know him. He can work in the small lab downstairs, and I'll make sure he stays there. What do you say?"

"It's bad enough having to socialize with him, but to have him here every day? No." Mitch sat back and rubbed his chin. "Isaac could look at it. He's going on holiday soon, so I don't know if he'll complete it. But he can start it. I'll make sure he documents everything in case we assign someone else. You and Isaac will get along fine. He doesn't like Weber either."

"When can Isaac start? I'm meeting Colter for an early dinner today, and I'd appreciate it if Isaac could start before I have to leave here. By the way, you want to join us?"

"I'll pass, but give Colter my best."

It happened quickly. Mitch had Isaac meet us in the downstairs laboratory.

"Let me give you some background, Isaac. My wife became fascinated with the idea that we now have the capability of encrypting messages onto the double helix. I'm thinking she may have left a message inside Cold. It may be difficult to locate. Do you think you'd be up for something like this?"

"Sounds intriguing."

"Focus on chromosomes 14 and 15. That's where she coded other messages."

"That's a lot of geography to cover: a billion codons. Whatever possessed her to alter DNA like that? It's dangerous."

"Catherine and I debated often on this very point. She held that, of the one hundred thousand genes in a cell, only a third of them are active. She stored messages in dormant genes only. I contended that altering any gene was, as you pointed out, dangerous, dormant or not. We may one day access dormant genes to regrow a hand or an organ, so no gene should be violated."

"What did she say to that?"

"That I was paranoid. But here's what you need to know. Her alphabet is based on the four DNA nucleotide symbols: *A*, *C*, *G*, and *T*, with six alphabet letters attributed to each one. So, letters A through F are assigned to symbol A, letters G through L are assigned to symbol C, G has the next six letters, and T has the last eight alphabetical letters assigned to it. It's as simple as numerology. When Catherine wanted to code the letter A, she would place one A in the DNA double helix. The letter B would have two As in a row. C would have three As in a row, and so on. The same theory applies to all the groups. To decipher the message, you simply count the number of As, Cs, Gs, or Ts in a row, and decode them. That's the simple part, but finding where the message begins and ends will be the tricky part."

"Let me poke around and see what I come up with. Mitch told you I'm leaving for holiday in a couple of days, so I'll do the best I can before leaving."

"Document your research, Isaac," Mitch said, "in case someone else needs to take over."

"Absolutely. If you two will leave me alone now, I'll get started on it."

Chapter Twenty-nine

Bastianich was late. He was supposed to have been at Rosetta an hour ago. I was surprised, because he very much wanted to give me a list of biotech drugs being kept off the market, along with the name of the multinational buying these drugs up. I went to Mitch's office and told him all about meeting Bastianich and also about the list of horded drugs he was supposed to be bringing me this afternoon. I made an error in judgment, because the more I explained to Mitch about Bastianich's list of drugs, the whiter he became. Mitch thanked me for making sure he'd stay awake a second straight night.

I told Mitch to reach me at *La Vie en Rose* if Bastianich showed up. With that, I rushed out of Rosetta to meet with Colter.

* * *

Colter arrived at *La Vie en Rose* shortly after I did. He shook the snow off his jacket and kicked ice from his boots before joining me at the table. For a man in his mid-thirties, he was remarkably lean and toned. Most scientists work long hours, never exercise, and succumb to a diet of junk food and soda, but Colter had bucked that trend in spades.

"What's up?" He tossed the *Times* on the table. "I thought Mitch was coming?"

"He's got work piled on his desk."

"I see. You told him I was going to be here."

"I did. I don't know why you two don't get along better."

"I've got nothing against Mitch. The bad blood started at a party a couple of years ago. Mitch had brought this fiery brunette and the next thing I know she's hanging all over me. The party was boring and I decide to leave. She decides to go with me. I said okay, and Mitch never forgave me. Anyway, I've got news to share with you."

Petri approached their table. "Monsieur Jack, how are you?

"I'm doing well, thanks for asking."

"Something to drink?"

"A cup of fresh-brewed Colombian for me."

"And for you, sir?"

"I'll have a Stella Artois."

"Is Michelle here?" She had called and left messages for me, but I just hadn't been able to get back to her.

"No, Monsieur. She will be disappointed to know you were here. If I had to guess, she is in her studio creating a sculpture of some kind." Petri handed us the menu. "Take your time, I'll tell you the specials when I return with your refreshments." Petri left for the kitchen.

"There's a clinic in Honduras that's developed a new cancer treatment. Quite a few patients diagnosed as terminal have gone there and returned clean," Colter said.

"Is the treatment FDA approved?"

"I didn't ask. Probably not, but FDA treatments don't work anyway."

Petrie returned with our coffee and announced the day's specials.

"Just the house salad for me."

"And for you, Monsieur?"

"The Steak au Poivre."

"An excellent choice." Petrie left for the kitchen.

"Only a salad?"

"I'm not very hungry today."

"Anyway, I think you should look into this treatment, Jack."

I asked Colter if he had any documentation on the treatment and he said the clinic was being *hush hush* about it. Just as I thought, another quack scam to bilk poor souls who had exhausted every other medical avenue possible. Some probably handed over their life savings and then died a week later. If I had thought for a single moment that there was a legitimate cure, I would jump on the first plane. I thanked Colter, but said *no thanks* to Honduras.

The kitchen door swung open and Petrie carried our food to the table. Outside, the snow continued to fall, and I found it soothing to watch the flakes flutter down. The large snowflakes were thick and dense and I was barely able to see through them to the buildings that stood across the street. My eyes picked up on a man hurrying down the block without a coat, which I thought odd. It was difficult to make out his face and features, but as he approached the restaurant I realized it was Mitch. He must have decided to join us after all. Rather than enter the restaurant, however, he stood outside the window and looked at me through the glass. I knew something was wrong by the alarmed look on his face. I got up from the table and walked outside. "What is it? What's happened?"

"I'm sorry, Jack. It was just on the news. They found Peter Bastianich. He committed suicide."

Chapter Thirty

"I'll come back for you in an hour," the nurse said as she locked the brake on Heinrich's wheelchair. He was glad to be out of his room and sitting in the hospital's enclosed garden. An odd sensation crept into him as he gazed down at the flora. He realized that, for the past fifty years, his imprint had remained firmly on the pulse of the family business; he had thought of nothing else. Rarely had Heinrich ever leaned back and relaxed without a worry in the world, and for the first time in years, his mind traveled back to the events of 1947.

The inner tube was on the floor. Picked it up and wrapped it around Herr Schneggenburger's neck. Used every ounce of strength. It only took minutes before...

"Nurse!"

She hurried over. "Is anything wrong?"

Heinrich looked up at her. "Take me back to my room and get my clothes. I'm checking out."

* * *

With Rutger seated beside him, Heinrich waited in a parked limousine just off the West Side Highway. He had refused the doctor's advice and left the hospital after just two days, choosing to convalesce at the mansion. The pain in his shoulder was constant from the bullet that had careened off his clavicle and come to rest in the deltoid muscle. After the doctor had removed the bullet, he told Heinrich that tissue damage to any major muscle group was serious, even moreso for an eighty year-old.

"More seltzer, Grandfather?"

"No, Son, I've had enough. I just don't understand why we conduct business in a place like this. We'd all be more comfortable back in the office."

Rutger didn't answer. Nor did he explain why they were parked in an unpaved lot on the waterfront side of the highway. The light from uptown traffic glared through the side window and bothered Heinrich's eyes. He hated being here, but Rutger was by his side, and that was what mattered most to him.

The West Village streets bustled with business during the daytime, but when the sun set, this part of the Village was quite a different matter. This stretch near the highway turned into a living fresco of homosexuals, prostitutes, and transvestites, as if darkness itself transformed the neighborhood into an aberrant sex market. Men in cars circled the blocks to find a quick release before returning home for dinner. Truck drivers picked up hookers on the New York side of the Holland Tunnel and dropped them off on the Jersey side. The hookers would then find different *johns* and head back into Manhattan with them. Heinrich never understood the perverted, the deplorable risk takers and the death wish they lived with from one day to the next.

"I will have a little seltzer, Son. My throat is dry again."

"You should have stayed in the hospital, Grandfather. You're still very weak."

"I'm all right. Two days in that place was all I could take."

Rutger poured the seltzer. As he handed it to his grandfather, he was distracted by a sudden movement outside the window, where the eyes of an attractive, young woman commanded his attention. The woman stepped back and executed a perfect plié in the snow, contorting her body to give him full view of her barely clad loins. Her performance continued as another limousine entered the lot and pulled up alongside. The driver of the second limousine shut the engine down and turned the headlights off.

Rutger glanced out the side window, but the young woman had disappeared. Only the swirl of footprints made by her nocturnal dance remained in the snow. He shifted his attention to the newly arrived limousine. The driver stepped out and opened the rear door. A short, dark-haired man exited. The man looked at the Hudson River for a moment and then turned to Heinrich's limousine. His driver opened the door. The man stepped inside and seated himself across from Heinrich and Rutger.

The two limo drivers walked to the river where they each lit a smoke near the rotting pier.

"I don't know why you select such scandalous places to meet, Heinrich. It's ill repute and unsafe after dark," the man said.

"Walk on the wild side of human nature," Rutger said to Vincent Renn Pierce, Chairman of the Board of Synogen, a small but highly publicized pharmaceutical manufacturer of Hiverom, one of the more successful AIDS drugs on the market.

"I can live without that, thank you very much," Renn Pierce said. "Enough about that. How are you feeling, Heinrich?"

"I'm fine, Vincent. It's you that I'm worried about." Heinrich's piercing eyes were like magnets Renn Pierce could not avoid. Heinrich looked down at the sheet of paper resting on his lap, and with his good arm, turned it over. He gave Renn Pierce a cold stare. "Vincent, how much money have you made on that AIDS drug this year?"

"Well, I don't carry figures around, but it's been a good year."

"How *much* Vincent? Round it to the nearest million."

Renn Pierce wiped his nose with a tissue. "I would say a hundred million."

"One hundred million. Your drug's been on the market for how long?"

"Let's see. It's twenty-two months since Hiverom came out."

"And your projection for next year?"

Renn Pierce cleared his throat. "We project doubling this year's numbers."

"And the year after that?"

"Without a serious competitor, we could reach a billion."

"Very commendable," Heinrich said. "There's no limit to your success, wouldn't you say, Vincent?" When Renn Pierce failed to answer, Heinrich pointed out the window at a group of transvestites strutting alongside the highway. "You see them? *That's* your market. Dope addicts that stick needles into themselves, and who knows what else. You'll make a fortune, won't you?"

Renn Pierce moistened his lips as Rutger poured a glass of seltzer and handed it to him. Renn Pierce gulped the water down.

"You disappoint me, Vincent," Heinrich said. "We had a deal. I agreed to secure the FDA approvals for your drug, and in exchange you would submit *one* new drug application to the FDA each month. From where I'm sitting, it appears I'm the only one living up to our bargain."

"It's not easy to submit a new application every month."

Heinrich's face hardened. "Nothing is easy! It wasn't easy to get your drug approved in six months, but it happened. Otherwise, this drug of yours would still be sitting on a shelf somewhere."

"I don't have the resources. It takes a team of twenty people to submit one drug application, and we're going through growing pains right now." Renn Pierce avoided Heinrich's stare. "I expect things to stabilize soon, maybe in three or four months. I'll get things back on track—"

"Not good enough, Vincent. I've been in the drug business for sixty years, and never once have I failed to keep my word." Heinrich paused. "I don't care what it takes for you to submit drug applications. I don't care if it costs you one hundred million a year. You do it, or else."

"Or else?" Renn Pierce said.

Rutger placed his hand on his grandfather's arm to calm him. He looked at Renn Pierce. "Vincent, try to understand what my grandfather is saying. These are challenging times with this biotech mess, and you and many others play an important role. There *is* a master plan at work here, and you're a link in that chain. Don't underestimate the importance of these drug submissions. You've been given a great gift by my grandfather, Vincent. Your children and your children's children will prosper because of his generosity. We never asked you for one penny of your profit. We asked only for your loyalty, and to keep your end of the bargain." Rutger reached over and took the empty glass from Renn Pierce's hand. "Is your mouth still dry, Vincent?"

"I'm fine, thank you."

Rutger placed the glass down. He reached into his coat pocket and pulled out some notes. "I want to read you something. It's a patent we filed last year for an FDA-approved drug called Amelgalis, which has not yet been released to the market. Your drug keeps AIDS from spreading to CD4 T-cells. It has the ability to alert the immune system when the AIDS virus invades the body, and in so doing, causes antibodies to be produced earlier in the infection stage. The result being that Hiverom limits the AIDS virus from entrenching itself into healthy CD4 T-cells. And Hiverom is effective in about forty percent of its patients. Is that correct?"

"Yes, that's right," Renn Pierce said.

"Let me tell you about Amelgalis. It does everything your drug does, but it also modifies the HIV virus and reduces the chance that it will ever turn into full-blown AIDS. In a double blind test, Amelgalis prevented AIDS from occurring in fifty-two percent of all patients. Healthy vector cells that contain Amelgalis are injected into the blood system to strengthen the immune system. Over time an infected body will repair itself. And, when Amelgalis is brought to market, it will become the most effective AIDS drug available. I'm afraid it will force you out of business."

"Does this drug really work?"

"It has for the past two years."

"Then why haven't you released it?"

"Would you want us to release it, or postpone it for a while longer?" Rutger watched Renn Pierce's eyes widen. "Relax, Vincent. We're postponing its release for now. You see, there's fierce competition among the biotechs to develop an AIDS cure. They're burning through their money at an incredible rate, and the more cash they burn, the longer we'll wait before announcing Amelgalis. If we announce it now, the biotechs will shift their research funds to a more promising venture. So you see, Vincent, you have the biotechs to thank. But heed my grandfather's warning, Vincent. Fail to live up to your end of the bargain and Amelgalis will be on the market thirty days after you default on your promise."

"I don't understand. You could make billions off that drug."

"If I were you, Vincent, I wouldn't worry about how we run our business. I'd worry about the survival of yours. We'll release the drug in twenty-four months. That should give you enough time to accumulate some decent wealth. But, fail us once more, and all bets are off. Can we expect your full cooperation?"

Renn Pierce swallowed hard without saying a word. He dropped his head and nodded.

"Thank you," Heinrich said. "You may go now."

Rutger turned on the cab light. The drivers took one last drag off their cigarettes, tossed them into the river, and walked back to the limousines.

Rutger saw the expression on Renn Pierce's face. It was an expression that said he felt dirty about himself. No one wants to discover that he lacks integrity. Renn Pierce was no different than the other small-minded men Rutger had recruited: always willing to take a gift, but full of excuses for not keeping their word. If Renn Pierce had simply submitted the drug applications, he would have lived his life believing himself to be a man of integrity.

Renn Pierce stepped from Heinrich's limousine and walked to his own. Rutger overheard him tell his driver to take him to the office—he was too upset to go home, and his wife always knew when something was wrong.

Chapter Thirty-one

"They'll be waiting for us when we arrive." Heinrich did not answer and Rutger looked at him. "You look exhausted. I'm dropping you at my apartment and going to the meeting alone."

"No, Son. I have to attend. They're expecting me."

Rutger admired his grandfather's courage, but Heinrich's face had turned pale and his voice had weakened. "I'm dropping you off. You've had enough excitement for one day."

Heinrich stared straight ahead. "Maybe you're right, Son. It's been an exciting first day back, and I—"

"Drop my grandfather at my—"

"No, I'll drop you and go home." Heinrich motioned for Rutger to close the glass partition so the driver would not hear them. "Tell me the final outcome on buying that cold drug from Jack Lewis. How much?"

"Two hundred and fifty million. That gives us complete ownership."

"That's a lot of money, Son. Did you bring Von Hoff in on this deal?"

"He did the analysis. His estimate to develop the drug with a marketing campaign came to a half billion. Projected profits over five years should reach eighty-five billion. When patent protection runs out on our product, we'll push it out to the market."

"And Lewis has agreed to the offer?"

"The contract is being drawn up now."

The driver pulled to the curb in front of Dobler Pharmaceutical, where six black limousines lined the street. Rutger stepped out and looked back inside. "Get some rest, Grandfather. I'll call you in the morning."

"Call me tonight. I want to know everything that happens."

"If we finish early, I'll call you."

Heinrich smiled. "Good luck, Son."

Rutger entered the large conference room where six men were already seated around an oval table. It was rare to find the leaders of the world's largest pharmaceutical companies gathered in one room. Only Heinrich was missing, but it was widely accepted that Rutger now spoke for the company.

Two of the corporate leaders, Jacob Greenberg of Ridgewood Drugs and Randall Whitestone of Whitestone Pharmaceutical, were in their late seventies, and both had started their drug companies as young men. Two other men, Lawrence Hines of Remington Drugs and Joseph Parlante of First Manhattan Medical, were in their sixties. The remaining two CEOs, Frederick Crutchfield III of Hurst Pharmaceutical and Edward Hoffman of Deutschen International, Inc., were in their early fifties. Rutger was the junior executive at the meeting, and he had the good sense to remember that fact. These men expected to be treated with respect, even if Rutger considered some of them to be dinosaurs.

Rutger had prepared for the meeting by placing a cigar at each seat around the table and ensuring the bar was well stocked so the bartender would be able to make any potable concoction these men desired. A fog of smoke now hung in the air. Rutger dismissed the bartender and closed the conference room door. He returned to the table and removed a copy of the Five Point Plan from his briefcase.

"I want to thank each of you for coming here tonight on such short notice." Rutger made it a point to look each man in the eye. "Our business is precious to us. Next to our families, we cherish it above all else. I have asked you here because we face serious challenges from the emergence of biotech companies. Genetic engineering is exploding in our midst, and if allowed to grow unchecked, these biotechs will take control of our industry.

"Five years ago biotechnology was considered a bad investment. Out of a hundred companies that emerged, only a handful had developed useful drugs. That's all changed. New biotechs are cropping up every day, and they develop drugs faster and at *one-third* of what it costs us to develop a drug. Biotechs will soon surpass our combined drug patent output. And in ten years, the FDA will be approving twice as many biotech drugs as all of our drugs put together."

Rutger paused. He knew he had their attention. "No one in this room has a war chest of new drugs to replace those losing patent protection. We have grown to believe there is no end to our ability to create new drugs. Let me assure you, gentlemen, our new drugs will pale in comparison to what the biotechs are creating. To survive in this new world, we must join forces and stop looking at each other as the enemy. It's time that we agree upon a code of conduct."

"A code of conduct?" Jacob Greenberg said. "I've never heard a Dobler use those words." Laughter erupted from around the table.

Rutger didn't react. This meeting was not about his ego. It was about getting a group of powerful men to agree on a plan. The remark was offensive, yes, but even more offensive was the fact that his grandfather had been shot days earlier, and not one person in the room had asked about his health.

"Let's stay focused, gentlemen. The issue I'm discussing affects us all."

"Get to your plan then," Greenberg said, "so we can get home at a decent hour."

There were rumblings around the table, and it was apparent to Rutger that he was losing control. "You can leave now, if that suits you," Rutger said to Greenberg. The room turned silent. "And if anyone else is inconvenienced by being here, you can leave as well."

No one spoke, nor did anyone leave. Greenberg sat back and puffed his cigar as Rutger scanned the faces of the other men. "Now, this plan might sound radical, but it will help us keep control of the drug industry. There are five parts to this plan, and I'll cover them now at a high level.

"Number one: Increase the number of drug applications now being submitted to the FDA. It will bottleneck their ability to approve new drugs. If each company submits two new drug applications a month, it will deliver a severe blow to the FDA, and more importantly, to the biotechs seeking drug approval. We have a number of small companies submitting applications, and already we can see the slow-down effect within the FDA. Time and money are not on the side of the biotechs, and this step will either force them to merger with us or it will drive them right out of business.

"Two: The FDA has lobbied for years to increase the drug approval fee from two hundred and fifty thousand to four hundred and fifty thousand. Stop fighting them. We can afford it, but the cash poor biotechs cannot. This will create another hurdle for them to overcome.

"Three: The FDA wants control over international drugs that come into the country. Again, stop fighting them; foreign drugs are not our competitors. Lobby Congress to support the FDA, and allow them to grow into an even bigger bureaucracy. While this will slow down the drug approval process for all companies, it will hurt the biotechs more.

"Four: We need a campaign that creates fear, uncertainty, and doubt about many of these new biotech drugs. Feed the Creationist, Christian Scientists, and other groups the information they need to paint these drugs as dangerous and unholy. Help support their belief that only God has the right to alter the genetic structure of living things.

"Five: We must identify important biotech drugs before they are fully developed and reach the marketplace. We need to buy them up, slow down their development, and use any means at our disposal to stop these drugs from reaching the marketplace.

"Now, in order for this Five Point Plan to work, it requires an investment from all of us. We'll need operating capital of a billion dollars. For starters, I am asking each company to contribute one hundred million—"

"That's collusion," Lawrence Hines yelled out.

"Label it what you want," Rutger said. "IBM did it when they dominated the computer industry. AT&T did it by controlling the state regulatory agencies. Show me a dynamic, high-growth industry and I'll show you powerful companies that control it."

Randall Whitestone spoke out. "You're asking every man in this room to jeopardize his reputation and risk going to jail. That's far too much to ask."

"If we don't act, you won't *have* a reputation," Rutger said. "The biotechs will take it from you. We'll be laying off employees and closing our plants. Is that what you want?"

"But you're talking anti-trust," Whitestone said. "That's treble indemnity if we're convicted."

"Take your choice," Rutger said. "Sit back and do nothing, or strike now while we still can. Powerful new drugs are being developed as we speak. They'll replace half the drugs we market."

"I'm quite aware," Whitestone said. "You're buying that new cold drug, aren't you?"

"Yes, and I'm glad you brought that up. Once we agree upon the Five Point Plan, we'll share ownership in new drugs like this one."

"Your grandfather's not known for sharing."

"My grandfather is a business man. He moves quickly so opportunities don't slip past him." Rutger looked around the table. "It's time to make a decision, gentlemen."

"Can we have a few moments alone, Rutger?" Whitestone said.

"By all means. I'll be in my office." Rutger left the room as the six men began to discuss the pros and cons of the Five Point Plan.

Thirty minutes later Whitestone called Rutger back into the room.

"There's one major concern," Whitestone said. "If you can satisfy it, then we'll meet one week from today to formalize an agreement."

"I had hoped to have a commitment tonight," Rutger said.

"That's not possible. We need at least a week to review everything. Now, here's our concern. It's with your grandfather, and, quite frankly, with you as well."

Rutger raised one eyebrow. "I'm afraid I don't know what you mean."

"When it comes to fair play, your family doesn't exactly have a sterling reputation."

"What are you implying?"

"Every man sitting at this table has done business with Dobler Pharmaceutical at one time or another. And we have all walked away with a bitter taste in our mouth. My dealings with your grandfather go back fifty years, to when he left Germany after the Schneggenburger scandal where his business partner was found drowned and a profitable drug company was cleaned out of millions. And then Heinrich shows up in New York with a pocket full of money and starts a brand new drug company."

Rutger looked at him in amazement. "I'm confused. What does any speculation about my grandfather's past have to do with the Five Point Plan?"

"Quite a lot," Whitestone said. "For openers, going into business with him is a huge risk. He was ruthless fifty years ago, and he hasn't changed one bit over the years."

Rutger controlled his anger. "In spite of your allegations about my grandfather, every man in this room knows he is a man of his word. He's never reneged on a business deal once he's shaken your hand. That's an accomplishment in an industry like ours."

"Let's cool down," Whitestone said. "I'm sure you understand our concern, and we've all heard and agree on the point you just made. But it will take some time for us to sort this out and determine how best to protect ourselves. Let's plan to meet one week from tonight."

Rutger walked to the door and shook hands with each man as he left. Still, not one asked about his grandfather's health.

Chapter Thirty-two

"Did I wake you?"

"No, Son. I've been waiting for your call. How did it go?"

"I think we're in agreement. We'll meet in one week to finalize everything."

"A week? Hmm. That may work in our favor."

"How's that?"

"I don't want Cold dragged into the negotiations. I know those vultures, especially Whitestone. Get the deal with Jack Lewis done before your next meeting with them."

"Good point. I'll get it done."

"I'm proud of you, Son. You're doing a good job. We'll speak in the morning."

"Goodnight, Grandfather." Rutger hung up and dialed another number.

A sleepy voice answered, "Hello?"

"I'm sorry. I didn't realize how late it was."

"Are you coming tonight?"

"I can't, darling. I still have work to get done."

"But you promised."

"I know, sweetheart. I'll make it up to you."

"I miss you."

"I miss you, too. I'll need your help tomorrow, but we can talk then. You sound sleepy."

"I love you."

"I love you too, Vanessa."

Chapter Thirty-three

I arrived at Doctor Frankfort's office for my next visit, and did so with the weight of the investigation resting solely on my shoulders. My ability to correctly interpret information from the file Julia had given me was paramount, but how well I functioned was in question. *Wait for her to return*, the doctor had said. *You lack the basic ingredients to effectively carry out an investigation. The left side of your brain has to compensate for the non-working right side, and that distorts your logic.* The doctor had made his point: I was prone to make errors. If I were to read the files five times, I would reach five different conclusions. *Concise analysis is the key ingredient for an investigator,* the doctor reiterated. I raised my hand to stop him. I got it.

Had I encountered mood swings? Was my mind clear one minute and disoriented the next? Yes, I told him, a couple of times a day. He jotted it all down and then asked me to tell him a story about Catherine and me. Once again, I was not certain why he had asked, but at that moment a story rushed into my mind, one I would never have shared with anyone under normal circumstances. It took place the morning after I had first met Catherine. I had awakened to find myself totally consumed by her. By late morning I was beside myself and could no longer contain my feelings. That afternoon I tracked Catherine down and confessed the spell she held over me. Moments later, with trepidation, I told her I loved her. I panicked in that instant with fear of pushing her away, since we barely knew each other. And yet, how could I go on without revealing my feelings to her? Then the most incredible thing occurred. Catherine told me that she had been suffering in much the same way, and that she loved me, too. We celebrated at *La Vie en Rose* that night, and were never apart from that day forward.

* * *

Outside Zalinsky's Funeral Home the wind whipped snow in circles. The death of Peter Bastianich had left me even more fragile. I was grateful that Mitch and Vanessa had come along to support me through yet another ordeal. When we walked into the parlor, we saw only a few people in attendance at the wake, and I recalled the photos Peter had shown me of his wife, Raija, and of his daughter Tanya. I also recalled what he'd told me—Tanya might have survived if Robert Farrington's drug had reached her.

I walked down an aisle of frayed carpet flanked by some rather shoddy furniture. Small, plaster-of-Paris lamps diffused a weak, yellow glow to light my pathway. For a funeral parlor it could have used a new coat of paint, or wallpaper, or something to spruce it up. When I reached the casket, I waited at a respectable distance while a silver-haired woman in a black dress paid her final respects. She genuflected on the kneeling board beside Peter's casket and repeated the Hail Mary a number of times while keeping count on the rosary beads clutched in her hand. She stood up and lightly touched his face before walking away. The sweet smell of gladiolas filled the air when I moved closer. It was subdued only by the spray of red roses that covered the lower half of the casket. Peter had a peaceful look on his face, and I knelt to say a prayer for him.

When I stood up to leave, I saw Raija sitting in the second row between two elderly women. She wore a black dress and had a pained look on her face. I walked over to her. "I'm Jack Lewis, a friend of Peter's."

Her eyes lifted. She was a petite woman with long, dark hair, and beautiful Mediterranean eyes. Her body shook when she let go of the two women and rose to her feet. The lost look in her eyes was in stark contrast to the brilliance that radiated from them in the photo Peter had shown me. "Peter mentioned you only this week," she said with a Slavic accent. "How did you come to know him?" She was unsteady and I took her arm and helped her sit back down. The two women stood and walked away.

"Oh, God," she moaned. "Peter's gone. Never will I hear his voice."

Vanessa and Mitch approached. "Raija, these are my friends, Mitch Cochran and Vanessa Boulay. They've come to pay their respects."

"My deepest regrets," Mitch said. He stepped aside and Vanessa moved closer to Raija. Her eyes welled up when she took Raija's hand, and it brought Raija to her feet. The two women embraced. I walked away and Mitch followed me. It was strange to mourn for a man I barely knew while I had been denied the right to mourn for my own wife in the same way.

"You okay, Jack?"

"Yeah, I'm fine. I just had some thoughts."

"What kind of thoughts?"

I was reluctant to share what I was thinking with Mitch, or with anyone else for that matter. Doctor Frankfort had suggested that it was more appropriate if I kept my thoughts to myself. "If you must know, being in this place reminds me that I missed Catherine's funeral. It's odd, though, because when I went to the cemetery I got the feeling she wasn't buried there." I looked at him. "Is she still alive?"

Mitch just stared at me for a moment. "You're asking me if Catherine's alive?"

The gravity of what I had asked him took a few moments to seep into my brain. Once it did, though, I realized the absurdity of my question. "Don't pay attention to me. I'm going to get this way from time to time."

Mitch didn't say anything, and before he had the chance, I changed the subject and told him my reason for attending Peter's wake. I explained that Peter had had contact with many scientists who developed drugs that ended up in the hands of the multinationals. My hope was that some of these scientists would show up today and pay their respects. Meeting them was the only chance to get my hands on the list of biotech drugs Peter had promised me. And maybe it would bring me a step closer to finding Catherine's killer. It was a long shot, but I had nothing better to do.

"You mentioned that list of drugs the other day."

"I did, and I think Peter was killed because of it."

"Killed? You didn't tell me he was killed. I thought he committed suicide."

"Keep it down. Raija and her family can hear us. I'll explain later. Right now, I need you to do something for me. Walk down and look at the flower baskets near the coffin and get me the names written on the sympathy cards. Some of those flower baskets are probably from Peter's scientist friends."

Mitch took a pen and a business card out of his pocket. He flipped the card over and headed down the aisle.

"Mitch." He stopped and looked back. "Do you think walking down there holding a pen and your business card might look a little conspicuous? Lose the writing utensil."

Mitch stuck them back into his pocket and spoke under his breath. "Okay, I'll try to memorize the names I can read. I'll circle back around and give them to you."

I sat down on a folding metal chair at the back of the room and waited for visitors to arrive. None came, however, and the parlor remained empty and quiet. I watched as Mitch casually strolled around the flower basket area and read names off the sympathy cards. He returned up the aisle, sat down, and scribbled the names down before handing them over to me.

"I'll have Julia track these down when she gets back."

"Does she know about Bastianich?"

"I left her a message, but haven't heard anything. I'm sure she's busy right now."

I looked down at Vanessa and Raija. They were steeped in conversation and I wondered what they possibly had in common.

"Vanessa gets along with everyone," Mitch said. He glowed whenever he mentioned her.

"How are things between you two?"

He leaned forward in his chair. "I'm open on my end, but I'm not feeling anything real strong from her. We're friends, so I'm happy about that."

"You haven't told her about my condition, have you?"

"Not a word, not to anyone."

"Good. Keep it that way." I looked at my watch and saw we had been there for over an hour. "It's late, and it doesn't look like any of Peter's friends are showing up tonight." We walked down and told Raija we had to leave.

The two women stood. "Thank you for coming, Jack, and you too, Mitch." Raija turned to Vanessa. "And thank you so very much." They embraced, and a minute later Mitch, Vanessa, and I were outside with the cold wind in our face.

"I'm starved. Anyone else hungry?" Mitch said.

"I could eat something," Vanessa said. "Let's get out of this cold."

The Greek diner we entered smelled of fresh feta cheese, olives, roasted peppers, and hummus. When we sat down I noticed the florescent lighting gave off a yellowish hue, similar to the lamps in the funeral home. I looked at Vanessa, and it was clear that even the poorest lighting could not diminish her physical attributes. She had been blessed with great cheek bones, beautiful blue eyes, an elegant nose, and full lips. She exuded confidence just in the way she sat straight in her chair and read the menu. The compassion she showed to Raija tonight was also impressive. There was little wonder why Mitch fawned over her the way he did.

"By the way, two more companies are interested in Cold."

"When did all this happen?"

"Yesterday. Vanessa has prepared an overview of all three companies who've shown an interest."

Vanessa took a sip of her tea and set the cup down. "That's right, Nakawa, a Japanese company; DNAtech, a west coast company; and, of course, Dobler Pharmaceutical."

"How serious are the other two?"

"Very. Let me summarize. Nakawa has deep pockets and is a company known for their great work ethic. They want to enter the U.S. market, and Cold would allow them to compete with the multinationals here."

"Interesting. Any concerns?"

"There is a potential downside. They want to retain Rosetta as their research arm. But, and don't take this the wrong way, Mitch, Rosetta is a minimally managed company by Nakawa standards. They will want to create a more rigid work environment to reflect what Nakawa has in place. Second, Nakawa wants to structure the deal so they have an out if Cold fails to reach its potential. In other words, cut their losses and walk. If that were to happen, Cold would be back to square one, and you'd be looking for another investor."

"What about the other company?"

"DNAtech is a smaller company that specializes in DNA research. They have an enormous upside, and may at some point become a major player in the drug industry. Their spreadsheet is not overly strong right now, but three of their drugs expect to receive FDA approval. That alone can turn them into a twenty-five-billion-dollar company. Right now they're cash poor, so that's why they're offering you a large chunk of stock for Cold. In time, the stock might be worth a billion dollars. Of course, Dobler Pharmaceutical has already offered you two-hundred and fifty million in cash."

"What's the downside for DNAtech?"

"There's no guarantee they'll ever achieve their potential. A few bad bumps along the way and this company may need to merge or fight just to stay in business. If that happens, they'll be forced to sell off assets, which might include Cold, and there's little you'd be able to do to stop Cold from being sold to another company."

"I get the picture. Who would you select, Vanessa?"

"Well, Dobler has money, power, and global distribution, which is where Cold needs to be positioned. And Dobler writes you a check and you walk away. Clearly, that's the safest offer for you and the drug."

Vanessa sipped her tea and picked at her Greek salad. With little effort she had outlined the strengths and weaknesses of each company. But this was not the time to select a business partner. Peter was in a casket down the street, and the vision of him clouded my mind. It had been a long day. My eyes burned and my body ached. I needed sleep more than food. "What do you say we get out of here?"

"Hold on. You were going to tell me about Bastianich."

"I'll tell you tomorrow. I'm burnt out tonight."

"You can't leave me hanging. Not after telling me he'd been killed."

Vanessa looked up, surprised.

"All right, then. I feel fairly certain that Peter didn't kill himself. I had spent an evening talking with this man, and he was as passionate as anyone I had ever met. This morning I went to the morgue and spoke with the pathologist who performed the autopsy. He told me that after his team had taken a closer look, they found scrapes and bruises on Peter's body not attributed to jumping off a building."

"Bastianich fell six stories, how could they tell?" Mitch said.

"The pathologist said Peter had finger mark gouges on his neck and arms."

"My God! Strangled in broad daylight?"

"Police are questioning people in the neighborhood to see if they saw anything. But there's something else." Mitch and Vanessa leaned closer. "His larynx had been crushed, which shows he was strangled first, then carried to the roof and thrown off."

A piece of food got stuck in Mitch's throat.

"You okay?" Mitch turned red as a beet, and managed to swallow it down.

"This is not good. I have the feeling I'm going to end up on someone's hit list or on a slab somewhere."

He gasped for air and I got him to his feet knowing the best thing for an anxiety attack was to get the person moving and breathing. "Okay, outside now."

Vanessa looked dumbfounded. It was a side of Mitch she had not seen. I handed him his coat and tossed a twenty on the table.

"A pattern is developing here!" he said. "I know things are only going to get worse."

"Try to stay calm." I pulled Mitch's collar up when we stepped outside. It was four degrees and steam rolled off his neck. Vanessa coiled her body to fight the wind. She was quiet and distant. I thought that if she had any affection for Mitch, she would have shown it at this point.

We wanted to get back to Manhattan but, as expected in snowy weather, there's never a taxi when you need one. I wished Eddie had been there for us, but he was no longer my driver. This afternoon, after my visit to the morgue, I informed him that his services were no longer needed. It was not fair to drag him into this mess. And, I thought, Mitch's anxiety attack was justified. Danger *was* around us. I felt it too. Mitch was right about another thing, too. Things were likely going to get worse, possibly much worse. I finally hailed a taxi and we returned to Manhattan.

Chapter Thirty-four

Rutger pulled a key from his pocket and unlocked the door. He went straight to the bedroom where he removed his clothes and slipped between the sheets, pressing up against her sultry back. He placed his hand on her thigh and slowly drew it up to her waist. Her fingers reached back and touched his cheek as his hand moved along the contour of her body.

Her breasts were warm and he kissed her neck. When his finger touched her lips she turned and faced him.

He rolled on top and her thighs opened. He wanted to penetrate her, but she resisted, teasing him. The more she resisted, the more it excited him, and with subtle, sensual force he pushed into her. She trembled and tightened around him. He lost control, and a moment later she did too. Her mouth opened and her head rolled back. Two bodies spent and motionless, the pounding of their hearts slowed to a quiet beat. It was the only sound they heard in the stillness and silence. His eyes met hers. She was sweet nectar to him, divine, light, and intoxicating.

He kissed her and sat up before lighting a cigarette. One long draw and he set it in the ashtray. He turned to Vanessa. "How did Jack react to the other offers?"

Vanessa slipped on her robe. "It's hard to tell. He needs to sleep on it."

"Was he impressed with either of those companies?"

Vanessa tied her belt. "Not especially. I presented the options just as you asked. I think he'll sign with you."

"Good. Things need to move quickly at this point. The attorneys have the contract ready, and we'll deliver it in the morning."

Vanessa winced and placed her hands on her stomach.

"Something wrong, darling?"

She sat on the edge of the bed. "My stomach's been tied in knots, and I was sick at work today. I can't do this any longer."

Rutger walked around and sat next to her. "We're almost there, darling. The contract will be signed soon."

"It doesn't matter."

Rutger pulled her close, so that her back pressed into him.

Vanessa looked up at him. "It's hell going into Rosetta every day. They treat me so well, and all along I'm—"

"Shhh. Don't torture yourself, darling. You'll only feel worse."

"I've decided to give Mitch notice."

Rutger stroked her arm. "If that's what you want, darling, then do so."

"I have no choice."

Rutger placed his hand on her forehead. "You may have a fever, darling. Have you anything in your medicine cabinet?"

"Nothing that can cure me."

He rubbed her shoulders. "Can we speak about this?" He helped her to her feet and walked her to the sofa in the living room. "I love you and would never ask you to do anything against your will. But these are difficult times and the drug industry is being transformed. Even our way of life will change if something isn't done. Grandfather has spent his life building this business, and I don't want to lose it. Can you give just a little more, darling? Stay there one week more?"

Vanessa pulled away and leaned into the sofa. "Okay, I'll stay one week more."

"Thank you, darling." He kissed her on the lips and held her close to him.

"It seems like ages ago that I first told you about Catherine's drug."

"It's only yesterday to me."

"When I told you about Catherine's research?"

"No, darling, meeting you."

"Oh, it's one year this week, to be exact."

"I know. It was my good fortune to attend the opera that night. And to find you."

Vanessa rested her head on his chest. "What are the odds of two people meeting at the opera and falling in love?"

"A million to one."

"Yes, I think so." Vanessa pulled his arms tightly around her. "I was all alone, and now I'm filled in every way."

"Are you tired, darling?"

"Not too. I heard something disturbing tonight. That man, Peter Bastianich. He didn't commit suicide after all. He was killed."

"How tragic. Have they any idea who did it?"

"I don't think so. I met his wife at the funeral home. It was just horrible. Jack said the man was thrown off a building."

"You look exhausted, darling." Rutger lifted Vanessa from the sofa and carried her back to bed. She closed her eyes and slept until morning. Rutger was already gone when she awoke. She read the note left on the nightstand. *I adore you, darling. See you tonight!*

Vanessa rolled out of bed to begin her day when a horrid thought flashed into her mind. Shortly after she had told Rutger about Cold, Catherine Lewis was killed. And the break-in at Rosetta had occurred the night after Catherine was killed. Vanessa walked into the bathroom and her foolish thoughts dissipated. Rutger would never harm a fly. These events were a coincidence. When she stepped into the shower she became sick to her stomach and ran to the toilet. The nausea did not leave and she decided to call her doctor, who told her he wanted to see her. Vanessa went to his office, and after her physical she waited in the reception area for the results.

"Vanessa, the doctor will see you now."

She walked into his office.

"Well, Vanessa, I think we've found the cause of your illness."

"Is it anything serious?"

"That depends on how you look at it."

"What do you mean?"

The doctor smiled. "You're pregnant."

Chapter Thirty-five

Eddie stared through the driver's side window and flashed me his wide smile. Behind that smile I was certain there was disappointment from being let go as my driver. I approached Colter, who was waiting at the curb in his vintage 1972 Alfa Romeo Montreal. Colter kept his car in meticulous condition. I climbed inside and he sped off. Peter Bastianich was going to be buried, and I had promised Raija that I would attend. Mitch hated funerals and his nerves had gotten the best of him, so Colter had agreed to drive me there.

Colter and I arrived at St. Mary's and joined a handful of people in the church. The Mass lasted forty-five minutes, and when we left the church we followed the funeral procession to the cemetery. Colter parked his car alongside a galvanized chain-linked fence. We walked a short distance and joined the small group of people that encircled Peter's casket. The Brooklyn-Queens Expressway was less than fifty yards away, and there were moments when the priest's voice was drowned out by the noise of the cars and trucks speeding by.

Colter leaned over. "It doesn't really matter, I suppose, but this cemetery would be my last choice."

The casket rested on four shiny brass rails. Two silk straps ran under the casket to lower it into the ground when the time came. The mound of dirt removed from the grave had been piled like a pyramid and covered with a carpet of green AstroTurf, probably in an effort to lessen the pain of family members who might not want to see the dirt destined to encase their loved one.

Only a dozen people squeezed under a canvas canopy to join the priest in a prayer. Raija stood on the other side and motioned for me to join her. I had shown up on the second day of Peter's wake, as well, and spent time with Raija. I was there out of respect for Peter, but again, to try to make contact with any scientists that might show up. Not one attended his wake, and when I looked around the cemetery, not one of them had come to his funeral either.

Raija was fragile, and I found myself monitoring her every move. She held my hand tightly, and also the hand of the woman standing on her other side. The priest began a prayer and a new pain found Raija's face. I feared she was on the brink of failure. She had been able to remain close to Peter's body for two days, but on this morning she would leave this cold, barren cemetery without him. There was a whimper when she stepped forward and laid her hand on the casket. "Peter! Peter! My Peter!" Her body trembled and she was on the verge of collapsing. I reached out to steady her with one hand while my other hand rested on top of the casket. The image of Catherine rushed into my mind, and in that moment I was now attending Catherine's funeral. The prayers spoken by the priest were for her. The weeping of those gathered around the site was also for Catherine.

The cemetery began to spin. I felt Raija's arm wrap around my waist and bear the full weight of my body. We stood, each supporting the other, and each with one hand touching the casket, as if drawing strength from both the living and the dead.

Colter walked over. "Do you need help with her, Jack?"

I looked down at Raija. She smiled at me reassuringly. "I think we're okay."

After the service, Raija guided me into her limousine. "Come to the house and eat with us, Jack. You're very weak."

"I would like to, but I have to be in Manhattan."

She took my hand. "Don't push so hard. I asked Peter not to push, but he never listened. Now the drug people have taken my daughter and my husband."

Her words surprised me. I had spent two evenings with her at the funeral home and could not bring myself to ask questions. She had now just opened the door to that possibility. "Did Peter ever discuss his involvement with the other scientists?"

"No. He kept everything from me, but I knew what he was doing."

"Have you ever met any of the others?"

Raija looked at me with worn eyes. "I know what you want, and why you came to the funeral. But I have nothing to give you."

I couldn't tell if she knew more than she was saying. I wanted to ask another question, but she had lived through her share of tragedy. So I ended the discussion there.

"I need to go." I stepped out of the limousine and stood firmly on my own two feet. I took a couple of steps before turning back. "Take care of yourself."

A smile crossed her face. "Be careful."

Colter was waiting at the car for me. "How is she?"

"She's fine. Can we drive for a while?"

He gunned it out of the cemetery and took the entrance ramp onto the Brooklyn-Queens Expressway. I opened the window to allow the cold air to hit me. Soon the cold hurt, but it felt good. My face went numb all too quickly, however, so I rolled the window back up. "I screwed up. My head's throbbing and I left my pills back at the Towers. I won't have time to get them before my meeting with Rutger."

"Cancel it. You're in no condition to meet with anyone."

"Mitch will be there and I promised we'd go through the contract with Rutger. Take the Williamsburg." Colter sped across the bridge and down the Bowery. "Pull over." I jumped out. "I need to walk a while."

"I'll walk, too,"

"No. I need to clear my head."

"Before you leave ..." Colter reached out and took hold of my arm. "Another clinic is getting rave reviews for their cancer treatment. This one's in Arizona. You could fly there in three hours and get evaluated. Maybe stay a day or two for treatments, and you'll be back in New York in no time. You'll only be away from the investigation for a short while. Jack, you can't afford to waste any more time."

"You gotta stop, man. I have a grade IV tumor. It's malignant. It won't stop growing or spreading. Now, please, just stop it!" I turned and walked away. It was bad enough that Mitch hounded me with his talk of cryonics, and now Colter with his cure-all clinics. I needed to walk, maybe all the way to Dobler Pharmaceutical. Walking made my head feel better, and it helped me to think, too.

It angered me that Peter's friends had not attended his funeral. Where was the concern and outrage over his death? Not a single bastard had shown up to pay his respects. If I were them, this would be a coming-out party. I'd rally thousands from the research industry and have them carry protest signs all the way to the Capitol. I could see them now: *Don't Let*

Bastianich's Death Be In Vain, Free New Drugs, and *Down with Corrupt Drug Companies.*

Chapter Thirty-six

My head was back on straight after the long walk. I was cold and my teeth were chattering, but I had reached my destination. Over the edifice a billowing, white cloud hung in the blue sky. The sun appeared unexpectedly from behind it. Its warmth, even for a brief moment, felt good on my face. I entered the building.

My cheeks were flushed and burning when I entered the office of Dobler Pharmaceutical on the forty-sixth floor.

"You can wait in the conference room, Doctor Lewis. I'll let Mr. Dobler know you're here."

I removed my coat and looked around the room. On the wall was a picture of a man and a young boy. Though taken years ago, the boy was clearly Rutger and the man Heinrich.

"Jack." Rutger entered and extended his hand. "My God, man, you're half-frozen."

"I should've worn gloves."

We sat across from each another as Rutger's receptionist carried a pot of coffee into the conference room. She poured it for us and left the room.

"How's your grandfather?"

"As healthy and irascible as ever," he said with a smile. "Thank you for asking."

"Have the police found out anything more?"

"Yes," Rutger turned serious. "They know how the gunman entered the estate and managed to leave without being seen. Our security was focused on the front gate, but the gunman came from the sound. They tracked a set of footprints down to the water where markings showed that a small boat had been dragged out of the water and hidden there. The gunman left the same way he came."

"Any suspects?"

"No one, yet. The police said the gunman entered the mansion and perched on the balcony over the ballroom. When the lights went out, he fired. Gun powder residue was found on the drapes and the floor there, but we don't know who pulled the trigger."

"The truth will come out. It always does."

"I hope you're right. It's horrible to think someone can walk into your life, violate you and your family, and get away with it," Rutger said.

"Yes, it is."

The conference room door swung open and Mitch and Vanessa walked in.

Rutger rose to his feet. "Welcome."

"Good to see you, Rutger. You remember Vanessa Boulay, my chief administrator."

"I certainly do remember. You attended my grandfather's birthday party. How are you, Vanessa?"

"Just wonderful. Thank you for asking."

"Make yourselves comfortable."

Mitch and Vanessa sat next to me across the table from Rutger.

"If you don't mind," Rutger said. "I'll save us all valuable time and get right to the core of this agreement. Cold works in vitro. It's our contention that if the drug can destroy viruses in a test tube, it's not far from also working in humans. Of course, the agreement covers the possibility of the drug not reaching its potential, something I believe is unlikely. If that occurs, however, you keep any agreed-upon down payment, but the contract will become null and void at that point." Rutger handed us a copy of the agreement.

I spent the next five minutes flipping through the pages. "I don't see any mention of the biotech that will be needed for ongoing research."

"We didn't think it necessary to include a research partner in the agreement."

"It's important to know that Cold will be given every chance to succeed. That requires a top-flight biotech."

"Well, I do understand your point. We can look into putting a team together."

"Assembling a team of scientists doesn't guarantees success. A team with a track record, and one that has worked on this drug would be much better."

Rutger glanced at Mitch and then back at me. "Are you suggesting Rosetta?"

"Yes. They're qualified, I trust Mitch, and his staff works well as a team."

Rutger jotted it down. "I don't see a problem with this, and I don't believe our attorneys will either. I'll have them revise the agreement to add Rosetta."

"Thank you," Mitch said. "We'll get this drug working for you."

"I have every confidence that you will." Rutger looked across at us. "Now, here's how we would like to proceed. Dobler Pharmaceutical purchases all rights to Cold. Upon contract signing, you receive a check for five million. Once the drug proves effective, we'll pay the remaining two hundred and forty-five million."

"I prefer structuring it differently," I said. "Make the initial check for one hundred twenty-five million, with the balance due upon Cold proving itself."

Rutger never blinked. "Here's what I'll do. I'll pay you ten million upon signing the agreement, seventy-five million when the drug is fully effective, and the remaining hundred and sixty-five when Cold is released to the marketplace. I should add, these terms will only be available if you sign this agreement within the next seventy-two hours."

I looked at Mitch and then Vanessa. They both nodded for me to accept the offer. "Well, we have a deal then. Make the check payable to The Catherine Prescott Lewis Foundation."

Rutger hesitated for a moment. "All right, the check will be made out to your foundation," he said, writing it down. We stood up and shook hands. "I'll have the revised agreement to you first thing in the morning. As we walked to the door, Rutger walked beside me. "This gives you a level of financial security that few men know, Jack. I hope you live a long life and enjoy it. "

"Thank you. That would be nice."

Chapter Thirty-seven

Isaac was bent over examining the gene marker sheet when I entered the downstairs laboratory. He looked up. "If Catherine left a message, she did a good job of hiding it."

Mitch barreled into the laboratory. "Jack! Upstairs. *Now.*"

I hurried after Mitch to the upstairs conference room.

"Look at that!" A bead of sweat rolled down his forehead as he pointed out the window.

I looked out over Washington Square Park and saw a group of NYU students watching a chess match. A skinny dope dealer whispered to people passing him on the street. There was a police car parked in the middle of the square with two cops inside. From where I stood, it looked like they were eating doughnuts. To me, everything looked perfectly normal in the park.

Vanessa heard the commotion and ran into the room. "What's going on?"

"I knew I was being followed the other day," Mitch said. "Well, *that's* the guy right there."

"Where?"

"The guy in the blue coat sitting on the bench."

"Are you sure?"

"I caught him checking out our building the other day. And when I went to lunch, he followed me. Now he's back in the park again."

Given Mitch's edginess over the past several days, I was skeptical about most everything he said. For his sake, however, I thought it better to err on the side of caution. "Is the front door locked?"

"The front door is always locked," Mitch said. He picked up the phone and called downstairs. "Make sure the front door is locked, and don't let anyone into the building."

"Are you sure that guy's been following you?"

"Positive. I know that face, and he's wearing the same clothes. Watch how he'll stare at our building."

"He's leaving," Vanessa said.

"Don't worry. He'll be back."

We waited five minutes and the man never returned. I didn't know what to make of it all. "Well, he's gone and I've developed an appetite. Anyone want anything from the deli?"

"Don't go out, Jack, Wait a while. He's still out there."

"I'll just pick up a bologna-on-white for you, then. That'll snap you out of it."

"Stop joking around. I'm telling you, don't take any chances."

I walked out of the room. Mitch remained at the window looking out at the park. I exited Rosetta through the back door, since it was the shortest route to the deli. Halfway through the alley, a sound caught my attention. I looked around but no one was there. When I turned back, the man in the blue coat was standing in front of me. His hand slipped into his coat pocket. Instinctively, I protected myself. There were two empty garbage cans nearby, so I grabbed one and hurled it. The man ducked and I grabbed the second can and threw it, hitting him in the head. While the blow did little to hurt him, it caused him to lose his balance and slip on the ice. I heard a thump when his head hit the ground. He was motionless when I bent down and placed my finger on his neck. I felt a pulse. As I went through his pockets and removed a .22 caliber pistol, he moaned and started to come around.

"Who sent you here?" He did not respond. "Answer me!"

"Uh, Jack Lewis."

"I'm Jack Lewis."

At that, the man passed out again. I stuck the gun in my pocket and carried him over my shoulder back to Rosetta. The receptionist let out a scream when I set him down on the floor in the foyer. Mitch, Vanessa, and most everyone in the building came running to see what had happened. I propped him up against the desk, then reached into my pocket and pulled out the gun. I had forgotten to check if it was loaded.

"Don't shoot him, Jack. It's not worth it," Mitch said running down the stairs.

"I'm not shooting anyone. I'm going to question him." I held out the gun and Mitch took it. "Put it some place safe." I slapped the man's face, but it did no good. Vanessa ran to my side with a glass of water and a towel.

"That's one big bump on his head," she said.

I splashed water in his face, but it failed to revive him. Vanessa helped me carry him into the downstairs laboratory, where we sat him in a chair. Mitch walked into the room as the man's eyes opened.

"Who sent you here?" I said. "And why are you carrying a weapon?"

"No one sent me. The gun is for protection."

"It's against the law in New York City. You know that, right?" Mitch said.

I looked at Mitch. "Can I ask the questions?" I looked at the man again. "How do you know my name?"

"Your name—I don't know your name," the man said, still groggy.

"It's Jack Lewis."

"Lewis, yes. I was given your name."

"By who?"

"Raija Bastianich."

"How do you know Raija?" The man stared into the distance. "And what's your name?"

He looked around at everyone. "Robert Farrington,"

"You're Farrington? Why don't you have identification?"

"I don't carry it. Someone is after me."

"What's Raija's husband's name?"

"Peter."

"What's their daughter's name?"

The man came more alive with that question. "Their daughter is dead."

"What's her name?"

"Her name was Tanya. She died a year ago from encephalitis. I know because I developed a drug that might have saved her."

I looked into Farrington's eyes. "My God, man, what happened to you?"

He straightened up in the chair. "I've managed to stay alive. When Peter was killed, I told Raija not to expect me at his funeral. They would look for me there. Raija said you were Peter's friend. You would know what to do. I've wanted to get out of New York, but now they've killed Peter and I'll never leave. I'll kill them, or they'll kill me."

"Who? Who's chasing you?"

"A large Japanese man is out there."

"Is he behind all this?"

Farrington looked up at me. "Peter didn't tell you?"

"Tell me what?"

"It's the Doblers. Heinrich and Rutger. And they killed Peter, too."

The water glass shattered on the floor, and Vanessa ran from the room.

Chapter Thirty-eight

Rutger called Vanessa twice and each time his calls were sent to her voice mail. "Darling, have you forgotten our dinner date? They told me you left work early today. I'll wait for you at the restaurant. Love you." He sat alone at the Four Seasons for another forty minutes, and when Vanessa failed to show up, he ordered off the menu.

Rutger returned to the Pierre but was too restless to work or relax. He decided to go to Vanessa's apartment. He let himself in and called out to Vanessa as he stood in the living room. There was no answer so he walked down the hallway and into her bedroom Her closet door was open and he saw that a large amount of her clothes were missing, along with the large suitcase that was kept there. A small, empty suitcase lay open on a side chair, as if Vanessa had planned to pack more clothing, but changed her mind at the last moment. Rutger returned to the living room and tried to make sense of it all. When he sat on the sofa he noticed a prescription lying on the coffee table. *Take one vitamin each day during the first trimester of pregnancy.*

The words Rutger read astounded him. Vanessa had never mentioned this. He waited in her apartment and fell asleep on the sofa. When he awoke at five a.m., he saw that Vanessa had not returned. He went back to the Pierre for a change of clothes and was at his desk by six.

When the telephone rang, he grabbed it. "Hello?"

"Good morning, Rutger. Randall Whitestone here. You're in bright and early."

"What can I do for you, Randall?"

"I'd like to stop by in, say, twenty minutes or so?"

"Is everything all right?"

"Yes. A few points of clarification, that's all."

"By all means, come up." He hung up and walked into the executive men's room. One look in the mirror revealed his stress over Vanessa's disappearance was taking a toll. A splash of cold water helped his burning and bloodshot eyes. When he returned to his office, he was surprised to see Whitestone already waiting there.

"Good morning, Randall. Coffee?"

"I can't stay." He sat in the chair across from Rutger's desk. "Let me get down to it. I met with the others last night to discuss your Five Point Plan. A few questions came up and I promised to get answers for them. I guess I'm the unofficial spokesman for the group."

"That's good to hear. We'll work well together."

"While we all agree your Five Point Plan makes sense, I'm sure you can understand that no one wants to get dragged before a Senate sub-committee either."

"If you're looking for guarantees, there are none. But the plan is solid."

"On paper most plans are solid," Whitestone said. "In real life, companies get crucified for carrying them out. The question is—can we block the biotechs and expect to get away with it?"

Rutger walked to the window and stood with his back to Whitestone. "We're not trying to get away with anything. Let me explain it to you once again. First, each company submits its quota of drug applications to the FDA. Second, let Congress increase the application approval cost. Third, support special interest groups that are opposed to genetic engineering. Fourth, help the FDA to expand their jurisdiction over foreign drugs. And fifth, buy up all promising new biotech drugs. There is nothing to fear about any of this."

"You don't think a group of multinationals putting a billion dollars into a slush fund will draw attention?"

Rutger turned and faced him. "It's called venture capital, Randall. It's what drives free enterprise in this country."

Whitestone scratched the back of his neck. "It sounds reasonable."

"The beauty of it, Randall, is that it's the American way."

"I got it. Let me discuss it with the others. It should give them a greater level of comfort hearing it explained that way. Oh, one more thing. About that Cold drug—we'd like to make it community property. You know, as a gesture of good faith on your part."

"We didn't discuss making this drug community property at our meeting. If you or any of the others want to purchase it, no one's standing in your way."

"So, the heat's on your grandfather then?"

"I'm not sure I understand what you're inferring."

Whitestone chose his words carefully. "I've known your grandfather a long time. He must be working at a fever's pitch to buy that Cold drug before joining forces with us."

Rutger walked to his office door. "Have a pleasant day, Randall."

"We'll just see what happens, then." Whitestone walked out.

Rutger sat behind his desk for nearly an hour, all the while expecting Vanessa to call. She never did. He walked down the hall to his grandfather's office.

"Good morning, Son."

"Randall Whitestone was here this morning."

"What the hell did he want?"

"He's the spokesman for the others now. He had questions about the Five Point Plan, but he really came with an ulterior motive. He wants Cold to be community property."

"What did you tell him?"

"To go buy it then."

"Good, but watch out for him. He's a liar and a crook. He'll stab us in the back the first chance he gets. I learned that fifty years ago when he spread more than a few lies about me."

"He attacked you at the meeting in front of the others. He said you murdered some man and stole millions from him. A man named Schneggenburger."

"He's a spiteful old man. Now, let's discuss some real business. Has the Cold contract been drafted?"

"It'll be delivered to Jack Lewis this morning."

"Make sure it gets signed today. I want to close the door on Whitestone. I'm sure he's got something up his sleeve. Now, Son, I've got work to do."

Rutger stood up to leave, but didn't move. Heinrich looked at him. "Is something else bothering you? You look troubled, Son."

"It's nothing. I didn't get much sleep, that's all." Rutger returned to his office and called Rosetta. "Vanessa Boulay, please."

"She's not in today. May I take a message?"

"No thanks." Rutger hung up the phone as Daniel Von Hoff poked his head through the doorway.

"The downsize meeting starts in five minutes. I'll be in the boardroom."

"Hold up. I'll walk down with you." Rutger started out the door when his secretary called.

"Vanessa on line two."

He ran behind his desk and motioned to Von Hoff to go ahead. "Vanessa, where are you?"

"I'm in the city."

"What happened to you last night?"

"I stayed at a friend's. Upstate."

"A new friend?"

"No. A girlfriend." She paused. "I won't be seeing you anymore."

"What? I can't believe that. Why?"

"Does the name Robert Farrington mean anything to you?"

"Farrington, sure, I know the man. What does he have to do with us?"

"I don't think you want me to discuss it on the telephone."

"Then meet me, darling."

"That's not a good idea."

"I don't know what you've heard, but you're not taking the word of a madman over mine, are you? Please meet me."

"The damage is done. Farrington told us how you and your grandfather masterminded everything."

"Farrington's a disturbed man. Grandfather and I did everything in our power to help him. His mind is gone, and he's turned into a vengeful person. He even came to the office last week and threatened the staff. My receptionist is afraid he'll come back. Lunatics are convincing because they believe what they say. Let me come and get you."

Vanessa hesitated. "I don't know. I'm tired and haven't slept since yesterday."

"Listen to your heart, darling. What does it tell you?" Vanessa did not answer. "Where are you? I at least deserve a chance. Tell me where you are."

"The Brasserie."

"Stay there. I'm leaving now." On his way out, Rutger motioned for Von Hoff to step out of the meeting. "Something's come up. I have to leave. Make sure the Cold contract gets into Jack Lewis's hands this morning." As Rutger raced to the door his receptionist held up a telegram that had just arrived for him. He opened it.

Attention: Rutger Dobler
The Catherine Prescott-Lewis Foundation has decided not to sell our drug Cold to Dobler Pharmaceutical. Let this letter serve as the final correspondence between our companies.
Jack Lewis

Chapter Thirty-nine

Vanessa was seated at a corner table and Rutger sat down next to her. She pulled away when he leaned over to kiss her, so instead, he took her hand.

"You're the most important thing to me. You must know that."

"I know you care," she said, avoiding his eyes.

"What exactly did Farrington tell you?"

"How you stole his drug. How you promised to get FDA approval, but never did. And how his drug would never reach the market because you have an inferior one that makes a lot of money. And then you hired a Japanese gang to do your dirty work."

"Listen to yourself! Can't you see he's disturbed? Did he mention that grandfather and I gave him money to keep a roof over his head?"

"You've had his drug for two years. Why hasn't it been released to the market?"

"We don't control the FDA. They dictate which drugs get approved and which do not. They're especially careful with drugs that affect the brain. We've spent millions on his drug. Does that sound like a conspiracy to keep it off the market?"

Vanessa hung her head. "I can't think about it any longer."

"Can we go somewhere? Anywhere. My car is outside."

"No, I need sleep. You can drop me at my apartment."

Rutger helped her into his car. Vanessa's eyes closed and her head fell on his shoulder. He placed his arm around her until they reached her apartment. "I'll take you inside."

"No. I need to be alone."

"I'll call you later, then."

"Don't call me. I need time to think."

Rutger was silent. "Of course, darling. I'll wait for your call."

Rutger instructed his driver to take him to Chinatown. He pulled out his cell phone and dialed the number given to him by Jito Sumataika.

"Hello." A man with a deep voice answered.

"It's me," Rutger said.

"Yes."

"I'm coming up. Make sure we're alone." Rutger had his driver drop him on Mulberry Street, and he walked from there to Yashida's building on Mott Street. For the first time, he questioned whether Tsai and Jito Sumataika had told him the truth about Catherine Lewis' death. The six o'clock news showed the face of an Asian man as he exited the back door of Memorial Hospital. This man, along with two other Asians were the only people captured on video the morning Catherine Lewis had been killed. Minutes after they left her laboratory she was found unconscious and beaten. As Rutger reached Yashida's building, the evidence had become clear and undeniable to him.

It was a five-story climb to the top floor. The door opened and a large presence stepped aside to let him enter. Yashida closed the door and when he walked across the floor the windowpanes rattled. He placed a chair in the middle of the room for Rutger, and then lowered his massive body onto the floor in front of him.

"Robert Farrington," Rutger said. Yashida lowered his eyes. "He's escaped you more than once. Find him. Tonight! Do you understand?"

"Hai."

"I'm going to ask you a question, Yashida, and it's important you tell me the truth. If you keep the truth from me, I will be forced to terminate my relationship with the Sumataika. Information has been released about the woman killed in the hospital. I know Jito is an honorable man and wants to protect me from knowing certain things. I respect him for that, but it's time I know the truth. An Asian man without his mask showed up on the hospital surveillance video leaving the hospital that morning. He was one of yours, wasn't he? And the Sumataika killed her, didn't they?"

Yashida lowered his eyes once again. He didn't say anything, but he nodded his head, and for the first time Rutger knew the truth.

"Thank you, Yashida. Thank you for the truth." He pulled out a piece of paper and wrote down a number of items. "Here. I need this business completed. Do you understand?"

"Hai."

Chapter Forty

"Let him stay here for now," Mitch said. "My staff is here during the day, but he'll be alone at night." He looked out the window. "It's time to call the cops. We can't protect him."

"What are you going to tell them? That Rutger Dobler and his grandfather stole Farrington's drug and hired a Japanese thug to kill him?"

Farrington overheard the conversation and begged us not to give his name to the police. In his mind it offered the Japanese man another avenue to find him. Then Farrington began to cough. Even though he was not a smoker, his hacking made him sound like a three-pack-a-day man. It sapped what little strength he had in his body, and he finally closed his eyes and passed out. We left the conference room and pulled the door shut. On the way to Mitch's office we tried to figure out a long-term solution for Farrington, because crashing on the couch in the conference room was not the answer.

Mitch walked to the window and looked up and down the street. "I still say call the cops, especially if that Japanese guy is looking for him. And who knows? Farrington may not be the only one he's after, if you get my drift."

"Calm down, Mitch. You know what happens when you get excited. Besides, I have my reasons for not wanting to call the cops." I removed a letter from my pocket and tossed it on his desk.

Mitch picked it up. "You're kidding me. Gravers completed his investigation on Catherine? It'll remain an unsolved crime?"

"Well, at least he advised me to hire a private investigator."

"Speaking of that, have you heard from Julia?"

"Not a word. I've left three messages for her, but I haven't heard back. She said she'd be back in New York in four days. Well, today's day four. Wait a minute. I just got an idea." I reached over and picked up the phone. "The day Julia left for Chicago I called Tuttles and asked for his help. He told me the FBI had no jurisdiction over Catherine's case, and that's what the NYPD gets paid to do. But if Catherine's case was tied to public corruption, terrorism, or white collar crimes, then the FBI would be obligated to investigate. Farrington's story opens that door very wide for us."

"Now you're talking, Jack!"

"John Tuttles, please."

"Your name, sir?"

"Jack Lewis."

"I'm sorry. John Tuttles is out for the holidays."

"When is he expected back?"

"After New Year's. Can someone else help you?"

"You wouldn't know how to reach Julia Marshant, would you?"

"Marshant, let me look. I'm afraid she's not listed in my directory. Does she work for us?"

"No. I just thought you might know how to reach her."

"Can I help you with anything else, sir?"

"I don't think so. Thank you."

"Have a Happy New Year, Mr. Lewis."

The telephone was still pressed to my ear when she hung up. "Tuttles is on vacation, and Julia has dropped off the face of the earth. That pretty much sums it up." I looked at Mitch. "Any bright ideas?"

"Call the cops." He reached into his drawer and pulled out Farrington's gun. "And if they won't protect us, we've got this."

"You'll hurt yourself." I reached over and took the gun from him. "Just our luck, a lousy .22-caliber pistol." I laid the gun on the desk and looked across at Mitch. "Sorry you got pulled into this mess. You had asked to stay out of it." Mitch didn't say anything, but he looked resigned to the situation. As if some force had latched onto him and was dragging him down a dark hole. I felt the same way, but my circumstances were different from Mitch's. I stood up and now it was my turn to pace and look out the window. "Let's accept the fact that we'll probably be on our own."

"I've been telling you that all along."

"Okay. So let's deal with one problem at a time."

"I agree. That's a good idea."

"Now, how do we trap Rutger?"

"Trap him? Did I hear you correctly? We're the ones being hunted."

"Maybe not. To us it might seem that way, but he's the one who's keeping those drugs off the market and who hired those thugs that killed Bastianich and Catherine. We need to put our detective hats on. "

"We're not detectives. Julia is the one who's highly trained in those skills. The only detective work we can do is look through a microscope at tiny things floating around. Please don't drag me into your scheme of trying to trap Rutger. Just leave me out of it."

"All right, I'll keep you out of it." Mitch leaned back in his chair and breathed a sigh of relief. "I'm going downstairs to see how Isaac is coming along with locating a message from Catherine."

Isaac was busy at work when I entered the laboratory. "Anything yet?"

"Nothing." He handed me the disc that detailed all the sections of the chromosomes he had covered to this point.

"Thanks. Mind showing me the process you're using to look for her message?"

Isaac led me to the workbench. "I'm using the Southern Blot technique. Chop the individual chromosomes into 6-cutter lengths and apply agarose gel to separate the fragments. Stain the gel with ethidium bromide to visualize the DNA fragments under ultraviolet light. By soaking each DNA strand with a re-neutralized solution, I keep them from re-annealing. I then immobilize the fragments from diffusing by blotting them onto the nitrocellulose membrane. When they fixate, I see the results."

"That's the way I would do it."

"You know, it would make my job easier if I knew the type of message Catherine might have left you."

"Good point. Her messages typically ended with 'Love always, Catherine.' Look for that pattern. Here, let me write it out for you:

5'...CCCCCCGGGTTTTAAAAAACCCCCCTTTTTATTTTTTTA
AAATTCCAAA AAGGGGGGCCCGGAAAAA...3'

Mitch stormed into the laboratory. "Jack, I need to see you outside."

"Give me five, Mitch."

Mitch waited in the hallway and looked frazzled when I finally joined him. I followed him upstairs and into Vanessa's office. I noticed all of her personal possessions were gone except for a piece of paper on her desk. When I walked over and looked at it, I saw it was a letter of resignation from her.

"She just took off? Without speaking to you first?"

"That's only part of the story." Mitch called his secretary into the room and asked her to repeat what she had just told him.

"Well, some man kept calling for Vanessa, but he wouldn't leave his name. So the last time he called I pressed star-six-nine on my telephone. A woman answered "Rutger Dobler's office.""

"Rutger and Vanessa?"

"And to think I introduced them," Mitch said.

I sat on the corner of the desk. "Maybe not, Mitch."

Mitch dismissed his secretary. "What do you mean?"

"Remember Heinrich's party? When Vanessa and Rutger danced, and looked so natural together? I'd say they already knew each other."

"I don't remember them dancing. I was in the men's room puking my brains out."

"It all makes sense. It's the missing piece. Catherine must have told Vanessa about her research, and Vanessa told Rutger. She was the mole planted here."

Mitch looked as though his heart had been ripped out. "I won't believe that. Vanessa would never deceive me like that. I know her." He took one more look around the empty office. "Let's get out of here. I'll throw up if I stay in this room."

We walked into Mitch's office and he slumped into his chair. "How did Vanessa ever get involved with someone like Rutger?"

Mitch's secretary walked into the room. "Jack, there's a call for you. Shall I transfer it in there?"

"Who is it?"

"Rutger Dobler."

You could hear a pin drop. I motioned for Mitch to let me sit behind his desk. I let the telephone ring twice before picking it up. "Why are you calling me?"

"Hello, Jack. I received your letter and was disappointed that you changed your mind about selling Cold."

"Did you kill my wife?"

"I beg your pardon?"

"Did you *kill* Catherine?"

"I did not kill anyone."

"You killed Bastianich, too, didn't you?"

"I never met the man. Nor did I kill him or anyone else for that matter. And before you destroy what little relationship we have left, you need to hear me out."

"I suppose you're going to tell me that Farrington's a confused man."

"Jack, someone's given you a poison pill to swallow, and you need to hear the truth. Meet with me so we can talk this over."

I placed my hand over the mouthpiece. "He wants to meet and tell his side of the story. What do you think?"

"Don't go," Mitch said. "It might be a trap."

I looked at Mitch a moment longer, and then removed my hand from the mouthpiece. "All right, Rutger. One meeting, just this one time."

"Thank you, Jack. You've made the right decision. Come to my office tomorrow afternoon."

"I'd rather you come here."

"I would, under normal circumstances, but the information I need to share with you is here. I can't transport it to Rosetta."

I thought it over for a moment. "All right, then. I'll be at your office at four p.m. sharp. You'll have ten minutes." I hung up.

Mitch placed his hand over his heart. I thought he was having a heart attack. "He did it. I could hear it in his voice." I looked at my watch. "I have to leave. Make sure this place is locked up airtight tonight. And leave a note for Farrington. He's not to leave the building for any reason." I stood up to leave.

"Hold on, Jack. I'm going with you to Rutger's office tomorrow."

"No. I want to be alone with him."

"Not a good idea. I'm going."

"Stay at Rosetta tomorrow. What if someone tries to get in here? What if Farrington needs you? A lot could happen tomorrow."

"All right, I get your point. But promise me you'll come straight to Rosetta after your meeting with him."

"I'll come back afterwards. And don't forget to lock this place down tonight." On that note, I walked out of the room. When I reached the front door, I heard Mitch yell down the stairway.

"Damn it, Jack. You took the gun, didn't you!"

Chapter Forty-one

"I'll need your driver's license and a major credit card, Ms. Boulay."

Vanessa tossed them down and waited for the rental agent to run her card through the machine.

"All we have left is a white Cadillac Seville. Will that do?"

"It'll have to."

The agent hit a button and the rental agreement streamed out of the printer. "That's our last car rental of the millennium." The woman smiled.

"My lucky day," Vanessa said.

"You'll find your car in space fifty-four. The key is in it."

Vanessa picked up the agreement and walked out. Twenty minutes later she pulled under the marquee of her apartment building and popped the trunk open. The doorman carried two suitcases out to the car.

"Just throw them in."

The gray-haired doorman gently laid her luggage inside the trunk. "Mr. Dobler called again. He asked if I knew where you were."

"Did you tell him what I told you?"

"Yes. That you've gone on an extended vacation."

"Is that all of it?"

The doorman thought for a moment. "Oh, your garment bag." He stepped lively back into the lobby as Vanessa waited by the car. She took the garment bag from him when he returned and tossed it on top of her suitcases, and then slammed the trunk closed. She pulled out a fifty-dollar bill and handed it to him.

"That's a lot, Ms. Boulay."

She tucked the bill into his lapel pocket and then kissed his cheek. "Happy New Year."

"Thank you, Ms. Boulay, and Happy New Year to you."

Vanessa stepped into the car, closed the door, and pulled away.

"Oh, Ms. Boulay," he yelled, waving his arms to get her attention. Vanessa never looked back.

"Darn it. I forget to ask when she was coming back."

Chapter Forty-two

Tsai returned to his hotel room and packed for his flight to Tokyo. He was grateful to Rutger for allowing him leave New York. He called his wife and gave her his arrival time, then double-checked the room to make sure he had left nothing behind. With suitcase in hand he stepped into the hallway and did not see the large presence standing against the wall. An arm reached out, latched around his throat, and dragged him back into the room before the door had time to shut. Tsai dropped his suitcase and tried to scream, but his air passage was closed. His efforts to peel back the fingers that were crushing his larynx were futile; he lacked the strength. Tsai tried to turn and face his attacker, but the fierce grip on his neck held him stationary. His lungs screamed for air as he weakened. He then crashed to the floor, dead.

Chapter Forty-three

"A call on line two, Mr. Dobler."

"Who is it?"

"He wouldn't give his name, but said it was important he speak with you."

"Hang up on him."

"Yes, Mr. Dobler."

Rutger's secretary rang back a moment later.

"What now."

"The gentleman told me to say it was about the sale of Cold."

He picked up. "This is Rutger Dobler."

"I'm interested in selling you a drug that I've developed. I believe you know it as Cold."

"Who is this?"

"I'd rather not say, but I will talk to you about Cold."

"I have no interest in speaking with anyone who won't tell me their name. Besides, I already know the people who developed Cold, so consider this conversation o—"

"Before you hang up, you should know that I am the creator of Cold. I am also in negotiations to sell the drug to your biggest competitor."

Rutger wanted to slam the telephone down, but he didn't. "Who is this?"

"You'll receive all the information you need in due time. That is, if you're interested in becoming the *legal* owner of Cold."

"What makes you the legal owner?"

"I worked alongside Catherine Lewis, and it was my breakthrough that perfected the drug."

"Your voice sounds familiar. Have we met?"

"I'll only remain on this call if you're interested in purchasing Cold."

"What's your proposition?"

"Seventy-five million dollars."

"You must be insane to ask for that kind of money!"

"You're already prepared to pay three times what I'm asking and, just so you know, I filed for the patent on Cold."

"Can you substantiate that?"

"Of course. If you're willing to pay me $75 million. Here's how we'll proceed. You have twenty-four hours to transfer the money into my escrow account. Otherwise you'll be disqualified, and I will negotiate with your competitor."

"It's too short of a timeframe to get that amount of money."

"Come on now, your bankers are at your disposal. We both know that."

"I'll need proof that you own Cold."

"You'll have it soon. What I'll be sending is a more advanced version of Cold, where viruses are unable to attach themselves to the surface of a human cell."

"Who else are you talking to about this drug?"

There was a brief silence on the telephone. "Randall Whitestone, for one."

"So, Randall managed to find you?"

"No, I found him."

Rutger's fax machine kicked on and several sheets of information poured out—a copy of the pending patent and a diagram of the chemical design. The name on the filed patent appeared to have been obscured by a magic marker. Rutger checked his watch and saw it was after five p.m., the time the patent office closed. That meant there would be no way to research the information until Monday. The mystery caller had planned every detail. "I won't do business unless we meet."

"We will never meet. Transfer the money into the escrow account, and my attorney will meet you at your New Jersey plant. Feel free to bring your scientists to authenticate the drug, but remember, you have twenty-four hours to transfer the money. Otherwise, Randall Whitestone will be the drug's new owner."

"You've orchestrated this very well, haven't you?"

"I believe so," the man said.

Rutger heard a click. He hung up and began reading through the patent. The information was legitimate, and the drug had been described in great detail. Rutger hurried down the hall to his grandfather's office and laid the patent information on his desk.

"What's this?"

"The patent filed for Cold. Jack Lewis doesn't own it."

"What?"

"I just hung up with the owner. He wouldn't give his name."

Heinrich looked over the information. "It looks like a legitimate filing. But why wouldn't he tell you his name?"

"I don't know. He wants $75 million for the rights to the drug, and we have twenty-four hours to transfer the money into his account. Otherwise, Randall Whitestone will buy Cold."

"Whitestone? He's involved? I told you he would worm his way into our business."

"This is your call, Grandfather. I'm prepared to walk away from it. Under the circumstances, maybe we should."

"And let Whitestone rub our face in it? I can't bring myself to do that."

Richard Bognar

"I'm not giving up now. I want it."

"All right. I'll make arrangements for the money transfer, but there's another problem."

"What's that?"

"Jack Lewis. He's on his way here."

"Cancel the meeting with him."

"I could, but the more I think about it, the more sense it makes to meet with him. Lewis believes we're responsible for his wife's death. The last thing we need is him going to the Attorney General. When he arrives I'll do my best to convince him we played no role in that. If I fail to convince him, and he threatens to go to the authorities, we may be forced to take other measures."

Heinrich hung his head and thought it over. "Make sure he doesn't hurt us, Son."

Chapter Forty-four

"Let's not waste a lot of time talking nonsense. Speak your piece so I can get out of here."

Rutger took a seat at the table and lit a cigarette. "For reasons I don't understand, Jack, you've taken the word of a madman over mine."

"Robert Farrington is probably the sanest man I know."

"He hasn't told you the truth. He's lied about everything; he can't help himself."

"So far, you haven't convinced me of anything. But maybe you can answer a question for me. How long have you and Vanessa been together?"

202

Rutger looked me straight in the eyes. "If I am guilty of anything, Jack, it's not disclosing my involvement with Vanessa. I met her before she ever worked at Rosetta. With my family name so widely known, Vanessa and I agreed that, for the time being, we would keep our relationship private. Small biotechs like Rosetta might try to leverage Vanessa's influence to reach me. That kind of thing would be uncomfortable for her and for me. I hope you now understand the reason we kept our relationship a secret."

"Did Vanessa tell you about Catherine's work?"

Rutger stamped his cigarette out. "Let's assume Vanessa did mention Catherine's work to me. Does that make me guilty of killing your wife? I just offered you $250 million for the drug. I would have offered the same to Catherine. Your argument appears to be that, because I had prior knowledge of the drug's existence, somehow that indicts me of killing her. Well, that argument doesn't hold up. Dobler Pharmaceutical is a $40-billion company. Why would I risk everything over one drug?"

"Then why did Vanessa leave Rosetta without a word?"

"I didn't know that she had left. She hasn't returned my calls."

"Frankly, I've heard enough, especially about your love life."

"Hold on, Jack. You came here to see information I've compiled." Rutger opened a folder and pulled out a stack of paper. "Farrington said that my grandfather and I stole his drug and never developed it. He said our intent was to keep it off the market." Rutger placed a sheet of paper on the table. "This printout is from our research department. It shows the investment we've made in Procelium. Look at the bottom line. Twelve thousand man-hours spent on it already—that's four scientists working around the clock for an entire year. Our investment on Procelium is well over $5 million."

"Numbers on a sheet of paper mean nothing to me. It doesn't change the fact that Procelium never received FDA approval and that it's not yet commercially available."

"Not true, Jack. Procelium received FDA approval two weeks ago. We expect it to be on the market in three months."

"Does Farrington know that?"

"We can't locate him."

"He was in your office less than two weeks ago, and you threw him out."

"He was here, Jack, but he was irrational, and I had no choice but to have him escorted from the building. My grandfather and I are distraught over the way things have turned out. Our hope is that the money from Procelium will help him get the treatment he needs."

"Why would Farrington fabricate this story?"

Rutger lit another cigarette and looked across the table at me. "Pathological liars lie. When we met Farrington, he told us Procellium was fully tested and only required FDA approval. We believed him, but then the truth came out—Procelium required millions of dollars of investment in order to gain FDA approval. Farrington manipulated us, and he's manipulated you. He knows you're going through a difficult time and he's using you the way only a madman can. We're both victims, I'm afraid."

Rutger had an answer for everything. I almost found a sick sense of pleasure in asking him a question, just to hear him manufacture another answer. "And what about Bastianich?"

"I never knew the man. He only came to my attention from the story in the newspaper."

Rutger continued to defend himself as I slid my hand into my pocket and wrapped it around the .22-caliber pistol. A scene from *The Godfather* flashed into my mind. Michael Corleone had just rejoined two other men at their dining table after finding a gun that had been planted for him in the men's room. Like me, he knows someone is speaking but barely hears a word because the pounding in his chest is much louder. In the movie, Corleone pulled out the gun and killed both men at short range. He dropped the gun and walked out of the restaurant. I sat across from Rutger, the man responsible for Catherine's death. He deserved to die, too.

Chapter Forty-five

The door to the conference room swung open and Mitch burst into the room. Rutger's receptionist was right behind him. "I'm sorry, Mr. Dobler. I asked Mr. Cochran to wait until I announced him, but he—"

"It's all right. Mitch is welcome to join us."

Mitch was breathing hard and beads of sweat showed on his upper lip. He looked first at me, then across the table at Rutger, and then down at the object protruding from my pocket.

"How you feeling, Jack? Can we speak a minute? You mind excusing us, Rutger?"

"By all means. I'll be down the hall in my office."

Mitch reached into my pocket and pulled out the gun. "Are you nuts?"

"Shhh." I pointed to the ceiling and walls.

"The room's bugged?"

I signaled to Mitch to step out into the hallway with me. Even after making sure no one was within earshot, I still kept my voice to a whisper. "It wouldn't surprise me if the entire building was bugged."

"I don't care about that. Why did you take the gun?"

"I was angry. I wanted to shoot him. I thought I could, but not in cold blood."

"Of course you couldn't. Only a real killer does that."

"Look, Rutger's spent the last half hour trying to convince me he had nothing to do with Catherine's death and that Farrington's insane. No matter what I ask him, he has an ironclad answer for it."

"Do you believe him?"

"Not for a moment."

"Let's get out of here, then."

"Not yet. Not before we trip him up. That's where you come in. Ask him some tough questions. You can't do any worse than I did."

"Do I look like Perry Mason to you?"

"Don't joke. Just try to drag the truth out of him. Be belligerent. I don't care. We've nothing to lose at this point."

"Jack, I'll crack before Rutger does."

"Just try to trip him up. Will you do it?"

Rutger was waiting back at the conference table when we returned. "I hope we've cleared things up today, Jack. Can we put this mess behind us now?"

My mind was turning into mush. I think my stress level had spiked and caused me to spiral downward to the point where I had become quite useless. Mitch had sat down next to me. I looked at him and saw an expressionless face. "Do you have something to say, Mitch?"

Mitch swallowed. "Yes, I have a couple of things." He cleared his throat. "You've been busted, Rutger. It was a big mistake hiring that Japanese gangster to kill Farrington. We found out who he is and where he lives. Pretend all you want, but when Jack and I go to the Attorney General, you're going to fry for murder, along with your Japanese goon."

Rutger sat calmly and listened. "But I don't know any *Japanese goon*, to use your vernacular. And you don't know what you're talking about."

"You keep thinking that, but that goon's going to pin this rap on you. We won't stop until you're strapped in the chair." Mitch leaned forward. "You're responsible for Catherine's and Peter's deaths. How many others have you murdered?"

Rutger stood and walked to the door. "Consider this meeting over, gentlemen. And, let me add, we are no longer interested in purchasing Cold."

Chapter Forty-six

Mitch and I hurried down Fifth Avenue not knowing what had just happened. "Yesterday, Rutger would have killed to get his hands on Cold, and today he walks away from it?"

"Slow down, Mitch. You're walking too fast." I stopped to catch my breath.

"Are you okay?"

"I don't think my brain's working too well right now."

We flagged a taxi and went back to Rosetta. It was dark outside when we arrived, and everyone had left for the day. We checked on Farrington, who was sound asleep on the upstairs couch. Mitch went around and turned off the lights. Afterwards, we walked to his office, where he reached into the top drawer and pulled out a bottle of Jameson Whiskey. He looked at me to see if I wanted a drink.

"Sure, why not. Pour me one."

He poured two shots. "Bottoms up."

Mitch drank his down. On second thought, I put my drink down. I could tell my mind had started firing on all cylinders again, and I wasn't going to do anything to chance it spiraling downhill at that point.

It was quiet in Mitch's office when a loud cracking sound startled us. Someone had just kicked in the front door to the building. We heard footsteps coming up the staircase.

"What's that? Did you lock the front door?"

"You came in last. I thought you locked it."

"Where's the gun?"

"Don't you have it?"

"You took it from me at Rutger's, remember?"

"Shit. It's in my coat pocket downstairs."

"Shut off the light."

The footsteps reached the top of the landing and started down the hallway. The door to Mitch's office was cracked open and I saw the presence of an enormous man walk past. He went to the end of the hall, to where Weber's office was located. We heard another cracking sound when the man kicked Weber's door open.

"It's him," Mitch whispered, "the Japanese goon. Let's run for it!"

Mitch ran out of the office and down the stairs. I hesitated for only a moment, but by the time I reached the staircase, the Japanese giant was behind me. He grabbed my shoulder and when I pulled away, I stumbled down the stairs and ended up on my back in the foyer. A hand reached down and gripped my neck. In the dark I kicked at him. The grip was vice-like, and I was lifted off the ground and slammed into the wall. I heard someone yell out, *"Release him!"* At that, the man's grip tightened on me, and I heard a gunshot. When his grip loosened, I fell to the floor. I then saw the giant turn and run out the door.

Someone was standing in the open doorway, but the streetlight from behind had blinded my vision. A silhouette of a tall, slender woman came into focus. She slipped her gun into her holster and placed one hand on her hip. I recognized that posture. "Julia, is that you?"

Chapter Forty-seven

Blood flow through my carotid arteries had been impeded and oxygen wasn't reaching my brain. Although dazed from the attack, I slowly regained my senses.

"Farrington! Help me find him, would you?"

"Is he a skinny, scared-looking man? If so, he ran out the front door just before I shot the giant."

Farrington was once again on the streets, but this time without his weapon. Mitch returned to Rosetta at about same the time the police arrived. He had run out of the building at Olympic speed and had run for five blocks before realizing I was not behind him. Two hours later the police had compiled all their information and left Rosetta. Only Julia and I remained in the conference room.

"How did you end up at Rosetta tonight?"

"You didn't get my message? I tried you at the Towers, and when I didn't reach you there, I left a message with Mitch's receptionist that I'd meet you here tonight."

"No. We didn't check messages when we returned." I looked over at her and was almost afraid to ask the looming question. Her response would either drive me into a deep depression or raise me to a state of euphoria. "Does this mean you're back on the case?"

"Well, I just shot someone for you, didn't I?"

That answered that question. A weight had been lifted off my shoulders. "Yes, you did." In spite of her response, I still allowed other feelings to surface. "Why didn't you return any of my calls?"

"I got them, and I apologize for not getting back to you. I also promised to mail you a background check on the Doblers, but haven't had time to do that, either."

"Don't bother. I know everything I need to know about the Doblers."

"Well, I bet there are a couple of things you don't know. But, there's been enough excitement for one day. I can tell you later."

"Actually, I'd like to hear them now."

"My people ran across this story while doing the Dobler background search. It begins in Heidelberg, Germany, where Heinrich Dobler lived as a young man. He was involved in one of that country's most publicized scandals of the 1950s. Most of what I'm going to tell you can be found in the public records there. Heinrich was a top salesman for a small pharmaceutical company owned by a man named Herr Schneggenburger. One morning, Herr Schneggenburger's body washes up on the banks of the Neckar River. After the burial, his widow Emma asked Heinrich to take the reins of the company. Three years later the company goes bankrupt. Shortly after that, Heinrich moves to New York and starts Dobler Pharmaceutical. That's when the scandal erupted. Emma accused Heinrich of murdering her husband and embezzling millions from the company. Nothing was ever proven, and over time the charges against Heinrich faded away—but the story doesn't end there. Emma Schneggenburger hung herself after losing everything. Five years later, her daughter Katrina hung herself in the very same room where her mother had taken her own life. That left only Alexander, the younger son, as the sole family survivor. He went on to become a well-known German scientist, and openly expressed his bitterness toward Heinrich. He swore that Heinrich would one day pay for his crime."

"It's an interesting story, but where's all this going?"

"Here's the important part. You once asked me to follow Franz Weber, to see what he does, where he goes, etc. While I was out of town I called a detective friend of mine and had him follow Weber. After Weber left Rosetta the other night, he went straight to a target range."

"Target range?"

"That's right. He was there for two hours. According to my friend, Weber's quite the marksman, or the next best thing to it."

"Weber and guns? I can't imagine his chubby little fingers pulling a trigger."

"Well, they can. And they did, repeatedly. He was never off target more than a hair on any of his shots. It gets even stranger. After he left the target range, he put on a pair of sneakers and jogged back to his apartment."

"Now I know you're putting me on."

"It's true. Weber may not look it, but he's in excellent physical condition. I might be stretching it a bit here, but I think it's fair to say Weber is using a false identity. We also know he's a brilliant scientist. I know for certain, too, that Alexander Schneggenburger disappeared from Heidelberg around the same time Franz Weber showed up in New York. I've asked a friend at the Bureau to produce a photograph of Alexander Schneggenburger. That will either prove or disprove my theory."

"Are you saying Franz Weber shot Heinrich Dobler at his birthday party, and he did it because of a fifty-year-old vendetta?"

"I can't say that with one hundred percent certainty. But I'll have a photograph in a day or two and we'll know then."

"This is all too much to believe. What are the odds Weber, or Schneggenburger, or whatever the hell his name is, ends up at Rosetta?"

"Actually, good odds," Julia said. "How many biotechs are located in Manhattan?"

"I don't know. Not many, I suppose."

"That's right. Biotechs can't afford Manhattan rents, so only a handful are located in the city. And if Schneggenburger wanted to stay close to Heinrich Dobler, where would he go? He'd work at a company in the city. I'm not a gambler, but I'll bet the odds of him ending up at Rosetta are pretty good."

I squeezed my temples with the palms of my hands to momentarily release the pressure that had built up. "These last four days haven't been a walk in the park for me. Leave it to Weber to complicate matters more." I pressed on my temples again. "I'm sorry, but I'm a little irritated right now, even though I know I shouldn't be. I can't help my anger from bubbling up, and some of it's directed at you. I should be grateful I survived being killed."

Julia stood up. "I think we're both tired, and a little rest wouldn't hurt either of us. Let's talk later tonight or tomorrow."

"Let's touch base later tonight, then."

"Sounds good. What if I told you I've got something that's going to blow you away? I'll stop by tonight."

"Wait. Tell me now!"

Julia grabbed her bag and headed for the door. "Get some rest, Jack."

Julia was halfway out the door. "Oh, and..." I said. She stopped and turned around. "Thanks for saving my life tonight."

A small smile crept onto her face. "Don't mention it."

Chapter Forty-eight

Jimmy called up from the lobby. "Sorry to disturb you, Doctor Lewis. Hotel security was throwing this loiterer out, but he says he's a friend of yours."

"What's his name?"

"Phil Farber."

"I don't know anyone by that name."

"That's what we thought. These bums tell us anything just to keep outta the cold. Sorry to disturb ya, Doc."

"Wait a minute, Jimmy. What does he look like?"

"Blonde hair, skinny, kinda raggedy clothes, and smells to high Heaven."

"Bring him up, Jimmy. I want to look at him."

"Are ya sure?"

"I'm sure."

Five minutes later there was a knock on the door. I looked through the peephole before opening it. "My mistake, Jimmy. I do know this guy. How are you, Phil?"

"So ya know him after all?"

"Yes, I do."

"Well, I'm glad I called up, Doc."

"Do me a favor, Jimmy. Order up a couple of steaks with all the fixings, and some fresh coffee, too."

Jimmy looked at Phil Farber, then back at me. "You got it, Doc. I'll make sure they're thick ones, too."

"Who's Farber?" I asked Robert Farrington after Jimmy had left.

"A guy I went to school with in Boston. Anyway, thanks for taking me in. And, uh, I hated running out when that giant grabbed you last night. Guess I panicked."

"I would've done the same." Farrington stood before me and I saw him in a different light for the first time. He was no longer just someone I needed in order to help catch Catherine's killer, but a living, breathing man. A man who had been stripped of his dignity, nothing about him was deranged. He was worn and tired. His body needed nourishment and his head a place to rest. Someplace secure. Beneath his drab exterior there was not only a brilliant mind but also a human heart.

"Jump in the shower, Robert, our food will be here soon. We can talk after we eat."

Robert was embarrassed, diffident, as if it had been a while since someone had offered a little kindness. I could tell he wanted to say something, but instead, he walked into the bathroom and closed the door.

The food arrived and the porter placed it on the table. Farrington was still in the middle of a steamy shower when I went into the bathroom, gathered up his clothes, and carried them out. "Can these be cleaned?"

The porter looked them over. "They're in pretty bad condition, sir, but the guys downstairs have been known to work a miracle now and then."

"Do the best you can." The porter took the clothes and left. I placed some of my own clothing in the bathroom for Farrington to wear.

Farrington cracked open the door. "Hey, where are my clothes?"

"Put those on for now."

He emerged from the bathroom a minute later. "Hope you don't mind, but I used your razor."

"Come and sit down." I removed the silver dome covering his plate. It was worth a million to see the expression on his face. "Hope you like steak, Robert."

"I'd forgotten how good a steak can smell." He ate voraciously. Neither of us spoke until we had finished our meal.

"Who are the others?"

"Others?"

"Bastianich told me there were other scientists."

"Oh, you mean the underground. That's what we call ourselves— better known as the-scared-to-death-of-the-multinationals scientists. The interesting thing is we've never met as a group. Bastianich knew everyone's identity and kept it confidential. No one expected he'd be killed."

"So you don't know the names of anyone else?"

"Not one of them. When Bastianich spoke to me about joining, we met alone, and then he reached out to the others and told them a new member was onboard. Once the underground was strong enough—and we felt safe—we'd meet and take action against Dobler and the other multinationals."

"What about the evidence to indict them? Where's that?"

"I don't know. Peter said the Doblers kept it in a vault somewhere, but he wasn't sure where."

The phone rang. It was Jimmy. "Those clothes you gave the porter won't be ready until later this evening, Doctor Lewis. I just wanna let you know."

"Is that men's store in the lobby still open?"

"Not for much longer. It's New Year's Eve you know."

"Would you come up and escort my friend down there? Let him pick out whatever he wants. Make sure he gets a warm overcoat, a hat, gloves, shoes, and a pair of dark sunglasses. Come up as soon as you can, Jimmy." I hung up.

"What are you doing, Jack? You've already done enough for me."

"Look, Robert, you're a sitting duck in those old clothes, and I need you alive. Your story is important and people need to hear it. One of us has to survive this mess and tell the world what the hell's going on."

Farrington stood up and walked over to me. "I know we can take them down, Jack."

I stood up. "I believe it too, Robert." A look of determination came to his face.

"We're in this together. Like brothers, right?" Farrington coughed a couple of times, and there was a knock on the door. It was Jimmy.

"Don't let him out of your sight. And remember, warm clothes and dark sunglasses."

After they left, I was certain Farrington was sick. No one can survive winter on the streets without food and shelter, and it had made his body anything but healthy. The best place for him was in a hospital.

Jimmy brought Farrington back an hour later. Sporting a pair of light gray slacks, a black turtleneck sweater, and a dark gray sport coat, Farrington looked like a new man. Draped over his shoulders was a black shearling coat. He slipped on his Ray-Bans and hat to show me his complete outfit.

"I'd never know you if we passed on the street."

"Pretty good, huh, Doc?" Jimmy smiled.

"Thanks, Jack. I don't know what to say." Farrington reached out to shake my hand, but another coughing spell stopped him short. This time his hacking was relentless. I sat him on the sofa and got him a glass of water. His face turned beet red from the coughing which abruptly turned into a wheeze.

"You all right, Robert?"

"It comes and goes. I'll be fine in a minute."

Only a respiratory infection causes that type of coughing. When I saw some blood trickle from his nostril, I knew something had to be done.

"Jimmy, I need one more favor."

"Just name it, Doc."

"Get Eddie to bring the Iron Lung around and take my friend to the emergency room. And Jimmy, tell Eddie to pick him up at the service entrance."

Jimmy looked at Farrington, then back at me. "Sure, Doc, I'll do that for you."

"Give us a minute, will you?" I scribbled some information on a piece of paper and handed it to Farrington. "I'll be working to get to the bottom of this while you're in the hospital. If something happens to me in the interim call this number and ask for John Tuttles. He's a Director at the FBI. Tell him everything."

Farrington stopped coughing long enough to get a word in edgewise "You're going after the Doblers without me, aren't you?"

"You're sitting this one out, Robert. You can join the fight once you're healthy again."

Farrington was dispirited. "Guess I've been sick for a while and didn't want to admit it to myself." He looked up at me. "Thanks again for the clothes." He waited a moment longer. Finally, he said, "Good luck." He shook my hand and walked out of the apartment with Jimmy.

My mind was getting mushy again, and this time my vision had begun to blur. In spite of the hour, I called Doctor Frankfort and caught him as he was about to leave the office. He told me to come straight over. When I arrived he examined my eyes. The blurring was from my deteriorating visual cortex. The largest system in my brain was losing its ability to process visual images. At some point, the doctor said, colors would change to black and white. In the final stage, I would only see black, and this condition would not reverse itself. It meant my time was coming near. I left Doctor Frankfort's office and returned to the Towers.

Chapter Forty-nine

Rutger grilled the doorman at Vanessa's apartment building. He found out that Vanessa had rented a Cadillac Seville and departed Manhattan. He called his investigator and gave him the information with orders to locate her whereabouts. All Rutger could do now was wait to hear back from him.

"Excuse me, Son, you busy?" William Dobler said, sticking his head into Rutger's office.

"No, Father. Come in, please."

"Your mother and I wanted to know if you had plans for New Year's Eve."

"I have tickets to the opera, but I don't believe I'll be going."

"I see. Then how about joining us tonight? After all, it'll be 2000, the start of a new century, and we'd love to spend the evening with you."

"That would leave Grandfather alone at the mansion. Maybe I can stop by tomorrow."

"Your mother hasn't seen you since his birthday party. Stop by, just for a little while."

Rutger looked at the stack of papers on his desk. "If I can finish all this at a decent hour, I'll try to stop by."

"Your mother would be thrilled. We'll be up late, so just come when you're finished." William observed his son gazing past him and out the window. "Well, Son, we'll plan to see you tonight then."

Rutger looked back at his father. "Yes, I'll try and make it." William left the office and Rutger walked down the hallway. Some events were about to take place, critical events that Rutger had decided not to share with his grandfather.

"You busy, Grandfather?"

"Come in."

Heinrich looked up at his grandson. "You've decided to get rid of Lewis."

Rutger was startled. He hadn't planned to have this conversation, but his grandfather had always been prescient, or maybe he had perceived something in his face or body language when he walked into the room. "I'm not sure we have a choice."

"You're still involved with the Sumataika, aren't you, Son. It's all right. I'm not angry with you for keeping it from me. You need to start making hard decisions on your own. That's how I learned. I just don't want you to go through life haunted the way I've been. I'm eighty years old and that Schneggenburger incident still hangs over me after all these years."

"Would I be overstepping to ask what really happened in Germany?"

Heinrich twitched, his eyes darting across the desk. He looked uncertain. Then, as if giving into something much larger than himself, he pushed his back in his chair and looked blankly up across the ceiling. "I never thought I'd tell this story, though I suppose I've always wanted to tell someone. It was so long ago. I was only twenty-two at the time. I had come off a farm and exploded into the business world. People told me I had a gift for sales, and in no time I helped turn a small company into one of the largest drug distributors in Germany.

"Herr Schneggenburger and I were good friends then. But with success came greed. He decided to incorporate his company, but made it clear that I was not to receive any of the stock. I felt I deserved something for all my work, so I confronted him. He admitted that my sales and marketing had been instrumental, but nonetheless, I would never hold an ownership position in his company. He stripped away everything. To argue with him was useless. One night, I was alone with him in his office. As usual, we argued, and I walked out half-insane. There was a large sink in the back room, which I filled to the top before calling him. This was a man I had once loved like a father. But I was in a blind rage that night, and when he entered the room I overpowered him. He fought hard, but I was younger and much stronger. Once the inner tube was wrapped tightly around his neck, he was at a severe disadvantage. I dragged him over to the sink and pushed his head under water. I held it there until he stopped fighting. Then I drove to the Neckar River and dumped him there, where his body washed up on the rocks the next morning. The newspaper reported it as an accidental drowning. In the weeks to come, Emma, his wife, asked me to take the reins of the company. I took them and everything else I needed. A year to that day I broke my ties with Germany and came to America. That's when I started Dobler Pharmaceutical."

Heinrich looked at his grandson. "Do you hate me, Son?"

"No, Grandfather. I could never hate you."

"My hope is that you never experience what I've been through, Son."

"I don't want you to worry. I know what needs to be done."

"I know you'll handle it." Heinrich looked at Rutger with admiration. "I'm leaving early tonight to avoid the New Year's traffic. They've predicted massive gridlock in the city."

"I have two tickets to the opera. Are you up for it?"

"I'll be more comfortable in Connecticut. Will you come home tonight?"

"Of course." Rutger stood to leave.

"Is she gone, Son?"

Rutger was surprised that his grandfather knew. "I'm trying to find her. Interestingly, we met one year ago today at the opera." Rutger turned to leave.

"Son," Heinrich said, "Keep a clear head. You still have the Lewis problem to deal with."

Chapter Fifty

Brilliant fireworks lit the sky above Manhattan while mobs of people crowded the streets. People had come to the Big Apple from all corners of the world to celebrate the new century. It was six p.m. on December 31, 1999, and in six hours the new millennium would be born. From my window I watched droves of people rushing about, and tonight a half-million more would gather to watch the ball drop in Times Square. The much-anticipated event would not be celebrated again for a thousand years.

The front desk sent up a package. When I opened it, I saw it was from Mitch. I thought, *not another push from him on cryonics*. He requested that I read every word of the twenty-five page document. I lacked the desire to read or hear anything more on the topic, but Mitch had anticipated my reaction and begged me to read the document in its entirety on the eve of the millennium.

I sat down and started reading Mitch's essay. To my surprise, the subject of cryonics did not come up. Instead, Mitch expressed his vision of what the future holds. He spoke about the pace of technological change, and how its impact would deeply affect human life: *First, let me say that one hundred and fifty thousand people die each and every day on this planet. We accept this curse because we know nothing else. Death is a horrible disease that, in time, will no longer be tolerated. Death will be eradicated sooner than most people think. The technology of the last century pales in comparison to the technology we will witness in the new millennium. Alzheimer's, cancer, and most major diseases will find their end. Biotechnology, artificial intelligence, and nano-technology will merge in the next thirty years and pave the way for immortality. People in horse and buggies laughed when they saw gas-engined machines leave tire marks in piles of horse manure. The same occurred with the inventions of the Wright Brothers and Thomas Edison. Then came the computer, and few men were able to conceive of where these innovations would take us or how they would transform human existence. Now we are evolving faster than anyone could ever imagine, and immortality will soon be upon us. Accept it; it's true. Place yourself in a position where science can restore life to you, and..."*

I had read enough. The essay was turning into his cryonics sermon. I placed the document down and closed my eyes.

The telephone rang, and the front desk informed me that Julia was on her way up. When I opened the door she breezed right past me with a bottle of champagne in hand. She walked to the window and looked out. "Wonderful view, Jack. Southern exposure, too."

I joined her at the window. "Can I take your coat?"

"Not right now. I'm still a bit chilly, but you can pour me a martini."

"Gin or vodka?"

"Vodka. Dry."

I went to the bar and poured Absolut and vermouth. I dropped a couple of jarred olives in each glass. A minute later I went back to the window carrying two martinis.

"Happy New Year, Jack. It's almost here." She clinked her glass into mine and took a sip of her drink while exploring my face. "Are you in a better mood this evening?"

"I think so. I've been having mood swings lately, and when you didn't return my calls it bothered me. I shouldn't get so angry, especially with you. But sometimes I can't control it. Anyway, I apologize. I'm grateful you're back on the investigation."

Julia smiled. "I'm not the type to just walk away, Jack."

"I should have known you were just busy and working your other case, and that's why I didn't hear back from you."

"To be honest, you didn't hear back because we decided not to return your calls, Jack."

"You intentionally ignored my calls?"

"It wasn't me. The Bureau asked me not to call you back."

"What has the FBI to do with this?"

"After you left the message about Bastianich, I shared it with John Tuttles. That gave him the green light to assign an agent to your case."

"My case?"

"Well, Catherine's case. The FBI is involved now."

"Why didn't you tell me?"

"You seemed a little irritable earlier. And besides, Tuttles doesn't need your approval to go after Rutger."

"Wait a minute. You said you spoke to Tuttles? They told me he was out until after the New Year."

"Tuttles is never out. If he's not in the office, he's operating in the background somewhere. And right now he's trying to figure this mess out."

I picked up my martini and almost took a sip, but I caught myself and set the glass back down. "Where do we go from here?"

"I'm not sure. You know what *habeas corpus* is, right? We can't hold a suspect for more than twenty-four hours. We're not going to arrest Rutger until we have hard evidence to convict him. The FBI recorded your phone conversation with Rutger earlier, and that should help."

"At Rosetta?"

"Yes, at Rosetta. It would also help to find that vault filled with the biotech records that Farrington told you about. That's the kind of evidence we need to convict him."

"That's a good place to—wait a minute, how did you know about Farrington and the vault?"

"Tuttles bugged your apartment, too."

"Without my approval?"

"Remember that document you signed before I left for Chicago, the one that authorizes me to act on your behalf?"

"In the event I couldn't be reached. Isn't that what you said?"

"Technicalities, Jack. Tuttles took the document to a judge and got approval to place the bugs. I told him you would understand." Julia smiled.

I looked around the room. "Are we being recorded now?"

Julia pointed to the lamp. "Tuttles wants you to leave it there, if you don't mind."

"Do you have any more surprises?"

"No more surprises. But, there is a topic we need to discuss. Our plans for this evening."

"Plans?"

"It's New Year's Eve, and I have not made plans, mostly because of you." She removed her coat, revealing a cocktail dress. "So here I am, all dressed up and looking for someplace to go." Her eyes were intense and very much alive.

"I'm sorry. It's a bad time for me. I'm half out of my mind lately. And even if I weren't, I couldn't handle the craziness on the streets."

"Put on your tuxedo, Jack. And don't say you don't have one. I know you do because you wore it to Heinrich's party. It's New Year's 2000, and I desperately want to go to SoHo tonight."

"What's in SoHo?"

"Put on your tux and I'll show you."

"I'm not leaving this apartment tonight, Julia. And that's final."

Chapter Fifty-one

I wasn't certain how we'd ended up in SoHo, but Julia was on my arm and we were strolling down West Broadway. "Where exactly are we going?"

"We're already there, Jack."

"Where?"

Julia smiled in the midst of the huge celebration taking place—on the street, in apartments, and in the packed restaurants that lined the block. "Just think. It will be a thousand years before this night comes again. Don't you feel the magic?"

"I feel wind in my face. And it's very cold."

"Then we'll just have to find a cozy restaurant and order a bottle of champagne and some caviar." Julia lifted her arms skyward and let out a laugh. "I'll remember this night forever. It may be the most important night of our lives."

"I'd like to share your enthusiasm, but I don't."

She stepped in front of me and blocked my path. Her face moved close to mine. "You're spent, Jack. Can't you see that? You'd have a hard time even getting through multiplication tables right now. How do you expect to stand up to Rutger?" The intensity in her eyes never wavered. "So, starting right now, this very moment, I want you to clear your head of every depressing thought. Let yourself go. Let me do the thinking. Forget about Rutger and the investigation for just one night."

"The problem is, the more I try to clear my head, the more cluttered it gets."

Julia was distracted by something she saw over my shoulder. "Look. They're serving champagne at an art show in that gallery across the street. How charming."

I turned to look. "But it's a mob scene. Don't even think of going..." I turned back and Julia was gone. I caught a glimpse of her disappearing through the front door of the gallery. When I tried to enter, the security guard stopped me.

"May I see your invitation, sir?"

"I didn't know you needed one to—"

Julia leaned out the door with a glass of champagne in one hand. "It's okay. He's with me."

"Very well, madam."

When I entered, Julia swiped another glass of champagne from a waiter's tray and handed it to me. Before I knew it, she had vanished again. I walked into the main room of the gallery and saw her admiring a collection of large paintings that hung on one wall.

"Look at the red elephants. Beautiful paintings. And I love the names of each one of them."

"I've never appreciated art that much."

"How could anyone resist them, with their large, sagacious eyes? Look how they exit the ocean under a moonlit sky. The clouds are so disquieting. Do you see the way the moon reflects off the dark water? I think I understand what the artist is trying to say, Jack. My God! These paintings capture the life and death struggle of the elephant as we enter the new millennium."

Her enthusiasm was contagious. It opened my sense of wonder. What started as a casual glance at a few paintings had turned into a full examination of each work. The clouds were ominous in each of the paintings, and they intrigued me. My interest shifted to the treacherous ocean and the full moon, and how skillfully the artist had depicted them to create her message. Finally, and what I found most appealing, was the use of vermillion-red elephants to symbolize their threat of extinction. "I think you're right, Julia. A life and death struggle is taking place here. It looks like the elephants are going to walk right off the canvas." I looked over at her. "You amaze me. Where did you get such an eye for art?"

"Listen to the names of the paintings, Jack." Julia walked along the wall. "They're wonderful—'A Moonlit Night,' 'Once in a Blue Moon,' 'Watch for Them by Moonlight.' And these: 'Ancient Mariners', 'Threshold to the Millennium,' and 'The Dawning of a New Day.'"

One painting in particular fascinated me. When I stood directly in front of it and looked into the elephant's eyes, she looked back into mine, as if she were trying to say something to me. "This one is remarkable. I wonder what it costs."

"Excuse me, sir," a saleswoman said. "Would you care to hear more about C. J. Barnard, the artist?"

"Not really, just the cost of the painting."

"The painting is a good value, given the artist's rising-star status. Investment in her art now will be—"

"Just the price, if you don't mind."

"Very well. The larger paintings are twelve thousand, five hundred, and the smaller pieces are eighty-five hundred."

I looked once more at the painting that intrigued me. Julia's eyes widened when she realized what I was about to do. "I'll take this one."

"'A Moonlit Night.' It's an excellent choice, sir. Isn't the sky magnificent?"

"Yes, the entire painting is magnificent."

"Will you take the piece with you now, sir, or shall we send it?"

"Deliver it to the Olympic Towers Hotel, care of Jack Lewis."

"Very well. And how will you pay for it?"

I handed her my American Express card, and she walked to the register to ring up the sale.

Julia touched the frame and then turned to me. "What a spectacular way to start the new century, Jack."

"I don't think I ever appreciated art with this level of detail until tonight. It's quite astounding. Thank you."

The salesperson returned with my credit card and receipt. "Thank you, sir. It's a lovely painting. I know you will enjoy it."

On our way out, Julia swiped another two glasses of champagne to toast my new painting. She drank hers down with gusto. I brought my glass to my lips, but resisted taking even a small sip. We were outside once more, strolling down West Broadway arm in arm. I looked at Julia.

"How about some more champagne and a mound of caviar? I know someone in the neighborhood who keeps a stash on hand."

"I would die for some caviar right now."

La Vie En Rose was wall-to-wall people. We could barely get inside the door.

"Jack!" Michelle pulled herself away from a group of people and ran across the floor. She kissed us and then twirled herself around to show how stunning she looked in her form-fitting, platinum-colored dress. Michelle had had a glass or two of champagne and was ebullient. And she was stunning.

"Happy New Year, my darlings." She took us by the hand. "I had hoped you would come tonight. I saved a table for you."

"Monsieur Jack! You made it," Petrie shouted from across the room. He worked his way through the crowd. "See, Michelle? I told you he would come." Petrie followed us to the table to take our order and Michelle dashed back to greet more arriving guests.

"A bottle of your best Veuve Clicquot and a tin of sevruga."

Petrie grinned as he wrote down our order. "A fine choice on the eve of the new millennium. I'll only be a moment."

To say the crowd inside the restaurant was zany would be an understatement. Even Petrie seemed out of control. He aimed a champagne bottle at the bartender and let the cork fly. The bartender retaliated by throwing an ice cube at him. All in all, laughter filled the restaurant and it was delightful. Petrie returned and filled our flutes with champagne. Moments later a platter of sevruga caviar arrived, garnished with chopped eggs and onions, crème fraîche, and toast points.

"Happy New Year, Monsieur Jack." Petri backed away gracefully and disappeared into the crowd.

"I feel so alive," Julia yelled to me across the table, and then stuffed a toast point heaped with caviar into her mouth.

People poured into the restaurant to the point where it became impossible to move about. Julia emptied her flute like a sailor. I refilled it, and then refilled it again as she devoured the last of the caviar. We attempted conversation a couple of times, but the noise level hindered any chance for us to converse. I remembered Michelle had called and wanted to speak with me, so I looked around for her but she was nowhere to be found. A short time later I motioned to get Julia's attention. "You ready to go? I told Mitch if I made it out tonight, I'd meet up with him at Hell's Kitchen."

"Sounds like fun. Let's go."

I tried, to no avail, to get Petrie's attention, so we left without settling the bill.

West Broadway was mobbed, and with Times Square forty blocks away, I prepared myself for the challenge of getting there. "I don't think a taxi can get through this crowd," I yelled. "Looks like we'll have to walk."

"That's fine with me." Julia clutched my arm as we pushed through the crowd. About twenty blocks from Times Square everything came to an abrupt halt. No matter which way we turned the streets were gridlocked with people crammed tightly against one another. Julia tapped my shoulder and pointed to a mounted policeman who was steering his horse through the crowd. I waded my way over to him. "Why the jam up?"

"Too many people," the officer said. "If you're heading uptown your best chance is to cross over to the East Side." With that, he pressed his heels into the horse and moved through the crowd.

I had begun to tire, and the thought that something might happen to me in the middle of this crowd frightened me. "We'll never make it to Hell's Kitchen," I yelled to Julia. "Let's get over to the East Side and go back to the Towers. We can watch the celebration from there."

"I'm right behind you."

For thirty blocks we squeezed through what seemed like the largest collection of humanity ever to assemble on one piece of terra firma. The mob ebbed and then flowed. Bodies surged and bashed. I weakened, but then persevered. When we finally reached the Towers, we fought the crowd that filled the lobby. We were packed inside the elevator all the way to the forty-sixth floor. Julia looked dazed by it all. We finally pushed our way off the elevator as I tried to locate my apartment key.

"Open the damned door, Jack!" She pounded on my back.

"I'm trying to find the key."

She stuck both her hands into my pockets and pulled it out. "Is this it?"

I took the key and unlocked the door. In a rush to get inside, Julia pushed me and we toppled onto the floor just inside the apartment. She climbed to her feet and slammed the door shut. "This is good," she said. "This is very good." Her face rested against the door listening, as if waiting for a mob to break it down and get to us. Only when she was convinced the world was locked out did she lean her back against the door and slowly slide to the floor.

I watched her every move and then let out a laugh.

"What?"

I laughed again. "You, on the floor in your cocktail dress."

Julia looked down at herself and began to laugh. I rolled on the floor holding my sides. Every time our eyes met, we laughed louder. Then Julia looked at her watch. "Oh, no! It's two minutes to midnight!"

"Not possible."

"Don't just lie there! Open the champagne!"

I scrambled to my feet and ran to the refrigerator. I grabbed the cold bottle of *Tattinger* and popped the cork. "Glasses! I need glasses!"

Julia flung cabinet doors wide open. "Got 'em!"

As I poured the champagne it bubbled over the tops of our glasses and ran down the sides and onto the floor.

"You're spilling it all over!" She looked at her watch again. "Oh my God! ...five, four, three, two, one. Happy New Year!"

She clinked her glass into mine. After one sip she placed her glass on the counter, threw her arms around my neck, and looked into my eyes. Her kiss landed firmly on my lips as a loud roar surged from thousands on the streets below. I looked into Julia's eyes and saw something I had not seen in them before. I wouldn't label it love or desire or even passion, but then, I could not tell for certain what she was feeling at that moment. I did not blame her for wanting what millions of other people wanted at that very moment. It was, after all, a special night. I hoped she knew that for me to offer any affection, in any manner, was simply impossible.

Outside the window the cheering raged on. Julia pressed her lips against mine once again. Her body pressed against me and her eyes met mine again, this time to see if I felt the same attraction. Everyone was kissing at this very moment. Romance was in the air. It was New Year's 2000.

I remained tentative, and with that Julia pulled away and walked to the window. The last thing I wanted was for her to feel spurned. Perhaps the long walk back had exhausted her, or maybe she had had too much champagne. Whatever it was, her knees almost buckled but she placed her hand on the window to brace herself. There was a rumble of thunder outside, followed by the tapping of rain against the windowpane.

"Rain?" I asked. She did not answer. "The reflection of the rain on the window looks like tears on your cheeks."

A blinding flash of lightning lit the sky. The thunder rumbled, loudly at first, and then it softened, as if a distant cannon had fired a salvo across the sky. I crossed the room. Julia turned to face me, and I saw the tears were real.

"Jack, I...I..." Her knees finally gave out.

My arm went around her waist, catching her fall. I carried her into the bedroom and placed her on the bed. A lone tear ran down her cheek, and I wiped it away.

"I had much too much to drink. I'm so embarrassed."

"There's nothing to be embarrassed about." I touched my finger to her neck. "Your heart is racing."

"Oh, is it?" She took my hand and placed it on her cheek, and her eyes looked into mine.

"Julia, I can't, I—"

Her finger touched my lips. "Shhh. Don't say a word. I know." The corners of her mouth curled into a barely detectable smile. She tugged at me gently, and I lay beside her. We heard faint bursts of laughter from the street below. Julia lay still, listening to the sounds of the night until exhaustion from our long night had finally won out. I lay awake beside her and wondered what the new day would bring.

Chapter Fifty-two

Silver-white fog streamed up past my bedroom window, giving the sensation that the Towers was spiraling down toward the center of the earth. With far too much to think about, I had not slept a wink all night. Next to me, Julia was perfectly at peace. Her head had sunk into the pillow and was barely visible. The contour of her body was thinly veiled by a single white sheet.

I lifted myself from bed and walked to the window. Outside, I saw no visible sign of life. The tops of only the tallest buildings peaked above the thick, silver-white substance. The sudden warming had caused a massive thaw, and snow and ice had converted into a billowing fog that scaled the height of the Towers. I became transfixed by the opaque substance, watching it glide past the window. It had direction while I had none.

Julia never budged when the telephone on the nightstand next to her rang. It rang a second time and her face soured from the disturbance. To escape the piercing rings she rolled to the other side of the bed and buried her head under a pillow. I walked over. "Hello?"

"Happy New Year, Jack!"

"Morning, Colter. How was your New Year's?"

"Let me put it this way: Dreams *do* come true. Need I say more?"

"Were you with Margo?"

"No. I went out by myself last night and met a brunette at the Union Square café. We got to know each other over a bottle of champagne. I'll tell you the rest later."

"I get the picture."

"Now that it's a new year, I'm calling to see if you've considered the clinic I mentioned the other day. We can fly to Arizona for a day or two and see what the doctors have to say. I want you to do this, Jack. They have a breakthrough treatment that's getting a lot of press. If you won't do it for yourself, do it for me."

Julia heard me speaking on the telephone and she began to stir. "Can I call you later? It's not a good time for me right now."

"Sure, Jack. Call me back. I'll be here."

I hung up the telephone and looked across the bed. Julia was now awake. "How do you feel?"

"I have a hangover. Was that Colter?"

"Yeah. He called to wish me a Happy New Year." The telephone rang again. "Hello."

"Happy New Year. I thought I'd see you last night. What happened?"

"The streets were too crowded, Mitch, so we came back to the Towers."

"We?"

"Let me talk to him," Julia sat up and grabbed the phone. "Good morning, Mitch."

"Julia? What an unexpected surprise."

"Don't let your imagination carry you away. Do you have plans for today?"

"Not really. Why?"

"Some things may come down, although I'm not at liberty to discuss them right now. Most likely, none of it will involve you. But if needed, are you available?"

"I'll be home or at the office. Jack has both numbers."

"Good. Thanks, Mitch."

"Oh, before you hang up, I need to speak with Jack again."

Julia held the phone between us. "He wants to talk to you."

"I've got some good news and some bad news for you," Mitch said.

"Is this where you ask which one I want to hear first?"

"No. I'll just tell you. The good news is that Isaac located an area on chromosome '15 where Catherine left a message. The bad news is it'll take a little more time to extract, since Isaac left for Jamaica this morning. He won't be back for a week."

"I knew Catherine had left one, Mitch! But if Isaac's gone, how do we extract her message?" There was silence on the other end of the phone and that told me Mitch wasn't going to volunteer anyone else to find her message. "That's okay. Right now I've got bigger things to worry about. Thanks for the update. You were right. That's definitely good news." Mitch said goodbye and we both hung up. I didn't let on how disappointed I was about the work stoppage on Catherine's message. Certainly, with all the craziness I'd experienced since returning to New York, reading a final message from Catherine would have lifted my spirits significantly. It wasn't Isaac's fault. He'd done his best under the circumstances.

Julia looked at me with raised eyebrows. "What's this about Catherine leaving a message in Cold? You never told me about this."

"It happened the day you left for Chicago. I noticed scribbling on Catherine's file, and I remembered that she'd created a language to store messages in DNA. It's nothing to do with the investigation, but it would be a nice boost to be able to read anything she would've wanted me to see."

Julia stared at me a moment longer. "We'll talk more about this later." She stood up and wrapped the sheet tightly around her body. "I need a change of scenery." She walked into the living room and picked up the phone and dialed a number. "John, it's me."

I walked out to listen.

"Uh huh...yes...he's at the Pierre...want him to meet Jack here...your man will bring the equipment. Okay, John. I'll have him do it." Julia hung up and turned to me. "Tuttles wants you to call Rutger and set up a meeting."

"Why would I do that?"

"Tell him you want to clear the air. That you had thought about speaking to the Attorney General's office, but that maybe an arrangement can be made where both he and you walk away whole."

"No. I won't do it under any circumstance."

Julia picked up the phone. "Fine, then. I'll call Tuttles back and tell him not to send the agent over. That you're not willing to cooperate or help entrap Rutger for murdering Catherine." Julia began to dial the number.

"Hold on. Tuttles wants to entrap him?"

"What do you think? Tuttles is inviting him to a barbecue? A lot of people are working hard here. The least you can do is help out, unless you have a better idea?"

I took the phone from Julia and called the front desk. "Connect me to the Pierre Hotel, please....Hello, Pierre? Rutger Dobler, please. Tell him Jack Lewis is calling."

"Good morning, Jack. Happy New Year. To what do I owe the pleasure of your call?"

"Well, we ended our last meeting rather abruptly and I've had time to think things over. My first thought was to contact the Attorney General, but the more I thought about it, the more it seemed there might be a solution that benefits us both."

"What do you have in mind?"

"Can you come to the Towers? I'd rather not discuss it on the phone."

"I'll be in my office this afternoon. Why don't you stop by and we'll chat?"

"I have this thing about large, empty buildings. They make me nervous."

"Sounds as though we've reached an impasse."

"How about some place neutral—*La Vie en Rose*, around six p.m.?"

"The restaurant on West Broadway. That'll do. I'll see you there at six. Oh, and make sure Mitch Cochran is there, too. Any arrangement we agree upon has to satisfy him as well."

"I'll make sure he's there." I hung up and looked at Julia. "How did I do?"

"You couldn't have done better. Okay, I need to run home for a change of clothes. I can't work in a cocktail dress."

"Hold on." I walked to the closet and pulled out Farrington's old suit. I laid it on the bed for her. "This might fit."

"You're kidding. I'm not putting that on."

"It's just been cleaned."

"It's not mine."

"Try it on. If you don't like it, you can go home and change."

Julia picked up the suit, looked it over, and walked into the bathroom. When she emerged, Farrington's clothes had taken on an entirely new look. The suit looked fashionably baggy, but she had cinched the pants at the waist and tucked in the shirt. When she slipped on her heels, the outfit was complete.

"All right, I'll wear it. Only because we don't have much time, and I need to tutor you before the agent gets here. Here's how your conversation with Rutger should flow when you meet him..."

Chapter Fifty-three

Two loud knocks on the door had startled me. I looked through the peephole and saw a man in a dark suit with a black suitcase in each hand. "Yes?"

"Michael Cheney, FBI."

He held his identification badge close to the peephole. I looked it over carefully before opening the door. Cheney was average looking, of medium build, with straight brown hair combed to the side. All in all, he was non-descript, although some might say he had the appearance of an accountant or insurance agent. He walked to the middle of the room and set the suitcases down.

"I'm Jack Lewis, and this is Julia Marshant."

Julia walked over and shook his hand. "We're glad you're here, Michael."

"Thank you. Tuttles briefed me earlier." Cheney looked at me and then turned back to Julia. "Have you explained everything to him?"

"Yes. Jack knows what to do."

"Good. I brought the surveillance equipment that I'll set up in the restaurant."

I looked at the suitcases. "What if Rutger changes the venue to a parking lot?"

"I've brought an extra set of equipment as backup, in case there's a change of plans and the meeting doesn't take place at the restaurant. If you do end up in a car somewhere, be sure to open the window. I can capture your conversation up to five hundred yards." Cheney opened his jacket and pulled out his .38-caliber issue. He checked the hammer and the cylinders before slipping the weapon back into his holster. "Things don't always go as planned, so make sure you follow my directions."

He walked to the window where fog still clouded our view, and then turned and faced us. "My job is to keep everyone alive. Just remember one thing—I'm in charge the moment we walk out that door. Understood?"

"Understood," I said.

Cheney gave me the once-over, sizing me up. "Are you carrying a weapon?"

"No, I'm not."

He turned to Julia. "If you're carrying one, leave it here."

"Why?"

"Tuttles's orders. He wants you on the sidelines, out of harm's way." Cheney turned back to me, "Gun play isn't likely, but if it occurs, just drop and hug the floor until I tell you to let go. Is that clear?"

"Clear."

Cheney gave us one last, hard look. "Any questions?" We had none. Cheney checked his watch. "Traffic is a mess. We should leave for the restaurant now." He slipped on his coat and picked up the suitcases. Julia and I followed him out of the apartment. When we reached the main lobby, Cheney received a call on his cell phone and stepped off to the side to answer it. Julia and I walked out of the hotel and waited for him out front.

* * *

Eddie was sitting in the Iron Lung across the street from the Towers. He saw Jack and Julia emerge from the hotel just as a car pulled up and parked in front of him. There were two Asian men sitting in the front seat, and Eddie saw one of them reach into the back seat and grab what appeared to him to be a weapon. His instincts told him something was about to come down, so he slouched down in his seat and pretended to be reading the newspaper, never once shifting his attention from the two Asians.

Pulling black hoods over their heads, the two men stepped into the street. Eddie froze, not knowing what to do. Almost without thinking, he threw the Iron Lung into reverse. The screech of the tires drew the attention of the Asians as they were about to cross the street. They stopped for a brief moment and glanced at Eddie. As they didn't sense danger from him, they continued on their mission. When they were halfway across the street, Eddie saw them draw their weapons. He jammed the car into drive and pulled away from the curb, fish-tailing the Lung to block their path.

Eddie leaned on the horn. His window rolled down and he yelled to Julia and me, "Get in the car!"

One Asian ran around the car, and that was when I saw his weapon. I shoved Julia toward the car and into the back seat, then jumped inside and pulled the door shut.

"You'll be safe in here!" Eddie said, as gunfire pelted the exterior of the vehicle. "Don't worry, the Lung's bullet-proof!" At that moment a bullet hit the rear window and shattered glass all over the back seat. We ducked for cover as Eddie pulled away, staring in disbelief that his rear window had been blown out.

Julia looked through the rear window. She saw Cheney emerge from the hotel with his weapon drawn. He raised his .38 and put a bullet into the forehead of one of the Asians.

"Nine o'clock! Nine o'clock!" Julia yelled, but Cheney was too far away to hear her. Another shot exploded and Cheney was hit. The impact knocked him backward into the revolving doors. The Asian who shot him fled down the street.

"Turn around, Eddie! Go back!"

"I can't. The Lung's not bullet-proof!"

"Cheney's hit. Turn this thing around!" she yelled.

Eddie spun the Lung around and returned to the Towers. I pulled out Farrington's .22 as we exited the car and ran to Cheney's side.

Cheney looked up and spoke in a whisper. "Thought you didn't have one."

I did not answer him. I just slipped the gun into my pocket. "Let me look at you."

A crowd had gathered around Cheney and another around the dead Asian who lay in a pool of blood.

"Call an ambulance," I yelled into the crowd.

Julia ran to my side as I opened Cheney's coat. "How bad?"

"There's heavy bleeding." I looked at Farrington's suit coat that Julia was wearing and told her to rip out a piece of the lining. "We have to stop the bleeding." The tourniquet slowed it down, but I still needed to press both hands on the wound. Within five minutes an ambulance pulled onto the sidewalk and shut down its siren. Two paramedics leapt out and motioned for me to step aside.

"Most likely the bullet's lodged beneath the clavicle and the first rib, and it may have struck the auxiliary artery. The bleeding's severe."

One of the paramedics examined the wound and then took out his short-wave radio. "Emergency, this is C7. We are requesting Priority A, I repeat, Priority A in six minutes. Gunshot wound to the auxiliary artery. Will determine blood type within ninety seconds. Copy please."

"Copy C7. Priority A is a go. Will stand by for blood type."

The other paramedic had already placed the gurney next to Cheney.

"We'll stay with you," Julia told him. "I'll call Tuttles and let him know."

Cheney reached over and grabbed Julia by the jacket. "Cochran. Stop him from going to that restaurant."

"My God!" she yelled. "Mitch!"

Cheney wanted to instruct us on how to proceed, but the paramedics were lifting him onto the gurney and moments later he was in the back of their vehicle. The ambulance door was shut and they were soon speeding off down the street, the siren wailing.

I ran back to the Iron Lung. "Eddie, does that phone on the dashboard work?"

"It did this morning." Eddie swept his hand across the front seat to clear the glass. I slid into the passenger side and called *La Vie en Rose*.

"Good evening. *La Vie en Rose*. May I help you?"

"Put Michelle on. It's an emergency."

"Hold on, sir. I'll see if I can find her," the young woman said.

"Don't see, just fi—." The woman had already placed me on hold. "Shit!" I looked back at Julia. "Get in the car!" I turned to Eddie. "How fast can we get to *La Vie en Rose?*"

"Twenty minutes in this traffic."

"Go then! We need to get there before Mitch does."

Eddie stepped on the gas and sped down Fifth Avenue as I waited on the phone.

"This is Michelle."

"Listen to me, Mich—"

"Jack?"

"Yes, yes! Just listen. Has Mitch arrived?"

"No. Are you meeting him here?"

"Yes. I mean no. Place someone outside the restaurant. Don't let Mitch in. Tell him it's a trap, and to get as far away from there as possible. Do you hear me?"

"A trap? What are you saying?"

"It's bad, Michelle, very bad. Better yet, just close the restaurant and leave."

"I have a room full of people here. I can't close down."

"Michelle, listen. Some bad people might be on their way to the restaurant. If I'm right, they plan on killing Mitch."

"I can't believe what you're saying."

"Listen! Has anyone out of the ordinary come into the restaurant?"

"This is New York. All kinds of out-of-the-ordinary people come in here." Michelle paused. "Wait a minute. A huge man just walked through the door."

"What does he look like?"

"He's Japanese."

"Oh, shit! Get out of there, *now*. That man's there for Mitch." There was silence on the telephone. "Michelle, are you still there?"

"Yes, I'm here."

"Are you closing the restaurant?"

"I'll tell Petrie to inform the staff."

"I'm hanging up and calling the police."

"All right, Jack. Please call the police!" She hung up.

Chapter Fifty-four

Michelle headed to the front of the restaurant. Before she had a chance to speak, however, Petrie was leading the Japanese man to a table and handing him a menu.

"Something to drink, monsieur?"

"Tea," Yashida said.

"Very good. I'll take your order when I return."

Michelle was furious with herself when she returned to the kitchen. "Why didn't I just say the restaurant was closing?"

"Talking to yourself?" Petrie said as he poured tea.

"Yes. I mean no," she said. She stopped one of the busboys. "Go outside and wait for Mitch Cochran. Tell him Jack said not to enter the restaurant. Do you understand?"

"What did Mitch do?" he asked.

"Don't ask questions. Just get out there." Michelle grabbed Petrie's arm as he was about to carry the tea into the dining room. "Wait." She opened her purse and emptied the contents onto the counter. "Thank God for this horrible cold." She opened capsule after capsule of Contac and emptied the crystals into the pot of tea.

Petrie placed his hand on her forehead. "Have you lost your mind?"

"Start opening these capsules. We haven't much time."

Petrie grabbed her hand. "What are you doing?"

Michelle grabbed him by the lapels. "Don't ask questions, Petrie! Do exactly as I say! That giant out there has come to kill Mitch. If the police aren't here in time to stop him, then we'll stop him!"

"Eddie, what the hell's wrong with this phone? There's no dial tone. I need to get through to the police."

"Jiggle the wires under the dashboard. Sometimes they come loose."

"And why the hell aren't we at the restaurant yet?"

"Stop yelling at him, Jack," Julia said. "He's going as fast as he can."

"Just step on it!"

* * *

A frightened look came over Petrie's face. "We need to call the police."

"Jack's calling them now."

Petrie went to a locked closet. He unlocked the door, reached in, and brought out a can of paint thinner. He began to open it.

Michelle looked at him. "What are you doing? I said we need to stop him, not kill him." Petrie set the can down and watched as Michelle poured the last capsule of powder into the tea. "That's twenty of them, enough to bring down a Clydesdale."

Petrie placed the teapot on his tray. "Well, here goes."

Michelle watched as Petrie placed the teapot on the table and filled the giant's cup. They watched him take a couple of sips.

"How is your tea, sir?"

Yashida nodded. Petrie filled his cup to the brim and returned to the kitchen. Ten minutes had passed and Michelle expected the giant to topple over, or at least to show some effect of being drugged. Instead, he looked unfazed and poured more tea into his cup.

"Damn it! One capsule knocks me out, and he's not even drowsy." She turned to Petrie. "Okay, here's what we do. Remove a side of beef from the walk-in cooler and carry it out the back door. Have the two chefs help you."

Petrie looked at her. "I'm not even going to ask."

241

Chapter Fifty-five

Petrie and the two chefs lugged the huge vacuum-packed slab of beef out the back door and around to the front of the restaurant. Michelle waited at the front door as they labored to get the beef into the main dining room, within eyeshot of the large Japanese man. Without warning, Petrie let go of the beef and allowed it to crash to the floor. "Oh, my back!" He gingerly hopped around the dining room.

"Oh, Petrie, not your back again," Michelle said.

"I really did it this time."

Michelle looked at the two chefs. "You two, get this beef into the kitchen. Do it quickly."

Two short, wiry-looking chefs made a feeble attempt to lift the meat, but they failed to even budge it. By now, the diners were voicing their displeasure at having to view the raw slab lying on the dining room floor.

Michelle got everyone's attention. "I'm so sorry for the disruption. The millennium has brought a great deal of people to our city, and these provisions are needed to feed our many guests. Please accept my apology. For the inconvenience, everyone will receive a complimentary drink." Upon hearing that, applause erupted.

Michelle wasted little time executing the next step of her plan. "Monsieur," she said, "you are very big and strong. Would you be so kind as to help us remove this animal from my dining area? I will prepare an extraordinary meal for you, compliments of the restaurant, of course."

Yashida sat quietly. A dining room full of people awaited his answer. Michelle flashed a charming smile when he looked at her. Yashida glanced at the front door, and then rose to his feet. With both hands he reached down and hoisted the side of beef onto his shoulder. Applause broke out, and Michelle led him into the kitchen where she opened the walk-in meat cooler.

"Just hang it anywhere."

He paused at the entrance to the cooler and looked at Michelle. She flashed another smile and motioned for him to proceed. He walked into the cooler and hung the beef on a hook. Michelle rushed the door, pushed it closed, and locked it. "Bon appétit, monsieur."

She had pulled it off. She was exuberant. A moment later, however, there was a loud crashing sound. The giant had smashed his body into the door. The vibration shook the dishes that were piled on the shelf near the door. The second crash quieted the guests in the dining room. Fear swelled inside of Michelle when she realized that her plan had one fatal flaw: This giant was too powerful to be contained by her meat cooler. His body pounded into the door once again, and this time Michelle watched the paint crack around the edges of the cooler door. If he escaped, he would kill her, and he would most likely kill some customers, too.

The next time he bashed into the door the walls rocked. A hinge on the cooler door began to pull loose. Michelle ran over and turned the temperature down to zero degrees. She began to pray when he rammed the door once again. Petrie was now standing beside her. He removed his apron and untied Michelle's. "I closed the restaurant. Everyone's gone."

"What did you tell them?"

"That we sprang a gas leak and Con Edison ordered us to evacuate everyone from the premises."

Michelle and Petrie stood frozen as Yashida crashed his body into the door once again. Petrie went to the closet and got their coats. "Come on. It's time to leave."

"My restaurant's going to be destroyed, isn't it?"

"Forget the restaurant." Petrie led her by the arm into the back alley and out to West Broadway, where he flagged a taxi. They had driven no more than two blocks from the restaurant when they saw Mitch walking down the street. "Stop the cab and pick that man up!"

Eddie pulled the Iron Lung to a stop and I jumped out. The front door of *La Vie en Rose* was locked, so I walked through the alley to the back entrance. The door was wide open. The kitchen was dark when I walked past the meat cooler and into the dining room. I saw all the plates of half-eaten food still on the tables. A loud crash in the kitchen caught my attention. I began to walk back there, but was stopped by the noise of someone banging on the front door.

"Jack!" Julia motioned to me.

I opened the door and she pulled me outside and back into the limo. "Let's get out of here," she said. "I have a bad feeling. Just drive, Eddie." He took off down West Broadway.

At that moment it sunk into my head that Rutger had attempted to kill me. I leaned back into the seat in a state of shock. It was spine-chilling to think someone had actually attempted to end my life. It frightened me to no end, but as the Iron Lung sped down the street, I became enraged.

"Pull over at Grand Street." Eddie pulled over in front of the *Le Strenge* restaurant, and when he looked at me, he had a blank stare on his face.

"Get out," I said.

"Get out? What do you mean?"

"How much do you want for the Lung? I'll write you a check."

"Sell you the Lung?"

"It's not worth much now. It's smashed and apparently not even bulletproof."

"I don't care if it's bulletproof or not. It's still the Lung, and it's mine."

"Get out. Open the door and get out."

Eddie stared at me in disbelief.

"Jack, what are you doing?" Julia didn't understand what was happening.

"I'll explain later," I said, and turned back to Eddie. "I'm not going to tell you again, now get out!"

Eddie looked at Julia and then back at me. He opened the door and stepped out. I slid into the driver's seat, pulled the door closed, and sped off. I glanced out the rearview mirror and saw Eddie standing in the street. A moment later, he disappeared in the fog.

Chapter Fifty-six

"And you'll need to leave the drug industry, and we'll live abroad. Those are the conditions. Otherwise, I can't do this," Vanessa said.

"I understand, darling. Come to Grandfather's this evening. We can make our plans there."

"I'll have something else to share with you this evening, too."

Rutger smiled, as he already knew about the baby. "I'll see you tonight, darling. And don't worry about a thing."

He hung up and called Yashida. There was no answer at the Chinatown flat, which gave him reason for concern. Rutger looked at his watch. In thirty minutes he was scheduled to meet with the multinationals to ratify the Five Point Plan. He called his grandfather.

"Where are you, Son?"

"Still at the Pierre. I'm leaving now to meet with the multinationals."

"It's been a busy day for you. The Cold deal is completed and the Five Point Plan will be finalized soon. I'll assume that that other matter we discussed has been resolved as well. I'm very proud of the way you've handled things, Son. Call me when your meeting is over."

"I will, Grandfather. Also, Vanessa will be arriving at the mansion tonight."

"Wonderful. I'll be here to greet her. See you tonight, Son."

Rutger hung up and he thought about Vanessa. She would come to realize that leaving the drug industry was not the solution, nor would it be possible to live abroad. He tried Yashida again, but there was still no answer, so he left the apartment to meet with the multinationals.

* * *

"Why did you throw Eddie out of his own car? And slow down! That's the second red light you've run."

My foot remained hard against the pedal. I refused to let up. There would be blood to pay for this. I had a plan, and I went over it in my mind to make sure it would work.

"Please tell me what you're doing."

I pulled over and threw the car into park. "I've figured it out. I know where the vault is located. If I'm right, it'll contain records on all the biotech drugs the Doblers bought and are keeping off the market."

"Bastianich's vault? Where?"

"It's in the dungeon."

"In Manhattan?"

"No. In Connecticut, at Heinrich's mansion. It's the logical place for them to store the information. Remember Heinrich's birthday party, when I left the table to speak with Rutger? We went down to the wine cellar, and while he was selecting champagne, I explored the dungeon. Every door had a window except this one room at the end of the corridor. I wanted to look inside, but it was locked. By then, Rutger appeared and we returned to the party. The mansion is the perfect place for them to store the biotech records."

"Let me see if I've got this right. You saw a locked door without a window in Heinrich's dungeon, and you've brilliantly deduced that that's where a load of biotech records are hidden. Has the pressure gotten to you?"

"There's more than just that. Why does Rutger live at the mansion with his grandfather? So he can keep an eye on everything, that's why. Remember the night of the party? Why so many armed guards? They were deployed everywhere. Even the twelve-foot-high gate had an armed guard."

"Suppose for a moment that you're right about the vault being in Heinrich's mansion. How, pray tell, do you propose getting past the guard at the gate? Not to mention the electronic surveillance system that's wired to the police station? If you're successful at all that, you'd then have to break into a vault with a combination that probably contains more digits than your social security number. Answer that."

"I'm still working on it." I threw the car back into gear and sped off.

"Well, you're not lacking for confidence. I'll give you that much."

I allowed the limo to roll to a stop in front of a luxury townhouse on East Sixty-Eighth Street. "Actually, I do know how to get inside the mansion. We'll take William Dobler hostage."

Julia gave me a queer look. "Don't even joke about that."

I wondered myself if I was blindly insane. "I'll do whatever I need to."

"Have you lost your mind?"

Having Julia with me was a mistake. She was too close to the law. "You're right. I'm overtired. I should get some rest. Just forget what I said."

"You scared me half to death. Thank God you've come to your senses."

"Can I drop you?"

"No need. I'll catch a taxi on the corner." Julia got out of the car. She walked down the block and disappeared around the corner.

I sat in front of William Dobler's townhouse a minute longer before speeding off. This time I parked in front of an apartment building on East Forty-Eighth Street. Unwittingly, Julia had pointed out a flaw in my plan. There were obstacles to overcome and I needed assistance in order to be successful.

I entered the building and took the elevator to the fourth floor. When I knocked on the door, Franz Weber opened it. My presence rendered him speechless. "I'm breaking into the Dobler mansion tonight, *Alexander*. Care to join me?"

Chapter Fifty-seven

"Don't ask how I know your name. I know most everything about you, even that you're the one who shot Heinrich Dobler. But let's not waste time on such trivial matters."

The Iron Lung came to a stop in front of William Dobler's townhouse once again. "Stay in the car. I'll handle this." I got out of the car, walked up the stoop, and pressed the doorbell. A man descended the staircase from the second floor and looked out through the wrought iron bars. He turned on the porch light to get a better look, and asked what I wanted. "I'm Jack Lewis, a friend of Rutger's. My car broke down and I wondered if I might use your phone to call a tow truck."

William swung the door open and unlocked the metal gate. He smiled and welcomed me into his home. We stood face-to-face in the hallway, and without a moment's hesitation, I pulled out Farrington's gun and grabbed William by the arm. His back arched and he was struck with fear. William's wife Elizabeth called down from the second floor and asked who was at the door. I placed the gun under his chin and stepped back so as not to be seen from the stairwell. Half frozen with fear, William did not answer right away. I pressed the gun more gingerly into the thick of his neck and he yelped out that a Jehovah's Witness had rung the doorbell, but they were gone now.

Elizabeth stood at the top of the staircase a moment longer, but then returned to whatever she had been doing. William's coat hung on a hook near the door. I removed it and handed it to him, and then motioned for him not to speak a word. He slipped on his coat and we left the townhouse. I walked him to the driver's side of the limousine and pushed him in the middle of the front seat next to Weber. That was when I saw Julia. She was standing behind a tree across the street from the townhouse. I should have known she was too smart to be deceived. She had circled back and waited, which is what a good detective does. I had no idea what was going through her mind, and I wasn't going to hang around to find out. I jumped into the Lung and gunned it, but Julia leapt out from behind the tree, forcing me to slam on the brakes. Before I had a chance to drive off, she opened the back door and jumped inside.

"I want everyone to know that I am *not* here as an accessory to this crime," she said. "I'm here to arbitrate your release, Mr. Dobler, and to make sure no one gets harmed. Jack Lewis will not harm you!"

"What in the hell are you doing?"

"Keeping you from spending the rest of your life in jail."

I pulled to the curb. "Get out, Julia."

"I'm not leaving. I'm going along as an observer."

Weber turned and looked at her. "Leave while you have the chance, young lady. And just so you know, there is no category as 'observer' when it comes to kidnapping. You're either the kidnapper or the victim, or you're an accessory to the crime. That's it."

"Everyone is better off with me in the car."

I sped off toward the Henry Hudson Parkway with no idea how to deal with Julia. She was a wild card at a point when time was running out for me. My thoughts turned to Weber and I glanced over at him. "How well did you know Catherine?"

Weber looked straight ahead. "She came to Rosetta one day, and Mitch introduced me to her."

"Did you assist her with her drug?"

"No, I didn't. I had neither a personal nor a professional relationship with your wife, if that's what you're asking."

The Lung moved at a pretty good clip as we crossed the Connecticut state line. In my head I kept going over the details of how the break-in should take place.

"Well, Jack, add another federal charge to the list. Kidnapping is bad enough, but carrying your captive across state lines adds twenty more years to your sentence."

"Julia, I don't need a play-by-play announcer." I glanced at William, who was stiff as a board. I guess the .22 pressed into his side was partly the reason. I jabbed his ribs a little harder to get his attention. "Where does your father hide those biotech records?"

"I have no earthly idea what you are talking about."

"You wouldn't lie to me, would you?"

"I don't lie. Not even to kidnappers. What is this all about?"

"Well, your father and son have developed a bad habit of murdering people and keeping life-saving drugs off the market. That's what it's about. Now, for the last time, where are those records hidden?"

"You're deranged, Lewis."

"Deranged? When your son is the one who tried to kill me tonight?"

"Rutger is not capable of killing anyone. Now stop this foolishness and release me before someone gets hurt."

Heinrich's estate came into view. I lifted the gun so William got a good look at the barrel, and then stuck it back into his ribs. "Tell the guard you're here to visit your father. Nothing more, understand?"

I stopped the car at the security gate and lowered the window as the guard approached.

"I'm here to see my father," William said. The guard looked into the limo and pulled out his log. "I'll need everyone's names." He looked in the back seat first.

"Helen Reddy," Julia said

"And your names?" addressing the men in the front.

"He's Franz Weber and I'm Jack Lewis."

He wrote our names down and pressed a button to swing the gate open. As I drove onto the estate, the guard noticed the blown-out rear window. I saw him hurry back to the booth and pick up the telephone.

* * *

Six men were seated quietly around the conference table when Rutger entered the room. The only reason these men had left the comfort of their homes on New Year's Day was to do what was necessary to maintain control of their industry.

"Thank you, everyone, for coming. Your presence shows you're committed to our cause. I know we—"

"We understand all that," Whitestone said. "Let's get to the important issue. Our concern is about entering into an agreement with your grandfather. If history serves me, he usually walks away with the lion's share, and everyone else gets the table scraps."

"I thought we were beyond that kind of rhetoric, Randall. I explained to you in my office that each man here receives an equal share, and no single person will control our joint venture."

Whitestone looked at his colleagues, then back at Rutger. "In order to protect ourselves, we've formed a sub-committee that includes everyone except you and your grandfather. The sub-committee will control the voting power of the new corporation."

"How can we trust each other if—" Rutger's mobile phone rang. When he saw the calling number he answered it. "Yes."

"Mr. Dobler, it's Harold, the gate guard at your grandfather's mansion."

"Yes, Harold?"

"You said to call if anything out of the ordinary happened."

"And?"

"Your father just arrived to visit your grandfather, and three other people came with him. The fellow driving looked a bit edgy, and the back window of the limousine was blown out."

"What's his name?"

"I got it right here. Let's see. It's Jack Lewis."

Since all eyes were upon him, Rutger remained calm. He looked at his watch. "I'll be there in thirty minutes."

"Should I call the police?" the guard asked.

"No, that won't be necessary. Lock the gate so no one leaves, then go to the mansion and stay with my grandfather." Rutger hung up and dialed another number. "Bring the helicopter to the top of the building. I need to leave immediately." He hung up and turned his attention to the men sitting around the table. "Well, gentlemen, it appears that my grandfather and I are not credible enough partners for you, so I see little reason to continue this meeting."

"We didn't say you couldn't negotiate better terms."

"It's too late!" Rutger leaned over the table. "Neither my grandfather nor I accept your conditions. You've allowed one man at this table to lead you like sheep, so let him lead you against the biotechs!" Rutger grabbed his coat and headed for the door. He turned to Whitestone. "Oh, and Randall, I purchased Cold this morning. Dobler Pharmaceutical now owns it lock, stock, and barrel. I thought you might want to know."

Randall stood and followed him to the door. "You filthy bastard!" he yelled. "I hope you and your grandfather rot in hell!"

Chapter Fifty-eight

Heinrich looked up and saw his son William standing in his office with three other people. "What is this?"

I pulled the gun from William's ribs and pointed it at Heinrich. "We just stopped by for some holiday cheer."

"What do you want, Lewis?" Heinrich said.

As Heinrich spoke, it appeared that he had slid open his desk drawer and removed something, but with my failing eyesight and his desk being such a distance away, I was unable to tell with certainty. I re-focused and answered Heinrich's question. "I want to know why you killed my wife. Then I want you to tell me where you keep those biotech records."

"Jack!" Julia screamed. I turned and saw Weber holding her from behind with a gun stuck in her ribs.

"Put your gun down, Jack."

I placed the gun on the floor.

"Now, everyone, move to the far wall. Slowly."

Heinrich began to wheel himself out from behind his desk.

"Not you," Weber said, letting Julia go and pointing his gun at Heinrich.

Heinrich sized him up. "And who are you?"

"You surprise me. You used to have an uncanny mind for details."

"Have we met?"

"You were once so certain of yourself, and now you're just a feeble old man."

"Heidelberg. Is that where we met?"

"You dumped my father's body in the Neckar River. You knew my mother, too, and stole everything from her, including her sanity. She and my sister went mad. In the end you destroyed them all but me."

Heinrich's eyes grew large as he rose from his wheelchair. "Alexander Schneggenburger."

Weber's expression hardened. "I've waited a long time to hear you speak my name."

"Are you the coward who shot me?"

"I'll make sure I'm more accurate this time."

Heinrich jerked a gun from his jacket. He aimed it at Weber and squeezed the trigger, hitting him in the chest. Weber fired back twice, hitting Heinrich in the neck and stomach. The impact knocked Heinrich back into his wheelchair. It rolled backward and slammed into the wall. Heinrich slumped forward, his arms falling limp at his sides. The gun slipped from his hand and made a thud as it hit the floor.

An odd but satisfied smile crossed Weber's face. All I could think was that his life-long ambition had been fulfilled. The front door opened and the gate guard raced into the room. He saw Heinrich motionless with blood streaming from his neck. Noticing Weber holding a gun, the guard did not hesitate to draw his weapon and fire two shots, hitting Weber both times. Weber fired back once, hitting the guard in the head and dropping him. He turned once more and looked at Heinrich with an expression that can only be described as gloating. Weber then collapsed to the floor.

Julia ran to the telephone and I knelt beside Weber, who was barely conscious. "An ambulance will be here soon."

"No." His eyes wandered and he struggled to pull air into his lungs.

"The truth," I asked. "Did you help Catherine?"

Weber gasped for air. "No."

"Can I call anyone?"

"They're all gone. I'm the last—" He coughed, and an eerie smile crossed his face. "You—You brought me here. You brought me...." His eyes closed. He exhaled one last time, and then he was gone.

"John, it's Julia. I need people at Heinrich's estate. Fast."

"Heinrich's estate? What are you doing there?"

"I'll fill you in later. Three people are down and I'm not comfortable calling the local police."

"Why not? What's going on?"

"Heinrich probably owns them, and the last thing we need is a bunch of trigger-happy cops storming this place. Can you get some people here?"

"I'll have two agents there in thirty minutes or less."

"Thanks, John. I have to go." Julia hung up before Tuttles could ask her any more questions.

William knelt next to his father who, incredibly, was still breathing. Heinrich whispered something and William placed his ear near his father's lips to hear his last words. I walked over, and when Heinrich saw me he ended the conversation.

"Yes, Father. I'll tell him."

"And... tell him...I love him...he's been a...good s..."

Heinrich's body went limp, his head dropping onto William's shoulder. William allowed it to rest there for a minute, and then gently pushed his father back into the wheelchair. "Funny, I don't recall us ever touching before," William said, as he looked into his father's face. He stood and turned to face me. "This is your fault!"

I reached down to see if Heinrich had a pulse. "He's dead, and I still need to find that vault."

"There's no vault in this place. Even if there was one, do you think I would take you there?"

Julia stepped between us. She addressed William in a more consoling manner. "I'm sorry you've lost your father, but you know very little about his dealings, and probably even less about the biotech records. But we need them. Where would your father have hidden them?"

William looked at his father, and back at Julia. "Leave us alone. Have you no respect for what's happened to him?"

I tapped Heinrich's pants pocket and heard the jingling of keys. "I need those keys, William." Just then, a loud noise shook the mansion.

"That's Rutger's helicopter," William said. "You'd better leave before it lands."

"Give me those keys, or I'll take them myself."

A look of disgust came to William's face. He then reached into his father's pocket and removed the keys.

I grabbed them. "Come on, Julia. There isn't much time."

Chapter Fifty-nine

We took the stairwell down to the dungeon and went straight to the large door at the end of the corridor. I found the key that fit the lock and swung the door open. The room was dark, dingy, and dusty. It was filled with old furniture. It contained exactly what Rutger had said it did. A stack of cartons were piled high against the wall. I opened them and began scanning their contents. They were old records and none of them had anything to do with biotech drugs. At that moment the truth hit me. There was no vault, and I was naïve to have believed my own incessant, delusional, confused ramblings. I sat down on a sofa covered in white sheets as the full force of reality crashed down. Three men lay dead on the floor upstairs, and the blame rested solely on my shoulders.

Rutger jumped out of the helicopter the instant it touched down. He ran through the arched doorway and into Heinrich's office, where he saw the bodies of the guard and a stranger on the floor. "My God! What's happened?"

William looked up. "They're dead," he said. He then pointed to the wheelchair against the wall. "So is your grandfather."

Rutger crossed the room and knelt before his grandfather, taking hold of his hand.

"That man is Alexander Schneggenburger. He shot your grandfather."

"Schneggenburger?" Rutger looked down at the man who had claimed his grandfather's life.

"Before your grandfather died, he said that he loved you. He wanted me to tell you. He also said something else, something I didn't understand."

"What was it?"

"For you to destroy it all. Whatever that means."

Rutger looked at his grandfather and whispered, "I will, Grandfather. I promise."

William heard him. "What did he mean? I want to know what you two have done."

Rutger looked at his father. "Has Vanessa arrived yet?"

"I don't know. Answer my question."

"Seal off this room before Vanessa arrives. I don't want her to sees this. Where's Jack Lewis?"

"Down in the dungeon looking for biotech records."

"What? Why didn't you tell me?" Rutger grabbed Heinrich's gun and ran down stairs. Jack and Julia were walking back along the corridor. Rutger heard them and ducked into one of the rooms to wait for them. As they approached, he sprang out into the hallway. "Leaving so soon? That's not very polite. Drop those weapons!"

I had become disoriented, and Julia was assisting me out of the dungeon when Rutger surprised us. We dropped our weapons not knowing what lay in store for us.

"Rutger!" William ran downstairs. "A black car has just come onto the estate."

"That would be the FBI," Julia said, "and I'm sure they've brought a search warrant. They'll rip this place to shreds to find the biotech records."

The wheels in Rutger's head started to turn. He motioned at us with his gun. "Back inside that room, you two. Father, you stay out."

Rutger followed us in and closed the door behind him. He ran to the corner of the room and opened what looked like a large, fire-proof container. He removed a five-gallon can of gasoline from the container. He then reached up and twisted a light fixture, causing the back wall to slide open. He motioned to us to enter. The room was not a vault, but it was filled with file cabinets that were indexed from *A* to *Z*. One by one, Rutger opened the cabinet drawers and doused them with gasoline. That was when I remembered what he had told me the night of Heinrich's birthday party. The dungeon had been built with hundred-year-old oak. If it ever caught fire, it would go up like a tinderbox.

"You can't be serious," Julia said. "You're going to burn this mansion down?"

Rutger ignored her until the last of the gasoline had been poured into the cabinets. "It'll be a terrible loss, but what's inside these cabinets can never see the light of day."

"And us?" Julia said.

Rutger paused for a moment. He looked at her and then at me. "You've left me no choice."

"Did you have a choice with Catherine?"

"It was unfortunate. It might be of little consolation to you, but the man responsible for her death has found a similar fate."

"Of course you're not responsible."

Rutger stepped toward us. His eyes filled with anger. "My grandfather is dead and all this will be destroyed! You don't think I'm paying a price, too?"

Rutger removed a cigarette lighter from his pocket and turned and looked at me. "Just so you know, Lewis, we acquired the full patent rights to Cold from its legal owner. You almost swindled us." We first heard a popping sound and then saw the flames. With lighter in hand, Rutger proceeded to ignite each gas-soaked cabinet.

The door crashed open and William burst into the outer room. He ran back to where we were and saw the flames shooting from the cabinets. "What are you doing? We have to put that fire out!"

"Leave, Father! You don't belong here. It's too late. What's done is now done."

"Are you mad?" William yelled. "Is this what your Grandfather wanted destroyed?"

The flames leapt from the cabinet to the walls. Julia and I looked at each other. My survival was immaterial, but Julia had her whole life ahead of her. I needed to take action. I waited for my moment as flames began to crackle and the room filled with smoke.

Julia leaned toward me and said, "When I rush Rutger, go for the door."

"No. I'll rush him. You go for the door."

William watched in horror. He could no longer take it. "No, Son. I can't live knowing what you're about to do!" He lunged for Rutger's gun and tried to wrestle it away from him. With that, Julia took hold of my arm and pulled me toward the door. A moment later we were in the corridor, then up the stairs and out of the dungeon. We ran out of the mansion expecting Rutger and William to follow, but neither appeared behind us.

I can only imagine what William would have said to his son after we left the dungeon. Maybe it was the heart-to-heart talk he should have had with Rutger years ago. Maybe William told his son that he had never known him, just like he had never known his own father. Or maybe that he was a blind fool for not seeing that Rutger had turned out just like his grandfather. Whatever he said, it was clear that by now flames were consuming the wood panels in the corridor, and a layer of black smoke was most likely hovering above their heads.

William begged Rutger to leave with him before they both died in the fire. Instead, Rutger grabbed furniture and threw it on the fire. William walked to the door and looked back at his son. He made one more plea, but Rutger told him to get out. William waited, even as flames and smoke streamed out of the room and into the corridor. They looked at each other, and William cried out to Rutger, telling him that he was still his son, and that he loved him. With tears in his eyes, William ran down the corridor to save himself. Rutger watched as his father disappeared from the smoke-filled doorway. He tossed one last chair onto the inferno and watched as the flames engulfed it.

Cold, crisp air filled our lungs as we watched the flames surge up the side of the mansion. The FBI and police had the building surrounded when William ran out the front door and fell onto the snow. He buried his head in his arms and sobbed. Just then a white Cadillac pulled up and stopped in front of the mansion. Vanessa stepped out, not believing what she was seeing. She stared at the mansion for a moment and then ran to William's side. "Where's Rutger?"

William pointed to the mansion and buried his head in his arms once again.

"Rutger!" she yelled, as flames consumed more of the mansion. "Rutger!" Vanessa ran in the direction of the mansion.

"Stop her!" Julia yelled. Two firemen ran across the lawn to keep her from entering the mansion. Vanessa was able to get inside before they reached her. Julia and I ran to the door, but the smoke kept us back. A portion of the mansion collapsed and I thought I heard someone scream, but maybe it was my imagination. I looked at Julia, who stood with her hand over her mouth.

In the background I heard an EMS medic say that William was in shock. They placed him in the ambulance and drove off the estate. Julia and I kept our eyes on the front door the entire time, hoping that Vanessa, and even Rutger, would emerge.

Fire now engulfed the entire exterior of the mansion, and the heat from the dying structure forced us to retreat. Our eyes remained fixed on the front door even though we both knew that only a miracle would allow someone to walk through it. Ten minutes later the fire had spread to the structure's core, and black smoke poured from every orifice. Julia looked at me and, without saying a word, we both knew that no one inside could possibly be alive now.

Firefighters began to remove the water hoses from their trucks, but the Fire Chief instructed them to stand down and allow the structure to burn itself out. The burning brick and stone turned into glowing red embers. Those embers then crumbled and turned into dark ash. The brilliant array of colors that spewed from the wreckage mesmerized us all as we stood helpless and watched the destruction occur. The burning was relentless and it raged for hours, until the last glowing wall collapsed and the mansion no longer existed. Julia and I left the estate after the last of the bricks and stones had lost their orange glow and turned to sooty ash.

Chapter Sixty

Julia and I arrived at the Towers late the next morning. The sun was full in the sky. Without saying a word, Julia went straight to the bedroom. Minutes later I looked in and saw she had crashed on the bed. I sank into the sofa with visions of torrid flames and burning embers playing over and over in my mind. I was abundantly alert, more so at this moment than I had been since returning to New York. The telephone light was blinking, so I checked the messages. Doctor Frankfort's office had called to remind me of my twelve o'clock appointment. My first thought was to call and cancel, but if there was ever a time when I needed to speak to a psychiatrist, it was now. If I hurried, there was enough time to take a quick shower and still make the appointment.

Doctor Frankfort sat on the other side of his desk with his hands folded on his lap. There was little he could say or do for me at this point, other than to explain what would occur in the coming days. He plugged in his stethoscope and walked around the desk to give me a perfunctory physical. He asked how I felt. Was I having dizzy spells? He bent my arms and pressed on my joints. Was I in pain? He offered to increase the potency of my medication. When he finished the examination, he sat back down in his chair behind the desk.

It was now time for me to share another vignette about Catherine, Doctor Frankfort said. Once again, I was not sure why he wanted to hear these vignettes, but I didn't ask him to explain. Besides, I had grown comfortable speaking to him about Catherine. It was as if time had stopped and the entire world was shut out while I spoke about the intimacy we once shared. I questioned whether or not to disclose the vignette that had first surfaced in my mind, because it was both painful and haunting. To talk about it, though, might help reduce the pain, so I began to tell him about the day I had left for the Brazilian Rainforest. I was standing in the hallway of the condo with my suitcase in one hand. My other hand rested on the doorknob. I yelled upstairs to let Catherine know I was leaving, but she didn't answer. We had quarreled earlier that day, and when that happened, neither of us would give an inch to the other. Catherine had a stubborn streak—not a horrible one, but enough to keep her upstairs. I stood in the doorway a while longer, and when Catherine refused to come downstairs, I walked out. I expected her to run down the street after me, but she never did. It hurt now because I know I should have been the one to give in to her that day.

Doctor Frankfort took notes and then gave me his private number. He said to call him anytime, day or night. I left his office and got in the elevator to go downstairs. I inadvertently pressed the wrong button and the doors opened onto the second floor rather than the lobby. I did not step out but rather pressed the lobby button a number of times. For some reason, the elevator door failed to close. Finally, I stepped off the elevator. At that moment the doors closed and left me stranded on the second floor. I looked up and read the sign on the wall: Pediatric Oncology. In other words it was the children's cancer ward. I walked down the hallway and looked through a glass window where a roomful of children were playing with dolls, climbing on monkey bars, painting, rolling on the floor, and just making a lot of noise.

Childhood cancer is different from adult cancer. It mostly affects children's white blood cells and attacks the brain, bone, and lymphatic system. Most of the children playing in the room had lost their hair and were wearing hats or bandanas. They had gone through, or were going through chemotherapy, bone marrow transplants, and radiation. I noticed one small boy sitting by himself. Our eyes met and he got off the chair and walked over to where I was standing at the window. "Did you come to play with me?" I walked into the room. "Why, yes, how did you know?" He ran to the toy shelves, picked up a box of blocks, and carried them back over. I sat on the floor and we built a house together. Every so often I glanced at the boy. There was something familiar about him, but I couldn't place where I might have seen him.

"What's your name?"

"Michael."

"How old are you?" He held up four fingers. "Is your mommy coming to see you today?" He dropped his head. "I live in a fuster home," he said. We played a while longer. Before I left we shook hands and I took a moment to look at him closely once again. He had translucent blue eyes and blonde hair, and I was now certain I had seen that face somewhere before.

Chapter Sixty-one

I returned to the Towers drained of strength and desire, and yet sleep was unattainable. The one thing I would have liked at that moment was to talk to someone. I checked on Julia; she was still out like a light, and I chose not to wake her.

Catherine's file was lying on the coffee table. Up until now I had refused to look at the pictures of her, and even then I thought I might not be able to handle it. I picked up the file and started by reviewing the testimonies from the hospital workers, and then I read through the background checks. With purpose, however, I continued to avoid looking at the pictures. Over the next hour I managed to consume the entire report. All that remained were the two sets of pictures taken of Catherine. It required courage if I was to see how the Crotalus had disfigured her, and I realized I had finally run out of excuses for not looking at them. The first picture showed her swollen face. She was completely unrecognizable. I only glanced at it quickly and then turned the entire set of pictures face down. Ten minutes passed before I found my courage once again, but this time I looked at the second set of pictures. They had been taken by the hospital staff while Catherine was in a coma, still alive. "Oh, my angel." The picture I was holding was poorly taken but it captured the classic beauty of her long, lean, milky-white body. She was the vision of a fallen Greek goddess. My body began to shake, and even after I set the picture down and walked to the window, I was unsettled. It was not just these pictures, but also the lack of sleep, the burning of the mansion, and so many deaths. I was lonely, melancholic, disquieted, nervous, and more awake than ever. Once again I thought to wake Julia, but decided against doing so.

I collected myself and returned to the table where I picked up the pictures once again. Trembling, I was determined to view each picture down to the smallest detail. One picture in particular caught my attention. I saw two small, faint bruises on the crook of Catherine's left arm. I looked at this photo more closely. My heart almost stopped beating. I skimmed through the rest of the pictures to see if any showed a better angle of those two bruises, but only that one picture had captured it. To make sure my mind wasn't playing tricks on me, I pulled out the photo that showed the bruise on Catherine's back. In the instant I held the two pictures side by side the truth burst wide open for me to see. I now questioned whether Rutger had any involvement in Catherine's death at all. The time had come to wake Julia.

I ran into the bedroom and gently shook her. "You awake? I need to show you something."

Julia raised her head from the pillow and looked at me, then at the clock, and then dropped her head back onto the pillow.

"Julia, wake up. It's important."

"Just give me five minutes." She turned her back to me and sunk deeper into the pillow. "I'm so tired."

Her deep breathing told me that she had fallen back to sleep. "I don't think Rutger killed Catherine," I said. There was no response from her, so I held Catherine's picture in front of her face. Her eyes remained closed and she was not responding, so I tapped her nose with the picture. She squinted, then lifted her head and pulled away to bring the picture into focus. "Oh, my God, Jack. What's wrong with you?" She sat up and finally I had her attention. "This picture proves that the men Rutger hired to break into Catherine's laboratory are not the ones who killed her, and it validates what I've believed all along."

Julia rubbed her eyes. "I'm still half asleep, so you'll need to start at the beginning and take it slow."

"Okay. Rutger hired common thugs who knew nothing about medicine. But the Crotalus was injected precisely into Catherine's brachial artery. That could only have been done by someone who knew what they were doing."

"Brachial artery? I thought Catherine was injected in her back?"

I held the picture up. "See the faint discoloration marks in the crook of her arm? Well, those are baby bruises from two puncture marks. They were made by a very fine needle. Now look at the injection made on

Catherine's back. See the much larger bruise? It was made with a standard gauge needle, an obvious attempt to mislead her doctors and the forensic team into thinking she was accidently injected there. The fatal blow, I'm certain, was delivered by the two tiny injections into her brachial artery. It was done by someone who was medically trained and who knew the brachial artery would transport the poison quickly and effectively. They didn't want Catherine to survive, not even for an hour, but she outsmarted them and hung on long enough for her body to bruise. Maybe she even watched as her killer injected her, and was determined to stay alive long enough for bruising to occur. Do you understand what I'm saying here? She was leaving a trail for someone to compare the different size bruises and then realize that her death was no accident—that she had been murdered. Only Catherine would think to do that."

"If that's true, she's even more remarkable than I thought."

"If my theory is correct, I just walked myself through a scenario that proves Catherine really is gone. A small piece of me wanted to believe she was still alive. I know it was foolish to think that. Just forget it."

"Your feelings are understandable, under the circumstances. But, where do we go from here?"

"Think about it. When we were in the dungeon, Rutger said he had bought Cold from its rightful owner. Well, whoever sold it to him has to be Catherine's killer." I grabbed the telephone.

"Who are you calling?"

"Someone who I hope can help us."

"Fourth floor nurse's station. How may I help you?"

"Is Frances McQueen on duty today?"

"She comes in at four o'clock. Can I take a message?"

I looked at my watch and saw it was already two-thirty. "Tell her Jack Lewis called, and that I'll be at the hospital at four o'clock." I hung up and walked out of the bedroom.

Julia came out, draped in the bed sheet. "Why Frances?"

"She spoke to Catherine at least twice a day. She knows more than she thinks she does. Besides, I don't know where else to start." I went into the bathroom and Julia followed me.

"You think she's involved?"

"We can't rule her out."

Julia stared at me for a moment and then shook her head in confusion. "I have to say something here, Jack, and I need you to listen to me. Either you've lost your grip on reality or I've lost mine. Last night you kidnapped someone, and now people are dead. You don't show the slightest bit of concern for them or for the consequences you face. Don't take this the wrong way, Jack, but I think there's something truly wrong with you. And to make matters worse, I'm an accessory to everything you've done. The DA is going to fry us both." Julia searched my face and waited for an answer that had some semblance of logic to it.

"There *is* something wrong with me, Julia." I took a deep breath. If anyone deserved to know the truth, it was Julia. "It's hard for me to tell you this, because I still struggle to believe it myself."

"What? Tell me!"

"I haven't been truthful with you from the beginning."

"What is it?"

"Cancer. The malignant type. And it's in my brain. It's just a matter of days."

A somber look came over her face as she stood there looking at me. She said nothing.

"So you see, that explains the little regard I have for the consequences of my actions. And the bad news for me is that I'll probably never find Catherine's killer before my time runs out."

Julia's eyes turned glassy. "I'm not sure how to react to what you just told me."

"I didn't expect you would."

"To find Catherine's killer in even a week will take a miracle."

I nodded. "I know. I've never been a big fan of miracles. But on the other hand, it's still the holiday season, so maybe there's one floating around out there for me."

Julia smiled. "Maybe. You know I'll help anyway I can." She tugged at the sheet wrapped around her body and used it to wipe a tear that had started to fall down her cheek.

"You'll come to the hospital with me?"

"Of course I will."

"In that case, would you mind leaving the bathroom so I can shower?"

Chapter Sixty-two

Traffic had caused Julia and me to arrive at Memorial a little later than we expected. We took the elevator to the fourth floor and went straight to the nurse's station. Frances had already begun her shift and I tracked her down as she was taking a patient's blood pressure in a room in the west wing.

"Jack. I waited for you as long as I could, but I had to start my shift."

"Sorry we're late. When you're finished here, can we speak?"

Frances jotted something down on the patient's chart and removed the stethoscope from around her neck. "Follow me." She led us into an empty radiology room and closed the door.

I wasted no time. "I have a couple of questions about Catherine. Do you know if she was seeing anyone on a regular basis when I was away?"

"You asked that, Jack, remember, and I walked out. I won't discuss Catherine's personal business."

"I'm not asking if Catherine was dating anyone. I'm asking if anyone visited her at the hospital on a regular basis."

She glanced at Julia, and then back at me. "Well, Mitch stopped by a couple of times a week."

"How long would he stay?"

"Not too long. But it wasn't my place to keep tabs on everything Catherine did, so I don't know for sure."

"Anyone else visit her?" A look came over Frances's face and it made me suspicious. "You're holding something back, I can tell."

"I've never been one to talk about other people's business, especially Catherine's."

"It's important, Frances. Really."

"All right. Catherine may have been seeing someone while you were away."

"Who?"

"Colter Malone. They spent a lot of time together. Sometimes late into the night."

"Colter and Catherine? Why didn't you tell me this before?"

Frances avoided looking at me, but then our eyes met. "And make Catherine's personal life public? So people can gossip? Never. And there was no reason to hurt you, either."

I tried to imagine Colter and Catherine. Complete opposites. Catherine loved classical music and jazz. Colter blared his rock and roll. Catherine was a workaholic, and Colter, well, he worked when the urge grabbed him. "How long had they been seeing each other?"

"Maybe we should speak privately, Jack?"

"You can speak in front of Julia."

"She was seeing Colter before you left for South America."

Her words stunned me. It didn't seem possible.

"Catherine shared a lot with me. I knew her better than anyone, and maybe even as well as you did, Jack. She even told me about the day you left, when she stayed upstairs, and you called to her from the door. She never forgave herself for not coming downstairs. After you left, she ran after you, but it was too late. You were already gone."

Frances had brought up the one subject that I'd played over and over in my mind. I had to fight to keep my emotions in check. "Did she tell you anything else?"

"Not about that day. But we had lunch together a couple days later, and Catherine asked if I knew the best place to hide."

"To hide?"

"I asked her what she meant, and she said the best place to hide is close to a bright light. The brightness makes you invisible, she said. I didn't know what she meant right then, but later I thought about it. She was talking about you, Jack. Your light created a glare and made it hard for others to see Catherine for who she was."

"I don't understand."

"Did you ever stop to think how difficult it was for her with the spotlight always on you, Jack? Catherine wanted to be your equal, your partner, but you blocked her."

"I never blocked her. Catherine *was* my equal. She knew that."

"In the weeks before you left, Catherine said she tried to talk to you, but you had stopped listening to her. That wasn't even the worst part. You had turned cold toward her, like she wasn't even in the same room with you. The sparkle in your eyes was gone, and you stopped touching her. A wall existed and she didn't know how to reach you. That's why she didn't go to South America, and it ripped at her every day. She even had a feeling that something terrible would happen if you two ever parted." Frances pulled out a tissue and wiped her nose. "My God, somehow Catherine always knew. In her heart she knew something bad would happen."

Frances turned away to wipe her eyes. Julia approached her.

"Why did Catherine keep her research from Jack?"

"She said because if Jack knew about it, he'd want to help her. People would think *he* was the creator of Cold, and that he was being the nice husband and bringing his wife in on it. Don't you see? To Catherine, her research made them equals. Believe me, it killed her to sit at the dinner table every night and not tell him, but it was only a matter of days before Cold was to be completed. She couldn't wait to share her success with

269

him." Frances's lips quivered. Then she added, "After what I've told you, I guess you won't be attending Colter's going away party tonight."

"Going away party?"

"Didn't he invite you? His co-workers are throwing a party for him on the third floor. It starts at five-thirty, and then he's off to the airport."

"Last I heard Colter was staying in New York for another week." Maybe it was the revelation about Catherine or that Colter was leaving town, or the combination of the two, but at just that moment I became dizzy. I was disoriented and had to sit down in order to get my legs back. Doctor Frankfort had cautioned me about trying to process large chunks of information all at once. *It would have an adverse effect on me*, he had cautioned.

"You okay, Jack?" Julia said, and glanced at her watch. "We should leave." She turned to Frances. "Thanks for telling us what you knew." Julia walked out of the room.

I stood up, wobbled momentarily, and turned to Frances. I wanted to say that telling me about Colter last week would have made all the difference in the world, but Frances didn't deserve that kind of treatment. "Thanks for helping me." She hugged me and I left the room. I did not let on to Frances, but I was staggered by what she had told me.

Julia waited for me in the hallway. When I joined her there she placed her hand gently on my cheek. "I realized something while Frances was talking to us. It's something neither you nor Catherine knew the day you left for Brazil. The love never died, Jack, but I'm afraid the sparkle in your eyes may have. You see, you were already sick before you left for Brazil. Had Catherine known just how sick you were, she never would have let you walk out the door."

I heard the words Julia spoke, but in my state of mind I found it hard to comprehend the meaning of what she was trying to tell me. I wanted her to explain it to me again, but she turned and hurried toward the hospital exit. "Where are you going?"

Julia turned and looked at me. "Are you coming? We've important research to complete."

"Research?"

When I caught up to her, she looked at me and said, "I know you're still a little foggy. I can see it in your eyes. Stay strong! And one more thing: Catherine wasn't having an affair with Colter. But I do believe he was her collaborator. If I'm right, it was Colter who sold Cold to Rutger. Let's prove it."

"How?"

"You should've told me about Catherine's DNA messages earlier. Good thing Mitch mentioned it on the phone yesterday. If Isaac was successful at isolating her message on some chromosome, it may give us the proof we need. It's up to you now!"

Julia suddenly stopped talking. I could see the wheels turning in her head.

"I've grown to understand Catherine quite well over the last week. I'll bet anything that she left quite an impressive message for you to read. What a beautiful way for her to tell you she created an important drug. It doesn't get much better than that for a scientist, especially a female scientist. And maybe, just maybe, her message has given credit to her collaborator. We need to get our hands on that message before Colter boards his plane tonight."

"You expect me to find her message? I can't even get my head to stop spinning."

Julia's lips tightened "You *will* do it, Jack! This is the miracle we hoped to find. Now stay *strong!*"

Chapter Sixty-three

Rosetta was cold and dark when we entered. Julia pointed me in the direction of the downstairs laboratory. Before heading off, she grabbed me by the arm and asked, "How long will it take?"

Looking for Catherine's message was no less than daunting for me. "You mean if my eyesight holds out?"

"How long, Jack?"

"I don't know. I'll do my best. That's all."

She stared at me for a moment. "Okay. Just remember that we're playing for all the marbles. You understand that, right?" She looked at me long and hard. "I'm going upstairs to call Tuttles. It's not going to be a pleasant call, especially when he asks me about the kidnapping."

Julia climbed the stairs and went into Mitch's office. She played his phone messages, went through his desk, and rifled through his papers. There was nothing suspicious there, so she decided to check out Franz Weber's office. The radio had been left on from the day before. The bright, lilting waltz it played made Julia think that Franz's life was anything but bright or lilting. In fact, his life had been quite tragic, in almost every sense. She leaned over and turned off the radio. A minute later she summoned the courage to call Tuttles, wondering if a warrant for Jack's arrest had been issued yet, or, for that matter, one for her arrest, too.

"Hello, John. It's Julia."

"Where are you?"

Julia detected a sharp tone in his voice. "I'm at Rosetta Laboratories. Jack's downstairs looking for a coded message that may be hidden in the Cold molecule."

"In a molecule?"

"I'll explain later. This might sound strange, but it seems that Rutger may not have been responsible for Catherine's death after all."

"What? Then who is?"

"No hard facts yet, but Colter Malone may be our man."

"Keep me posted. I'm going to be needing testimonies from everyone who was at the Dobler estate last night, including you. We need to know how Franz Weber ended up at the mansion. William Dobler was released from the hospital this afternoon, and two agents will be going to his home tonight to question him. I'll be at Heinrich's estate first thing in the morning, and I want Jack and you there. Nothing is adding up and I need to sort through everything that happened last night."

"I'll let Jack know."

"You sound a bit distant. Is everything all right?"

"I'm fine, John. Just a little tired."

"I'll be home this evening. Call me if there are any new developments."

"All right, John, I will." Julia hung up. She realized the FBI had few facts of what had actually occurred the night before. Apparently they didn't even know that Jack had kidnapped William Dobler. But, she thought, when they question William later, he'll tell them everything. An idea occurred to her. Anything was worth a try at this point. And, if she could pull this off, it might keep both Jack and her out of jail.

Julia made her way back downstairs. She looked into the laboratory and saw that Jack was still engrossed in the search for Catherine's message. She left Rosetta, allowing herself an hour to accomplish her mission. Fifteen minutes later she arrived at William Dobler's townhouse, and rang the doorbell.

William Dobler looked out the window and saw Julia. "What do you want here?"

"I need to speak with you, Mr. Dobler."

"Go away. I'm not talking to anyone. Now leave us alone."

"Please, Mr. Dobler. It's important that we speak."

William opened the door a crack. "What could we possibly have to talk about?"

"May I come in? I'll take only a moment of your time."

"No, you can't. My wife is in shock. Have you no respect? Don't you realize what we've been through?"

"Please, just one minute of your time." To Julia's surprise, he opened the door and allowed her to step into the hallway.

"You have one minute."

Julia placed her hand on his arm. "I can only imagine what you and your wife are going through. Please accept my deepest sympathy."

William looked at the floor for a second, and then back at her. "Thank you. But I'm sure that's not why you're here."

"You're partly right. The FBI is on their way here to question you. They want to hear your side of the story of what happened last night. I hate to think that there could be more casualties before this evening is over."

"What are you getting at?"

"I need you to understand. Jack Lewis was not in his right mind yesterday when he kidnapped you. It was a terrible thing to do, and I'm sure you were terrified. Jack has not been stable for some time. I won't go into the details, but as things stand right now, he'll be arrested and charged with kidnapping."

"And?" William said.

Julia swallowed. "Last night, there were six people who knew that Jack had kidnapped you. Four of them are now dead. Only you and I remain. I haven't told the authorities what really happened, and I suppose that makes me an accessory to his crime." Julia swallowed again. "It's a lot to ask of you, or anyone, but I am asking you not to tell the FBI that Jack kidnapped you."

William's eyes opened wide. "You have some nerve! My son and father are both dead because of him!"

"I realize that," Julia said, "but I'm asking you to try to understand. Jack Lewis kidnapped you as a last resort. His wife was murdered, and Jack and I both would have been killed if you hadn't stepped in and saved us. You must know that Jack had nothing against you." Julia paused. "There's been so much tragedy, Mr. Dobler, and it would be even more tragic for Jack to go to jail."

"Jack Lewis should walk away? And my wife and I should be the only ones to suffer in all this? Is that what you're asking me?"

"William!" Elizabeth said, appearing in the hallway. She walked over and stood in front of her husband. "We lost Rutger to your father when he was a child. He stopped belonging to us at that point. All these years, we've been lying to ourselves. Never once did we question him on his business practices. We were afraid to learn the truth: that our son was a monster, just like his grandfather." Elizabeth turned to Julia. "Young lady, my husband and I have lived honest and respectable lives. Tell Jack Lewis that I am sorry for the pain my son may have brought to him, but William has no choice but to tell the authorities the truth when they question him."

Two men in dark suits appeared on the stoop and rang the doorbell.

William went to the door. "Yes?"

"William Dobler?"

"Yes."

One of the men showed his badge. "FBI. We'd like to speak with you about the events of last night."

William turned to Julia. "You'll have to leave now."

Julia reached out and took Elizabeth's hand. Their eyes met for a brief moment, and she turned and walked to the door. "I hope you both find peace." She left the house.

Julia returned to Rosetta at six p.m. and went straight to the laboratory. I was standing in the middle of the room, a little glassy eyed from having read the message a number of times. She walked over and I handed her the sheet of paper that I had transcribed it on.

CCCCAAAACCCCCGGGGGTTTTTTTTTTTTTGGGTTTTTTTTTG
GAAAAAAAAAGGGGGGTAGGAAAATTTTTCCTTTTTTTCCCTTT
ATTTTTTTAAAAAAAAAAAAAGGGGGGGAAAAAAGGTAAAAGGA
AAGGGGAAAAATTGGGGGGTTTAAAAACCCCCGGGTTTTAAA
AAACCCCCCTTTTTATTTTTTTTAAAGGGGCCCCCCTGGGGGAA

AAAAAACCCACCCCCCTTCCAGGCCCCCTTTGGGAAAGAAAAA
AGGGGGGGGGCCCCCTAAGGGGGGCCCCCCCCCCCCCCCCC
CAGGAAAAAAAAA

"What does it mean? You expect me to decipher this?"

"Sorry. Turn it over. I spelled her message out on the other side."

Julia turned the sheet over. *jack   I did it   you and I   shoulder to shoulder   my dream come true   forgive me darling for keeping this from you   love you always and forever   cpl*

thanks to cm for his help

She lifted her hand to her mouth and read the message a second time. "Catherine has spoken to you from her grave." Just as Julia was about to hand me the sheet, she pulled it back and read aloud, "*Thanks to CM for his help*! Colter Malone! She did thank her collaborator!"

"And Colter said he rarely saw her."

Julia looked at her watch. "There's still time to crash his going away party."

"I can't wait to get my hands around his neck."

"No, Jack. That's not what we're about. I'm going to call Tuttles and ask him to send some agents to the hospital and the airport."

After Julia made the call, we walked back out through the dark foyer to exit the building. We heard the sound of footsteps coming toward us.

"My God!" Julia screamed.

Chapter Sixty-four

Julia and I were frozen in our tracks, standing in the darkness of the foyer when someone emerged.

"Mitch! You scared us half to death. Where've you been?"

"I was on my way to *La Vie en Rose* to meet you on New Year's, and the next thing I know Michelle yanks me into a taxi cab. She tells me about locking a Japanese giant in her meat cooler and closing the restaurant because she thought he was going to bust out and kill her. You were supposed to call the police."

"The car phone went dead. What happened to the Japanese guy?"

"We went back this afternoon and found the building still in one piece. The meat cooler door was closed and locked, so I knocked on it a couple of times and asked if anyone was in there. There was no answer. Petri refused to open it, as did Michelle. In the end I mustered up the courage to swing the door open. It was the scariest thing I'd ever seen—this Japanese guy still on his feet leaning against the wall. It looked like he was posing for a picture, but he was frozen solid—solid as a popsicle. His eyes were still wide open, and you'd swear he was still alive, but it was clear he was stone dead."

"Why are you here tonight?"

"I could ask you the same question, but I came to get Tuttles' number. Michelle is calling the cops, and I promised to reach out to the FBI."

I studied Mitch with great detail. First, his eyes—did they reveal he was being anything but straight with me? Next, I looked for any quick or jerky facial gestures. I glanced down to see if his hands were twitching. Lastly, I checked to see if he was shifting his weight from one foot to the other, as he usually does when he gets nervous. I noted nothing apparent in his body language to make me think he was covering something up. "Mitch, is there anything you haven't told me that I should know?"

"About what?"

"About Catherine. About anything."

"I tried talking to you when you got back from Brazil, but you didn't want to listen. Then in my office, the day I assigned Isaac to find Catherine's message, I tried talking to you again, but it was useless. You've become pretty hard to reach."

Julia stepped forward and cut Mitch off. "I'm going to ask you only one question, Mitch, and I want the truth. Did you have anything to do with Catherine's death?"

"No. I loved her. I would never harm her."

Julia stared at Mitch a minute longer. "I believe you." She turned to me. "Jack! If we're going to stop Colter from getting on that airplane, I suggest you and Mitch pick a different time to hash out your problems. We've got to leave now!"

Julia was right. Without another word, we turned and headed for the door.

"Where are you going?"

"To crash a going away party," Julia said. "Colter's."

"I never got an invitation. But if it's Colter going away party, I'd enjoy seeing him off, too. Wait up. I'm going with you."

Catherine's message had lifted my spirits, and my head was clear when we reached Memorial. Actually, I felt quite normal. And I now understood aspects of Catherine that, for some reason, up and until this time, had evaded me. Never in question was her inner desire to achieve, and I had no doubt that she enjoyed the pleasure her accomplishments brought her. These were attributes well known to me and to most others. But the degree of her desire was, well, a magnitude higher than I had ever imagined. Catherine's message opened me up in a special way. It allowed me to shed my biggest doubt and in so doing, to lift an enormous weight from my shoulders. The moment I read that she loved me I felt much lighter inside. What a fool I had been to mistrust her intentions. Catherine was the most truthful person I had ever met, and reading her message more than reminded me that her nature was incapable of expressing anything but the truth.

Before entering the hospital, Julia gave Mitch and me our marching orders. "Listen, our goal is to keep Colter from leaving the hospital until the agents arrive. Mitch, you stay at the front door to wait for the agents. Tell one to go to Colter's party on the third floor and have the other one watch the back door, in case Colter makes a run for it." She looked at me. "Ready?"

We followed two women off the elevator and onto the third floor. We entered a room filled with people. I scanned the room for Colter, but didn't see him. "Excuse me. Have you seen Colter?" I said to a young nurse.

"He was here a couple of minutes ago." She shrugged her shoulders before turning away to chat with her friend.

I walked over to where Julia was standing. "I'm getting a little nervous. I'll check the hallway."

"All right, but don't leave the floor, okay?"

I nodded and walked out of the room. Two people had gotten off the elevator and I stopped them. "You didn't happen to see Colter, did you?"

"He just got on the elevator going down," the woman said.

I pressed the button, but there was no guarantee an elevator would come soon, so I ran down the stairwell to the main floor where Mitch was stationed. "Did you see him?"

"He hasn't come this way."

"He must have gone to the basement. Stay here, Mitch."

A minute later I was standing outside Catherine's laboratory. When I entered the room, the first thing I saw was her handwriting on the blackboard. No one had ever erased it. A noise from Colter's laboratory next door distracted me. I left Catherine's room and pushed open his door. Colter was removing some items from the refrigerator and talking to himself when he noticed me standing there.

"Jack! What are you doing here?"

I just stood there looking at him. "Why aren't you at your own going away party?"

He regained his swagger. "I needed to get away for a while."

"Saying your last good-bye to Memorial, huh?"

Colter smiled. "Yeah, a little clean up before I'm off. How are you? That fire at the Dobler mansion has been all over the news."

"Yeah, a real tragedy." I walked to the bench and lifted a flask that Colter had just set down. "Smells toxic."

"It's just a chlorine solution. They want me to empty everything out before I leave."

I set the flask down and decided not to beat around the bush. "You never told me what company you're going to work for on the west coast."

"Actually, I've decided to take some time off."

"You're just going away, then?"

"I plan to travel a bit. I'll figure the rest out later." Colter hesitated and glanced at me. Well, I'd better get back to the party. Are you joining me?" He started to walk toward the door.

I looked at my watch and wondered how long before the FBI would arrive. What if Colter really didn't go back to the party but left the hospital instead? Once he's on that airplane, he could go anywhere on the planet and never be found.

"Sit down, Colter. I want to ask you something."

Colter sat behind his desk. In typical fashion, he remained calm and cool. "Sure. What do you want to know?"

I placed my hands on his desk and leaned over toward him. "Why you killed Catherine."

His eyebrows furrowed. "Are you insane?"

"You made too many mistakes."

"You're losing your grip, Jack."

"I know Catherine confided in you. My question is, did you file for the patent before you killed her, or afterwards?"

"Now I'm beginning to feel sorry for you."

"You made three mistakes. Your first was creating a diversion—a red herring—by puncturing Catherine in the back with a standard-sized needle, and then cleverly using a finer needle when injecting her brachial artery. You thought she'd die quickly, didn't you? It must've made you nervous to find out she was still alive hours later. You never expected Catherine to survive long enough for those injections to bruise, did you?"

"So this is how delusional people process information."

Your second mistake was selling Cold to Rutger. I would never have known except for the fact he told me the night the mansion burned down

280

that he'd purchased Cold from its rightful owner. That would be the person who filed for the patent, the person who was also Catherine's collaborator. The problem is, you can't hide a huge sum of money from the authorities anymore. First, they'll track down the attorneys who handled the transaction, and then they'll locate the money, even if it's sitting in some off-shore account or hidden in a bank in Podunk, Switzerland."

"Now you're throwing crap against the wall and hoping something sticks."

I reached into my pocket and pulled out the piece of paper. "Then there's your third mistake, the most damaging. I held up Catherine's message so Colter could read it. For the first time, I saw a look of concern creep onto his eyes. A bead of perspiration formed on his forehead and trickled down the side of his face. "You see, this evidence proves you were Catherine's collaborator, and it's enough to hang you. For such a brilliant guy, you sure made a lot of mistakes."

Colter stood up. I didn't notice the gun right away, not until it was pointing in my face. "Talk about mistakes, Jack. Walking in here to show what a great detective you are was a mistake. Put that note on the desk."

"There's a million copies more where this came from."

"Turn around and walk over to that wall."

When I didn't move quickly enough, Colter jammed his gun hard into my back. As we passed the refrigerator he ordered me to stop. He removed a vial and laid it on the bench. I looked around as he filled a syringe. I had a pretty good idea what was coming next.

"People are going to be heartbroken, Jack, to hear that you took your own life. First, you were depressed over the loss of Catherine. But it was the brain tumor that pushed you over the edge."

"Make sure you do it right this time. Don't screw up like you did with Catherine."

"Huh. Catherine. You cared for her even less than I did. I told her you would leave someday, and you proved me right. I told her you would shortchange her, too, Jack, like you did me. Two years I worked side by side with you on the LEC Enzyme project. Once *we* figured it out, you dismissed me as though I were your water boy. *You* won the award. *You* collected the money, and *you* got the fame. Then Catherine asked me to help her. Next thing I knew she told me she was ready to patent Cold. Does she offer to give me any credit? Not a thing. Can you *imagine* that? And I came up with a genetic design to push that drug over the top. In the end, Catherine turned out to be just as selfish as you. All I ever got from either of you was a pat on the head. Well, not this time. You see, Jack, I *am* a brilliant scientist, and everyone knows it."

At that point, I didn't care if Colter stabbed me with the syringe or shot me full of holes. I turned around. "You pathetic little man. Catherine created Cold. She was the visionary. You were nothing more than a technician that followed instructions. And if you think getting a virus to slide off cells makes you a genius, then you're more pathetic than I thought. Catherine created the most elegant drug I've ever seen, and that's an achievement your sick, little, woman-beating, abusive mind will never fathom." I never saw the butt of the gun coming. It was sudden, and it caught me just above the right temple. Next thing I knew I was on one knee and holding the wall with both hands. Colter tried to stab my brachial artery, but I turned away and he stabbed me in the side instead. Within seconds I felt hot liquid spreading to the far reaches of my body, and shortly after that I was sprawled out on the floor.

"Drop that syringe!" I rolled my eyes to catch a glimpse of Julia standing in the doorway. Her legs were spread evenly apart and the weapon was held away from her body in both hands. "Step back!" She ran past Colter and came to my side. I tried to warn her that he had a weapon, but the Crotalus had worked its way into my facial muscles and I was unable to speak. My body began to spasm from a seizure brought about by the Crotalus. I moved my eyes from side to side to warn Julia when Colter quietly moved to the counter and grabbed his gun.

Julia sensed I was attempting to tell her something. She rose to her feet and pointed her gun at him. "Don't be a fool, Colter. I can drop you this very moment. Place the weapon on the floor!" He took one ill-fated step toward her, and Julia fired her weapon, hitting him in the shoulder. It jarred the gun loose from his hand and he turned and ran from the room.

Everything became muffled when the security guard entered the room. When Julia gave him instructions it was all a blur. She then disappeared into the hallway which was when I lost consciousness.

The door leading to the stairwell closed, signaling to Julia that Colter was headed upstairs. She ran into the stairwell and heard him climbing to the next landing. When she reached the second floor landing there was no sign or sound of him. She started to climb to the third floor, but stopped. Would Colter really go to the third floor, with his party in full swing? She walked back down a landing and took hold of the door handle that led into the second floor hallway. Colter heard Julia coming and timed it perfectly. He slammed the door into her as she was about to open it. The force hurled her across the landing and into the far wall. Dazed, she saw Colter standing over her with a syringe in his hand.

"Say good-bye, sweetheart."

Julia's hand fumbled into her pocket and gripped the Beretta automatic. Without removing it, she pointed the gun toward Colter as he jabbed the syringe toward her neck. "Good-bye," she whispered. Three shots echoed in the stairwell. There was a hard thud and the weight of Colter's body fell on top of her. She heard people rushing into the stairwell. Still dazed, she remembered they had, after all, come to Colter's going away party.

Chapter Sixty-five

The doctor tried to calm Frances down after explaining to her the severity of my condition. My eyes were closed, but I heard her implore him to do everything possible for me. He told her he was an internist, not a miracle worker. With that he left the room to make his rounds.

"Oh, dear God! Don't let it to be true! Sweet Jesus and Mary, please hear me."

Frances walked to the side of the bed and said a prayer over me. She removed the compress, rang it out in a basin, and laid it back on my forehead. When the telephone rang, she picked it up.

"The doctor just left, Mitch." Her voice was hoarse. "Yes, the antivenin is working...No, the doctor can't say how much longer he'll hold out, but his eyelids flicker every so often, and I think he's getting stronger...No, Julia's not here now. She went home to rest after staying up most the night talking to him—and her with a concussion and all. Sweet Mary and Child. I never met such an angel...What? Okay, I'll see you when you get here."

Frances hung up and whispered one more prayer before picking up the water basin and leaving the room.

My eyes were still closed when I sensed a *presence* moving about in the space above and below me. A feeling of well-being came over me and I was not frightened by it. A face oval and classic, and flawed only by the wisp of bangs that covered her eyes, appeared. And when she brushed her bangs back, two intelligent eyes gazed down at me. The corners of her mouth turned up into a smile. She walked toward me, forever walking toward me. I beckoned to touch her, to hear the richness in her voice, but her eyes spoke without words and to say only that she was now different from the vision that had come to me just days earlier in the condo. I resisted the idea and yearned for her to lie beside me. But her message was lucid and unmistakable: She was beyond that now. Strangely, as I lay there, it began to matter little to me. I understood why she had come. She was the beacon of light, and her light had entered my body to immerse me with strength. And with this new found strength I had the gift to live once again and to settle what needed to be settled.

My right arm twitched and I lifted it and placed it on my chest. Then, I drew one knee up. My eyelids were heavy, as though glued together and the brightness of the room hurt when I finally opened them. I was alive with senses that worked. Out of the corner of my eye I saw a shadow appear.

"Jack! You're awake!"

Mitch had startled me. "Yes, and I can tell you it's great to be awake." The last thing I remembered was Julia leaving my side and running after Colter. "Is Julia all right? What happened with her and Colter?"

"She's fine. Just a mild concussion and a few bruises. Colter was less lucky." Mitch made a gesture with his hand and when I squinted to see what he was doing, he held the thumbs down sign. The light was too strong so I closed my eyes again.

"A lot's happened in three days, and I still can't believe most of it."

I opened my eyes. "Three days? Is that how long I've been here?"

"Yeah, but you're doing fine." Mitch stepped closer. "Listen to this. The Dobler story has been on the front page of every newspaper in the country. The Attorney General filed fraud, restraint of trade, and who knows how many other charges against them. In all, there are roughly thirty counts against the company. William is barred from setting foot on any company property, and his personal assets have been frozen. And dozens of biotech companies have come forward to tell the Attorney General how they were cheated by the Doblers." Mitch poured a glass of water. I reached out for it because my throat was parched, but Mitch, preoccupied with telling his story, didn't notice me, and drank it down.

"And, just as you predicted, Memorial claims they own Cold. Rosetta received a cease and desist order on all research and development. Meanwhile, attorneys for Dobler have filed a counter suit, stating that they purchased Cold legally, and hold the patent on it. It all has to be worked out in the courts now." Mitch poured himself another glass of water. "But I saved the shocker for last. Two days ago Tuttles had everyone meet him at Heinrich's mansion, well, former mansion. I wanted to see the ruins, so I drove up. Boy, I never thought stone could burn so hot it turns into soot. But anyway, I'm standing there telling Tuttles about the expression on the Japanese guy's face when I had opened the meat cooler, and all of a sudden this FBI agent walks up with Heinrich's groundskeeper. The agent asks him to repeat his story to Tuttles. The groundskeeper says that he was outside the mansion the night it burned to the ground when he saw what appeared to be a ball of fire running toward him. He watched some person fall on the snow and roll over four or five times, until the flames were snuffed out. Then this guy stands up and starts running again. The groundskeeper didn't recognize him at first, because it was dark outside. But when the man ran past him, he did. It was Rutger. He said Rutger climbed over the fence that led to the back road and disappeared into the woods. The FBI found the story incredulous, but why would the groundskeeper make up a story like that?"

"Jack! You're awake," Frances placed two fingers on my wrist and checked my pulse. "Your blood pressure is almost normal. How are you feeling? Can I get you anything?"

"Actually, I'm thirsty."

She poured water from the pitcher and handed me the glass. She then turned to Mitch. "You need to get out of here so he can rest. I don't want him overdoing it."

"Okay. I'll be back later, Jack." Mitch started to leave, but he returned to the side of the bed. "If, in fact, that was Rutger who ran out of the house, he must know by now that Vanessa had run into the mansion after him. I wonder what he's feeling this very moment. Well, get some rest." Mitch turned to leave.

"Hold on, Mitch."

He walked back again. "Need something?"

"Yes. To visit Catherine's grave again."

Mitch was caught off guard. "Well, okay. When they release you from the hospital, I'll drive you to the cemetery. Now get some rest, and I'll see you later."

I closed my eyes and rested a while. When I woke up a tray of food was on the table next to the bed. Fishcakes, a pile of plain unbuttered corn, and apple sauce, but it didn't matter. I ate it all down, even the tapioca dessert. I dozed off again, and woke up some time later to see someone looking down at me.

"You must be feeling good today. I see you've cleaned your plate."

"Doctor Frankfort. I didn't expect to see you."

"I stopped by yesterday to check on you. It's much better to see you awake."

"I feel like I'm getting stronger. My eye sight's not that great, but I have energy."

"That's good to hear. Are you considering, at this point, to stay in the hospital? You'll get all the care you need here."

"I hadn't really thought about it. But since you've brought it up, I don't believe my time is up yet. There are things I need to get done, and I'd like to write down everything that's occurred over the past two weeks. It might be too much to hope for, but I want to try."

"I can't answer whether you're capable of achieving that goal or not. I can only say what I told you before. When you recall events, many of them will be distorted. So if you do write your story, events you recall may seem perfectly real, but it's possible they never occurred at all. It will be a challenge to get your facts right. I'm not discouraging you from writing your story, but as your doctor, I just want you to know what to expect."

"I think I can get this story straight."

"Well, I like your confidence." He looked at his watch. "I have to leave in a few minutes, but how about telling me a vignette first?"

"Is there's some medical reason for hearing these stories?"

"Yes, an important reason. I'll tell you what it is after I hear your vignette."

I placed my arms behind my head and gazed at the ceiling. "It was our second wedding anniversary and I'd taken Catherine to the Waldorf. We were a little old fashioned in some ways, a throwback to earlier times, a quality we had recognized in each other right from the beginning. Anyway, after a couple glasses of champagne we went out onto the dance floor where a small orchestra was playing classic torch songs from the 40s and 50s. Catherine kicked off her heels and stepped onto my shoes. We danced the rest of the evening looking into each other's eyes. When it had come time to leave it was raining cats and dogs. We found ourselves stranded because taxis were at a premium. Catherine insisted on walking home in the rain, even though I resisted walking half the length of Manhattan. In the end I gave into her. Bare foot and beautiful she began stomping in every puddle we passed. The more she stomped, the more soaked we became, the harder we laughed. We were drenched head to toe when we reached the condo. The feel of Catherine's skin was soft as satin as we lay in our bed that night and loved each other. I mean, we really loved each other that night. The euphoria carried over into the morning, even as Catherine whipped up eggs and bacon, the smell wafting into the bedroom where I lay and drew in the aroma. I remembered thinking that every night should end like that one, and every morning should begin this way." My throat locked up.

"What's wrong, Jack?"

"Oh... To know these memories will soon be ripped away."

"I see... It's a beautiful story. Let me tell you why I've been so intrigued with your vignettes. Some things you've told me during our appointments have been, well, skewed in places. As a doctor, I have been trained to spot them. But whenever you speak of Catherine, your stories always ring true. I find it fascinating, and I sometimes wonder if memories such as the ones you recall about Catherine are stored somewhere else inside of us—a place where they can't be ripped away, a place where they remain pure and true forever."

"My wish is to have my last thought be about Catherine."

Julia walked into the room. "Hi. Remember me?"

"Julia! Say hello to Doctor Frankfort."

"No need for introductions. I'm leaving. Patients are waiting." He smiled and laid his hand on my shoulder before leaving the room.

I motioned Julia closer and whispered. "Is there a guard outside my room?"

"No," she whispered back. "Why do you ask?"

"When you kidnap someone, you don't expect to get away with it."

"You were rescued."

"Can you explain that in more detail?"

"Okay, but I'm going to stop whispering now. William Dobler told the FBI that his wife, Elizabeth, had driven him to the mansion."

"Why would William say that?"

Frances walked into the room carrying another tray of food. "Yum, Jack. Look what I've got for you. A nice piece of liver, mashed potatoes with gravy, and I saw that you ate all your tapioca earlier, so I brought you a large bowl of it. What do you say to that?"

Chapter Sixty-six

Not everyone agreed with my decision to check out of Memorial the following morning, but I was lucid and felt reasonably strong. Doctor Frankfort had told me that some terminal patients experience a sense of normalcy in the days leading up to their death. Something in the chemical makeup of the human body allows the mind, senses, and aspirations to come alive to a greater degree. When he told me that, I thought about how a light bulb brightens moments before it burns out.

I was determined to put my affairs in order and, if time allowed, to write my story.

Jimmy called up from the lobby and informed me that a Mr. Tony Miranda was on his way up. He was from the law firm of Delmont, Miranda, Miller, and Graham, and he was here to prepare my Last Will and Testament. At the core of my will was Cold. A legal battle was about to be waged over the ownership of the drug, and this law firm had a sterling record of winning virtually every case they touched. I wanted to make sure the Catherine Prescott Lewis Foundation retained ownership. Miranda asked if there was anyone else I wanted to bequeath property to. I told him about the four-year-old boy at Sloan Kettering Hospital with the translucent, blue eyes. I had racked my brain trying to recall where I had seen the boy's face before, and all I could think was that his may have been the face on the portrait Catherine had painted that weekend we were in Woodstock. Maybe her painting only reminded me of the young boy. In any event, I set up a trust fund for the boy and asked Miranda to find him and to see that he was well taken care of until his twenty-first birthday. The remainder of the profits from Cold I bequeathed to the *Memorial Sloan-Kettering Cancer Center for Children*. Executors to administer the foundation would be Mitch Cochran, Julia Marshant, and Michelle Chavier.

Once the will had been completed, I had Jimmy and one other person from the hotel come up to witness my signature on the document. Jimmy also brought up the ream of paper and box of pencils I had requested be delivered to the Towers. With my affairs in order, it was now time to embark upon the story that had begun on December 16, the day those three extraordinary events had occurred, when I killed a man, heard Catherine had been taken from me, and received the grave news about my health.

There was limited vision in my left eye, but I soon learned that my hand knew perfectly well how to scribe without the use of sight. I spent the next two days writing my story with as much detail as my memory allowed. I went over the story again with a fine-toothed comb to be as certain as possible that my facts were accurate. I did this mainly because

Doctor Frankfort had said my brain could not help but distort the facts, and I wanted to prove him wrong.

On the third day Julia arrived at the apartment in the early afternoon. I selected our entrées from the menu of the Towers restaurant. I ordered pheasant with a grape and port sauce, string beans, and baby potatoes. Crème brûlée was our dessert.

Julia lifted her glass to my toast, and this time I tasted the Châteauneuf du Pape before setting my glass down on the table. I located my silverware, but soon found that cutting the pheasant was an obstacle for me. I was relegated to holding a baby potato in one place on my plate and stabbing it with my fork before popping it into my mouth. Julia saw my dilemma and walked to my side of the table, where she removed the utensils from my hands. She cut a bite of pheasant and fed it to me. She waited as I devoured it. She proceeded to cut the next piece of meat for me, and so on. Neither of us spoke the entire time, and she remained at my side until my plate had been cleaned.

"Your dinner is cold by now."

"I wasn't that hungry."

"To be with someone and not have to speak a word. It's, well, I don't know how to explain how good it feels."

"I know. I feel that way, too."

I placed my napkin on the table. "Come to the window with me." Julia took my arm and we walked across the room. I placed my hand on the windowpane. "What does it look like outside?"

"Well, the sun is out, casting its reflection on the Hudson."

"Wait here. I have something for you." I fumbled my way into the bedroom and carried back the red elephant painting. "Take this when you leave."

"'A Moonlit Night.' Oh, Jack, I—"

"Not a word." I had no need to see Julia's face. It was glowing, and her eyes had turned misty. "We had a wonderful night in SoHo. I knew then you had fallen in love with this painting."

"I really do love it."

"That makes me happy. Now, I want you to do me a favor in return."

"Anything."

"Leave me now. Take the painting and go. I want to remember this moment."

The room became silent. Then Julia's arms wrapped around me and her lips caressed my cheek. She kept them there for a while as she continued to hold me. When she let go, I heard the rustle of her coat as she slipped it on, the sound of the painting being lifted, her footsteps walking to the door, and the turn of the doorknob. But mostly, when she turned around to look at me for the last time, I felt her gaze upon my face.

"Good-bye, Jack." The door closed.

I caught the inflection of Julia's last words to me. There was a slight crack in her voice when she spoke, but she managed to hold herself together. I repeated her words over and over in my mind until I had forgotten the point at which her voice had cracked. Only silence filled the room as I stood at the window with the knowledge that the sun was out and its reflection was cast upon the Hudson. I stood there for quite some time, until the rush of my story filled my mind. What had compelled me to write all this down? I had no desire for anyone to read it. What interest would anyone find in the senseless killing of a young woman and a man slowly growing blind before the arrival of his own death? Then, in a flash, I realized why I had put pencil to paper. I did it to find the answer to one simple question that had eluded me until this very moment: Had I failed to give respect and allegiance to you, Catherine? "I believe so. I deserted you for a greater gift, or so I thought. Only now do I see it all so clearly, the right and wrong of it all. They tell me, my angel, that my decisions, my judgments, are outside of my control. I am crippled in mind and body, and even my image of you is fraught with distortion. Can you hear me, my angel? Are you out there listening to me? If so, then you know that madmen can sometimes see the truth more clearly. I know now that each cell that lives in my body holds thoughts of you. So you see, my angel, both beauty and truth run through my veins and gives pleasure to my last hours. I also—only now—accept that you lay peacefully in your grave.

Because I accept that truth, I feel at one with all things living, all things beyond life, and all things that will become. Only now can I say that death will be a welcomed blessing for me."

Chapter Sixty-seven

There was a quick knock on the door and Mitch let himself into the apartment. He carried my coat to the window and helped me on with it.

"The car's downstairs."

He had called the caretaker at the cemetery to get the exact location of Catherine's gravesite. When we arrived, he took me by the arm and led me to the headstone. I squinted to see facets of Catherine's name. This time I brought a bouquet of red roses, and Mitch set them at the foot of her headstone for me. I kneeled on the snow and, for the first time, tears flooded out of me. My body had finally let go, and I prayed that if there was a God in Heaven, that He allow me to die in this place at this very moment. "I want to be buried with her."

"You mean alongside of her?"

"No, inside Catherine's casket. Figure it out. I know you can."

"That's one thing I won't be able to do."

"Why not?" Mitch didn't answer me, so I turned my head in his direction and waited.

"Because this is where I finally tell the truth, Jack—the truth I tried to tell you on more than a few occasions. It's going to hurt you, and you're going to hate me for it."

"What are you talking about?"

"If I were to have you buried in this grave, you would lay for all eternity next to a stranger."

"Who's in this grave?"

"It's the Jane Doe. She's buried here."

"What? Where's Catherine?"

"She's in the Cryonic Institute."

Slowly, I rose to my feet, lost. I searched for refuge from the stabbing pain. I did not deserve it. "Have I ever told you this story, Mitch? The evening we went to *La Vie en Rose*? Hah. You'll love this one, Mitch. Catherine had ordered a glass of orange juice, and I asked if she was feeling okay. She turned to me, her face glowing, and said she felt wonderful. I knew at that moment that our dream had come true. I told Petrie to bring me an orange juice, too, and we spent the night planning the next chapter of our lives. Six weeks later Catherine lost the child. She was heartbroken. We both were."

"Let me talk, Jack. I really did try telling you a couple of times, but you never gave me a chance. You need to hear it from the beginning. It'll make more sense once you hear the whole story. Just listen. It began when I had taken Catherine down for x-rays after arriving at Memorial. Everyone told me it was hopeless, that the Crotalus had done too much damage, but I was half out of my mind. After the x-rays were taken, it finally sunk into me that she was going to die. There I was, standing beside her gurney in the basement, waiting for the orderly to come take her back to her room. Then, another orderly parks his gurney against the wall and walks into the men's room. It had a body on it, so I walked over and lifted the sheet. It was the Jane Doe. Her body was swollen almost beyond recognition. It was a horrible sight. But even in that condition I saw an uncanny resemblance to Catherine, like a bad caricature or something. And it struck me at that moment. Catherine was near dead, and she deserved every chance to live again. I know, to you this is irrational thinking, but I would've hated myself for the rest of my life if I had just walked away at that point. I was determined to go through with it, even if I got caught, even if I was disgraced. When you care about someone, really love and care about them, you'll do everything in your power for them. That's how I felt at that moment, and there wasn't much time so I had to move quickly. I lifted Catherine from the gurney, set her in a wheel chair, and placed my coat around her. Then I switched gurneys so Jane Doe was waiting near the x-ray room, and I placed the gurney that Catherine had been on outside the men's room. When the orderly who had come for Catherine showed up, it was Jane Doe he took back to Catherine's room. Once he left, I wheeled Catherine out of the outpatient door and took her to my car. I was certain someone would catch me leaving the hospital, or discover that Jane Doe was in Catherine's bed, but I guess no one paid much attention. After I left the parking lot I…"

"After she lost the baby, we spoke about trying again. We even had a conversation about the type of house we'd get. Catherine said if she became pregnant again, she'd leave Memorial for good."

"Let me finish this, Jack, It needs to be said once and for all. After leaving Memorial, I took Catherine to a location in the city where this team prepared her body for cryonics. We had to wait for her heart to stop, for her to be legally dead, before they started the process. I never left Catherine's side for a moment, and she was in my arms when she took her final breath. Only then did I hand her over to the team. I stayed with her until she was placed in the refrigerated truck and transported to the Cryonics Institute in Michigan."

"No! No! No! Who gave you the right! Condemned her to that! Violated her! Took her dignity!" I fell to one knee. "How could you? Catherine would never have wanted this!"

"That's not entirely true, Jack. Listen to me. Catherine and I talked about a lot of things while you were gone, including cryonics. Of course, no one ever thought any of us would die this young, but Catherine told me that she believed in science more than anything, and that one day we'll find cures for all these diseases, and we'll overcome death, too. Catherine was a pioneer and wanted nothing more than to blaze trails. If given the choice, I believe she would've wanted me to do exactly what I did. And if you can get past your anger, Jack, if you can just put yourself inside Catherine's mind for a moment, you'll admit that I'm right: Catherine would have chosen this for herself."

Neither of us spoke for quite some time. I finally got to my feet and rested my hands on the headstone. "Maybe Catherine would've chosen this, but maybe not. We'll never know, will we?" I rubbed my hands across the top of the headstone. "And what's to become of this poor soul?"

Mitch walked over and stood beside me. "People will bring flowers to this place and pray. They will mourn at this gravesite, and Jane Doe will receive more love in death than she found in her troubled life."

I stood there a moment longer before walking away. I was not steady and Mitch took my arm. We did not speak until we were halfway back to the City.

"Were you able to write down everything about the last two weeks?"

"I think I captured most of it."

"Someday someone will read it and understand the truth of what you've captured. In fifty years it will be ancient history. The world as we know it will be changed. What's waiting around the corner will annihilate what you've lived through—what we all are living through."

I wasn't sure, but for the first time I think I understood what Mitch meant. He had pounded me over the head so often with his future crap that some of it had begun to stick. If we lived an extended life we would be less inclined to throw it away. And who knows, an extended life might be a deterrent from stealing a bag of money, killing someone, or cheating them out of a cure for the common cold.

"I met with Michelle yesterday, Jack. She told me you made her your legal guardian. We talked quite a while. I eventually told her the truth about Catherine, and also that a cryonics team will be on call for you." He paused for a moment. "This is hard for me to say, Jack, so I'm just going to say it. In the hours before your death, you'll most likely fall into a coma. And when death does come, there'll be only a small window of time to stabilize your body before your brain dies. If we miss that window you will no longer be suitable for cryonics."

"I'm sick of hearing about cryonics. Michelle will decide what happens to me."

"I know. She told me."

"What did she say when you told her about Catherine?"

"That I'm insane, and that I need to check into a mental institution."

"You told her you want the same for me?"

"I did. She said she'd burn in hell first."

Chapter Sixty-eight

When we reached the condo Mitch helped me out of the car and up the sidewalk. I stopped halfway and pulled out an envelope. "It's for Eddie. Tell him I'm sorry about wrecking his car, but this will allow him to buy another one. He really loved the Iron Lung."

Mitch raised his eyebrows. "Eddie who?"

"You know, the limo driver who took us to Heinrich's birthday party."

"What are you talking about, Jack? I hired the limousine that night."

The condo door opened and Michelle stood in the doorway. When I turned back to Mitch, a black van had pulled up to the curb. Mitch turned and waved to the men inside.

"Before I go, tell me. Did the mansion burn to the ground?"

"Every brick and every stone."

"And did Colter, did he...?"

Mitch remained silent for a moment. "And he paid the ultimate price." He walked up and placed his hand on my shoulder. "Anything else you want to know?"

Michelle had walked down from the condo and taken my arm. She pulled me away from Mitch and led me back to the condo. From the doorway I looked back, but wasn't sure if Mitch was standing there or not. Michelle closed the door and we went into the bedroom. I lay on the bed with my head on her lap and dictated what had taken place at the cemetery and outside the condo. Michelle promised to capture all future moments, and she assured me that my story would be completed.

My throat was parched. I drank some water and rested a while. Michelle asked to read my story, and I allowed her to do so. At one point, her body shivered, and I wondered what part she had read. A couple of hour later she laid the story down without commenting on it.

"Parts are not true, I now know. I guess Doctor Frankfort was right after all. Promise me, though. Not to change a word, or let anyone change it. I lived every moment of it the way it's written."

"I will guard it for you, darling."

I rested again, and later that evening when I opened my eyes the room was pitch dark. "Are the lights on, Michelle?"

"Yes, my love. I left them on for you." I ran my fingers through his hair.

"So many people."

"What, darling? What about the people?"

"Peter Bastianich was a brave man, And Robert Farrington was fearless."

"Yes, my darling, they were all that and more." I took his hand in mine.

"Franz Weber had a kindness about him, and how he lived through the tragedy that befell him, I'll never know."

"Yes, my dear." I gently stroked his hair.

"It was Weber, I found out, who had sent the white roses to Catherine's grave. He thought the Doblers had killed her. And I'm sure he carried roses to his mother and sister's graves in Heidelberg."

"He was a thoughtful man."

A long spell passed before another word was spoken.

"Michelle!"

What is it, darling?"

"I feel something happening inside."

There were no words I could say to him.

"Michelle!"

Yes, darling."

"I should have been here for Catherine. I... I... loved..."

My vision blurred as the last word failed to leave his lips. "I know you loved her, my dear." I was not certain he heard me. His eyes had closed and he lay silent on my lap. I accepted the inevitable, that his lips would never speak Catherine's name again. I was grateful that his last thoughts were for his beloved, and I recalled a passage in his story that had sent a shiver through my body. I now wished for it to be true. Catherine had appeared in his midst. Her face oval and classic, and flawed only by the wisp of bangs that covered her eyes. When she brushed them back, two intelligent eyes gazed out at him. She began to walk toward him, forever walking toward him.

ABOUT THE AUTHOR

Richard Bognar was born in Buffalo, N.Y. He attended Canisius College and received a Bachelor of Arts Degree in Philosophy. Richard and his wife Cynthia live on a small farm in Milton, Georgia.

You can e-mail the author at: rich@richardbognar.com

ISBN: 978-0-9890962-3-2

www.ingramcontent.com/pod-product-compliance
Lightning Source LLC
Chambersburg PA
CBHW050557260626
47157CB00002B/604